ADVANCE PRAISE FOR
Roll for Romance

"Sweet, charming, and wonderful! *Roll for Romance* is written with such affection for its characters and for D&D that you'll feel like you've made friends for life!"
—Sarah Beth Durst, author of *The Spellshop*

"What a delightful debut! *Roll for Romance* is full of wit and charm, with a satisfying side of finding yourself while pretending to be someone else. Watching Sadie and Noah—as well as their in-character counterparts—fall for each other was as satisfying as rolling a natural 20!"
—Jen DeLuca, author of *Well Met*

"As cozy as it is utterly charming, *Roll for Romance* is a loving ode to the bonds formed between D&D players and the magic of finding your own community. Lenora Woods lands a critical hit with this adorable romance."
—E. B. Asher, author of *This Will Be Fun*

"This swoony and nerdy romance had me kicking my feet and blushing the entire time. Sadie and Noah's real life and in-game romance is full of charm, healthy communication, and genuine friendship. This book is such a beautiful love letter to all things fandom, nerd culture, and gaming."

—Mallory Marlowe, author of *Love and Other Conspiracies*

"A scintillating, sexy romance filled with spells and self-discovery, *Roll for Romance* will charm you and have you willingly failing your saving throw. The alchemy between Sadie and Noah is out-of-this-world electric, and their adventures at and away from the D&D table will have you whipping through pages to find out what happens next. Hold on to your dice, because Woods's debut will absolutely disarm you."

—Tara Tai, author of *Single Player*

"*Roll for Romance* has me fully under its spell! With a sweet love story and charming friendships, this delightful debut will make readers fall in love with both the human characters and their D&D alter egos. A completely successful campaign!"

—M. Stevenson, author of *Behooved*

ROLL FOR
Romance

ROLL F🎲R
Romance

a novel

LENORA WOODS

DELL

NEW YORK

Dell

An imprint of Random House

A division of Penguin Random House LLC

1745 Broadway, New York, NY 10019

randomhousebooks.com

randomhousebookclub.com

penguinrandomhouse.com

While this novel is written with great love and affection for
Dungeons & Dragons, it is in no way official, sponsored, or endorsed.

A Dell Trade Paperback Original

ISBN 978-0-593-97541-1
Ebook ISBN 978-0-593-97542-8

Published in the United Kingdom by Arcadia Books, an imprint of Hachette UK.

Printed in the United States of America on acid-free paper

1st Printing

BOOK TEAM: Production editor: Christa Guild • Managing editor: Saige Francis •
Production manager: Erin Korenko • Copy editor: Laura Dragonette •
Proofreaders: Nicole Ramirez, Taylor McGowan

Book design by Alexis Flynn

Adobe stock illustrations: DesignToonsy (sparkles), Marina Zlochin (menu border)

The authorized representative in the EU for product safety and compliance
is Penguin Random House Ireland, Morrison Chambers, 32 Nassau Street,
Dublin D02 YH68, Ireland. https://eu-contact.penguin.ie

To the Triboar Trio, and our brave DM:
Will, Tomoko, and Nathan.

Thank you for your friendship, and for all of the adventures.

ROLL FOR
Romance

CHAPTER
One

"Your first set of dice should come as a gift. It's tradition."

Liam fishes into the pocket of his chinos and draws out a small velvet pouch. I shift from where I've sunk into the plush cushions of his couch, suddenly uncomfortable. My palms start to sweat, the can of beer slick in my right hand.

"You've already given me too much, Liam," I say. A plane ticket from New York to Texas. Groceries for the last two weeks. Free rein to drive his grandpa's old Civic. His guest room to stay in for the foreseeable future. I smile crookedly and shake my head. Finally agreeing to play Dungeons & Dragons with my best friend for the first time after years of him begging is a small price to pay in the face of such generosity. "Really, the least I can do is buy myself some dice for your game."

"Oh hush, Sadie. This is my favorite part." He holds the bag aloft, obviously waiting for me. Eventually I set aside my beer and hold out my hand, and he shakes the dice into my palm. I'm immediately charmed. They're sparkly and shimmering, made of clear resin with specks of gold and white glitter suspended inside. They look like little gilded nuggets, seven in total, all different shapes. I'd only ever seen six-sided ones when playing old-school board games, but apparently you need all sorts of dice for D&D.

"I'll explain what they each do later, but take the d20 for a spin," Liam says.

"The big one?"

His lips twitch with amusement under the fluff of his ash-blond beard. "The big one, yes."

I pluck out the large twenty-sided die and swirl it around in my palm, testing its weight. Without ceremony, I drop it onto the coffee table, where it bounces noisily among the stacks of D&D guides, stray papers, and cartons of takeout noodles. When it lands, the number 17 is face up, inked in bold white lines. I turn to Liam. "That's good, right?"

He looks pleased. "That's good, especially for your first roll. The closer to twenty you get, the better." He reaches for a fortune cookie from our pile of snacks and shoots me a grin. "Maybe they're lucky dice. Or maybe *you're* lucky."

I can't help it; my mood immediately darkens, like a cloud blotting out the sunny giddiness of my first roll. The beer turns sour in my stomach, and I glance away, tossing pale curls out of my face. "Unlikely. But it'd be nice if my luck swung in the other direction for once."

Liam is quiet for a moment, fiddling with the end of the paper fortune sticking out of the cookie. He cracks the cookie in half, pops it into his mouth, and spins the slip between his fingers. When he finally lets out a slow, measured sigh, I know he's about to hit me with some hard truth. We've been friends for fifteen years; I recognize his tells.

"People get laid off all the time, Sadie. It happens."

"I know," I say sullenly. "But that doesn't make it suck any less."

Since college, I'd lived the dream. For years, I'd trekked every morning—in *heels*—through the grimy streets of Midtown Manhattan to a gleaming beacon of a skyscraper where I'd worked as an associate at Incite Media, one of the top marketing agencies in the nation. I'd loved throwing that name around, loved seeing the raised eyebrows from Tinder dates and my parents' fancy friends. *So impressive!*

It had seemed too good to be true. Sometimes I felt like I was dressing up in someone else's pencil skirt and magenta blazer, showing off someone else's flashy résumé full of glowing recommendations and compelling statistics. I kept waiting for somebody to out me as an impostor, to yell, *Who let her in here?* But I stuck around, and I did good work. My campaigns were inventive and effective. I was devastated when I was let go.

I was also—just *slightly*—relieved.

But I wasn't ready to admit that out loud. And I definitely wasn't ready to tell Liam the whole truth about why I lost my job.

It was his idea for me to leave New York and stay with him in Texas for a while. He'd known something was wrong after a week of me ignoring his texts. He'd known something was *really* wrong when I stopped sending reactions and emojis to dumbass memes he sent me through social media. So he'd made up an excuse to fly up to visit his mom, who still lives on the same street my parents did in the small town in Connecticut where we'd both grown up. He'd hopped on the train and shown up at my apartment building in Queens one Sunday morning, stale donuts from my favorite hometown bakery in one hand, a couple of duffel bags in the other. I'd opened the door with a scowl and a messy bun, wearing sweatpants I'd had on for four days. After a few hours of stuffing my face and crying, I hashed out a half-assed plan with Liam, and we decided I'd finally take the trip down to visit his new place in the Wild West.

Just a month, I'd told him. *Just a month, and I'll be back on my feet.*

But with another look at my blotchy eyes and the state of my neglected apartment, Liam had put a hand on my elbow and gently encouraged me to stay for the summer.

"I know it sucks," he soothes, bringing my attention back to the present. "But try to look at it as an opportunity."

"Is that the advice your fortune cookie gave you?"

Liam gives me a flat look. "No. But it's stale advice, I know. Listen. It's awful, and it's going to hurt for a while. But think of it as a forced vacation." I wince, but he presses on. "That job was running you ragged. You never took time off, never explored the hobbies you said you would, never came to visit me . . ." He's smiling now, teasing, but guilt pinches at me. He'd moved to the tiny town of Heller, Texas, five years ago, but since college, I'd only ever seen him on his trips back to New England.

He squeezes my shoulder. "Enjoy it. Take a pause. Think about what you want to do next. Let me show you around, introduce you to my friends, and distract you with a fantastical adventure."

It's the perfect subject change, because I'm certainly not yet ready to think about any future further than this D&D game. "The adventure. Okay. Remind me how this is going to go?"

Liam leans forward, and the light of excitement in his eyes nearly makes the lenses of his glasses flare. He's played D&D since high school, and nothing gets him fired up more. "At this stage, all you need to do is create a character," Liam explains. "You can play as whomever you like—a haughty wizard intent on learning new magic, a farmer who decided to pick up a sword and seek out fame and fortune, a sneaky thief who dreams of stealing a crown . . . anyone." He sets before me a pencil and a sheet of paper covered in an overwhelming number of tiny blank boxes. I adjust my glasses and squint at the paper as Liam continues. "Once we fill out this character sheet, it will tell you everything you need to know: what spells your character can cast, how strong they are, whether they're dexterous and good at picking locks or charismatic enough to persuade a crowd, and so on. I'll walk you through the details, and then over the next week before our first game, you can think through your character's backstory."

I nod and tap the pencil's eraser against my lower lip. "What types of characters are the others playing?"

"So far we've got a barbarian with a big axe, a clever knife-wielding rogue, and"—he briefly pauses, then huffs out a quick laugh—"a bard."

I narrow my eyes. "Like a musician?"

"Sort of. You'll see." Liam bends over the character sheet again. "The guy playing the bard is new to town, too, and he seems like a good egg. I think you'll like him." His tone is entirely too nonchalant in a way that makes me immediately suspicious.

And then, like he's dangling a carrot, Liam adds, "He's cute."

Fine. I'm curious.

"I'm excited to meet everyone," I say evenly, fighting the smile that tugs at my lips as I take another drink of beer. Warmth spreads to my limbs, chasing away some of the tension from earlier. "And you're not playing a character, right?" I clarify. I still haven't wrapped my head around how the game works. "You just run the game?"

"Right. I'll be the Dungeon Master."

"Sounds kinky."

Liam shoots me another flat look. "I run the game," he explains. "I build the world, create a compelling plotline . . . think of it as the storyteller role. I create the map, and the players choose which paths to explore. Does that make sense?"

"Not really, but I'm sure it will next weekend." I let out a rush of air and nod. "Okay. It sounds like this adventuring party could use a healer. A cleric."

There's something like approval or pride in the way Liam's eyes light up. "That's a great idea."

I smile. "Good. Let's call her Jaylie."

For the next hour, Liam walks me through filling out my character sheet, and together we sketch out the bones of who Jaylie is. We pick out her spells, determine her background, and sprinkle in some charisma for fun. Drafting out our ideas reminds me in some ways of my old job, where I'd begin campaign planning by first brainstorming a handful of words I wanted the project to capture. *Adventurous, curious, bold,* I think. Jaylie is someone who's embarking on something new and exciting—someone who hasn't royally fucked up her life. Someone with luck on her side.

Someone I'd like to be again.

I'm still scribbling ideas down when Liam stands to stretch, not bothering to cover his loud yawn. "Early day tomorrow," he says. He's teaching summer school again this year. "Let's take a pause here?"

But ideas for the game still flood my thoughts; it's the most inspired I've felt in months. "I might keep noodling away for a bit, actually."

"Of course." Liam disappears into the bathroom, and as the whine of his electric toothbrush drones in the background, I take another look around his new home. It's so unlike the apartments we shared in college. The house is fucking massive, frankly, and Liam's given me full rein of the second floor, while the first-floor master bedroom and game room are his. He inherited the house from his late grandpa, and it's still furnished with an odd mix of Liam's clean, modern taste and his grandpa's rugged old country boy aesthetic. I look up the stairs, and a mounted deer head gazes imperiously down at me from where it's positioned next to a fantasy landscape I painted for Liam as a birthday gift years ago.

I frown at the landscape. I haven't painted in ages, but still— I could do much better work now.

Liam's elderly orange cat, Howard—another inheritance from his grandpa—lumbers carefully down the stairs and curls up at my side. In just the last couple of weeks, we've become good friends. He croaks a meow at me, sounding like a growly old engine. I run my thumb along the cat's forehead, between his eyes, and he immediately begins to purr.

"Hey," I call down the hallway. "Thank you again, Liam. For everything. I mean it."

The sound of running water cuts off, and the buzzing stops.

"Josephine Sadie Brooks." Liam comes out of his room with

one hand on his hip and the toothbrush gripped menacingly in his fist. He always uses my full name when he's pretending to be cross. "You're my best friend. It's nothing. I'm glad to have you here."

His expression softens.

"You'll figure it all out. We can't control the wind, but we can always adjust the sails," he says sagely.

I narrow my eyes at him. "Now that's *definitely* from the fortune cookie."

Liam's eyes sparkle. "You caught me." He passes me the small slip of paper before disappearing into his bedroom.

I look at the fortune then set it aside and turn back to my notebook and Jaylie's character sheet. I can't ignore the itch that there's something missing, some aspect of her character that I haven't captured yet. Again my eyes skim the painting I made for Liam all those years ago.

Even as a knot of apprehension tangles in my chest, I trudge upstairs with Howard close on my heels. Ignoring the mess I've made of Liam's guest room—bed unmade, clothes scattered on the floor—I dig into the bottom of my duffel bag and retrieve my sketchbook. It was the last thing I'd grabbed before Liam shepherded me out of my apartment. I hadn't touched it in months, but I remember that tug of uncertainty, the feeling that I couldn't bear to leave it behind.

I sink to the floor and open it in my lap, flipping about midway through to a blank section. Already I imagine Jaylie coming to life on the page as colors and lines swim behind my eyes.

Before I begin, I tape Liam's crinkled fortune to the top of the page and read it once more.

We can't control the wind, but we can always adjust the sails.
Lucky Numbers 34, 23, 67, 5, 40, 17

As I set my pencil to the empty page, a brief flash of optimism settles in my chest. Maybe my luck is turning after all.

CHAPTER
Two

The morning of our game's first session, it's easier to get out of bed than it has been for weeks. Rather than having the day stretch out before me, intimidatingly empty and directionless, I've got an agenda. I've got—

"Coffee, Sadie!" Liam calls up the stairs.

That, too.

I roll out of bed, careful not to disturb a still-sleeping Howard—whose alliance with me I suspect might have Liam feeling jealous—and trot downstairs to the kitchen, where Liam stands leaning against the counter. He's got on dark shorts and a green button-up, short hair already carefully combed in a stylish sweep to the side. Liam has never dressed casually a day in his life.

"Morning." He's not entirely successful at hiding the surprise in his tone when I appear so shortly after his summoning. He's probably grown used to me reheating my coffee closer to noon—but that's when today's game starts. "You excited?"

"Something like that," I tease. I grab for my coffee, which isn't in its usual mug, but in a paper takeout cup. "What's this?"

"A latte from Busy Bean down the street. Best in town, and I thought we deserved a treat today." He pauses. "You should check them out sometime—or we can go together."

I nod distractedly and take a sip, not registering much taste beyond *hot*.

I hadn't picked up on it the first time, when Liam asked me a couple of weeks ago to water his plants in the backyard while he was at work. Or the day after that, when he asked me to drop off a few letters for him at the post office. But eventually I noticed how he seemed to have one small, innocuous errand for me every day. Some tiny excuse to get me out of the house—or even just out of the guest room. I'd resented it at first and ignored it more than once. But somewhere along the line, I'd started to look forward to my little daily quests.

"Wake me up next time," I offer. "I'll go with you."

Liam straightens and smiles. "Okay."

But those errands are small potatoes compared to the big weekly commitment I've signed myself up for—participating in fantasy-improv with a bunch of strangers. I glance toward the front door, half expecting them to barge right in.

When I take another drink of coffee, it's bracing.

"Walk me through who's playing again?"

Liam rolls his own cup between his palms. "They're all beginners like you—never played before." It was the first thing he'd assured me of when he initially pitched the idea of starting a summer D&D campaign. "I recently met the bard, Noah, and we connected over online gaming; the other two I know from work. Julie teaches orchestra at the middle school, right down the hall from me." He winces at what I'm guessing is the memory of children sawing away at out-of-tune stringed instruments. "And Morgan works at the bookstore downtown. After summer school hours, I like to pick up shifts there to keep myself busy."

I huff out a laugh through my nose. Running ourselves ragged for work is something Liam and I have in common.

Well. *Had* in common.

Before my sullen silence has a chance to stretch and fill the kitchen, Liam continues seamlessly. "Should probably get dressed, Sadie. I told Jules she could come early to prep snacks."

I glance down at my cotton PJ shorts and oversized high school marching band shirt. Maybe not the best choice for my very first adventure. "I'll fetch my cloak and sword," I tease dryly.

I hike back to the guest room, and as I tug on a tank top, a car pulls up outside of the house. Curious to catch my first glimpse of the other players, I inch up the window blinds with a fingertip and peer down at the driveway.

But it's not Julie who's arrived early—instead, a burly man climbs out onto the pavement and waves at the driver before the car pulls away.

This must be Noah.

The bard.

I can't help but snort. I would never call this lumberjack of a man *cute*—at least, not in the boyish, clean-cut way that Liam normally means.

Brawny, maybe, I think, noting how the thin fabric of his green flannel stretches across his broad shoulders. His hair, long and bound in a messy bun at the back of his neck, shines copper-penny red in the sunlight, darkening to a muted red-brown as he steps under the shade of a tree. I can tell he's tall just by the way he has to duck. He scrubs a hand over his red beard as he glances down at his phone and then up at the house, probably to make sure he's in the right place.

Just as I decide on the scientific classification of *ruggedly handsome,* I swear he hears my thoughts and tips his head up to meet my gaze—surely I imagine the way his teeth flash a white smile in the tangle of his beard. I jerk back from the window just as another car arrives.

I shake my head, feeling chagrined. No more spying. Time to meet this adventuring party face-to-face.

"I'll make you rich."

The merchant drops a burlap sack on the table—where it lands with a heavy thud—and slides it toward Jaylie. The clink of coins inside is enough to make Jaylie inhale sharply in surprise. But it's not enough to convince her.

"I've heard that before, Dorna," she says airily. "But I'm not after the money."

Dorna smirks and rolls her eyes upward toward the dusty rafters of the old tavern. "All you priestesses are the same, claiming you're above earthly temptations, hm? But I know the church of Marlana could use the money, and you won't turn away a donation of this size. You take this job, and there's much more than that in your future. I suppose it's your lucky day, isn't it?"

Jaylie withholds a sigh. As a cleric of Marlana, the Goddess of Luck, she's heard that joke many times before. But Dorna's not wrong. She *could* use the money.

"Anyway," the older woman continues, tracing the pad of one ring-laden finger around the rim of her mug of ale, "this job is specially made for you, Jay. And I'm even giving you a *team*." Dorna's muddy brown eyes spark as she leans forward, resting the bulk of her well-muscled figure on top of the table. Her leather armor creaks with the movement.

Interesting. Jaylie isn't used to working with others. "When can I meet them?"

"Right now."

Jaylie's brows shoot up, and Dorna looks smug to have caught her off guard. "Wait here, aye?" Before Jaylie can protest, Dorna's already on her feet and out the door of the small private dining room. The wood of the door is so old and warped that she can't shut it all the way behind her.

Jaylie winces. Dorna has brought her solid job opportunities before, but it's always a wonder that she insists on conducting her business in such an absolute shithole.

On a whim, Jaylie reaches for the merchant's mug and takes a quick swig of liquid courage—or liquid sewage, from the taste of it. *Marlana's mercy, that's awful.* Trying not to gag, she presses the back of her hand to her mouth and shoots up a prayer to her goddess instead, hoping she can make a good impression on this group of strangers. She *needs* this to work out—every coin counts. Suddenly aware of her travel-worn appearance, she twists the messy golden waves of her hair into a quick bun just as the door creaks open again.

Dorna reenters and steps aside as an assortment of dusty travelers files in. Jaylie is surprised to discover that she and Dorna are the only humans in attendance, but from the way the newcomers size one another up, Jaylie assumes this is the first time they're meeting, too. Good—she's not at a disadvantage. As everyone moves to find a seat, Jaylie casts a sidelong glance at the purple-skinned giant of a man who sinks into the chair to her immediate left. He bares his fanged teeth at her, and Jaylie can't tell if he is smiling or snarling; she's far too distracted by the obsidian bull-like horns jutting from his temples to get a good look at his face. A *tiefling!* She's heard stories about tieflings, and how you can recognize them by their horns or pointed tails. Supposedly they're the descendants of the devils of Hell, or the products of dark infernal magic. Spooky as the stranger might appear, though, she knows this man's devilish heritage gives him power—and rippling muscles, it seems. Badass.

"My friends." Dorna stands at the head of the table and spreads her arms wide. All eyes swing to look at her. "How glad I am to finally get you all in the same room. I know we've had our separate business relationships, and all of you have worked with me as mercenaries for years. But for an opportunity like this, well—we could use a bit of *teamwork.*" She straightens suddenly and snaps her fingers. Annoyingly on cue, a tired barmaid sweeps in with a tray full of new mugs of ale. Internally groaning, Jaylie prays for a strong constitution to face such poison again while Dorna smiles beatifically. "Introductions are in order. First off—"

"That's sweet of you, Dorna, but it's unnecessary. I'm sure I need no introduction."

The elven stranger speaks with a smooth, lilting accent before Dorna can continue, and while the merchant's smile freezes on her face, she seems unsurprised. Amused, Jaylie turns toward the speaker sitting across from her, and she swears his green eyes twinkle as they meet her gaze. He rises from his seat and regally inclines his head toward the crew like a lord presiding over his court. "But, if I must—I am Loren. Loren Rosewood."

He pauses dramatically, as if waiting for applause. But Jaylie has never seen this man in her life; she would have remembered someone so striking. She's met many pretty elves in her time—*all* elves are pretty, with their ageless features and bright eyes—but he's got to be the handsomest one she's ever seen.

Loren looks like he belongs on a stage, not in some dank room in the basement of a tavern. His clothing favors shades of green, brown, and gold in a combination of silks, delicate embroidery, and fine leather. His polished boots come up to his knees, and his frilly shirt is unlaced practically to his navel, showing off an impressive collection of necklaces and overlapping pendants. He has a ring on each finger and several gem studs pierced through his pointed ears. But it's his hair that draws Jaylie's gaze—it looks as if it's on fire. At first she thinks it's a rich auburn, but when he leans forward, the table's lantern highlights threads of vivid copper and gold. Half of his wavy hair is pulled into a loose knot, leaving the rest to tumble over his shoulders, deliberately styled to look effortlessly messy. Jaylie strains not to roll her eyes at the pretense.

But before she can do that, her gaze narrows on the neck of a polished lute peeking over Loren's shoulder.

Bard.

Of course.

"I've never heard of you," Jaylie announces sunnily, flashing him a sweet smile. The others murmur agreement, their tones reflecting varying degrees of agitation and amusement.

Loren is unfazed. "Ah, then someday down the line, you can tell my fans that you were among the *first* to know me." His gaze flicks down to the holy symbol strung on a thin chain around Jaylie's neck: an amulet with the gold coin emblem of Lady Marlana proudly displayed. He winks. "Lucky you."

Jaylie snorts, but her smile lingers on her lips. Arrogant asshole.

Handsome, though.

"Well, if you're quite done . . ." drawls a smooth voice to Loren's right. The dwarven woman sports a small half smile as she toys with one of the rings braided into her long, dark beard. Her hair is much shorter, braided close to her scalp and threaded with gold clasps. An assortment of leathers hugs her dark skin, and Jaylie spots a couple of knives sheathed at her thighs. "It's a pleasure to meet you all, loves," she quips. "I'm Morgana. I'm looking forward to working together."

A beat of silence stretches out and hangs uncomfortably in the air, but once Jaylie realizes that the tiefling man to her left is in no rush to fill it, she speaks up. "I'm Jaylie Amberlight. I'm a priestess of the Church of Marlana." Calling it a *church* is a bit of a stretch. The Lady of Luck is hardly as uptight as some of the realm's other deities, and her places of worship aren't the traditional lofty and expensive cathedrals that other gods boast but cozy temples scattered across the land. "Dorna typically hires me for my healing abilities. I'll keep you alive—if my Lady wills it," she teases.

"And what if I'm looking for luck in other areas of my life?" Loren, of course.

Jaylie arches a brow and fixes him with a stare. "You'll admit you can't get by on skill alone?"

He only grins. Morgana lets out a ringing laugh, and the tiefling flashes a fang in what might be a smile. Jaylie counts it as a win.

Dorna clears her throat and gestures to the tiefling. He's the only one who has touched his ale, and he makes the group wait as he drains the mug dry. Then he tosses his head with a grunt, his long ink-dark ponytail swaying with the movement. His voice is a rumble in his chest. "Kain."

A few seconds pass.

He says nothing more.

Jaylie jumps when Dorna claps her hands together, bringing everyone's attention back to her. "Well, then! I'll give you all time to get to know each other, but before that, I know you're waiting for me to cut to the chase." Jaylie feels the air shift slightly as everyone at the table takes in a breath at once, and Dorna smiles slowly, savoring the suspense. "We've got our muscle, one of the realm's most talented rogues, some *entertainment*, and our very own lucky charm. I imagine you're all wondering what in the Hells I have planned for such a diverse group of talent."

With a flourish, she withdraws an envelope from her pocket, its blue wax seal already broken. As Dorna slides out the thick card and lays it flat on the table for everyone to see, Jaylie catches the delicate scent of lilies wafting from it. Reading the looping cursive letters embossed on the parchment, she lets out a puzzled laugh.

It's an invitation to a wedding. Tomorrow.

"And that's a wrap on session one! What did we all think?" Liam asks.

I have to shake my head for a second to clear it. I put so much effort into embodying Jaylie that it takes some time for my imagined tavern scene to fade, revealing Liam's game room. In place of what I pictured as the worn wood of the tavern table is a white fold-out piled with character sheets, multicolored dice, and empty cans of craft beer. Liam stands just as Dorna had, with his hands braced on the tabletop and his bearded face stretched into an expectant grin.

"I loved it." I'm surprised that Julie is the first to speak, considering that she barely strung together five words for the entire three-hour session. "I want to play more, right now. I don't want to wait another week for next Sunday." I immediately liked her when she arrived with a tray of brownies and a pitcher of sangria. I had complimented her sweater—it had little cats all over it—and she'd proudly claimed that she knit it herself.

She is absolutely adorable, which makes it that much funnier that her character is Kain. He's all brooding purple muscle and devilish menace, while Julie is all sunshine, pastels, violet cat-eye glasses, and curly, pink-streaked brown hair. Her voice is also delightfully high-pitched, so I'm impressed that she gives such a convincing performance of Kain's gravelly masculine tone.

Even with her head bowed low over her notebook as she scribbles down the last of the session's notes, Morgan looks amusingly like a taller, beardless version of Morgana—which I suspect is the point. According to Liam, she decided to join the game last minute, so most of her character-building involved little more than tacking on an extra letter after her name. Long braids frame her face, and her beauty is enhanced with sparkling, bold makeup. She finally looks up at Liam with a smile. "You know, I had my doubts about D&D, but . . . it was a good time. A really good time."

I open my mouth to say something, but the bard beats me to it.

"Fucking epic, man. I'm excited. Invested! Absolutely here for it." Even though Noah has dropped Loren's Zorro-esque Spanish accent, his deep voice draws my attention back to him in the same way Loren's had drawn Jaylie's. His grin is bright, and he stands with his hands gripping the back of his chair, buzzing with excited energy. If anything about him is cute, I'll admit it's his contagious enthusiasm for the game.

Liam's about as short as I am, and seeing them side by side, I can tell Noah's got at least a foot on us both. Frankly I'm surprised he isn't playing a warrior-type character or a great big bear of a druid to match his bulk, but I'm charmed by Loren.

And maybe his player, too.

"Sadie?"

I dart my eyes back to Liam, hoping he didn't notice how I was staring. But Liam just looks at me expectantly, and I can see a little tension in the way his brows knit together, despite his smile. He won't be satisfied unless he's assured that everyone had fun. It's what makes him a great host—and an even better Dungeon Master.

"All right, fine." I lean back in my chair as I raise my half-finished glass of sangria, toasting him. "Fantastic stuff, Liam. I can't believe I held out on you for so long. I wish I'd been playing for years."

He does a little fist pump of victory. "Good. Excellent. I'm so glad to hear it—and it only gets better from here." He takes a long look at each of us, pleadingly, as if afraid we'll ghost him after one session. "We'll meet again next Sunday?"

"You know it," Noah booms, clapping Liam on the shoulder.

Liam and I follow the others as they shuffle toward the front door and out onto the driveway. While Morgan and Julie chat animatedly as they walk to their cars, I linger near the doorway and marvel again at the way Noah's hair lights up as he steps into the sun. He catches my eye and gives a friendly wave before Liam shuts the door.

With everyone gone, I turn back to Liam for his honest opinion. "Was that a good game?" I ask. "Did we do all right? I don't really have a frame of reference."

Liam stands in the entryway, staring out toward his front yard. I let him process for a minute before he finally turns toward me with a wide grin on his face. "Oh, it was fantastic. Beginners are my favorite. I get to use all my old tricks that my veterans usually see through."

My shoulders sag slightly. "You've told this story before? The whole wedding invitation setup?"

He presses a palm to his chest, offended. "What? No, of course not. I create a new story for each group." His eyes twinkle. "But still, new players are easier to surprise."

I'm not sure what he means, but I assume it's something like reading too many books of the same genre. After a while, you get used to the same old plot twists. I elbow him as I follow him back to the game room. "Maybe we'll surprise you, too."

Swirling the last dregs of sangria in my glass, I meander around the room as Liam cleans up the mess from the table. It's the only room I hadn't been in until today, and from what I can tell, it's the one room that Liam has fully claimed for himself. The bookshelves are full of brick-shaped fantasy paperbacks, game figurines, chess club trophies, and old photos. I smile at the framed pictures of our friend groups from both high school and college, dressed for academic competitions, anime conventions—god, I'd really fucked up that cosplay—graduation, and more. My blond hair had been much longer then, before I'd chopped it off after college to curl in a bob right at my shoulders. In one photo Liam and I pose after a middle school Quizbowl tournament, and with our matching pale hair and glasses, we almost look like siblings. There's even a picture of Liam and his first boyfriend at our high school scholarship ceremony, though neither of them had been out at the time.

The walls are decorated in the nerdiest way possible, with beautifully illustrated special-edition maps from books and video games, a tapestry from *Skyrim,* and another Sadie Brooks original: a painting of Garzoth the Wise, Liam's beloved character from the MMO *Legends of Lore,* posed in his fancy wizard's robes as he holds a glowing orb aloft. It had been my college graduation gift to Liam, and when I first arrived at his house, I was touched by how many of my pieces he'd kept and shipped here all the way from Connecticut.

"They were great," I say eventually. "The other players, I mean. I loved everyone's characters." Liam hums a happy agreement, and my gaze strays to Garzoth's shining green eyes, which remind me of Loren's own playful wink. "Tell me again how you met Noah?"

Liam waggles his eyebrows. He knows I'm intrigued.

Asshole, I think fondly.

I huff and busy myself with gathering the dishes into a pile. Liam follows me into the kitchen, where Howard greets us with an offended meow; he hates being shut out. But if we let him in, Liam says he'll knock all the dice off the table, turning critical hits into critical failures. I set the plates down and soothe the cat with chin scritches.

"I met him at a bar," Liam says, his mouth quirking up at the corner.

". . . On a date?"

"Yes. Well—no, not on a date with *Noah,* but . . . yeah. I was there on a date a few months ago. Noah was bartending."

"Bartending?" I swing to face him, grinning. "And you, what— you just invited him to play after meeting him for the first time?"

Liam spreads his hands wide and lets out a surprised laugh. "Look, I know it's random, but he seemed cool. Honestly, I had a better conversation with him than I did with my date. And he's new here, too, Sadie. He seemed eager to make friends." He pauses. ". . . And he also likes *Legends of Lore*."

The fastest way to Liam's heart.

"Well, as long as you're sure he won't axe-murder us after earning our trust," I tease as I snatch up the keys to the Civic. "I'm going to go grab a few groceries for the week. Do you need anything?"

Liam hesitates. "I've still got leftover pasta and some frozen pizzas, if you want them."

But he's been more than generous enough—especially on his teacher's salary—and I've got an unexpected urge to cook for myself. I'd thought socializing with strangers for the first time in weeks would be draining, but I haven't yet come down from the unexpected high of how much fun I had. Besides, Sunday has always been grocery day for me, and a step back into a routine feels . . . good. Maybe next week I'll even get back into running. "Thanks, but I'll be fine for this week, Liam. I appreciate it."

He gives me a quick nod and a plea to pick up some toilet paper as I swing open the front door. The Texas summertime heat is like a slap in the face, and the sticky, oven-like humidity is almost enough to make me turn around. Instead, I persevere.

CHAPTER
Three

Speak of the devil.

Or, well, the elf.

Noah sits on the curb next to Liam's Prius, scrolling lazily through his phone. It's been at least twenty minutes since everyone else left, and his flannel lies discarded in the grass. Seeing him in just a tank top, I can tell he's no stranger to the sun, with his tanned, freckled (and wonderfully broad) shoulders. I bet he's regretting wearing flannel and jeans, too. Maybe he's waiting on his ride—or maybe he waited for everyone to leave so he could axe-murder Liam and me, just as I suspected.

He turns and sees me hovering behind him before I can make up my mind about his motives.

"Sadie!"

We've known each other for only a few hours, but Noah greets me with the enthusiasm of a big fluffy dog who can't help but treat every stranger he meets as a potential new friend. He unfolds from the curb like a pop-up book, rising to his feet until he looms over me. Privately, I'm thankful for the shade provided by his silhouette. His smile is bright, and his eyes are the same hue as the cloudless sky above him.

It's hard not to smile back, so I do. "Noah. Your ride bail on you?"

"Not quite. I usually bike, but she's in the shop today, so—I Ubered."

I wince.

"Exactly," he confirms with a sigh. "Heller's so tiny, there aren't any available drivers at all. The one I matched with is still . . ." He checks his phone again as he runs one hand over his thick hair. The sunlight catches on a little silver hoop pierced through his left ear. "Eighteen minutes away."

"Bummer. Good luck with that, yeah?" I turn on my heel and head toward the Civic.

Kidding.

I set my axe-murderer concerns aside and take pity. "Do you want a ride?"

Noah's eyes go soft at the suggestion. "Would you?"

"I would." He bends to grab his backpack and flannel off the grass and follows me to the car. "Where to?" I ask.

"I've actually got work in an hour, and not much time left to change, so straight to Alchemist Brewing, I suppose."

"Where's Alchemist?"

"Sadie, you haven't been yet?" He feigns a wounded tone.

I like how often he uses my name—how often he uses everyone's names. There's an immediate familiarity to it. As I fish the keys from my bag, I say, "Just haven't had the excuse to yet, I guess." Or the expendable income. Or the will to leave the house.

But today's a new day.

As soon as I get the car started, I blast the AC—the interior is hot enough to bake cookies in—and key the brewery's address into my maps app. The inside of the car seems to shrink when Noah sinks into the passenger seat, his long legs bending awkwardly around the discarded cups and tote bag I'd left on the floorboard. Good-naturedly, he helps me transfer most of it into the back seat along with his backpack, though he pauses with my sketchbook in hand.

I press my lips together. I forgot I'd brought it with me on one of my Liam-mandated side quests to return his books to the library. I'd paused in the shade of their small backyard garden, doodling mindlessly as I sat on an old worn bench.

"You draw?" Noah asks.

I keep my eyes on the road as I pull out of the driveway. "A little."

It's something of an understatement.

"Like what? Moody still lifes? Graphic design sketches?" He pauses. "It's all naked anime men, isn't it?"

That earns a half grin. "How did you know?"

"I know your type." There's a smile in his voice, and when I glance at him, the playful glint in his eyes suggests *I am also the type.* "Can I see?"

Despite the many years I've spent creating art, it never gets easier to share it with anyone. Of course, it's easy to post to social media, where I can share pseudonymously with a crowd of fans, friends, and mutuals. And in Liam's house, no one knows any of the pieces he has are mine because I hate signing art; a little scribbled "S" at the bottom feels like it's subtracting from the piece. With Noah sitting close enough that I can easily gauge his reaction as soon as he opens the cover—close enough that I'm getting distracted by whatever woody cologne he must be wearing—well. It could be awkward, if he doesn't like it. He doesn't strike me as a good liar.

But I can't help feeling like I want to impress him, so I take the risk.

"Sure."

As he opens the worn sketchbook, I glance over at the pages, though I already know all the drawings within. It's my moodiest sketchbook, with a sticker on the cover spelling out VIBES in bubbly letters. In this one, I draw whatever makes me happiest. I have others, of course, for figure studies, concept work, and more—but there's a reason why this was the only one I'd brought with me to Texas. The Vibes book is just for *me*. It's both the worst place Noah could start, if he wants an idea of what I'm truly capable of, and the best place, if he wants to get to know me.

For one, he's not totally wrong about the naked anime men. I've doodled plenty of my favorite cartoon and video game protagonists, drawn in a series of different poses or in compromising positions with other characters. But alongside sketches of Kylo Ren with his pants pulled up to his nipples are charcoal drawings of my mom, tiny watercolor wildflowers, and one painstakingly rendered floor plan of what my dream apartment in New York might look like.

"These are really good, Sadie."

I make a noncommittal noise as I keep my eyes on the flat road before me, though I sit a little straighter, pleased.

"No, really. This is modern art at its finest."

The road's clear, so I risk a sidelong look. Noah holds up a page with a series of portraits of the beloved wizard Gandalf: Gandalf the Blue (sad Gandalf with a drooping hat), Gandalf the Black (Goth Gandalf with thick black eyeliner), Gandalf the Pink (Barbie Gandalf with a bow in his beard), and Gandalf the Green (stoner wizard, obviously, complete with swirling pipe smoke).

"You're too kind."

"You could do it professionally, if you wanted to. Honest."

"Oh yeah? You think the Tolkien estate would be interested in my work?" I turn an earnest, hopeful gaze toward Noah as the car rolls up to a stop sign.

I like the way his eyes crinkle at the corners. "*I* would. I'd pay you for this."

I chew at the inside of my cheek, biting back a smile. I'm flattered, even though his comment doesn't take root in my mind. I know better than to give too much hope to ideas like that. "Turn the page."

I'm rewarded with a sharp inhale of surprise as Noah takes in my latest sketch. A woman lounges lazily on her side across the span of the page, her chin cupped in one beringed hand, a glass of wine balanced in the other. Wild honey-blond curls escape from a pink-and-turquoise headscarf, spilling over the revealing folds of a cream-and-gold-colored robe. Her telltale golden amulet nestles between her breasts. I'd used lots of different colors and quick, free-form lines to sketch out her curves, lazy perch, and coy half smile. It's not the sort of practiced and perfected drawing that I could *sell*, as Noah suggested, but I like the way I'd captured her for the first time. She's a jumble of scribbled lines, full of possibility and potential, waiting until I'm certain enough of her character to out-line her in bold, sure strokes.

"Jaylie," he says, recognizing her immediately. "She's lovely."

My cheeks warm as if he had complimented me instead.

"Thank you," I hum happily. Another stop sign. There's a field to my right and two houses to my left, and I'm struck by how far I can see toward the horizon. I'm still getting used to how wide the landscape feels—how *flat*. I peek at Noah again.

As his finger hovers over Jaylie, his lips part. It's like he's got something to say, but then he shakes his head and it's gone. After a beat of silence, he continues, "So you don't do this professionally, then, as shocking as that is to me. What *do* you do, Sadie?"

"I'm in marketing." I've said it so many times, my answer is automatic. But then the pain of realization hits, a sharp reminder that—"Well, I *was* in marketing. I lost my job a few weeks ago."

I wait for the sympathetic wince I've seen on every face since I've started admitting that fact, but Noah's expression stays open and curious. "Trying something new?" he asks.

"I'm . . . taking some time off."

"That's good."

A bolt of annoyance flashes through me. How could he know whether it's a good thing for me? The harsh disappointment at losing what I'd thought was my dream job twists beneath my ribs again, and I have to clear my throat before I continue. "Just for the summer, though. I'll be back to work in New York soon enough." I nod once—sharp, decisive—and try to relax. "What about you? Liam said Alchemist has only been around for a couple of months. Is that when you moved here?"

"Yeah. A buddy of mine from college always dreamed of opening a brewery. Dumbass kept trying to brew in our dorm room before they caught him," Noah says fondly. He shrugs one shoulder. "I didn't really have anything else going on, so I said I'd help out."

I stare at the license plate of the car ahead of us to hide my surprise. Until recently, I hadn't known what it was like to *not really have anything else going on,* so I just ask, "Do you like it?"

"So far! It's so new to me, it's hard to tell. But I like meeting new people. And the free booze doesn't hurt."

"And how do you like Heller?"

"Heller's great!"

I don't try to suppress the laugh that bubbles up. "Really?" I say dryly. "Liam says that Alchemist is the most exciting thing to happen to this town in the past decade."

"That makes me something of a local celebrity, then, doesn't it? No wonder I'm enjoying myself." Noah's tone is light with amusement, and it reminds me briefly of Loren.

Finally we reach the brewery, and as I weave around cars in its half full parking lot, I'm afforded my first glance of Heller's newest gem. A wide deck wraps around the front of the building and extends into the back, with twinkling fairy lights and hanging orange canopies stretched over top. Paired with the late afternoon sun now warming the horizon, the budding lights and neon "A" sign buzzing over the door paint a welcoming invitation.

But Noah hasn't moved yet. He's still lounging in the passenger seat, elbow propped on the center console. "What about you? Do you like Heller?" he asks, his head tilted.

"It's so new to me, it's hard to tell," I say, echoing his earlier assessment. "It's . . . hot," I add helpfully. Grumpily.

He laughs, but his smile lingers. "Maybe we can explore it together." His tone lilts up at the end, turning it into a question. His gaze skates across the horizon like he's mapping it all out.

And then he trains his clear blue eyes on me.

His suggestion hangs in the air between us, humming with possibility. I'm caught off guard, but I can't help the flash of intrigue that blooms in my chest. It would be nice, maybe, to explore this town with someone who's as displaced as me—someone who looks at Heller as an adventure to be had, ripe with undiscovered magic and opportunity. Already Noah's cheerful company has been a welcome distraction, and it doesn't hurt that he's so easy on the eyes, either.

Maybe I could use some of his sunshine to chase away my stormcloud perspective.

Noah tosses his chin toward Alchemist. "Start here. Come in for a minute and see the place." The brewery's fairy lights reflect in his eyes when he offers, "First drink's on the house."

I consider it. Even from my car I can hear the jaunty crooning of a folk song carrying from the speakers set up outside, and the temptation of a beer to relax the tension in my shoulders almost has me reaching to turn off the ignition. I can't lie and say I'm not eager to quiz Noah about how he ended up in Heller. I wonder, too, if I'm imagining the hopeful note in his invitation—but then again, Noah's overt friendliness is likely what entices many patrons through those glass doors in the first place. It's probably the same charm he turned on Liam, enough to be invited to our D&D group.

It's hardly a charm I'm immune to, but for today, I've reached my quota for new experiences. Reminders of my joblessness and all the groceries I said I wanted to buy circle my thoughts, and I shake my head. I'm just not there yet. Anxiety pools in my stomach.

"I've got to make a grocery run," I say lamely, my smile feeling forced as it stretches my cheeks wide. "I told Liam I'd pick up the TP this week. I'm his only hope." Unwilling to completely shut the figurative door, I add hopefully, "Next time?"

"Next time." Noah reverently sets my sketchbook on top of the dashboard before reaching to pat my forearm. He gives it a brief squeeze. "Drive safe, Sadie. And thanks for the ride."

He shrugs back into his flannel and exits the car, giving a two-fingered salute before he disappears into the brewery.

CHAPTER
Four

I'm running calculations. Midway through my fourth week of unemployment and a third of the way through my fifth cup of instant ramen this week, I sit at the guest room's tiny desk and squint at my bank account totals. Although I've always kept some savings set aside for emergencies, it turns out that my rainy-day fund accounts for only a light drizzle—not the steady downpour of facing a whole summer with no work. Even with Liam's generosity and weeks of ramen and PB&Js, I won't last longer than another month or two at best without some additional income. Not when I'm still paying my roommates rent for the NYC apartment that I'm not even living in.

I need a new plan.

When I lost the job at Incite, I had only a handful of options. In theory, I could have stayed with my parents in Connecticut, but that was immediately out of the question. I wouldn't be able to handle the pressure of the old high school medals hanging above my bed, my mom peeking through my door and softly asking, "Are you all right, Sadiebug?," and my dad's stormy glances from across the kitchen table . . . it was too much to think about. As an only child, I felt that the weight of their expectations for me was heavy enough. I could have gone back to my manager and asked her to reconsider her decision to let me go, but the thought of that had filled me with cold dread. I'd considered trying to find something else in the city, something I could work part time until I got back on my feet again. But instead, I'd stared blankly at my ceiling for a week, paralyzed by indecision and disgust until Liam came to the rescue.

Among my banking and budgeting browser tabs, I spot the threatening bubble of an unread email. But it's just from an old nosy co-worker.

Subject: Just Checking In!

Josephine!

How are things going?? I know it's been a while since we've had the chance to catch up over happy hour (you're in TX now, right?) but I miss having you around. I told my manager about you, and he said he reached out a couple of weeks back to set up an interview but hasn't heard back from you yet. You should hit him up—you know I'd KILL to work with you again.

I'm not sure what happened at Incite, but I'm here if you need anything. I'll keep you posted if I have any other leads. We'll have you back in the city in no time!

x Darcy

Despite spending a few lunch breaks together and sharing a cubicle wall, Darcy and I had never been close while she'd worked at Incite. I know this outreach is only her attempt to fish for juicy details to pass around at her next office happy hour. I don't bother to look at the link she's attached to the recruiting website.

Instead, I sit with the email for a few heartbeats, allowing the anxiety to grip my chest in an icy fist. When I first got the job at Incite straight out of college, my manager had called me Josephine by mistake, referring to my HR paperwork. No one except my grandma ever called me Josephine. I'd always been Sadie. But in the moment, I'd liked the sound of it and hadn't bothered to correct her. Josephine seemed like a chic big-city gal, ready to take on the world—a name I could grow into. Seeing the name again now just adds another layer of sour resentment.

I roughly scrub one hand through my hair. Ignoring a handful of other emails like Darcy's, I pull up the social media accounts I created for my art and idly scroll through, looking for any distraction. I used to be proud that my accounts were fairly popular, as I'd kept up-to-date with posting fanart for trending shows and games. It wasn't unusual for superfans to reach out and ask me to draw their faves, and I'd taken on a few paid requests when the mood struck. So, despite half a year of inactivity, I've still got a backlog of DMs and requests: *Are you currently accepting commissions?*

I tilt my head slowly to the side and then go still. Into the quiet silence of the room, I let out a single contemplative "Hm."

There are plenty of ways I could make enough money to get through the rest of the summer. I could be the Uber driver Heller so desperately needs, or pick up shifts at the grocery store. *Since they're brand-new, Alchemist is probably hiring,* I think wildly, before waving away that idea—even though working at Alchemist would be a safer plan than the one currently taking root in my mind. Everything has felt so foggy lately that this small seed of inspiration feels like a ray of sun piercing through the clouds—impossible to ignore.

Before doubt can poison my sudden rush of enthusiasm, I accept all of my pending commission requests, including a pet portrait for a birthday gift, a bust of someone's *Legends of Lore* character, and a NSFW drawing of my least favorite Marvel hero, Captain America. But hey, the spicy art will undoubtedly bring in the most money—and even the most boring of the Avengers will be a treat to draw nude. For years I've done commissions just to keep my skills fresh, but this is the first time I might actually be relying on the income. And despite my nerves, it feels *good*.

I smile to myself. Is this what Noah imagined when he suggested I pursue art *professionally*?

Regardless, America's ass is a lot easier to focus on than my real career falling apart.

I carefully close my laptop and set it to the side, trading it for my drawing tablet and pen.

"Hi, Sadie."

Noah stands silhouetted in Liam's doorway, early Sunday afternoon sunshine beaming bright and merciless behind him. His face is shiny with sweat, loose curls sticking to his temples as he lifts off his helmet and clips it to his bike. I open the door wide enough for him to roll it inside and rest it against the wall of the entryway.

"Just in time, Noah. Can't have a wedding without any music," I tease. It's not that he's late—everyone else just arrived sheepishly, eagerly early, to Liam's delight.

"Worst case, Kain would fill in for me."

I laugh. "You think so?"

"I'm sure he's got a nice baritone."

"Bass," Julie calls from the kitchen, correcting him. "But he'd kill you first before ever agreeing to perform."

Noah and I share a grin, and he slides a drawstring backpack from his shoulder. I frown at its awkward bulkiness. "What's in the bag?" I ask.

Surreptitiously, Noah glances to either side before he leans close enough for me to feel the heat of his sun-warmed skin radiating against my cheek. He holds the bag out, almost in offering. But just as I reach for it, he snatches it away and laughs.

"It's a surprise. You'll see."

He disappears down the hallway and into the game room while I lean against the wall, pretending not to be flustered. After a moment or two, I return to the kitchen to finish helping with today's snacks.

Apart from my growing curiosity about Noah, Julie—who upon meeting her for the second time this morning insisted that I call her Jules—is swiftly becoming my favorite member of the group. My affection can be won with little treats, and Jules is the queen of little treats. Again she arrived early, with iced tea and cookie dough, insistent on using Liam's oven to bake the cookies so that they'd be as fresh as possible when everyone arrived.

Bless her.

I stack cups for the tea while she removes the last batch of chocolate chip cookies from the oven. "So, Jules," I ask, "what big secret is Liam blackmailing you with to get you to play D&D with us? Is it the recipe for these cookies?"

As she laughs, her eyes crinkle with delight behind her glasses. "I don't look like I play, do I?"

I pause to give her outfit a once-over: black denim overall skirt over a white-and-red-checkered button-up shirt. There are hearts embroidered on the lapels, and the skirt flares outward in a way that accentuates her curves. "You look like you're too cool for us, actually," I say.

She pretends to flip her hair over her shoulder, even though she's got it pinned up in space buns today. "Truthfully, I asked to play." I lift the pitcher of tea, and she follows behind with the cookies as we walk to the game room. "I've been exploring new hobbies and trying to find new outlets, you know? And Liam and I have always been buds."

I imagine if I had to listen to middle schoolers play out of tune all day, I'd need an outlet as a big, muscled barbarian dude, too.

We join the others in the game room, where Morgan and Noah

have their heads bent together across the table, discussing what elaborate outfits their characters are wearing to the wedding. Jules is quick to chime in as she hovers over them, pouring drinks and arranging her cookies. As the others go on about their wardrobe selections, I sit and jot down notes in my journal alongside rough sketches. I'd already drawn Jaylie—why not the others? As Morgan laughs at something Noah says, I keep my eyes on the page and outline Morgana's confident smirk.

I wonder if Noah's asked her to show him around town, too.

"All right, all right—are we ready to get started?" Liam asks. Everyone settles in and pulls out tiny velvet bags identical to the one holding my own dice—we'd rolled only a few dice during our first session, and I hadn't noticed them in detail. My heart melts to realize that Liam must have gifted everyone their first set. Morgan's dice are a dark, decadent red with swirls of gold threaded throughout, and Jules's are a stormy purple. Noah's are a mix of different clover-green tones, and he energetically passes them back and forth between his hands. I marvel at how thoughtfully chosen they all were. When Liam first gave me my set, I'd simply admired how pretty they were, but it occurs to me now that they look just like the Goddess of Luck's gold coins.

As Liam prepares the last of his notes, Noah's voice floats toward me from across the table. "Which color? You should ask Sadie, not me. She's the artist."

Morgan turns to me from where she sits on my left. Her perfume is a sharp, citrusy cloud around us. "Are you really, Sadie?" She glances at my notebook, and her brows climb her forehead in surprise. "Is that my girl?" She taps a pointed red fingernail over my sketch of Morgana.

"I—yeah. I like to doodle." Internally, I wince. *Doodle?*

"She's perfect," Morgan gushes.

I look up to find Noah smiling at us—at me. His eyes dance

over my features, lingering on the side of my face. "Picked those out special for today, didn't you?"

I twirl one of my dagger earrings between my fingertips. "Maybe."

"So thematic," Morgan says with a laugh. "Can you draw some for Morgana, too?"

"I'm on it."

"Well, if we're all set, then?" Although he addresses the whole table, Liam's gaze is pinned on me. He's using his teacher voice. I'm the kid in the back of the class who won't stop talking.

"I've got all my spells. Let's do it," I say.

"And I've got my songs picked out." Noah reaches under his chair and produces a cheap-looking ukulele out of seemingly nowhere. The table collectively groans good-naturedly, and Jules claps her hands together with a laugh. Liam looks pleased to have inspired such a high level of participation.

Noah meets my eyes across the table and grins.

"Excellent," Liam says. "Then allow me to paint a picture of where we left off . . ."

CHAPTER
Five

"You have until the count of ten to explain to me why I'm dressed like this before I introduce you to the sharp end of my axe."

The threat drips off of Kain's fangs with menace, but Jaylie is more surprised to hear the man string together so many words at once.

"Oh hush," Loren chides. "I think you look rather handsome." With a flourish, the bard expertly ties off the black bow tie around Kain's neck. It appears comedically tiny when situated atop the tiefling's broad chest and shoulders. Below it, the fabric of his smart black butler's suit strains against his muscles, two sizes too small. They'd had to rip a hole in the seat of the pants to make room for his tail, which snaps back and forth with annoyance. Jaylie is reminded fondly of her grouchy kitten, Charm, waiting for her at her Lady's temple.

Teeth bared, Kain continues to hiss out his countdown. "*Seven. Eight. Nine . . .*"

"It's part of the plan, Kain," Jaylie stresses. "Remember?"

Back at the tavern, Dorna had laid out every detail. Their mission is simple: ensure nothing goes wrong at the wedding of their eccentric and rich employer, Lord Aurelio Donati.

Although Jaylie herself is no mage, even she's heard of Donati, the city of Belandar's most beloved wizard. He boasts a seat on the Arcane Assembly, a professorship at the Arcane Academy, and a reputation for having boundless generosity and deep, deep pockets, so it's no wonder Dorna is quite eager to please her newest client. To stay in line with the groom's wish not to have obvious armed guards in attendance on the happiest day of his life, each member of Jaylie's party is given a disguise and a perfectly good reason to be at the wedding.

"Really, we gave you the easiest job of all. And the best opportunity for scouting," Loren adds.

Morgana snorts from where she leans against the doorway, picking at her nails with the blade of her dagger. "It's an empty threat anyway, Kain," she says dryly. "You already hid your axe by the tree, in case you actually *need* it during the ceremony, gods forbid." She's dressed the part of a noblewoman, with delicate chains woven into her oiled beard and eyelids streaked with silver. The slit in her blue skirt is provocatively high. Jaylie suspects it's more for ass-kicking practicality than to draw eyes, though she imagines Morgana is probably quite good at both.

Kain mutters something about not needing an axe to make them bleed for forcing him to suffer the indignity of a bow tie.

Casting one last glance around the perimeter of the small guest room Donati allowed them for their preparations, Morgana nods to herself. "Let's get going, then. I could use a drink." She swings the door wide, and Kain stalks behind her with a silver tray stacked with treats and champagne.

"Wait," Loren murmurs.

As the others wander off, Jaylie turns.

"Your pendant's crooked."

Loren steps close and begins to fuss with the chain strung across Jaylie's forehead and pinned into her curls, a gold coin medallion depicting Marlana's winking face—her order's symbol—hanging slightly off-balance above her left eyebrow. As the bard presses his fingertips gently against her temples to tilt her head straight, Jaylie inhales slightly, her shoulders and neck tensing.

This close, she can tell his eyes aren't fully green. They're threaded through with warm brown, tiny spears of emerald, specks of amber . . .

His mouth curls into a teasing smile. "Nervous, priestess? You've got the most important role of all."

The reminder grounds her, and her gaze slides past his face to the mirror behind him and meets the eyes of her reflection.

She's dressed in ceremonial garb befitting her position as a priestess of Marlana. Her robes are the color of flower petals, beginning with a pastel pink at her chest that deepens into a wine red near the ends of her skirts. More tiny gold coins are strewn in chains all over her body: encircling her neck, draped across her bare shoulders, strung to her wrists, and wound in the newly straightened circlet that binds her free-flowing hair.

Jaylie offers a little smile to her reflection. She loves a bit of ceremony. She *loves* to dress up. And admittedly, none of her party would look even half as good without the bard's skill for cosmetics and flair.

She exhales in a rush, standing tall. "I've officiated dozens of weddings, Loren. Nerves are long behind me."

His brow arches in amusement. "Dozens?"

"Of course. Who wouldn't want to start off their marriage with a little luck?"

"I can't argue with that."

He offers her his arm, and they step out into the sun.

The sprawling gardens of Lord Donati's estate stun Jaylie for the second time that day. She and her party had toured them that morning when making last-minute security preparations, but now that all the guests have arrived, the grounds are bursting with life. Nobles draped in jewel-toned dresses and coats flutter among the hedges and rosebushes like butterflies while wizards stand in clusters near the fountains, heads bent together in scholarly conversation. A group of young students in formal black robes pauses to stare at the pale towers of Donati's small castle, its iron gates bookended by pale blue banners, emblazoned with his sky lily crest in white, swaying in the breeze.

As they meander through the crowds, Jaylie turns to regard the statue at the center of the nearest fountain. This figure, like at least half of the statues in the garden, is sculpted in Donati's likeness. Although Jaylie hasn't met Donati yet, she doubts that he could possibly be as handsome as the piece makes him out to be. Here, he poses with his arm outstretched, water bursting from the tip of the wand clutched in his fist. His stone hair is perfectly coiffed, marble teeth clenched in a grin. It's better than the one of him standing atop the back of a galloping unicorn, at least.

Arrogant prick, Jaylie thinks.

"Cocky bastard," Loren murmurs under his breath.

She doesn't stop the laugh that bubbles out, and Loren smiles conspiratorially.

As they make their way toward the ceremony tree, Jaylie's ears perk at the sound of music drifting from a different direction, and she turns to see another fountain with water spouting from a pointed wizard's hat atop Donati's smiling stone face. There, a group of nobles lingers near a trio of musicians plucking out the gentle chords of a love song. Morgana, deep in conversation with two halfling women, catches Jaylie's eye. She nods to Loren and juts her chin to the side. Jaylie squeezes the bard's arm briefly. "I think that's your cue."

"So it is. Best of luck, Jaylie."

She smiles. "Of course."

With the sun almost at its highest point in the sky, Jaylie knows the ceremony is about to begin, and she quickens her pace to the base of the large tree at the garden's center. When she steps into its wide pool of shade, a wistful sigh escapes her lips as she pauses to admire it. It was clever of Donati to hire a group of druids to decorate for his wedding, using their connection with nature to conjure a scene of such beauty. The tree is so large that even if Jaylie's whole party stood in a ring around it and held hands, they wouldn't be able to encircle its entirety. Facing an array of benches, two of the tree's roots have been magically coerced to rise from the ground to form an arch, their ends twining together in the middle. Dozens of sky lilies bloom impossibly from the roots in bursts of blues, whites, and pinks, gently swaying in the wind. A tall elven druid in leafy green skirts casts one last spell over the arch, summoning a handful of illusory blue butterflies and glowing orbs of soft light. Although Jaylie had nothing to do with the decorating, she's gratified to see strands of Marlana's coins threaded throughout the arch and to hear the gasps and coos of amazement from the guests as they arrive and take their seats.

Jaylie takes her place at the center of the arch and prepares to wait, but it doesn't take long. Near the back of the crowd, Jaylie spots Loren and the musicians murmuring together. The half-orc violinist taps their bow once, twice, and then launches expertly into the music, right in time with the rest of the group. It's a grand song, full of power and pride, though Jaylie thinks it's a touch too upbeat for the soft ambience of the setting. It's only a few moments after the first measures are played that she gets her first glance at Donati.

If the man looked anything like his garden statues, the song would be a fitting entrance.

But he doesn't.

He looks sweet. *Approachable.* While his statues scream might and strength, the professor himself exudes an air of gentle charm, friendliness, and come-to-my-office-hours-for-tea energy. Still, he looks very proud as he paces toward the ceremony tree, dressed handsomely in a deep navy suit and subtly platformed boots that still don't get him to the height of his supposedly life-sized statues. His light brown hair is styled in its signature coif, carefully gelled in place. As he nears the tree and stands to Jaylie's right, he gives her a small bow of his head. "Thank you again for your services today, priestess."

"It is my pleasure." Before she can say anything further, Loren's lute takes the lead, and the music swells into a melody more romantic—and much more beautiful.

Flanked by her parents on either arm, Donati's bride-to-be, Alora Clare, strides gracefully between the pews. *She's a riot of lace,* Jaylie thinks unkindly. It's exquisite lace, of course, and Jaylie suspects that magic was involved in the creation of the dress, but there's so much of it that the woman herself is buried under layers of the ball gown. The veil is thick, hiding Alora's eyes behind sparkling thread. All Jaylie can see are her pink-painted lips—and the small, polite smile she wears.

Even as guests beam and hold their hands to their hearts as they behold the bride, Jaylie suspects that not everyone is pleased to see her. As she wandered the gardens before the ceremony, Jaylie had caught some of the rumors.

One of his own students! one gnome whispered to another, both dressed in the red and gold of the Academy. *It isn't appropriate, is it?*

I've heard she's with child. There's no other explanation for such a swift union, a tall elf tutted, scowling jealously at a stone statue of Donati blowing a kiss.

Money, a dwarf grumbled appreciatively, stroking a long blond beard woven with heavy golden rings. *It's always about money, and I can't blame him. Her parents are the wealthiest family in the Great North, did you know? All thanks to their sorcerous inventions.*

Whatever the truth of the matter is, Jaylie watches as Donati's features soften at the appearance of his bride. He squeezes his hands together to stop himself from reaching for her. Alora's veil flutters as she releases what sounds like a wistful sigh, and the music softens. The last lines of the melody are plucked sweetly from the lute, and Jaylie suppresses a laugh.

Damned bard always has to get the final word in.

There's a moment where all that can be heard is the breeze as it weaves through the greenery and the tinkling coins, which chime gently. All gazes shift to the couple, and then to Jaylie.

The priestess inhales, and then begins.

"*Mawiage*—"

"Okay, Sadie, come the fuck *on.*"

Liam looks positively distraught to have had his gorgeously described scene interrupted by such an obvious joke.

There's a roar of laughter from Noah immediately followed by the girls dissolving into fits of snickering.

"You were literally asking for it, giving me this kind of responsibility!" I protest.

Noah is *rolling,* clutching his ukulele to his chest as tears of laughter gather in the corners of his eyes. He has one of those loud-ass, wholly genuine laughs that are immediately endearing, and I'm smug to be the cause of it.

Liam rolls his eyes skyward, probably sending up a prayer to the D&D gods, before returning a steady gaze to me.

I hold up my hands in surrender. "All right, yes, let me try this again."

I catch a small dimple in Liam's beard—a concession—as he gestures for me to continue.

Earlier, Jaylie was a little disappointed that she was not given the opportunity to write the script for the ceremony herself. As a priestess of Marlana with a decade of service under her belt, she has found that marriage officiate is one of her favorite roles to play.

But Dorna stressed the importance of sticking to the lines provided by Donati, who even seems to laugh on cue, as if he planned every reaction. But despite her strict guidance, Jaylie makes sure to sprinkle in a little of her Lady's wisdom.

"There's always a bit of luck in love."

Donati's eyes flash to Jaylie at her words, but his smile is wide and encouraging, and his eyes crease happily at the corners. Jaylie catches the sparkle of a grin through Alora's veil.

"To exist within the same lifetime as someone, the same universe—to be more than fleeting glances across the road, or ships passing in the night . . . there is no greater fortune than for your stars to align with the one you love. There is no greater blessing than for the Lady of Luck to connect two souls as she has here." Jaylie smiles beatifically at the couple and lifts her upturned palms toward them both.

Donati squeezes Alora's hands, and Alora strokes her thumbs over his knuckles. Jaylie reaches to where a lily grows from the cluster of flowers embedded in the arch. The petals unfurl at her touch, revealing two rings.

"Lord Aurelio Donati," Jaylie intones, turning back to the couple. "Do you take this woman to be your wife? Do you promise to love her, comfort her, honor and keep her, in sickness and in health, as long as you both shall live?"

"I do."

"And Alora Clare, do you take this man to be your husband? Do you promise to love him, comfort him, honor and keep him, in sickness and in health, as long as you both shall live?"

"Unlikely."

Jaylie flinches at the venom in her tone. It's the first time she's heard Alora speak, and the strength of her deep voice catches the priestess off guard. But when she sees the girl's lips part in a surprised "O," it occurs to her that Alora never spoke at all.

Gasps echo throughout the garden as a clawed hand curls around the back of Jaylie's neck, nails piercing through the silk of her gown to press into her skin. Gingerly, Jaylie turns just enough to see a sharp grin set into the long, angular face of a human woman. The woman's violet eyes glow with magic, and her long black hair, shaved on the sides of her head, whips in the thrall of an unseen wind. Behind her, a newly conjured portal yawns within the arch, undulating with glowing black-and-purple energy.

"She'll be making no promises to you today, Aurelio." The witch seethes, biting off every syllable of his name with barely contained hatred.

"*Guards!*" Donati shouts.

It takes Jaylie a few moments to realize that he's referring to *her*. The wedding erupts into chaos, and several things happen all at once.

The witch snakes her arm around Alora's waist and tugs her forcefully toward the portal. The arch itself begins to decay at an alarming pace, mushrooms and jagged thistles replacing the spring blooms. The druids from earlier descend on Donati, revealing thornlike blades hidden under their leafy skirts. While most of the guests add to Donati's enraged yell with their own yelps of terror and shock, a number of darkly dressed mages join the druids and summon shadowy pools of magic between their hands. It looks remarkably like the same sinister power the witch wields.

We weren't the only ones undercover.

"Well, fuck," Jaylie says helpfully.

Just as Kain rips his buttoned shirt off—unnecessarily, but to Jaylie's great amusement—and flies into a rage, Morgana lurches toward the druids with daggers gripped in her fists. Jaylie's brows draw together in confusion as Loren launches into a bawdy tavern song, but to her surprise, the music has a magic of its own. From the bowl of his lute, tiny bolts of fire launch toward the dark sorcerers. As her party flies into action, Jaylie realizes just how skilled they all are—and just how far away they are from what matters most.

Goddess, what a *mess*.

Desperately, Jaylie wraps her fingers around the witch's flexed upper arm—*Ooh, she's strong*—and sends a prayer up to Marlana. A spell forms in her palm, one that would freeze the woman in her tracks. But it fizzles out almost immediately, useless. Behind Jaylie, Donati roars, and lightning crackles between his fingers—only to dissolve into a shower of sparks. The witch snorts, and Jaylie realizes just how easily the woman dispelled their magic. *That's very advanced spellcraft*, Jaylie worries.

Jaylie swears the woman's smile is almost apologetic as she pulls the bride tight to her side. "I'm terribly sorry, but we've got to be going."

"I'd really appreciate it if you stayed. It would make my job a lot easier," Jaylie says sweetly, her words high-pitched. Desperate.

The witch pretends to consider that. "I think not," she decides, turning back to Alora. "Come, sweetling."

And then, meanly, to Jaylie: "*Good luck.*"

Within three strides, Alora and her captor disappear into the portal. Immediately the glowing magic disappears with a sudden *pop*, and the archway returns to normal. Although the fighting continues in the gardens, Donati stills, his hands dropping uselessly to his sides. In slow motion, he swivels his head and meets Jaylie's gaze.

"You will find me my bride," he snarls, and it's his wide, white-toothed smile that's the most unnerving. "Or I will have your *heads.*"

CHAPTER
Six

Liam picks up on the second ring. "Hello?"

"Hey!" I say cheerfully, phone tucked between my ear and shoulder as I smear peanut butter onto toast. It's almost noon, but it's never too late for breakfast in my book. "What's up?"

"Just working. You know. *Teaching.*" It's Tuesday. "Summer school's not out till three."

"I know damn well this is one of your off periods or I wouldn't have called, friend."

"Yeah, yeah. Still, if you're just calling to try to get me to tell you where Alora went—"

I'm tempted to give it another shot, but even after I harassed him for answers for the last two days, he remained tight-lipped. I smile at the memory of the stunned silence that had settled over the table after Liam's plot twist, the way Noah had knotted his fingers in his hair in shock, and the Kain-like rage that had set Jules's eyes on fire. I'd thought she was going to flip the table.

Suffice to say, we're totally invested now.

But I have something else on my mind. "I wanted to see if you were game for happy hour after work today."

"Where? Chili's?" he asks. It's embarrassing, but Liam and I are sluts for Chili's. It helps that there's always one within a ten-mile radius, and I suspect that the Texas locations aren't too different from Connecticut's.

But that's not where I want to go. I don't really have the budget for happy hours at all, frankly.

But for a free drink?

"I was thinking we could try Alchemist." I keep my tone cool, nonchalant.

I can hear the smile in his voice when he speaks again. "Uh-huh." He sees right through me.

"Do they have any . . . happy hour specials?"

"If by that you mean to ask if you can claim your first beer on the house . . . Yes, he's working today."

Excellent. "See you at six?"

He barks out a quick laugh. "See you at six, Sadie."

I hang up, finish the rest of my toast, and sip at a yogurt smoothie as I think through the afternoon's agenda. For the second morning in a row, I managed to get outside for a run—or, if we're honest, a brisk walk. It wasn't anywhere near the hour-long jogs I used to take when I was at my peak, but it's a start. Now I want to shift my focus to the state of the guest room. I'm still living out of my suitcase, and coffee mugs and forgotten dishes have started to clutter the desk. But when I arrived at Liam's, I swore to myself I wouldn't let the guest room reach the state I'd left my New York room in, so as soon as I finish my Captain America pinup commission, I plan on spending time cleaning it up.

My phone buzzes in my pocket, and I wonder if it's Liam wanting to change plans. But it's my mom's face that flashes across the screen.

I consider pretending to be busy, which has been my go-to strategy over the last few weeks with her, but I jam the answer button at the last second.

"Hi, Mom." My voice is all careful neutrality. "What's up?"

"Sadiebug, I am so glad you picked up," she croons. "Do you have a sec? I have *got* to tell you what Meatball did this morning."

"I've always got time for Meatball."

As my mother regales me with a story about their latest pit bull foster—a habit she and my dad have gotten into since becoming empty nesters—I wander back up to the guest room and start organizing my dirty clothes to wash later and collecting my dishes to take downstairs. There's something calming about listening to my mom chatter on about the mundane and sometimes hilarious aspects of her newly retired reality, and a pang of homesickness takes me by surprise.

"The whole thing, Sadie. The lasagna, the broccoli—he licked the container clean! I had to send your poor father to work without his lunch!"

"I'm sure he'll live," I say with a laugh. "He's always looking for an excuse to visit the pizza place on the corner."

"Don't I know it." She pauses, and I listen as she noisily sips what I know is coffee. It should be a crime to consume as many cups as she does each day. She exhales a sigh, and I straighten instinctively, bracing myself. "I miss you, honey," she says, her tone more wistful now. "It was so much easier when I could just hop on the train and come see you!"

"I know, Mom," I say. She used to visit at least once a month during the summer. We'd take our time walking from Grand Central up to Central Park, where we'd find an empty bench and people-watch as we talked for ages, catching up on gossip, work, and family drama. In the evening I'd get us discount Broadway tickets through Incite's benefits program, and then we'd end the evening sipping overpriced cocktails and tipsily befriending tourists in Times Square. My mom has a talent for making friends with anyone, which is fun until she tries to set me up with any bartender who pauses long enough to listen to her. It's a tradition we won't get to have this summer, and I'm horrified by the way my throat tightens at the thought. I have to swallow a few times before I speak again. "I miss you, too."

"I'll see you soon enough." I can't tell if she's saying it to soothe me or to assure herself. "And how's my boy doing?"

"Liam's great," I gush. "His house is beautiful, Mom. You'd be really proud of him."

"You'll give him my best, won't you?"

"I always do."

"Good." I can hear the smile in her voice. "Well, I've got to take this big lug on a walk, but I'll check in with you later."

I'm surprised that she hasn't pressed me on my job hunt progress, but perhaps she's realized that I'll answer her calls more often if she doesn't bring it up. "Okay. Tell Dad I said hi."

"Of course. Take care, honey. And—" There's a brief twang of tension in her tone. "Let me know if you need anything, okay? Anything at all."

"I will."

We exchange I-love-yous and goodbyes, and when we hang up, I stand alone in the kitchen with a dirty mug in my hand, forgetting what I meant to do with it. I set it aside and reach for my tablet where I'd left it on the countertop, but instead of pulling up my half-finished commission, I open my inbox again.

Feeling nostalgic, I begin to page through the industry-related emails I'm still subscribed to. There are a few mentions of promotions at Incite, and discussions about the challenges and ethical issues of new tech being introduced in the marketing world. I glance through the hiring boards, hardly ready to begin applying but letting myself imagine what it might be like to work somewhere new. Perhaps I'd have less oversight and more freedom to be experimental and bold with my campaigns. Perhaps my new manager would be more flexible, and I'd get a salary that would let me live closer to the city. I could take my mom out to Broadway shows without needing the discounts.

There's an ad for a position at Paragon Media, and the name rings a bell of recognition in the back of my head. Although Paragon is something of a new kid on the block in the city's media marketing scene, the startup already has a reputation for creativity, innovation . . . and great pay. Even while at Incite I'd considered applying to them, curious about their strategy.

After a few minutes of pacing the kitchen, sipping my smoothie, and avoiding Howard's judgmental stare from where he sits perched on the countertop, I retrieve my laptop from upstairs and pull up my old résumé and cover letter. In a month or so, I'll have to get more serious about job hunting. Applying to Paragon while the stakes are still low will minimize the terror I feel every time I think about returning to New York—right? Before I can talk myself out of it, I click open Paragon's application. At the very least, I have a tall glass of beer to look forward to as a reward.

Alchemist looks just as welcoming as before, with its stylized neon-green "A" glowing like a beacon above the entrance. Heller's still solidly in the grips of summer, but we got lucky tonight— there's a hint of coolness in the air, and the brewery has plenty of customers happy to take advantage of the break from the heat. On the deck, people cluster under the shade of the canopies, laughing with friends or winding down with a beer in hand, their voices carrying over the breezy bluegrass music humming from the speakers. I spot Liam leaning against the railing and wave as I head toward him.

"You look nice," he says, his tone teasingly accusing.

I've paired ripped jeans with a cropped green tank top and my favorite combat boots, though I've thrown a cardigan on top of it all to soften the look. It's the most care I've put into an outfit in weeks—and it's not Liam's attention I'm hoping to catch. Even the dagger earrings are in again. I'm on a mission.

"Thanks. You look like you're trying to convince your students you're cool."

Liam looks down at his Vans, khakis, black button-up, and denim jacket. "My kids *do* think I'm cool."

"Uh-huh," I deadpan. "No math teacher can be cool. It's against the rules."

Privately, I *do* think Liam's the coolest. The prospect of helping hormonal, angry middle schoolers navigate the trials of growing up scares most people shitless, so I've always admired Liam's dedication to the role he plays in his students' lives.

He shoves my arm playfully as we turn and walk inside.

My immediate thought is that it looks just like a fantasy tavern. Several dark wooden picnic tables stretch out along the middle of the floor, while smaller tables and rocking chairs are set up to create cozy reading nooks, a gaming setup, and perfect little corners for dates. Large kegs sit in clusters along the walls, and everything is lit by soft yellow lights hanging from the rafters above. To our left is a dark green wall with a few scattered posters pinned up and an electric fireplace burning merrily in the middle. It's far too early in the year for a fire, and their AC must be working double-time to counteract it, but damn does it set the mood. Already I have the itch to settle in at a corner table and sketch the whole scene out.

To our right is the bar itself, manned by Noah and a bald man with an unfortunately long blond mustache. He sports a beanie and a black shirt with the brewery's logo on the front: the same stylized "A" but stuffed into a bubbling conical potion bottle. It's an excellent logo. Both my marketing and my artistic sensibilities agree.

Noah is wearing a black-and-red flannel—*how many does he*

have?—rolled up to his elbows, and he's tied half of his hair into a little knot on the back of his head. He's already wearing a customer-service-friendly smile when we walk in, but as soon as he recognizes us, his expression brightens into something warmer.

"Sadie, Liam!" He circles around the bar and tugs Liam into a friendly side hug before turning to face me, arms outstretched in that universal *Are you a hugger?* invitation. Totally game, I welcome the embrace, and Noah bends to fold me into his chest. The height difference between us is comedic and undeniably cozy. He smells like beer and the outdoors, and his beard tickles my forehead.

"You came," he says cheerily, gesturing for us to sit on the barstools. "What can I get for you two?"

Liam points to one of the stouts on the brewery's menu. "I'll have the Flask of Storms again."

I glance through the draft list, marveling at the names of the different beers—Elixir of Love, Firebreathing Potion, Brew of Poisons, Draught of Demons—and laugh a little under my breath. Within seconds I know what I want, but I can't help myself. I turn my most charming smile onto Noah. "What do you recommend?"

He leans forward on the bar, perching on his forearms. "I'm so glad you asked."

He launches into a series of pitches for every drink on the menu, and after a good bit of back-and-forth, it's obvious that he's great at his job—or at least that he knows a lot about beer. What am I in the mood for? Something dark and heavy? An IPA? No, absolutely not. Okay, so something summery, right? Light and breezy, something I could crush while lounging on the beach? Maybe. We're getting closer. He doesn't want to assume that all women go for fruity drinks, but he has to ask . . . do *I* like fruity drinks? My sheepish grin is enough of an answer. What about something a little tart, with a burst of flavor at the end?

Perfect.

"Sunshine Spirits," he declares, naming the sour I knew I was going to order all along. "You should start there." Noah fills a glass for me—it's charming, shaped like a wider-mouthed version of the logo's beaker—and slides it in my direction. He leans forward and whispers, "And it is, as promised, on the house." He flashes me a lopsided smile, and I try to ignore the way my face heats.

I clink my glass with Liam's and raise the drink to my lips. As the name guarantees, it's a bright, sunny sour, with tart notes of passion fruit and peaches. The bubbles settle alongside the butterflies in my stomach, and immediately some of the stress of this afternoon eases out of my shoulders.

Noah leans against the edge of the bar, his eyebrows perched expectantly high on his forehead.

"It's good," I say. "It's really good."

"I knew you'd like it." His gaze slides past me and over my shoulder, and the carefree crookedness of his grin shifts into a more reserved customer-service expression as he welcomes in the newest patrons. To Liam and me, he says, "Let me get them settled and then I'll come hang, yeah?" We nod and wave him away.

I turn back to Liam, who's watching me with an infuriatingly sly, close-lipped smile. His eyes bounce to where Noah ran off to then pan slowly back to me. I can practically see the equations he's running reflected in his glasses.

He takes a sip of his beer. "So—"

"Don't."

"Very well." His eyes sparkle with mischief as he releases me from his searching gaze and eyes the other patrons curiously.

We used to frequent happy hours together, though it's been a long time since we've done it with any sort of regularity. The last time was during Christmas, when we were both in Connecticut. Back in high school, we were annoyingly straitlaced, and the only times we ever drank were when we snuck some of his mom's wine after his first breakup and my first college rejection. We both ended up going to UConn, and in college . . . well, we'd gone a little wild. In the way of sheltered nose-stuck-in-textbook academic kids, we'd frothed at the mouth at the first taste of freedom and tequila.

But we've grown up since then, and in the five years since we graduated with our bachelor's, my move to New York has meant fewer opportunities for happy hours with Liam. I went to plenty in New York, of course—with my loud co-workers, or on bad dates, or by myself on the worst days—but the ones with Liam were always the best. Now, instead of a virtual happy hour over FaceTime with us gossiping about the people we'd gone to high school with, him detailing his frustrations with his school administration, and me needling him about his recent dates, we finally get to have another one in person.

Speaking of.

"So the first time you came here was for a date?" I tease.

Liam exhales a laugh and self-consciously runs a hand through the sweep of his sandy-blond hair. "It seemed like a safe bet. You know—the location was new to me, new to him . . ." A good strategy; it's always a risk taking a first date to your favorite spot. If it goes badly, it might mar the memory of your go-to haunt.

It makes me want to stay in town long enough to find out what Liam's favorite spots are.

"And it went badly?"

"We didn't have much in common. He only stayed for one drink." Liam shrugs it off, unbothered.

"That seems rude."

"I didn't mind," he says, and I wonder if he's underselling it. I've always known Liam to be notoriously picky. "He didn't want to waste my time."

"And *I* was a much better conversation partner." Noah slides back into his spot behind the bar. I'd seen him out of the corner of my eye as he made his rounds, and though I pitched this outing in the hopes that he would hang out with us, I'm glad to see that the brewery is bustling enough to keep him busy.

"I've been meaning to ask," I say, drumming my purple nails on my glass. I hadn't cared enough to paint them in months, but I somehow found time to do it after my commission this afternoon. "Liam's hard to impress, Noah. How did you get from being a total stranger to securing an exclusive invitation to the D&D table?"

Immediately Noah begins to unbutton his flannel.

I'm surprised, but I don't complain.

He shrugs off the shirt, revealing a dark green Alchemist tee underneath. I try not to let my eyes linger on the way the logo stretches over the wide expanse of his chest. Turning to the left, Noah braces his elbow on the bar top and rolls up his sleeve to show off a flexed arm, his biceps covered in ink.

It all makes sense now. I nod sagely and turn to Liam.

"You invited him for his muscles," I say. "You wanted to challenge the insidious stereotype that jocks don't play Dungeons & Dragons."

Liam scoffs at the same moment that Noah barks out a laugh. I smile into my beer.

"No, Sadie, his *tattoo*."

I turn back to Noah and pretend to adjust my glasses for a closer inspection.

It's gorgeous work. It depicts a warrior wielding a glaive like a walking staff, their face shrouded in the depths of their hood save for the glint of a smile. A midnight cloak flows from their shoulders, and the artist did a wonderful job of inking out the dozens of intricate feathers covering the cape. I tilt my head to the side, realizing that each feather is distinctly unique, like they all came from different birds. Liam grins at seeing the tattoo again, but I don't recognize the character.

"Who are they?"

"It's the Wayfarer," they answer at the same time. "From *Legends of Lore*," Noah adds, for my benefit. Liam looks disappointed at my ignorance, while Noah just looks happy to have the opportunity to explain. "He's not one of the main characters in the game," he continues. "There's really only one questline with him, but everyone agrees that it's one of the best. He's almost impossible to find because he only spawns in the game every couple of weeks, and always in a different location. When you talk to him, he tells you that he's trying to cast a spell to find his way home, and the spell requires the feathers from a hundred different magical creatures."

I wince. A quest like that sounds tedious to me, but Noah's bright blue eyes are lit with avid interest.

"As you help him gather more feathers, you learn more about him and his travels. When you hand off the last part of the quest, the phoenix feather, he just . . . flies away."

I sip my drink. "Does he fly home?"

"You never know!" Noah says it like it's the best part. "I like to think that he fell so in love with the journey that he kept exploring."

"At the end you're rewarded with a version of his cloak, for your character to wear," Liam adds.

"Does it give you the power to fly, too?" I ask.

"Of course." They're talking in unison again.

I nod. I've played *Legends of Lore* only a handful of times for Liam's sake. It didn't stick, but I've been hearing Liam gush about it and its stellar storytelling reputation for years. "I love it. The art's gorgeous, too—beautiful work. Where did you get it done?"

"My buddy's shop in NOLA. He does a lot of fantasy stuff, so I knew he'd kill it," he says. "Do you have any tattoos?" Noah's searching gaze touches on where he can see my skin—neck, wrists, collarbones.

I have to wet my lips with another sip of beer before I speak again. "Just one." I draw up my sleeve to show him where I have a very subtle and pretty tulip tucked near the crook of my elbow, and Noah circles his fingers around my arm to get a better look. I tap on my glass with my free hand to distract myself from the feel of his calloused fingertips on my skin. His hands are warm.

"Pretty," he hums, tracing the outline of one petal with the pad of his thumb. For a few heartbeats, the gentle circling of his finger is the only thing I can focus on.

"My old job didn't really encourage us to have tattoos. But I'd like to get more one day. More flowers, maybe? My mom had this whole garden that I loved when I was a kid, and she taught me to take care of it. I could get tons."

Oh god, I'm babbling. Liam's biting the insides of his lips, trying not to grin.

But either Noah doesn't notice or he's just too kind to point it out. "Now that you're free from work, you could really go all out," he says. "A face tat, huge chest piece, everything."

I want to laugh, but my stomach clenches at the thought, the bubbly feeling of giddiness from the beer quickly turning into the churning of anxiety. "Probably not. I plan to return to the industry this fall," I say, deflating slightly. I draw my arm into my lap and tug my cardigan back into place. "But I like having a secret up my sleeve."

Liam idly scratches at the skin on his inner forearm. "Do you think the kids would respect me more if I had some ink?"

"Depends on the ink," Noah muses.

"I was thinking the Pythagorean theorem."

"Oh hell yeah. That'll do it," Noah says dryly, flashing me a look that has me snickering. "Anyway, round two?"

I opt for the Draught of Demons this time, while Liam orders another Flask of Storms. The Draught is heavy and I don't like it as much, but I don't mind, as it means I'll savor it more slowly. I haven't had anything to eat since the peanut butter toast, so the

Sunshine really went to my head. Out of the corner of my eye I see Liam analyze Noah's next pour as he tilts the glass at an angle until it's half full before setting it straight again. Liam nods to himself in satisfaction.

"Been bartending a long time, Noah?" he asks.

Noah exhales a short huff of a laugh. "Nope, Alchemist is my first go. Why?"

I arch a brow in surprise. "What did you do before Alchemist?"

"Man, what haven't I done?" Noah grins wryly to himself and shakes his head, curls brushing his shoulders. "I interned at a swanky financial firm in school, then worked at an animal shelter after college for a while. Spent a summer as a park ranger in Washington— that one was the best, probably. Then a couple of soul-sucking months at Best Buy was all I needed before I quit. Even tried my hand at starting my master's, but . . ." He shrugs. "Nothing's really stuck yet."

"What would you study?" I ask. At the same time, Liam mutters something under his breath about a "jack-of-all-trades" D&D feature.

"Something brand-new. Maybe environmental science." His tone is wistful. "Maybe I'll go back to it eventually, but it just wasn't the right time."

I sneak a sideways glance at Liam. He has on the studious, blank look of his famous poker face. The poker face makes him an excellent teacher and an even better Dungeon Master, but occasionally I can see through it. In this moment, I assume he's thinking the same thing I am. We've had the same dreams since middle school— and we've both followed extremely straightforward, single-minded paths. He's always wanted to teach, and I've always wanted to make it in the big city. For Noah to have such varied interests, to have chosen no clear path in favor of trying a hundred different ones . . . I bet that Liam is surprised and a little suspicious, while Noah's many experiences only make me feel curious and somewhat jealous. There's a part of me that wishes I'd tried more things before landing on marketing.

"Well, we're glad to have you, Noah," Liam says, raising his glass in a *cheers* fashion. I nod enthusiastically and mirror the gesture. Quickly Noah gets himself a clean glass and fills it with just enough beer for a swallow.

"To new friends," Noah says, his eyes flicking to catch mine.

"Good beer," I add, clinking my beaker against his.

"And my two favorite spellcasters," Liam finishes.

We all take a sip, and as I watch Noah knock his drink back, his neck flexing from the action, the warmth that spreads through my chest isn't all due to the alcohol.

CHAPTER
Seven

We spend the rest of the evening like that, talking through Liam's struggles with his class clowns, trying to convince him to bring another date to Alchemist so Noah and I can play wingmen, and Noah asking Liam about different D&D builds. I zone out for this last conversation; I want to be good enough at the game to do justice to my character and heal my party when they need it, but I have no interest in "winning." I suspect Noah, with a character as charmingly chaotic as Loren, isn't motivated by that, either, but with his and Liam's backgrounds in *Legends of Lore*, it's clear that game mechanics are a shared love for them both.

"Fuck."

My attention snaps from the flames of the electric fireplace back to Liam.

He downs the rest of his beer and fishes out a few bills from his wallet. It's enough for both of our drinks, and I flash him a grateful smile. "I forgot I had quizzes to grade," he says apologetically before glancing at his empty glass; he huffs a laugh. "Maybe I'll be more lenient with them tonight. But hey, it's been fun. I'll see you both for the game on Sunday, and let's do this again soon." He pins me to my stool with his eyes. "Don't get up to too much trouble without me."

"Okay, *Dad*."

Noah swoops in for the bro hug, reaching to clasp Liam's hand before bringing him in for the shoulder thump, but Liam dodges it awkwardly and goes in for a side hug instead. Even I still get the same treatment, though with a little more warmth. He's not the touchy-feely sort, even after fifteen years of friendship.

For a moment Liam gives me a look, double-checking whether I mind being left alone—something we've done for each other since going to our first bar in college. After a reassuring nod from me, he grins and gives us a quick wave before ducking out of the brewery.

When I turn back to Noah, he's got me fixed in an unblinking, thoughtful stare. His brows are drawn together in a puzzled line, and his mouth is ticked up to one side in amusement. He circles around the bar until he's standing next to me, hip pressed against the polished wood.

I freeze, feeling somehow caught. "What?"

He drums his fingers once, twice atop the wood before his hand wraps around my empty glass. His voice is low and teasing. "A jock? Really?"

I laugh suddenly, remembering my earlier comment.

"Noah, you look like you could casually pull a tree out of the ground." I try not to look at his shoulders. I'm always looking at his shoulders. "You look like you lift . . . heavy things." *Well said, Sadie.*

He's fully grinning now. "If anyone's the jock in our group, Sadie, it's you."

I scoff. "Hardly."

"How many marathons have you run?"

"How do you know I run?"

Noah holds my gaze for another moment before his stare drops. Those lake-blue eyes, somehow darker now, slide slowly down my body in an assessing way that doesn't feel entirely clinical. The path of his eyes traces a line of heat down the side of my leg, and his gaze catches on where my jeans are ripped and lingers there. You can hardly tell the shape of my legs in these pants—*and it's certainly no way to judge who does or doesn't run,* I think dimly—but Noah looks for all the world like he's trying to picture them bare anyway. "Lucky guess," he says dryly. "How many?"

"None," I say honestly, though I have to clear my throat before I do. In truth, this was the second year I'd entered and lost the drawing for the NYC marathon. Begrudgingly, I admit, "Just a few halves."

He doesn't bother to brag; the twinkle in his eyes and his softly exhaled "*Uh-huh*" do it for him.

Noah strides back behind the bar with my glass in hand, and I look to where his bartending partner is cashing out the last group down the bar. I begin to gather my own things, ignoring the goosebumps on my forearms. After a moment, we're alone.

"Listen, Sadie, I've been meaning to ask you."

I swing to face him again. He stands grinning with his thumbs tucked into the pockets of his jeans, rocking back onto the heels of his Docs. His smile is like sunshine.

My bones buzz with anticipation.

Do you have any plans this weekend?

Would you still like to explore Heller with me?

"Would you be interested in painting the wall?" he asks.

". . . What?"

Smiling sheepishly, Noah gestures at the dark green wall on the other side of the brewery.

I blink twice. I'm caught in a swirl of confusion before the unmistakable stomach drop of disappointment and embarrassment anchors me.

Had I really thought he was about to ask me out?

A date? I scoff internally. *Very silly, Sadie.* And even if he had wanted to explore—which had been his suggestion in the first place—it was presumptuous to assume that he meant it in any context other than friendly. God, he was probably asking everyone else the same thing. Maybe he'd already checked out the gaming store with Liam, or has plans for Morgan to show him the bookstore . . .

I've let the awkward silence hang for so long that some of Noah's smile has dimmed, his hand dropping back to his side. Forcing some humor into my tone, I tease, "You don't like the green?" Anyone can paint a wall. Why is he asking me?

"We want a *mural*," he clarifies. "My boss, Dan, has some directional ideas, but not much. There would be a lot of artistic freedom. I'm not sure if it's the sort of project you do, but after looking through your sketchbook, well . . . I thought I'd ask if it's something you'd consider." His smile is endearingly crooked.

I'm intrigued, but hesitant. "When does he want it done by?"

Noah rolls his shoulder in a shrug. "He's not in a rush. It's more important we find the right fit, y'know?"

"Mm." I look back to the wall. Shapes and colors dance before my eyes, forming the wisps of different ideas for how to fill such an expansive space. It's been so long since I've worked on anything other than my digital drawing tablet. Though I have some traditional experience with the few art classes I allowed myself in college, I haven't done a mural since high school, when a friend and I were hired to paint a couple of exam rooms at the local children's hospital. I open my mouth to say as much, but on second thought, I close it. I don't want to disqualify myself so quickly. I've grown used to shrinking back and saying no these past few weeks, so I'm surprised to feel the tug of *want* to do this project.

"Thanks for thinking of me, Noah. I didn't realize Kylo Ren's cleavage left such an impression on you."

His smile is indulging, but his eyes are serious. "It's true, 'twas the dark side sad boy who drew my eye. But I saw some of your other sketches—the lighthouse, the cliff face, the campfire . . . and they just seemed so perfect, Sadie." He dips his chin to meet my eyes. "You've really got something special."

"Oh." Suddenly I'm wringing my hands to keep them busy, and some of my earlier disappointment fades. His compliment leaves me feeling flattered and soft. "Thank you, Noah. I'll consider it," I say, already nervous—but excited, too. "What would you need from me? My portfolio?"

"That would be a great start."

"I'll text it to you." This is a *professional, friendly* endeavor, I remind myself. No need to feel so eager to get his number.

But we're both smiling as he keys it into my phone, and his fingers brush the inside of my palm when he hands it back. "Perfect," he says. "Thanks, Sadie. I'll see you soon?"

"Soon," I agree. There aren't many things that can distract me from his carefree smile, but as I look to the wall again, I'm flooded with ideas. A small part of myself screams that I'm not a professional, that I've never taken on a project of this size, that I'm not at all cut out for it.

But my longing to put a lasting mark on this place—or anywhere, for that matter—is enough to keep the inspiration flowing. For now.

I spend the better part of Saturday afternoon updating my portfolio website, and I'm embarrassed to realize that it's been more than three years since I posted anything new. I first built the site back in high school when I still daydreamed about pursuing art in any sort of serious capacity. I'd since squashed out that desire—most of it, anyway—and before today I'd updated the site only whenever I was feeling nostalgic. I didn't need my website for commissions, since most of them came through fandom sites or my anon social media accounts. But since those are full of NSFW doodles and dumb memes, and I'm not yet willing to share the hellscapes of those feeds with Noah (and especially not his boss), I resign myself to sprucing up my site instead.

I'd finally taken Liam's advice to get out of the house and visit Busy Bean, and I'd been relieved to find the tiny, plant-filled coffee shop to be quiet and calmer than its name suggested. As I settle in with my second cup of the day, I add recent pieces to my portfolio that give a good impression of my style, skill, and range. I decide against adding in Spicy Cap and Green Gandalf, opting instead for other works, like a moody tree study I'd done of the park I like to run in near Liam's house, a grim portrait of a warrior from a fantasy book series, and a scene of a witch standing before her inviting, vine-wrapped forest home.

After a moment of hesitation, I add in the sketch of Jaylie as well.

My stomach twists as I scroll through the new additions. Save for Jaylie, they're all digital pieces. Nervous that I don't have any recent examples of traditional art, I page through some of my older pictures on the site, back to the coral reef–themed mural on the pediatrician's walls, a forest landscape I'd been assigned back in college, and the painting of Garzoth from Liam's game room, backlit by flames and smoke.

Well. These are all I've got, so they'll have to be enough.

I put the finishing touches on my website and publish it, then pull my phone from my pocket and drum out a text. Noah hasn't texted since we exchanged numbers earlier this week, but in all fairness, he left the ball in my court.

> Hey! Here's my site, SadieSketches.com. Would love to be in the running for the mural 😊

Noah's response is almost immediate, which makes my chest feel light and bubbly in a way I refuse to think too hard about.

> where's Gandalf the green?

I snort a laugh.

> kidding ☺
>
> these are great, Sadie! the witch cabin one is my favorite. I'll send these all through to Dan and let you know what he says

> thanks! Hope he likes them :)

For the thousandth time, I paint ideas for the mural in my head. I could do a portrait of a mad alchemist, but despite the name, it doesn't feel like the right fit for the brewery's vibe. Maybe a rendition of the cliff at Bear Hill, the town's most popular hike and every kid's favorite spot to smoke weed after dark, according to Liam. Or perhaps a fantasy scene of green and purple vines climbing the walls, the silhouette of a stag perched in the distance . . . I imagine what it would feel like to sweep my arm in a wide arc, dragging a swath of color across the brick wall. Would they have me paint while the brewery's open, or after hours? Would it be Noah staying with me until the sky grew dark? Maybe while I worked, he'd let me taste the new beers before they were added to the draft list. Maybe he'd hold the ladder while I painted the highest corner of the mural, or reach up to steady me with his broad hand warm against my lower back. Maybe he'd—

The jingle of Busy Bean's front door opening startles me out of my daydream, and I blink several times—hard. It's a dangerously alluring train of thought that I'm tempted to let run off the rails— and a complete, utter waste of my time.

I glance at my phone again. No new texts from Noah after our exchanges about my website.

Perfectly professional. Perfectly friendly.

Without the rose-colored lens of two drinks on an empty stomach, I force myself to take a cold, sober look at the way I felt that night at Alchemist. Sure, I can admit to Noah being *objectively* cute and ruggedly handsome, but I'm kidding myself if I think a distraction like him is something I should be indulging in this summer, as much as I'd like to. I have a thousand and one other things to worry about—like preparing to return to the city and getting my shit together—and I'm fairly certain my interest is one-sided anyway. Noah is always smooth assurance in the face of my flustered nerves, and he's just as friendly with the other players as he is with me. And even if he were being sweet to me specifically, well—who can really trust a bard's charm, anyway?

Better to just focus on the mural. Better to focus on what's really within my grasp, as I've gotten carried away before with things I couldn't handle. Too recently.

I sip at my lukewarm coffee; some of its sweetness has faded.

It takes a while to calm my thoughts about Noah, but once I start to daydream about the mural again, I'm surprised and almost uneasy about how optimistic I feel. This project feels *big*, somehow—like something I hadn't known I'd been waiting for. For one, a job of this size would sustain me financially for the rest of the summer, combined with the steady commissions and my savings. On top of that, this opportunity just feels wonderfully *indulgent*. It's exactly the sort of thing Liam had sold me on when he'd convinced me to take the summer off: a chance to rest, recharge, spend time with him, and unearth old hobbies and joys that had slipped through my fingers when I told myself I no longer had time for them.

And if I allow myself to be honest, to listen to the quiet voice I thought I'd snuffed out months ago—I think I could do a damn good job with this. I really think I could do it justice.

Determination surges through me at the thought, and I tell myself it's just the coffee at work.

Either way, I'm getting ahead of myself—I have no idea how long Dan will take to consider. To distract from premature brainstorming, I pull out my tablet and open the scan of my original sketch of Jaylie again.

Feeling more certain of my own direction, I begin to ink in her outline.

CHAPTER
Eight

"We must be really bad at this game, huh?" Jules has concern painted all over her wide gray eyes and scrunched-up nose. She wrings her hands nervously, warming up a d20 between her palms.

Liam's mouth quirks into a small, amused smile. "What makes you say that?"

"We failed our first quest," she groans. "Who's going to hire a group of adventurers that failed their *first quest*?"

Morgan tugs at her braids irritably. "The witch lady escaped. Where the hell are we meant to go from here?"

"Is it because we rolled so bad?" I ask, recalling how poorly last session's combat had gone for us—or, more accurately, how poorly it had gone for *me*.

I remember Liam calmly walking us through each step.

Okay, Jules, so you want Kain to rush up and try to slice at one of the evil druids, right? Roll a d20. What's that—an eighteen? Excellent. Kain rushes forward and cuts the druid down, badly wounding him.

And you, Loren, your rays of fire pierce into the druid's armor, set-ting it aflame. Liam had pointed to a handful of six-sided dice. *We'll need you to roll those and add them together to see how much dam-age you do . . . eleven points? Beautiful.*

Jaylie. You want to try to cast a spell on the witch to stop her from escaping? Big roll for you here. Let's see. A . . . nine? He'd paused and given me a gentle, pitying shake of his head. *Not quite good enough.*

Liam opens his mouth to answer my question, but Noah beats him to it. "Failing is half the fun, isn't it? We leave the story up to the dice—good rolls and bad." His folding chair squeaks in protest as he leans back on its two rear legs, lacing his broad hands behind his head. He's sitting next to me today, and I'm tempted to reach over and catch him before he falls. But he rocks forward again, planting the chair on the carpet. His tone is serene. "Maybe we'll have better rolls this time. What happens next is up to us. Right, DM?"

Liam nods sagely, looking pleased.

"Teacher's pet," I scoff under my breath, not unkindly.

Noah cants his head toward me and winks.

Liam spreads his hands before him. "Let's take it from the top, then, friends, and see where we end up."

Jaylie swallows nervously, and the bob of her throat very nearly brushes the sharp edge of the blade held at her neck.

"Come now," she says, sounding calmer than she feels as a guard roughly binds her hands behind her back to prevent her from casting spells, "there's no need for all of this. I'm sure we can work it out, yes?"

Without turning her head, she casts her gaze at her party. Morgana stands with her arms crossed, armored men flanking her on either side. Kain bares his long fangs dangerously at the five guards who circle him; Jaylie notices that their leader holds her sword at his sternum with the slightest tremble in her grip. Loren helpfully holds his wrists out before him, and the guard tying them together looks decidedly uncomfortable with just how much the bard seems to be delighting in the experience. The guards all wear the blue and white of Lord Donati's household, and though their armor is polished and their swords gleam, they don't seem especially skilled. Or clever.

No, that was why Donati hired Jaylie and her team. He wanted undercover *specialists*. It's why he kept the guards back at his estate.

Fat lot of good that did for him.

Donati paces in front of Jaylie with his hands clasped neatly behind his back. If he heard her plea, he doesn't give any sign of it. Eventually he stops, sighs, and pinches the bridge of his nose. Jaylie swallows again, and she swears the sword at her neck draws blood.

"How do I know you're not working with her?"

His words are so soft Jaylie barely hears him. "I'm sorry, what did you—"

"How do I know you're not *working with her*?!" he thunders. Lightning crackles up Donati's arms, and his eyes spark with barely withheld violence. He has to clench and unclench his fists for several heartbeats before the electricity sizzles out. Every hair on Jaylie's body stands upright.

"I don't know who that woman is," Jaylie protests. "I've never seen her in my life."

The party grunts and murmurs their agreement, and Morgana mutters, "I would have remembered a woman like that." She almost sounds admiring.

"Lady Shira Soros?" Donati mocks. "You really expect me to believe you're unfamiliar with her reputation?"

There's a pause.

"She was the wizard kicked off of the Arcane Assembly last summer."

Every head turns toward Kain at his revelation. Jaylie never would have thought that the politics of Belandar's most powerful wizards and sorcerers would be the sort of thing that Kain would keep up with, but he continues to surprise her.

Kain gives a shrug, causing the muscles of his huge shoulders to ripple. "Everyone was gossiping about it. She was using the Assembly's resources for dark magic. Even my father caught wind of it." Glancing at Kain's massive curling devil horns, Jaylie resolves to save her questions about his parentage for later—but she winces as Donati turns a suspicious gaze on him.

Hastily, she speaks up. "Clearly we're not on any sort of professional or working basis with her." She clears her throat delicately. "If you like, my lord, my Lady can vouch for me and my companions. She's gifted me with a spell that has the power to tell truth from lies. I can cast it, if you wish."

Donati scowls, then shakes his head. "Your offer is enough. I can tell from your blank, foolish stares that you're not involved with her."

Morgana's mouth thins to a grim line, but she says nothing. She looks sidelong to Jaylie.

"Then why all of the dramatics, my lord?" Loren lifts his bound hands toward the wizard. "We failed to protect you and your bride, and for that we are deeply apologetic, but as much as I enjoy being tied up by a pretty woman . . . this is not the right context, and it's unnecessary. Allow us to give you your initial deposit back, at the very least."

"Or allow us to right our wrongs."

Jaylie feels all eyes swivel to her.

Donati's lip curls. "You were unable to stop Shira today. What mark of confidence would I have in you to stop her tomorrow? To get Alora back?" His voice cracks on his bride's name, and Jaylie's posture softens.

"I don't like to leave a job unfinished, and I cannot walk away from here in good conscience without doing everything I can to set things right," she says.

Morgana mutters, "Doubt we'd even be *allowed* to walk out of here anyway."

Jaylie coughs once, and Loren jumps in. "Tell us everything you know about Shira and Alora, Professor Donati. Give us context to work with, backstory on the politics at play, motives that she might have for capturing your bride. We came into this job with nothing to work with save for an overarching order to try to prevent any chaos that might ensue. That sort of guidance works fine if we're simply hired to guard a caravan or patrol a festival, but this plot absolutely *reeks* of drama. We're clearly missing something important."

Jaylie thinks he should have worked harder to hide his enthusiasm for said drama.

"This was personal, wasn't it, Donati?" Loren continues in a low voice, leaning forward. "Perhaps if you and Dorna had prepared us better for what might happen, we could have protected your interests more successfully. But there's still time. Tell us what's going on. Tell us how we can help. I assure you, we're of more use to you alive than dead, and you won't find anyone else with better eyes on this situation than us."

Jaylie is convinced by Loren's persuasive words, but Donati's face is a mask of irritation and deep thought. Jaylie does her best to shift slightly to see her own companions' expressions: a mix of discomfort, anxiety, and a small amount of fear. No one is enthusiastic to continue working with Donati, but surrounded by the wizard's personal guard and no other wedding guests—no other *witnesses*—she doesn't doubt that Donati has the power to make their lives either very difficult or very short if they can't assure him of their usefulness.

"Keep them here," Donati orders. "See that they don't move while I'm gone." And in a shower of sparks, he suddenly disappears.

Jaylie exhales sharply from her nose. Obediently she stands still, hands folded behind her back as tense silence stills the air. A cheerful songbird sings in one of Donati's lemon trees, and Jaylie unsuccessfully tries to find some peace in listening to its melody. She can't lie to herself—she's scared shitless. She barely knows Donati, and despite his sweet first impression, she's clearly misread him. He could very well be coming back to kill them, and as one of Belandar's most powerful mages, he would be able to cover up their disappearances easily enough. Jaylie holds her hands together so tightly behind her back that she thinks her knuckles might crack—until Loren reaches his bound hands forward to lay a soothing palm over her fingers.

Immediately Jaylie's grip loosens, more from surprise than anything else. But his touch helps ground her, and after a heartbeat of hesitation, she laces her fingers with his. He doesn't say anything, doesn't even use it as an opportunity to make a pass at her. Instead, he just stands with her hand in his, rubbing soothing circles over the inside of her wrist with his thumb. Jaylie concentrates on the motion until Donati reappears in front of them with a sharp *crack* of thunder.

Everyone—including his guards—jumps to attention.

"All right," he snaps, striding forward to stand before the loose semicircle of Jaylie and her companions. "You are all going to get one more chance to make this right. But if you fail me *again*, well . . ." His expression is a storm cloud. "Let's not find out."

Loren slides his hand from Jaylie's and moves to stand at her side. "To do this the right way this time," he says, "we need to know everything you can tell us about Lady Shira."

"And as a show of good faith, maybe your man can sheath his sword, aye?" Morgana adds, narrowing her eyes at the half-orc guard with his weapon still outstretched toward her neck. "Took me near seventy years to grow this beard. I'll lose my shit if he nicks it."

Donati sneers—and then sighs. "At ease, then."

The guards lower their weapons and free Loren and Jaylie from their bindings. Half of them head back to their posts in Donati's estate while the others fan out to observe the group, settling in the pews still arranged for the ceremony.

Donati stands in the shade of the tree, in the same spot where he'd said his vows. His eyes are distant, his hands clasped before him. "Shira and I attended the Arcane Academy together decades ago," he begins. "We were the best in our class and very, very good friends."

"Oh?" Jaylie says. *Just friends? Or more, perhaps?*

Donati gives her a flat stare. "*Friends,*" he stresses. "Anyway. We were pitted against each other on more than one occasion, but we took it in good humor. As a team, we were the best. The perfect combination. I'm willing to admit that Shira has the kind of intellect that comes naturally with some people. She was a prodigy— effortlessly clever. Where she was all chaos and seat-of-her-pants innovation, I was . . . studious. Organized. I stayed up for hours memorizing concepts that came to her readily after only one lesson. She could conjure a bonfire with a mere thought, while I had to inscribe the spell over and over again in my spellbook before I got it right. But she inspired me to be experimental, while I kept her on track and punctual. Together, we were unstoppable."

Loren rocks back on his heels, close enough to Jaylie to murmur, "All of this chemistry, and you're telling me they *didn't* fuck?"

Morgana clears her throat. "I don't think he's her type," she says dryly. Jaylie jumps at the sound of the dwarf's voice; she hadn't noticed her sneak up to stand at her hip.

Kain cuts a glare at the three of them, and they all straighten at once, nodding for Donati to continue.

"But her experiments grew wilder with each new assignment. She began to, ah . . . *dabble.* In less savory magics."

Everyone avoids looking at Kain. Jaylie had never seen him use any spellcraft of his own, relying only on his skill with his axe. But who knows what infernal magic he inherited from his devilish father?

"She was convinced that the Academy was keeping the secrets of dark magic from us to limit our potential. She reasoned that they wanted us to become powerful mages in our own right—but not so powerful as to be able to challenge them. She wouldn't listen when I warned her about the stories of those who had tried necromancy, communing with the dark old gods, or trading their souls for wicked magics only devils could offer. She didn't care. She was confident that she was strong enough to bend such power to her will. And I was almost convinced, too. If anyone could have managed it, it was her.

"But as we drew closer to graduation, things got worse. She would come to class with dark circles under her eyes. Potion ingredients and spell components started to disappear from the storage rooms. Spellbooks she borrowed from the library were found with pages ripped out, or with indecipherable scribbles in the margins. When one of our professors, Lazlo, disappeared, she became . . . unwell. She wasn't eating, her hair was falling out. She rushed out of class once when blood began to leak through a bandage from a wound I didn't even know she had. I caught her before she made it to a cleric and demanded that she show me. When I pushed up her sleeve, I—" Donati coughs forcefully, struggling past some emotion caught in the back of his throat.

"Her arm was covered in symbols of the devilish tongue," he spits, "carved into her skin with the thinnest of blades."

Again, everyone avoids looking at Kain.

"She needed help. But I knew she wasn't going to like where she got it from." Donati pauses. He stares into the empty space within the twined root arch where he stood just a few hours ago, hand in hand with his beloved, before Shira stole Alora from his arms.

"They expelled her, of course," he says quietly, returning his gaze to the party. "Once I told the dean of my concerns. They offered her help through mage counselors and a team of clerics to cleanse her of whatever dark bargains she had made. But she couldn't be allowed to continue her studies, not when they posed such a danger to other students."

"You mentioned Lazlo before. Who was he?" Jaylie asks.

"He taught conjuration magics at the Academy—you know, summoning creatures from other realms, teleporting between one place and another. It wasn't Shira's school of specialty, but she loved him nonetheless. He was her favorite mentor. I think the loss of him . . . broke her."

Loren asks the obvious question. "What happened to him?"

"No one knows. The story goes that he teleported somewhere that he shouldn't have and never returned." Donati's tone darkens. "But after everything came out about Shira's experiments, some suspect that she was involved." He turns away and closes his eyes. "Even after everything that's happened, I still don't believe that she could have done anything to him."

"But how does all of that get us to where we are today?" Morgana sets her hands on her wide hips. "Do you really think a grudge from your school days is enough reason to crash your wedding and steal your bride out of, what, *spite*? Seems petty. Seems a stretch."

Donati levels an even gaze at her. "I'm expending a great deal of patience by allowing you my continued patronage and this second-chance opportunity," he says quietly. "Perhaps you can do me the same courtesy?"

Morgana flutters her fingers in the air sarcastically, gesturing for the wizard to continue.

"Shira's expulsion created an irreparable rift between us. Heart-broken, I tried encouraging her to take the help that was offered. But she refused. I still wanted to be her friend, but after months of trying, I stopped reaching out. I started teaching at the Academy. I worked as an archivist for the Arcane Assembly. I took all sorts of ambitious jobs because that was always our goal, mine and Shira's—to rise to the top. To get a seat on the Assembly."

Thanks to Kain's surprising knowledge of Belandar's history,

Jaylie and her companions know Donati now holds a seat. Shira had, too, at one point—until last summer.

"For every new initiative I had, for every goal or fucking *charity* event I held, she worked to undermine me. My students were endangered, my food drive was spoiled, my summer home on the coast was set aflame . . .

"Now, *those* actions I'm certain she did out of spite," Donati says, seething. "Thankfully she stopped her meddling after finally worming her way into a seat on the Assembly, using what I can only guess was a mix of blackmail, bribery, and a degree from that *other* Academy in Port Shecta. That blessed quiet was part of why I stopped seeing her as a threat. At that point, we both had what we wanted: our seats. Our goals were different, but we managed for long enough to stay out of each other's way. But when the Assembly discovered more of her dark experimentation last summer and removed her, she got desperate. Angry."

"But what does that have to do with Alora?" Jaylie presses.

"Alora is . . . special. In more ways than one. The rumors *aren't* true—she wasn't my student. She's a professor, and she traveled here from the Great North to teach an abbreviated winter course on the use of blood magic in dragon worship. Highly illegal now, but highly interesting to her students. And to me."

Donati pauses, tapping one perfectly manicured nail on the side of his nose. "I found out it was a bit of personal history that got her into the subject. She's a very powerful sorceress, due in part to her intense studies—and in part to the dragon blood that runs in her veins."

Jaylie nods with interest. Quietly, Loren murmurs, "Kinky."

Morgana and Kain simultaneously cover their faces with their hands.

"Her ancestry enhances her magic. It's not the reason I fell for her, but . . ." Donati's lips curl into a blissful smile, contrasted in part with the way his hand fists in excitement at his side. "We're a fantastic pair," he says earnestly. "We have so many dreams for our future—for our children."

Jaylie waves her hand mildly, cutting him off. "No worries about going into any further details, my lord." Loren has the gall to look disappointed. Jaylie continues, "So you think Shira wants her for her blood, then?"

Donati's expression clouds over. "Given how very rare it is, yes. Just a drop and she could perform feats of magic to level a small village. More than a drop and, well." He swallows thickly.

Jaylie turns to meet the gazes of her companions. From the wrinkles lining their foreheads and the way they shift their feet, Jaylie figures they are all thinking the same thing. *We don't stand much of a chance against power like* that.

After a beat of uncomfortable silence, Morgana asks, "Do you know where Shira might have taken Alora?"

"I most certainly do," Donati says, and Jaylie notices for the first time a slender leather folder tucked under his arm.

He opens the folder and dives into a thorough description of Lady Shira Soros's tower, several days' ride outside of the city. Her teleportation magic makes it easy for her to travel to and from the city as she likes, he explains, but she prefers the peace of life outside of it. Jaylie focuses as much as she can on the details about the travel route, the tower's defenses, and other bits of information about his rival.

Magic can do quite a bit to keep someone out. But if she and her party can get as close to Lady Shira as she is to Donati in this moment, well. Between Kain's axe, Jaylie's spells, Morgana's daggers, and Loren's charm . . . with Marlana's luck, they might have a chance.

CHAPTER
Nine

My phone buzzes, stirring me from my daydreams.

It's a wild Saturday night: I'm curled in bed with my tablet propped on a pillow, anime on my laptop, and a purring Howard pressed against my side, his orange eyes slitted in blissful half sleep.

Noah:

what are you up to tonight?

It's not the first time Noah has texted me since I sent him my website. That text came through shortly after our last D&D session, a stealthy pic of Liam scowling at a handful of poor dice rolls. Noah had captioned it *the wizard ponders his orbs*.

Since then, we've eased into a casual daily cadence of exchanging links to funny videos, theorizing D&D plot twists, and curious *how's your day going?*s. Perfectly friendly, I tell myself. Our conversations have been a nice distraction throughout the ups and downs of a fairly slow week, so I've avoided thinking about whatever intentions might be behind them—mine or Noah's. On the good days, when I was bolstered by the hope of receiving news on the mural front soon, I had enough energy to carry me through commission work, more sunny runs, and handling errands for Liam before he even had to ask. And though the bad days didn't come as often, I still had them—days where I lay in bed until lunchtime, scrolling idly through my phone until my eyes bled.

Today I find myself somewhere in the middle.

> Watching anime, drawing cartoons, you know the drill. You?

Brandon took my shift tonight, said he wanted some extra hours, so I've got nothin to do now

take me somewhere? :)

> where? do you need a ride?

lol no

i mean let's hang out, let's do something

we're both new here, let's explore!

Oho.

Whatever distraction-free promises I made to myself dissolve like clouds in the sun. I scrub a hand across my mouth as if to wipe away the smile already curling there. I start to type back, and—

And I take a breath, pausing first to wrestle down my expectations to something more manageable.

My phone vibrates again.

what do people do for fun around Heller?

> Allow me to poll the room.

I'm lucky Liam hasn't left yet. He's also got a date tonight—*not a date,* I correct myself, *I am* not *going on a date*—but when I open my bedroom door, I can still hear him crooning along with his playlist as he gets ready. I pad downstairs, through his room, and into the master bathroom. Again I'm startled by all of the fake fish mounted to the walls, as horrified as I was when Liam gave me the first house tour. I can't imagine what possessed his grandfather to decorate like this. People don't usually take nautical bathroom themes so literally.

"This is heinous, Liam," I remind him.

"I know."

"You have to take them down. They watch you while you shower."

"I know." He sounds resigned.

I sit on the edge of the tub and challenge a plastic catfish to a staring contest while I wait for Liam to finish cleaning up his beard. Finally he rinses his razor and turns to me with an expectant look.

But I stall. "Who is it tonight?"

He adjusts his glasses, and his eyes go unfocused as he tries to recall. "Andrew—no, he prefers Andy. Works for a consulting firm in Austin. He's taking me to a speakeasy downtown."

"Bit of a drive, isn't it?"

"Worth it. God, Sadie, you would *love* Austin. We're going, before you leave."

I hum my agreement, but I'm too distracted by my own plans for the evening. "I'm trying to go out tonight, too, but I don't know where to go."

Liam's brows bounce up. "In Austin?"

"In Heller."

He snorts. "With who?" Okay, rude. He turns back to the mirror and gets to work styling his hair in its usual wave. "Is it a *date*?"

"No," I say too quickly. "Noah and I are just . . . bored."

"Uh-huh," he deadpans. "Well. There are a few options for a not-date. The mall has movies and bowling, though it's ancient and full of preteens. You could grab blizzards at DQ, or hit up the

Applebee's happy hour. I've taken boys on walks around the park, but at this hour, that would come across as awfully suggestive." I'm sure he only says this so that he can snicker at my reflection as my cheeks glow red.

But then he slaps the green marble of the sink, and I jump.

"I've got it. Take him to the diner. It's open 24/7, has pancakes to die for, and it's cute as hell without being too oppressively date-y. It's called Mama's, it's down on . . ."

He keeps talking and giving directions, but I'm already bent over my phone, making the pitch to Noah.

listen I'd kill for some pancakes rn

fuck yeah

want me to drive?

pleeeeaaase i'll buy you pancakes

deal

how's 8?

see you then! 👋

Noah sends through his address. Liam laughs, and I look up again, suddenly aware of the smile that snuck its way back onto my face as I stared at my screen. "Oh hush," I say.

"I didn't say anything."

"I heard it all the same." I stand and smooth down a few unruly strands of hair on the side of his head. "You look nice—have fun, okay? I'll come pick you up if you need me to."

"Probably not, but thanks, Sadie." Liam pauses, and something in his expression softens. His eyes grow big and sentimental. *Here we go.* "Date or not, I'm glad you're going. I'm glad you're getting out more."

I roll my eyes good-naturedly, even though I'm internally grateful for the same. "*Bye,* Liam."

Back in the guest room, Howard and I stand in front of the closet. A few days ago I'd finally emptied my suitcase and shoved it under the bed. Putting my clothes into the closet felt a little too much like the beginning of setting down roots, but it wasn't an uncomfortable feeling.

That's what scared me the most.

"I don't know what to wear, Howard. Unless you think I should go like this?"

Howard blinks owlishly at my sweatpants and old tank top. I turn to inspect the hole that's forming right on my ass.

"Yeah, I didn't think so, either."

I opt for a flowy patterned maxi skirt paired with sandals and an oversized T-shirt from my favorite coffee shop back in New York—Athena's—which I knot behind my back into a crop top.

Staring into the mirror, I finger-comb through the loose waves of my bob until I deem them presentable and swipe on quick eyeliner wings over my brown eyes—it took me years to master that quick arch and pointed cat-eye style. My glasses with the gold frames make me feel the witchiest, so I keep them on.

Liam's on his way out when I get downstairs. We blow each other a kiss, hop into our cars, and drive away in opposite directions.

I pull up to a duplex right on time. Well, right on time after I circled the block because I arrived ten minutes early—it's a lot closer to Liam's than I thought. I shoot Noah a quick text and wait, glancing at the charming blue camper van parked in the driveway. It looks old as hell, but also like it belongs in some artsy Wes Anderson movie. Eventually the door to the left side of the duplex opens to reveal Noah and a cute girl with long dark hair silhouetted in the doorway. He wraps her in a warm hug before waving goodbye and jogging out to my Civic.

I don't like the way my stomach twists, the way the tips of my fingers prickle with anxious and annoyed energy. She's got to be his roommate, right? Is this even his house—is it hers? Did he linger in the doorway for a moment, stressing to her that I was just a friend from his D&D game?

I squeeze my thigh in an effort to ground myself, fingernails digging into the fabric of my skirt.

I *am* just a friend from his D&D game.

I jump a little when he opens the door and flash a quick, somewhat forced smile. "Hey!" Fuck. Too loud.

"Hey, Sadie." The way he says my name calms me a little, and the sharp edges of my smile soften. The smell of his sandalwood cologne or soap or whatever the fuck it is fills my nostrils as he slides into the passenger seat. He's wearing a pair of black pants and a dark red button-up shirt—not flannel!—and his hair is smoothed down into that same half-up, half-down look.

Pretty nice for the diner.

"Thanks for coming out tonight," he says.

"Thanks for inviting me." I hope the tension in my voice isn't obvious, and I try to relax as I pull out into the street. "From what I hear, these pancakes are worth putting on real clothes for." I tilt my head back toward the duplex. "Your roommate?"

"Sorta."

My stomach churns again.

Noah bends to retie the laces of his boots as he continues. "Roommate's girlfriend, Maura. She's been staying here on and off for the last few months. My actual roommate is Dan, the owner of Alchemist. Always feels weird calling him my boss, though he's that, too." He straightens, his smile wistful. "We were actually roommates back in college."

Just like me and Liam. I'm a little ashamed by how quickly I relax, my posture easing as I lean back into the driver's seat. "Which college did you go to?"

"University of Colorado Boulder. Maura was visiting us for the week, but she's heading back home to Boulder tomorrow. Not sure I'll see her again before then, so I said goodbye just in case."

"Oh! Are you sure you don't want to spend the evening with them?"

Noah turns a long-suffering blue stare toward me. His eyes are wide and pleading underneath his thick brows. "Please, no. It's their last night together before she leaves, and they're doing all sorts of romantic shit—cooking dinner together, lighting candles, *crying*." He winces. "They were sweet to invite me to eat with them, but they need some time alone. And some, ah, *privacy*."

I let out a low laugh and nod. We roll up to a stoplight, and I take a moment to glance around the Main Street area of Heller. It's old and charming in the way of all small towns. Most of the stores and little boutiques look closed already, but a few bars and ice-cream shops are still brightly lit from the inside. Couples and young families walk hand in hand down the sidewalks, illuminated by glowing yellow streetlamps. I look sidelong to Noah. His features are especially soft in this lighting—warm, inviting. Golden.

"Colorado's a long way from Texas," I say. "How did you and your roommate end up here?"

"Dan's from Texas, actually. Even in college he always talked about moving back one day. His parents are getting old, y'know, so I guess it seemed like the right time for him." Noah leans toward me conspiratorially even though we are the only two people in the car, his shoulder pressing up against mine. "Maura hates it here. This is probably the last time I'll ever see her."

"You think they'll break up?"

"I'm certain of it. Dan's not going anywhere anytime soon, not when he's just launched Alchemist. It's a bummer, and I'm sure it's all they'll be talking about tonight." He turns his smile back on me, looking guiltily relieved. "You see why I'd rather hang with you instead?"

"It's not just my winning personality and engrossing conversational skills?"

"Well, those, too."

I wonder if I was the first person he texted when he decided to escape for the night—or just the first to respond.

It doesn't matter, I decide. I'm here now.

Leaving the downtown area behind us, we set out on a long stretch of beautiful country roads. The landscape starts to blend together, and I'm far more interested in sneaking peeks of Noah's profile anyway, but it's obvious when we approach the diner. It's right off the highway and shines like a beacon from half a mile away, a blip of brilliant fluorescent light against the otherwise unbroken line of the horizon.

The sign that hangs over the parking lot buzzes with a neon glow, and though the lights of the first MA are out, MA's still gets the point across. When we pull in to park, I'm amused by how much the diner looks like—well, exactly how you'd expect it to. Through the large windows surrounding the building on all sides I see shiny red vinyl booths occupied by high schoolers sharing milkshakes with four red straws, truck drivers making late-night pit stops, and a few sleepy-looking families. Hanging over the double doors of the entrance is a hand-painted retro-style curvy waitress with curly gray hair and a wide grin. MAMA's, it reads in looping red-and-chrome lettering. WELCOME HOME!

The door squeaks loudly as I pull it open, and from behind me Noah reaches up to hold it ajar. Twangy country music drawls through the speakers, though two teens in the corner jam their fingers at the buttons on an old jukebox in a doomed effort to change the song.

A middle-aged waitress with wiry dyed-blond hair smiles at us as we walk in. "Evening, sweethearts. Table for two?"

"Yes, please," Noah says.

She leads us to a booth next to a window, where Noah and I settle noisily across from each other on the cracked seats. The waitress—whose name tag reads CRYSTAL—sets two spiral-bound menus and glasses of water on the table. "You two let me know when you're ready, okay?"

I take my bendy straw from its wrapper and fiddle with the flexible bit before sticking it into my glass. Noah smooths out the laminated menu across the table like a treasure map, tracing down the path to paradise with his pointer finger.

"Marshmallow swirl pancakes? Chocolate chip and mint pancakes? *Fruity pebble pancakes?*" He scrubs a hand down his beard before looking back to me, his eyes wild and bright. "Fuck me *up*, Sadie, I don't know where to go from here. There're too many options."

"Let's each pick one and we'll share," I say. "Try a little bit of everything. I want the cinnamon roll pancakes." As he scours the options, I eye the group of teenagers in the back sharing their milkshake. One of the boys is holding the stem of a cherry just out of reach of a girl trying to catch it between her teeth. "Can we get a milkshake, too?" I ask.

"You bet we can."

"What's your favorite flavor?"

"Vanilla."

I turn a deadpan stare on him. "Bit basic, isn't it?"

"It's a classic for a reason."

"Didn't peg you as a *vanilla* kind of dude, Noah."

"Oh, Sadie, that's unfair." He reclines into the booth, draping his arms over the back. His eyes crinkle at the corners. "I am anything but." The way he says it with such casually assured confidence makes the sides of my neck flare with sudden warmth.

Two can play at coy.

"Is that why you wanted to play a bard in the game?"

"What do you mean?" He feigns innocence, but I don't trust his crooked smile for a second. He knows exactly what I mean. He just wants me to say it out loud.

"Come on, Noah. This might be my first time playing, but bardic reputations extend far past the realms of D&D. Bards are persuasive, suave, charismatic, flirty—" I'm not quite ready to say *horny,* but it's true. Bards are undoubtedly the horniest class. They're musicians, but much of their magic relies on how well they can engage with their audience, entrance a crowd, or tug at someone's emotions—so of course they are associated with lust, love, and everything in between. "Lots of people play bards so that they can fuck their way across the kingdom and try to seduce the villain into letting the party run free. So, no. Bards aren't *vanilla.*"

Noah's eyes sparkle with mischief as he opens his mouth to say something—then closes it as Crystal approaches again. "You ready now, dears?"

He looks toward me as if for permission. I gesture for him to continue, and he leaps into our order: cinnamon roll pancakes, strawberry shortcake pancakes, and a vanilla shake with chocolate syrup and two straws. It's a fair middle ground.

After Crystal leaves, Noah leans forward and braces his forearms on the table, hands folded before him. "Would you believe me if I said I just wanted an excuse to bring the ukulele to D&D?" The light from the lamp overhead catches on the shine of his one earring and the brightness of his grin.

"No." I pause. "Though I was very impressed by how well you played it during the wedding scene," I say dryly.

He barks out a laugh, immediately clocking my sarcasm. "I learned the Beatles chords for the first time the night before. I think Jules was clenching her fists underneath the table, it was so bad."

"It was cute. Good effort."

His grin softens into a smile. After a moment he rolls his left shoulder in a shrug. "Truthfully, I just wanted an excuse to play a fun, boisterous character who would be outgoing and easy to start conversations with. I didn't know any of you guys, y'know, coming into this. I wanted to make a character who was approachable."

Admittedly, it's a good strategy. "Not one to play the brooding, misunderstood sad boy?"

That earns me a flat stare from Noah. I'm not used to seeing his features so serious, and it catches me off guard. "There's literally not a worse character personality type to play in D&D, and I'll die on that hill."

"So you have played D&D."

"Not exactly. I've played other tabletop roleplaying games, like Pathfinder and World of Darkness. I also did a good bit of role-playing on *Legends of Lore,* and in online forums and servers." He spreads his hands wide. "So I'm familiar with the type. Plenty of sad boys all over the internet."

"Point taken." Internally I note not to share any of my high school Zuko fanart with him. I love a broody man in fiction, but I can admit that they don't play well with others—which would make them difficult in a group setting like D&D.

Noah interrupts my thoughts. "Why did you play a cleric?"

My expression goes still, and I meet his gaze solemnly. "My faith means a lot to me."

His lips part in surprise, but before he has a chance to say anything—aha, Miss Crystal, back again. Her Crayola-red lipstick outlines a friendly smile as she sets our plates before us, followed by the milkshake. "Enjoy. Let me know if I can get'cha anything else."

Noah reaches for his silverware enthusiastically, but I stop him with an outstretched hand. "A moment," I say, boldly taking his hands in each of mine. *So warm*, I think as my fingers fold around his. "To say grace."

Noah hesitates for only a moment before he gamely closes his eyes and squeezes my hands.

"We give our thanks to the Lady of Luck," I say, my tone thick with playful earnestness. "For your unluckiness in being pushed out of your home due to your roommate's romantic endeavors, and for my luckiness in having an excellent excuse to share with you a feast fit for a king."

Noah laughs, and the deep, rolling sound makes me a little giddy. "Do I say 'Amen'?" he asks. "'Cheers'?"

"Cheers works." I immediately feel the absence of his hands as he slips his palms from mine, but we hold each other's gazes as we bend forward to sip from the milkshake at the same time.

The next few minutes are filled with blissful silence as we dive into the food, taking turns spearing fluffy bites of pancake from each plate. The cinnamon roll turns out to be a most excellent choice, dripping in gooey icing and shot through with swirls of cinnamon sugar, but the strawberries in the other stack are sweet and tart, pairing perfectly with the peaks of whipped cream that decorate the top.

As Noah washes down a bite with a sip from the frosty milkshake, I continue. "I chose cleric because I like playing support roles. I like helping people." I lick my knuckles where they accidentally brushed against whipped cream. "I thought about playing a big bitch with a giant fuck-off sword, but the idea of being thrown into the middle of combat, surrounded by enemies, when I'm only just now learning the rules of D&D . . ." I shudder. "Maybe next time."

"But why the Goddess of Luck?"

I purse my lips around the straw of the milkshake, pausing before I answer. "Maybe I was trying to get lucky."

His voice is heavy with joking doubt. "Is that right?"

I laugh and shake my head. "Nah, it's just—all of the other gods had themes like life, death, nature, storms, *torture* . . . I wasn't really drawn to any of them. I didn't want to play some good-girl stuck-up nun character, but I wasn't trying to sacrifice children to appease some fantasy god, either." I play with the red straw, twirling it between my fingers. "Luck sounded like fun. I liked how well it matched the theme of D&D—like how we leave everything up to a roll of the dice, right? And I suppose I was feeling a little unlucky when I first built Jaylie's character, so."

Noah winces sympathetically. "Bit of a dry spell?"

I roll my eyes toward the ceiling.

He concedes with a smile. "The old job?"

"Yeah," I say, smearing a pancake around my plate, trying to lance one stubborn soggy strawberry. I smile ruefully. "It felt like everything that could have gone wrong did. I thought dedicating my character to the Goddess of Luck might catch me a break."

"Has it?" He's sitting with his bearded chin propped up on his folded hands. After nearly clearing his plate, his eyes are blissfully half-lidded now, though they're still trained on me with interest.

I tilt my head from side to side, uncertain. "Sure," I say. "For now. I'm enjoying my break." I want to ask him if Dan has looked at my portfolio yet, but when I remember that he spent the week with his long-distance girlfriend whom he's about to break up with, I figure he's probably distracted.

God bless him, Noah takes my short answer to mean that I don't want to go into details (I don't) and changes the subject. "How well do you know the other folks in our group?"

"Not well at all, honestly; they're both Liam's friends. But Liam and I have been best friends since middle school. It's a wonder it's taken him this long to drag me into this D&D mess." Liam and I have a habit of constantly shitting on each other, in the manner of most close friends, but my tone is warm, my smile nostalgic. "We were inseparable all through grade school, and we went to the same college, too. We had plans to move to New York together, but . . ." I go quiet for a moment. Even now it still bums me out to think about whether I might have liked the city better with him there. Things might not have gone so wrong if I'd had him to lean on. "I think he was afraid of the big city. I would have thought small-town Texas would scare him more, but he seems to love it here."

"There's a lot to love," Noah offers.

I'm still skeptical—but maybe not as much as I had been when I first got here a little over a month ago. "What about you? Have you hung out with the others outside of game time?"

"No, just you."

Oh.

"Don't like them much?" I tease.

"Maybe I just really like you." He leans forward, keeping his eyes locked on mine as he takes a sip from the milkshake. It's the sort of look that challenges me to hold on to it—that dares me to look away.

It's the sort of look that invites me to meet it with the same blunt honesty.

My cheeks warm under the heat of his gaze. I can barely hear myself talk over the way my blood rushes in my ears. "It's a clever tactic," I say once I'm sure my voice won't come out breathy. "Charming the cleric so she makes sure your character stays alive."

"You think I'm charming?"

Fuck, he's good.

My flat stare is ruined by the smile I can't school into a mockingly serious frown. *Oh, Noah, you know you are,* I think fondly. "Not everyone can play a bard. You've got to have some measure of charisma to start with." I dip my long spoon into the milkshake for another bite. I'm slow about it, though, and I take my time licking along the spoon's edge as I hold his gaze.

Noah's dark brows shoot up, and a twinkle of amusement glistens in his eyes as he leans forward to swipe his thumb along my chin and bottom lip, catching a smear of whipped cream I'd missed while trying to play at flirty.

Immediate mortification.

But before the heat of embarrassment sinks into my bones, he sticks his finger in his mouth. "Missed a spot," he says, dragging the pad of his thumb down his tongue.

See? Charisma.

To distract myself from his shit-eating grin and the way my heart starts to thud painfully fast in my chest, I eat the last bit of pancake left on his plate. Even soggy with syrup and sticky cinnamon roll icing, it's still incredible.

I bet he would taste the same.

Holy hell, I've got to distract myself. "Whose camper van is in your driveway? Maura's?"

Noah straightens, looking surprised by the change of subject. He's got his shoulder pressed against the window to his left, and the casual lean has the buttons of his shirt straining harder than before. I keep my eyes on his clear blue ones. Does he ever blink?

"It's mine." His voice is an amused purr. I bet he sees right through me.

"I thought you only rode your bike."

"For the most part, when I'm staying in town. Biking is really the best way to get to know a place. That, or hiking."

I swirl my straw around my water glass. The ice is almost all melted. "Then what do you use the van for? Do you camp a lot?"

"I do, actually—though I haven't in Texas yet. But I move around a lot, too, which is why I got the van after college. She's been with me across the country more than once." He looks sidelong through the window, as if sketching out his next journey. I remember what he said about his travels. College in Colorado, a park ranger job in Washington, a visit to a friend in NOLA, and now Texas.

It stresses me out. He's lived in three times as many places as I have and had as many different jobs. It's adventurous and admirable, but nerve-rackingly chaotic, too.

I lost the only job I've ever had and I'm a wreck.

"You really are a traveling bard," I muse quietly. "Where to next?"

"Who knows!" God, he almost sounds excited. "I don't like to think too far ahead. And why bother? I love living with Dan again, love working at Alchemist. I'm trying new things, meeting new people, playing new games . . . Once it starts to grow stale, then I'll know it's time to move on."

Unease twinges at the base of my ribs, and I can't understand why. He's describing my exact situation, my summer of rest and recuperation before I return to the hustle of New York. The perfect small-scale adventure. And yet I don't know what he means—what it feels like for a place to grow *stale*. New York never grew stale for me. I'd always found it endlessly exciting, dynamic, and fast-paced—but when things got tough, I just couldn't keep up. And the city wouldn't slow down for me.

I withdraw slightly, pulling my hands under the table and pressing them between my thighs, suddenly cold.

The vinyl booth squeaks its protest as Noah eases himself forward. He catches on to the shift, and even as my energy dims, his eyes stay intent. Even as I retreat, he follows. His knuckles brush against the thin fabric covering my knee.

"It's hard to imagine, though, isn't it?" he muses.

I shift slightly, and my fingertips brush against his. Immediately he opens his hand, skating his rough palm against mine until he finds the smooth ring I wear on my middle finger. Cradling my hand between each of his, he twists the ring in slow, thoughtful circles around my knuckle. Already I've lost his thread of thought.

Every ounce of my focus is fixated on where his skin touches mine.

"What's hard to imagine?" I ask.

"That a place like this could ever lose its charm."

I try to see what he means—I really do. I give myself a moment to listen to the R & B song that buzzes out from the jukebox's old speakers, to watch Crystal teasingly swat a menu against the arm of an older man who's clearly a regular. My gaze slides farther out, through the window and into the night, and even from here I can pick out the pinpricks of stars that would be impossible to see in New York's light-polluted sky. But my attention keeps getting tugged back to the warmth of Noah's hands, to the twist of the ring, to the steady gaze he's pinned on me.

I smile, and he squeezes my fingers under the table.

"I'm glad we came out tonight, Sadie."

I hum my agreement. "We should do it again soon."

"I hope so."

CHAPTER
Ten

The next day, Sunday morning dawns through my window like a dream. Instead of pulling the pillow over my face with a groan like I usually do, I bask in the rays of light slitting through the blinds and listen to the birdsong outside of the window. Lazily I wind my arms around the only stuffed animal I brought with me from my New York apartment. It's a purple lavender-infused bear my mom gave me that's supposed to ward off stress and help people fall asleep. Until last night, it had never worked.

I'm disgustingly sentimental and bubbling with optimism, and it's all his fault.

Honestly, I'm surprised to be up so early. Although Noah and I left the diner at a reasonable time, and I'd dropped him off at his house soon after—following a sweet and woodsy-scented hug goodbye—he kept me up much later than that. The first text arrived midway through my drive back to Liam's.

Noah:

they're having a really heartfelt discussion in the living room and I super feel like I should not be hearing it

sadieeeee

> Sorry, sorry I just got back haha. What are you gonna do?

> can I watch anime with you?

The thought had crossed my mind to invite Noah over so we could keep talking and he could have an escape, but it's Liam's house, and . . . well, whatever's happening between two of his players, I should probably talk to him about it first. Soon.

> I'm already in pjs, I cannot possibly be convinced to leave the house again, even for you

> try this

He sent through a link to a website where we could watch my show—a supernatural anime about yet another high school fighting evil—while also typing our reactions and more with an included chat room add-on.

> oh hell yeah. this works

> do you want me to start the season from the beginning?

> ofc not, just pick up wherever you left off. I've seen it enough times I'll be able to follow along:)

I'd told him I had only enough energy in me for a couple episodes before the carb coma from the pancakes would inevitably take me out.

And yet, we binged the whole thing.

After an additional half hour of discussing theories for the next season and Noah begging me to share any fanart that the show inspired, I'd finally passed out.

This morning, I tiptoe downstairs, but there's no sign of Liam yet. I check my phone again to make sure I hadn't dreamed his late-night text to assure me he got home safe. In the kitchen, I'm greeted by Howard's gravelly meow, and I prepare us both breakfast before scampering back upstairs with my spoils.

Over my morning coffee and my standard PB toast, I doodle a winking face—not Noah's favorite pink-haired, tattooed villain, but a smirking Loren sipping a milkshake. It's a messy sketch, but hell, I've drawn so many elves over the years that it barely takes me any time at all. I text it to him along with good morning, bard, and immediately toss my phone onto the bed and jump into the shower before I can be tempted to wait for his response.

For the next half hour, I take my time getting ready, allowing myself a long shower and a thorough skin-care routine to follow it. I'm surprised I'd had the optimism to even pack all of my cosmetics, given how they've mostly gone ignored for weeks until now. After a refreshing mask, I run my fingers idly through my hair. Initially, the short hairstyle had taken a while to grow on me, but now I love how quickly my curls dry and effortlessly frame my face. I throw on some leggings and a cropped tee and do my makeup before finally checking my phone.

Noah:

my boy!

you're right, vanilla would be too basic for him. he seems like a red velvet motherfucker

good morning ☺

Ah, yes. Extremely satisfying.

☺ ready for dnd today?

you bet

> tho tbh I don't know where the hell we're supposed to go from here

> to Shira's tower right??

> there's no way in hell we're ready to fight her lmao

> I bet Liam's got something else up his sleeve

> bc we're way too low level to face off against someone on the assembly

Admittedly Shira does have Final Boss Energy, but I guess we'll find out. I collect my sketchbook, character sheet and notes, sparkling gold dice, and a few colored pens before trotting downstairs.

The whole world stretches out before Jaylie: sprawling fields of green, an endless expanse of blue sky, and a well-worn dirt road that disappears over the horizon.

This is the first time she's left the city since . . . before. Until now she had no reason to leave. She loves Belandar, especially the plush accommodations, the excitable people, and her close circle of friends at Marlana's temple. Though she's eager to win back Donati's favor, she's loath to leave the city of her heart—and her perfect feather bed. But she reminds herself of the teachings of her goddess: *Luck is out there where you least expect it, and opening yourself up to new experiences is the surest way to find it.*

But surely sleeping in the dirt and shitting in the woods aren't the sort of new experiences Marlana is referring to, are they?

Although Jaylie and Morgana squint skeptically at the wide-open sky, for the first time Kain and Loren are agreed: they're thrilled to be free.

A sudden rush of air stirs the pale curls around Jaylie's face as Kain bounds out into the grass the moment the gates groan open. It's almost cute; the scattering of blue and yellow wildflowers gives the impression that the big man is frolicking. Loren trails behind him, playing an energetic waltz to accompany the tiefling's leaping dance. Jaylie isn't surprised by Kain's reaction, as she expects he's more excited by the potential for some *action* on the roads than by the change in scenery. But Loren's enthusiasm catches her off guard. Jaylie assumed that for someone with such a love of fine things, he would be as reluctant to leave Belandar as she. But no—he's traded in his silk shirts for stylish and form-fitting leather traveling gear and pulled back his red mane of hair into a sporty tail. His grin stretches from pointed ear to pointed ear.

"Cheer up, Jaybird," the bard singsongs, blowing her a kiss. "You're finally getting the opportunity to fly the nest."

Jaylie grumbles under her breath and readjusts the pack's straps on her shoulders.

Donati gave the group detailed directions to Shira's tower, and for days all they have to worry about is travel. But while the main road might take them a good two weeks to reach their destination— crowded as it is with wagons full of fresh summer produce, arguing merchants, mages hoping to join the Academy, and more—taking the less traveled trails through the surrounding farmland and wilderness will cut their journey in half. With the help of his intimidating guardsmen and their very sharp swords, Donati had impressed upon them the importance of haste.

It quickly becomes clear that Loren is no stranger to travel as he marches ahead of the party, masterfully navigating them past a series of friendly, red-roofed farmhouses and deeper into wild rolling hills dotted with clusters of trees and flower-sprinkled fields. Eventually he stops them at the base of a slope circled by a ring of trees, summons up a merry campfire, and sends them to a restful sleep with a lullaby.

The next morning, Jaylie wakes to the sounds of bacon frying, eggs sizzling, and the guttural speech of devils.

She leaps from her sleeping roll and grabs her holy symbol to ward off evil only to see Kain leaning over a frying pan positioned above the campfire. He flips one of the eggs with utter gentleness, careful not to break the yolk. Jaylie blinks rapidly, looking around. The others begin to rise as well, Loren rubbing at his eyes while Morgana groans and pulls her dark red jacket over her face.

"What was that?" Jaylie asks earnestly. "I thought I heard . . . I thought I heard talking?"

"I'm catching up with my father," Kain explains, his eyes narrowed in concentration as he pokes at the bacon. There's a hissing, dark laugh that catches at the edge of Jaylie's hearing—but perhaps she's just imagining it.

"What do you *mean*?" Morgana asks, her voice muffled under her coat.

Jaylie moves to Kain's side to inspect the breakfast—*He really did not strike me as the cooking type,* she muses—and notices how the flames from the fire seem to curl around the frying pan with a mind of their own. She bends down closer to the heat and gasps when she sees it.

There's a face in the flames. The tongues of fire weave together to form the edges of a horrifically wide grin full of sharp kindling teeth under two burning black pits for eyes. Bull horns identical to Kain's sprout from a wide forehead and curl into smoke that spirals up between the leaves of the trees overhead. Immediately Jaylie's palms fill with holy light, an instinctive defense.

Kain looks decidedly unbothered.

"Priestess, I'd like to introduce you to my father: Lord Maglorbizel of Hell, Ruler of the Bone Pits, Prince of the Flames, Burning King of the Damned, Betrayer of Man." Kain lists off the devil's titles like he's reciting a nursery rhyme, they're so familiar to him. "We communicate through fire."

"*Any* fire?" Jaylie says. Her voice comes out high-pitched and wavering.

"Any fire," Kain confirms. "When I was a boy, staying with my human mother in her home on our dairy farm, he would come to me in the candle on my bedside table to tell me bedtime stories."

"What sorts of fucking bedtime stories were those?" Loren asks. He's standing now, green eyes wide with horror.

Kain smiles wistfully. "Tales of conquest and slaughter, legends of strength and vengeance."

"*I am a very good storyteller.*" The flames crackle and pop with the hiss of a deep voice.

The fine hairs on Jaylie's arms stand to attention at once. The sound is like clawed nails on metal to her ears.

"*I'd be very pleased to share one with you all sometime, if you would care to listen.*"

"He's an excellent cook, too," Kain continues. He lifts the pan from the flames and holds it out to the party for approval, leaving Maglorbizel's face on full display. Jaylie can't help but appreciate just how perfectly the breakfast is done. It's even shaped into two eggy eyes and a porky smile. "He taught me how to make these."

"From the stories I've heard," Loren says, his voice tight with fear, "devils are deceivers and tricksters. Give them room to talk and you'll find yourself unwittingly wrapped up in a deal with your soul sold and your dreams crushed, all for granting what you thought was your greatest desire."

"That's true in many cases," Kain admits as the flames hiss, "*Yesss . . .*" The tiefling shakes his head, his great horns swaying from side to side as he dismisses his party's protests. "But he's still my father. And so far he has done right by me."

"How did your mother get wrapped up with the likes of him?" Morgana asks eventually. By the way everyone but Kain shares a glance, it's a question on all of their minds. Morgana is just the only one brave enough to ask.

Kain's lips curl back into another one of his unsettling grins. "He wanted to sire a child. And Mother wanted to say that she'd survived a night with a devil."

Jaylie puts her palm to her face. Loren can't help but nod with grudging understanding and respect.

"Well, then," Jaylie says after clearing her throat several times. "I wouldn't want to come between you and your family. So long as he's not poisoning our food or whispering into our dreams at night, I suppose he is welcome."

"*Your approval is appreciated, priestess*," the flames hiss, dripping with sarcasm and bacon fat.

Jaylie swallows. "Let's get back on the road as soon as breakfast is finished," she says tightly, even though she's lost her appetite.

"*Go on—EAT*," Maglorbizel crows, and the fire suddenly surges upward. "*You may need your energy yet.*"

The second day of traveling does not pass as uneventfully as the first.

While her party pauses for a short rest, Jaylie offers to scout ahead with Morgana, though they soon split up to cover more ground. Jaylie has traveled for the span of only five minutes when she hears a rustle.

"Wot's a pretty thing like you travelin' through our forest for, eh?" a voice calls from the trees.

A group of dirty humans appears from out of the forest. Their cloaks are ragged and gray-green, blending effortlessly into the foliage around them. Even their boots shuffle quietly over the earth, and Jaylie curses herself for not having sensed them earlier.

She knows Morgana is nearby, but she doesn't want to give her presence away by looking for her.

The leader speaks again, lifting his knife to pick at his yellowing teeth. "Cat got yer tongue, priestess?" The group look young, barely adults. The speaker seems to be the oldest of them, around Jaylie's age, with wiry ginger hair that falls messily to his shoulders.

"I wasn't aware that these woods belonged to anyone in particular," Jaylie says airily.

Red scowls. "Well, they belong to *us*, earned fair an' square. And anyone passin' through, priestess or not, gotta pay the donation. For forest upkeep, y'see?"

"You don't look like druids to me."

"Wot, we've gotta be druids to love our land?" The woman who speaks has her hay-colored hair braided into twin tails down her back.

"I'm not going to pay your toll. I'll just go back the way I came."

"'Fraid that's not gonna be an option, dove. Everyone pays the toll, and if you're not gonna give it willingly, well—then we'll just have to take our due." Red finishes fishing out whatever gristle was stuck between his teeth and spits noisily to the side.

He does, however, keep his knife out.

Jaylie prays that her luck is strong. Pink sparkles gather in her hands as she prepares to fling a spell of light into the face of whichever ugly bandit approaches her first.

A piercing howl rings out as a black-cloaked figure dives from above. There's a clatter of breaking branches and rustling leaves as Morgana crashes through the trees, cushioning her fall by landing right on top of Red. Jaylie catches a glimpse of Morgana's bared white teeth gleaming through the depths of her beard as she wraps her legs around the man's middle from behind and buries two daggers into his shoulders.

If Morgana's battle cry isn't enough to summon their friends, then Red's screech of pain certainly is.

As Jaylie shoots a bolt of light into the face of the bandit with the braids, Kain rushes through the trees, axe lofted over one shoulder. The jaunty tune of a tavern song starts up behind him as the bard struts into the small clearing, unconcerned as you please.

Kain stops in front of the party, his long whiplike tail flicking with anticipation. The muscles of his back ripple under his purple skin as he hefts his axe over his head, and the damn thing is at least as tall as Jaylie. Morgana stands to his side, daggers dripping with poison and fresh blood. Jaylie and Loren situate themselves at the very back, with Jaylie on hand to heal as needed and Loren ready to do—well, whatever it is that he does. He seems confident, at least, and he winks to Jaylie before his fingers fly across the strings, striking up what she can only describe as a battle march.

Let's fucking go.

It happens so fast that Jaylie almost misses it. There's a rush of colors and screams and devilish laughter and the buzz of spellcasting and the wail of bandits and then, within the span of twenty-four seconds, it's over. The scavengers lie scattered around them, writhing as they clutch at their wounds. Morgana has one hand fisted in Red's tangled hair, holding the poor boy up as he weeps for mercy. As the rogue taps the corner of her mouth, debating Red's fate, Jaylie casts her gaze around for the others.

Kain is the first she sees, laid out on the ground under a tree.

"Are you all right?" Jaylie asks as she hovers over his prone form.

Kain is so doused in blood that Jaylie briefly considers whether he might be dead. But he coughs once, spits into the dirt, and lets out a boisterous laugh that rattles his whole frame.

"Do not worry for me, priestess," he says, fangs bared in his usual grin. "None of it is mine."

Jaylie swallows down bile and makes her way over to Morgana, who's knocked the boy out with a swift *thunk* of her dagger's pommel to his temple. Jaylie gently lays a hand on her shoulder. "Thanks for having my back," she says.

The dwarf woman relaxes as healing magic flows through her,

and she stretches and groans like a cat in the sun. "And thank you for having mine." She surprises Jaylie with a hug. Feeling the woman's bristly beard brush against her cheek, Jaylie warmly returns the embrace.

"Jay!" There's panic in the voice. It's an octave higher than usual. "Jaylie, *please!*"

"You weren't even in the melee," Jaylie mutters to herself.

She turns around to find Loren lying on the ground, curled into the fetal position. He clutches at his ribs with one hand while the other is pressed dramatically to his forehead.

"Oh, my savior, you've arrived just in time," he gasps through clenched teeth. His breathing is labored, and little beads of sweat gather at his temples, making his red curls hang limply around his face.

It's not a bad look for him, Jaylie notes, admiring the effort he must have put into the fight—or into his dramatics. *I'm impressed he managed to break a sweat at all.*

"What ails you?" Jaylie asks. Her painted lips are pressed into what she hopes is a pout but probably looks a lot more like a playful smirk.

"I've been struck!" With exaggerated difficulty, the bard pulls back the fabric of his billowy teal undershirt, revealing his grievous wound. The thin red cut is so shallow, so easy to miss, that Jaylie turns her attention to admiring his toned abdomen instead, his skin warm and lightly freckled.

"Caught in a thornbush, more like," Jaylie muses.

"Caught by an arrow that streamed past, more like!" He's got the gall to sound offended.

"And I suppose you're in need of my services, then?"

A flash of mischief lights his eyes. "Kiss it and make it better?"

"Great try, but no. Let's see if my Lady favors your health . . ." Jaylie fishes in her pocket for one of the stray coins of Marlana that she always keeps on hand. With a practiced flick of her thumb, she sends it spiraling into the air, and it falls to land face up with the goddess's winking face on full display. "Good for you, Loren. You're in luck."

Jaylie bends down. She's hardly about to reward his whiny behavior with a kiss, but she wouldn't mind teasing him a little. Concentrating the healing magic of a prayer on the very tip of her pointer finger, she slowly traces down the length of the shallow cut, from where it begins at the top of his ribs to where it curves down along the V-shaped line of muscle that disappears into his pants. The wound knits up easily, and the sparkling gold of the spell fades to reveal smooth, unmarred skin.

By the way he inhales sharply, she knows the magic burns. But by the way he regards her with heat in his half-lidded eyes, she knows he likes it.

Her work done, she crooks her finger under the waistband of his pants, deliberately tugs once, then stands.

"All better. Now, on your feet. We've got a long way to travel yet."

"And that's where we're going to end today's session," Liam announces as he laces his fingers and stretches his arms out in front of him, eliciting a satisfying *crack* from his knuckles.

I glance down at my notes—if you can call them that. Instead of jotting down helpful information, I'd doodled a grumpy Jaylie, a frolicking Kain, and the horrifying fiery grin of Maglorbizel.

Under the table, Noah's booted foot knocks against my sneaker. When I look up, I'm met with his wide, shit-eating grin. "Really saved my ass there," he says.

"More like a waste of a spell slot," I say with a sniff, but his expression begs for a smile in return, so I give it.

As the others move to pack up their things, Morgan leans over to check out my latest work. As always, her fancy journal is filled with her gorgeously loopy handwriting and meticulous notes. She juts one sparkly fingernail into the binding of my old notebook; it's nearly falling apart.

"Its days are numbered," she teases. "How many pages do you have left? Four?"

It's a good guess. I check.

It's an accurate guess.

"It's got one more session, tops."

"Come to the bookstore sometime this week," she offers. "We have a lot of journals to choose from, and I can give you my manager discount. Maybe Saturday?"

I'm touched. "Are you working then?"

"No, but he is." She bounces her chin in the direction of Liam, who's too distracted gathering up his own notes to notice. "We can get coffee and talk shit," Morgan says with a laugh.

"My favorite hobby. I'd love to."

As the boys file into the kitchen and Morgan packs her bags, Jules stands at the end of the table, humming idly to herself and tucking leftover cookies into bins. Morgan and I lock gazes, sharing a brief moment of telepathy. Morgan gives me a tiny, encouraging nod.

"Do you want to come, too, Jules?" I ask.

"You know where Bluebonnet Books is, right?" Morgan adds. "I feel like I've seen you there with your little ones for story time."

Kids? I had no idea Jules is a mom, or that Morgan is the bookstore's manager. There's so much I don't know about either of them, and it only makes me want to get coffee with them more.

"Oh!" Jules straightens. "I'd love to!" She beams, and then her expression falls. "We've got piano lessons Saturday. But maybe— maybe after? Late afternoon, if I can get away?" Her tone is hopeful.

"That's perfect," I say.

Morgan flashes us a smile, her teeth bright against her dark lipstick. "Great. See you two then."

I follow everyone outside. Liam always keeps his house at arctic-cold temperatures, so the sun feels good on my arms, thawing me out. But in the midafternoon heat, I can already feel sweat begin to pool under my bra and at my temples. After our goodbyes and more of Jules surreptitiously sneaking baked goods into everyone's bags, the gang all pile into their cars and drive off. Even Liam follows them out, heading to his shift at the bookstore. Noah rolls out his bike and comes to stand next to me in the driveway. I linger by his side, eager to put off chores for a little more time together.

"Shop got her back in good shape, then?" I ask, gesturing with my chin toward his bike.

"Sure did," he says cheerily, squeezing the brake. "As much as I enjoyed being chauffeured around by you, I'm glad to have an excuse to stretch my legs and get all this energy out before work." Casually and without warning, he peels his T-shirt off and stuffs it into his backpack. At my alarmed expression, he grins. "I can't show up to work with my shirt all soaked through." He *tsks*.

I worry that my glasses will fog up from the heat rising from my cheeks. Part of me wishes that they would, just so that they could conceal the way my eyes linger on Noah's skin. *He doesn't look like Loren*, I think, and I can't believe that's my first thought, but it's true. Noah looks like he could swing a sword or break a tree in half with his hands. He's not willowy and graceful like an elf—like Loren. Instead, he's all broad shoulders, big arms, and thick muscles bunching up underneath a layer of softness that makes him look incredibly huggable. Of course he's always towered over me, and I've seen hints of his bulk in the way his clothes tighten across his shoulders, but—it's entirely different to witness him in all his shirtless glory.

"Great timing," I say dryly. I try to say it sarcastically, but my mouth is literally dry.

"Oh, you think this show is for *you*?" He flexes playfully, and I almost pass out. I keep my eyes on the tangle of his beard instead of the trail of curly hair running down his chest.

"Any more of this and you're going to be late."

"Are you planning to delay me much longer?" he drawls, but when he glances at his watch, he jumps a little. "Oh shit. Hah! No, I do actually have to go." He reaches forward to squeeze my wrist. "I'll text you after work?"

"I'll be around. Have fun."

"Always do." He adjusts his backpack on the bike, hops on, and peddles off.

CHAPTER
Eleven

Nearly two months into my funemployment, I'm finally ready to admit that I'm bored out of my mind.

Just a few weeks ago, getting out of bed before noon was a Herculean task. Brushing my hair on any day other than Sunday seemed unnecessary. Running Liam's errands, given to me with good intentions, felt like a complete burden.

Now I sit in a corner booth at Busy Bean—my assigned seat, at this point—for the fourth time this week, laptop, tablet, coffee, and caprese panini spread out in a ritual circle of productivity before me. My hair is still damp after my post-run shower. For the last few days, I managed two miles each morning before the heat became unbearable, and this morning alone I already did two loads of laundry and vacuumed the whole damn house. Liam had run out of side quests for me days ago.

I trace my finger along the tablet's dark screen, and it lights up with my last commission—until more requests come in, at least. It's a pet portrait, and I glance at the reference picture. God, it's the ugliest little dog. One of those tiny yappy white ones with crusty red eyes. But I've done my best to make him look cute. I splash in a few extra details to the leafy background, and then that's finished, too.

Idly I pull up the proposed sketch I'd put together for Alchemist's mural, a project I'd tried not to throw myself too deep into considering Dan's weekslong silence about it. Even though Noah and I have established a daily, easy banter over text and spend evenings virtually watching anime together or playing online games with Liam, he hasn't brought up the mural again. It isn't his decision anyway.

There's a small ache under my ribs as I set the tablet aside and drag the laptop forward. It hurts to let the mural go for now, but I've still got an itch to occupy myself with *something*. And with only a month or so left in the summer, it's time to get more serious about planning.

It's time to start applying again.

The panic comes, and I let it—but this time, it's only a cold, nervous lapping at my feet, as opposed to the riptide that used to viciously sweep me out to sea every time I thought about approaching the job search. I brace myself against the pressure that builds in my chest then let it out in one long, slow exhale.

I can do this. I already sent in one application—what's ten more?

While researching opportunities and writing cover letters don't fill me with the same inspiration that the commissions do, I have to admit that there is something soothing in the familiarity of the exercise. As I scroll through options—a marketing position at a cute pet insurance agency, another at an athleisure company, one as a video game studio's community manager—the words flow easily enough. A cover letter is just another kind of campaign pitch, isn't it? Only this time, the product I'm selling is *me*.

Granted, it's a product I don't have a lot of confidence in yet, but risk is always part of the marketing game.

I zone out as I type away, not lifting my head until my phone vibrates with a text, minutes or hours later.

Noah:

> sadie! can you come by the brewery?

I glance at the time—only 2 P.M.—and huff a laugh.

> bit early for a drink, isn't it?

> lmao yeah, but it's not for that. I want you to meet dan.

> it's good news:)

> he really likes your work, wants to talk about it more

For a moment I can't tell if the electricity spiking down my skin is my second afternoon coffee or genuine elation. It feels like light.

> YES.

> can I come by in about an hour?

> no rush, we'll be here all day!

I try to fire off one more app, but it's useless—I'm too distracted. With little shame, I pick up the tablet again. After forty minutes of urgently adding broad strokes and excited lines to the sketch for the mural, I get to my feet and power walk out to the car. I don't wait for it to cool off before I jump in and gun it to Alchemist.

It takes me two heaves on their door handle to realize that it's locked because the brewery's not even open yet. I peer inside to where Noah stands in the taproom with his back to me, energetically waving his arms and talking to a familiar short, mustachioed man—I recognize him from my first visit with Liam. The man has on a thoughtful frown that tugs his mustache down hard toward his jawline, but as soon as he sees me through the door, he gestures for Noah to let me in. Noah greets me with his usual beaming smile before unlocking the door and pushing it open.

"Sadie! Great timing." He places his broad palm on my back—*how are his hands always so warm?*—and steers me forward. "Dan, this is Sadie, the artist and friend I've been telling you about."

Dan reaches out to shake my hand pleasantly. Although I know he and Noah went to college together, I can't help but think that the bags under his eyes and the strange choice of facial hair make him look a few years older.

His hand is cold, but his smile is genuine. "It's a real pleasure, Sadie. Thanks for coming by." He's officially the first Texan I've met with such a thick country twang. I struggle not to glance down to see if he's sporting a pair of cowboy boots.

"Noah tells me you're looking for someone to paint a mural," I say.

"Yeah . . ." Dan turns to study the forest-green wall across from the bar, the electric fireplace cold at its base. "The color looks nice and all, but it's a bit plain. Not very memorable, y'know?"

I rock forward on the balls of my feet, trying not to look too eager. My tablet feels like it's burning a hole through my tote bag. "What do you have in mind?"

"I'm open to suggestions," Dan says slowly. Noah stands behind him with his arms crossed. When he catches my glance, he gives me a subtle thumbs-up.

"I've done a little research on my own with the help of the other bartenders," Dan continues, "but we haven't come up with a whole bunch. We thought it might be fun to have the high schoolers come in here and go wild with it, but with Alchemist being a bar and all . . ." Dan smirks, the mustache wiggling like an inchworm on his upper lip. "And then the other artists we looked into were just too sparkly, or too cartoony, or too religious." He shrugs, and then his expression relaxes into a hopeful half smile. "But I like your stuff—especially the forest bits. I want this place to have that old-school tavern feel, right? A little magical, a little funky."

I nod and lean casually against the bar to distract myself

from excitedly tapping my foot. Sheepishly, I say, "If it's not too presumptuous—I-I understand you're still looking into your options, of course . . . but I already sketched out a vague idea. Can I show it to you?"

"Of course," Dan says at the same time Noah enthusiastically adds, "Please!"

I pluck out my tablet and pull up my sketch from earlier today. Noah had assured me that it wasn't necessary to arrive with a pitch ready to go, but who am I kidding? I've been excited about this opportunity for the last couple weeks, secretly sketching and hoping and wishing. I have plenty of ideas ready, but this is the one I love best. After a quick breath in and out, I maximize the picture so that it fills the screen and hold out the tablet toward Dan and Noah.

"It's just a sketch," I hurriedly assure them. "And if you're not connecting with this direction, I can return to the drawing board. It was just a feeling, a scene that came to my mind after I visited Alchemist for the first time . . . I'm not sure. Maybe it's not what you're looking for . . ." I trail off, suddenly aware of my rambling. *Goddamnit.* My manager at Incite used to praise me for my confident assurance and bright enthusiasm in my pitches. I've really lost my touch.

Or maybe this is just the first project in a while where I actually care about the stakes.

I carefully watch Dan's face as he regards the glowing screen with a squint. Behind him, Noah covers his mouth with his hand; his gaze keeps darting from the tablet to my face and then back again. His eyes are lit with honest admiration.

But he's not the one I have to convince.

Something in Dan's expression softens, and the tiniest corner of his mouth curves upward. He looks up at me.

"When can you start?"

After another half hour talking through the details of the piece (adding in certain elements), the payment plan (holy shit, Dan insists on paying me way more than I bargained for), and when I will be working on the mural (all day on Mondays and maybe some weekday mornings before Alchemist opens), we finally say our goodbyes.

Noah walks me out, and as soon as we get to my car he gathers me in his arms, lifts me off my feet, and twirls me around in two laughing circles. "Sadie! You did it!"

"I barely did anything!"

"You did it!"

I'm smiling so wide that my face feels like it's splitting in two, and when he sets me back on the ground, I distract myself from the giddiness by adjusting my glasses where they skewed off my nose from Noah's enthusiasm. He holds me at arm's length, gripping my shoulders excitedly.

"God, I'm so glad you'll be around on Mondays! It gets so dull here. It's usually just me and the brewing and the *cleaning*."

It's good for me that I hadn't known Noah spent his days alone at Alchemist on Mondays, or I might have done the project for a whole lot cheaper. Already Dan has transferred money into my account so I can shop for supplies next week. "I've got so much to do," I say, my pitch high. *And not much time to do it,* doubt echoes in my mind. But it's the first solid *plan* I've had in months, and it's calming to have an actual purpose and routine, even if it's temporary.

"Do you want me to go with you to buy stuff?" Noah offers.

I smile. "Yeah, if you're up for it. I could use the extra pair of hands." Hands that are still on my shoulders, lingering, fingers curling around my upper arms. "And your reach." I'll never get over the way he towers over me. "And your van, probably."

"Of course." I can see his dimples through his beard as his gaze shifts toward the tablet I tucked back into my tote bag. "Sadie, if this turns out anything like what you've drawn . . . Seriously, it's going to be incredible. It's perfect."

"I'm glad you liked it. I'm really excited for it."

Noah finally lets his arms fall, shakes his hands a bit, and then wraps me in another hug. This one I return, circling my arms around his waist. Every time he hugs me I marvel at the warmth of it, secretly delighting in the way my head tucks right underneath his chin. I want to stay here.

"I'm really excited for *you*," he says, his words vibrating through his chest.

Finally I let him go, and after a wave and a promise to let him know when I'm ready to go shopping, I unlock my car and slide into the driver's seat. After I turn on the ignition and queue up a song, I allow myself an excited, full-bodied wiggle, stamping my feet hard on the floorboard. Art has always been something I've done for fun, and though I take payments for small projects, this is the most money anyone has ever invested in me. I'm shot through with confidence, inspiration, and tingling enthusiasm.

It's almost enough to make me forget about the cluster of applications still open on my laptop.

CHAPTER
Twelve

It's a storybook Saturday afternoon.

Bluebonnet Books is nestled near the center of Heller, and I park far away so that I have an excuse to amble through the downtown area, decorated with perfectly manicured trees, bunches of flowers, and unlit strands of looping globe lights. I meander behind a group of tan blondes tipsy from brunch, parents tugging along kids with strawberry and chocolate ice cream smeared across their chins, and elderly couples shuffling along hand in hand. Clouds occasionally drift in front of the sun, offering brief periods of respite from the heat.

The bookstore is impossible to miss. Two windows stretch to either side of the double doors, showing off purple and pink pansies in the window boxes and thoughtfully curated book displays inside. Upon entering, I hear the jingle of a bell hanging over the doorframe, and I'm immediately hit with a blast of cold AC and the comforting smell of hundreds of bound books.

"Welcome in," Liam says cheerfully from his post at the information desk. His back is turned to me as he adjusts a stack of paperbacks on the shelf behind him. "Can I help you find anything today?"

"I'm looking for a how-to guide for breaking into a wizard's tower."

Liam swings around with a laugh. "Fresh out of those, sorry. Guess you'll have to figure it out on your own." He braces his palms on the desk. "But I'm glad you came, Sadie. She's cute, right?" With a broad sweep of his arm, he gestures to Bluebonnet's interior.

It's very cute indeed. Every time I walk into a bookstore, I tell myself I ought to come more often. Thanks to long runs, I prefer audiobooks to print, but still—there's no atmosphere more welcoming than a beloved indie. As I scan the shelves, I can tell where each genre is sectioned by the way they're decorated. Paper hearts are hung above the romance section, plastic starships and stuffed dragons prowl the shelves in sci-fi/fantasy, and embroidered tea towels and local hand-carved spoons are for sale near the cookbooks. Themed displays stand out on separate tables, boasting staff-recommended summer reads, vacation guides, colorful Pride picks, and more.

A man with graying sideburns and a backward baseball cap frowns at one of the rainbow flags. "Ain't that month over? It's July now."

Liam sucks in a breath as I stiffen beside him. But Morgan beats us both to the punch.

"Oh, they have that display year-round! It's my favorite," she says sunnily, walking up from the back of the store wearing a brightly patterned dress, cropped jean jacket, and wedge-heeled sandals that have her looming over the man. She's changed her hair, too, since Sunday; she's taken out her long braids, and her tight curls surround her face like a halo. Without her blue employee lanyard on, there's no way this guy could know that she's an off-duty bookseller.

Robbed of his chance to hassle an employee, the man mutters

an excuse of needing to find his wife and shuffles away. Morgan rolls her eyes, though she keeps him in her line of sight.

Liam huffs a laugh. "Always appreciated, Morgan, but you're off today. I've handled assholes before, I can do it again."

"Well, if he comes back and asks to *speak with a manager*," she says, mimicking a nasally demand, "you know where to find me." She fixes her smile on me. "Come on, Sadie, let me show you around. Jules said she'll be running a little late."

We do a lap around the store, and by the time we make it to the register, I've got a pile of unexpected purchases: two new leather-bound journals, a set of pens, one gorgeous graphic novel that Morgan swears is her favorite book of the year, a fantasy debut recommended by Liam, and a candle from a local business that is supposed to smell like a Brooding Love Interest. It was a tough decision between that and Incorrigible Rake—which I imagine is what Loren smells like—but I like the spicy scent of the one I picked. Even with Morgan's discount, it's an extravagant purchase I wouldn't have considered a few weeks ago. But with the mural's first payment sitting pretty in my bank account, some celebratory extravagance is warranted.

After we order iced coffees from the café near the back of the store, Morgan and I settle at a cozy table in the corner. Morgan sits with her back to the wall so that she's got the whole store in view. Even though she's not on the clock, I like to watch as the booksellers—Liam included—stand a little straighter, careful to be on their best behavior as they tend to their duties.

"How long have you been manager?" I ask, sipping my coffee. It's delicious. It's got cinnamon in it.

"For the last couple of years. I started while I was in college, worked my way up to the top." She props her chin up in her hands, tapping her pink-and-purple acrylic nails against her jawline. "She's my baby."

With all of the personal touches and staff recommendation cards littering the shelves, I can tell Morgan and her booksellers put special care into Bluebonnet. During the tour, I'd noticed that her recommendation cards were mainly reserved for highbrow literary fiction novels and wise memoirs—not rollicking adventure fantasy. I've questioned both of the other players at this point, so I ask, "What made you want to play D&D?"

Morgan purses her lips and dwells on the question for a moment. "I like stories," she says bluntly with a grin. "Any kind of stories. And I like Liam quite a bit." She looks toward him and nods appreciatively at the way he's enthusiastically hand-selling a middle-grade series to an enraptured preteen. "He's one of the good ones, isn't he?"

"The best," I agree.

She reaches into my bag of goodies and draws out the candle I purchased, taking an experimental sniff. "Yummy. Not what I thought you'd go for, though." She narrows her eyes wickedly at me. "Were we out of stock of the Burly Lumberjack with Expertise in Persuasion?"

I'm horrified, so of course I cough out a laugh. It's so loud I make myself jump. I lean forward, shoulders hunched, and my voice comes out as a stressed whisper. "Is it that obvious?"

Morgan is all smug coolness. "It is," she says matter-of-factly. "And it's cute as hell."

"I'm not seeing him," I say suddenly. I don't know why I'm so quick to explain myself. Worse—I don't know why my admission triggers a twinge of disappointment.

She shrugs. "Okay. But the flirting, the banter . . ." She touches her fingertips to her dark red lips. *Chef's kiss.* "I'm almost more invested in watching your little romance play out than in the actual game."

Just as I turn beet red, Jules arrives, striding forward in a pair of Converse and a daisy-yellow dress. As soon as she sees my face, she presses her hand to her cheek. "Oh no. Are you okay? What did I miss?" Instant mom-mode.

"Sadie just finished telling me how she and Noah are totally not dating," Morgan says helpfully.

"Oh." Jules pouts. "You're not? I thought for sure . . ."

"Right?"

As I dissolve into a boneless puddle on the table, Jules pats my shoulder gently. "Well, I think he's got a bit of a crush on you, honey. It's sweet."

I peek one eye out from where I've hidden behind my bag of purchases. *He does?* I'm ready to believe that *my* crush is obvious—I've always been a poor actress—but I'm not sold on Noah's. I shake my head. "I think that's just Loren's character peeking through," I say. "Noah's just—he's just friendly. He acts that way with everyone."

Morgan and Jules exchange a kind, pitying look with each other. Jules's laugh is like the tinkling of bells. "He most certainly does *not,* Sadie."

"Poor thing," Morgan soothes, her dark eyes lit with mischief. "We won't tease you anymore. Jules, let me grab you some coffee, and then we can all chat."

As Morgan goes to order Jules's iced mocha, Jules turns her warm smile to me. "So, Sadie—what's new? How are you liking Texas?"

The subject change is an out, and after a moment's hesitation, I take it. I've been looking forward to this girls' day out all week; the puzzle of Noah can wait.

There had been a brief moment this morning when I'd worried that today's hangout was going to be awkward. That maybe we were better off just being buds who met once a week, forging strong bonds between our D&D characters but holding one another at a distance as soon as our game was over. I wasn't sure that Morgan and Jules would have as much fun out with me as they might with a pile of dice forming a wall between us.

But they're quick to prove me wrong.

Rays of sunshine shift and span across the bookshelves as we chat from afternoon into early evening. I tell them how surprised I am by how much I've been enjoying Texas, and they quiz me about what it's like to live in the big city. "I've begged my husband to take me for years," Jules says, sighing wistfully. "I'm desperate to visit Broadway at least once before I die." I even catch her and Morgan up to speed about my current job—or lack thereof. They're sympathetic to my complicated feelings and excited to hear about my part-time project with Alchemist.

"That's where Noah works, isn't it?" Jules says musingly.

Morgan flashes me a sharp smile before seamlessly steering the conversation in a different direction.

We ask Jules about her family, and she enthusiastically gushes about her three young children and recounts her romantic saga with her high school sweetheart turned husband. Apparently she had been a stay-at-home mom up until last year, teaching private music lessons out of her living room until the school finally won her over when the previous orchestra teacher retired. "I got connected with Liam through the after-school clubs," she explains. "I run a little jazz band, and he runs, like, three other clubs. Chess club, book club, debate . . ." She releases a whistling sigh. "I'd heard he was thinking about a D&D club, too, but wouldn't start it until the school year. I didn't want to wait that long."

As we talk, we have to pause every so often whenever someone recognizes Morgan. She greets customers, booksellers, and even people she recognizes from college, and I swear she knows almost all of their names. "How is your partner, Eric?" she asks, or "Did you finish your thesis you were telling me about?" She's warm and friendly, and her laughs are loud and infectious. Morgan reminds me of the popular girls from high school. Not in the gorgeous stuck-up bitch sort of way, but in the I-can-make-friends-with-anyone and I-know-everyone-in-town way.

Only after she's asked me and Jules a thousand questions does she finally talk more about herself. How she worries about the store's finances, misses her brother who's traveling abroad, and hopes to host a book festival in Heller someday. How she's helping another bookseller with his script for a slice-of-life short film while also trying to work on her own novel. Her hands are in dozens of projects, yet somehow she still finds time for D&D.

Even as the sky darkens outside the window, I find myself hoping for an excuse to stay longer. There's a coziness to their company that I can't quite get over. It's not the comfort of a fifteen-year friendship like I have with Liam or the butterfly-inducing hangouts with Noah, but something different altogether.

As the conversation fades, I exhale a small sigh and begin to pack my things. Jules is staring at her phone, looking thoughtful. Her eyes bounce between me and Morgan curiously.

"What is it?" Morgan asks.

"My mom's just asked if she can keep the kids tonight for a sleepover." Jules delicately swirls her straw around her cup and sips up the last of her coffee. "What do you girls say we get out of here and treat ourselves to something a little *stronger*?"

"But why Kain?" I ask.

Two hours later we're sitting on the deck at Alchemist, three drinks deep. The sun is a smudge of dark pink on the horizon, and the lights strung above us seem more luminous than usual. The air still holds some of the weight left over from the day's heat, but it's not unbearable. It's a busy Saturday night at the brewery, and the conversations surrounding our table make for pleasant, buzzing background noise. I am blissfully, tipsily contented.

Jules is bopping her head in time to the music flowing from the speaker, counting each measure under her breath. When she realizes I'm talking to her, she shakes herself out of her daze and offers me a sheepish smile. "Sorry, what did you ask?"

"Why Kain?" I repeat. I splay my palms out on the sticky table. "Jules, I've only known you for a month, but you're maybe the sweetest person I've ever met in my life. So, help me understand . . ." I grin, waiting for Morgan to stop giggling into her fist before I continue. "Why are you playing a bloodthirsty, hellish, *raging* barbarian?"

Even now Jules looks like a total sweetheart. She shyly regards the two of us from under thick lashes, her hands clasped over her heart. Her curls bounce and her tulip-shaped earrings sway as she shakes her head.

Morgan and I watch as her mouth forms words, but I can't hear what she says. She's speaking too softly, and laughter from the neighboring table smothers her words.

"What?" Morgan barks.

"I said, sometimes I just get so *angry!*" Jules's already high-pitched voice goes up an extra octave as she throws her hands upward. The couple behind us look alarmed at the outburst, and the old man sitting by himself shoots Jules a withering glare.

But instead of withdrawing into her shell, Jules presses on. "Last semester, I had a mother threaten to sue the school because her son didn't make first chair cello. Last week, my daughter did a beautiful drawing of a dragon. On my living room wall. In *lipstick.* And this afternoon, my husband—my wonderful, handsome, talented husband—asked me for the hundredth time to remind him where I put the kids' overnight bag." Jules grips Morgan's forearm. "It was in the same place it always is," she stresses. "*The same place it always is.*"

"Oh girl." Morgan throws her head back as she laughs. "I get why you wanted to play a big angry beefcake. Just hearing about it makes me want to pick up an axe and break shit."

"Please don't, though."

His voice is so warm and so *low*, his tone all playfulness. Butterflies flutter around doing pirouettes in my stomach, and I spin to see Noah approaching with three glasses of water.

"No rolling for initiative in Alchemist," I promise solemnly, repeating the words Liam always uses to start in-game combat. Rolling for initiative determines the order in which each character gets to make an attack. It decides who gets to make the first move.

If the girls were being honest with me and there really is something there . . .

Maybe I *should roll for initiative.*

His eyes snag on mine, and for one horrified, wonderful moment, I wonder if he can see my thoughts painted across my forehead. But with a smile he's already gone, off to take care of some other customer. I'm left reeling, questioning just how reckless these last few drinks have inspired me to be.

Noah was so fucking thrilled when we arrived.

He did a double take when he first saw me, then his eyes widened when he spotted Jules and Morgan in my wake. He'd held his arms out to either side, a big grin splitting his beard. "Having a party without me, ladies?"

"Just a bit of a girls' night," Morgan teased.

All evening, he's taken special care of us. He'd bent over our table with his hand curled around my shoulder as he walked Morgan and Jules through the menu—"And that's Sadie's favorite, Sunshine Spirits"—brought out a gigantic pretzel with six different dipping sauces, recommended a few nonalcoholic options when Morgan told him she was our designated driver for the evening, and generally kept us company whenever he had a couple minutes to spare.

"Morgan," Jules whines, her fingers laced around her glass of Sunshine. "I feel bad that you aren't getting to have any *fun*."

"What do you mean? This is the most fun I've had in weeks." Morgan had gently nursed her own beer for the first hour but had stuck with sweet tea since. Jules and I safely left our cars at the bookstore to be picked up after tomorrow's game. "I don't mind, Jules. We're celebrating Sadie's new art job anyway, and your . . ." Morgan shares a look with me that has me biting the inside of my lip to keep from giggling. I suppose Jules isn't actually celebrating anything, but it's clear to us that she doesn't get a lot of opportunities to go out on her own without her kids in tow. She should enjoy her night off to the fullest.

"Anyway," Morgan says with a laugh. "It's getting late, ladies. Tell me what you want, and the last round's on me."

I hesitate, but eventually order a half pour of Jar of Bees, a honey ale Noah had recommended. "Made with honey from real local bees!" he'd buzzed. Jules orders the same.

Morgan strides inside to where Noah waits behind the bar. I prop my chin in my hand and watch them through the wide windows of the brewery, their bodies warped by the thick glass and hanging lights. Morgan's animatedly chatting about something, gesturing with her hands, but my eyes are on Noah as he pours. On the way his long fingers wrap around the handle of the tap, how his wrist swivels dexterously as he fills the glass underneath it, how his biceps flex under the fabric of his—

"Look at you," Jules says. I snap back to attention as she nudges me with her shoulder. She's got her chin propped just as I do, and behind the lenses of her glasses her gray eyes are big and round and soft. It takes me longer than it should to realize that she's imitating me.

"You're *pining*." She lets out a dramatic, wistful sigh for effect.

"I am not!" It comes out louder than intended. "I am simply . . . admiring. I am simply—tipsy, okay?" I am simply full of excuses.

"Okay, Sadie." She regards me with a small, knowing smile.

Morgan finally returns and passes two glasses to me and Jules, the beer inside richly gold and glittering. As the evening winds down, Jules questions Morgan about why she chose to play a dwarf, but I lose track of the conversation as I stare up at the budding stars in the sky.

I'm reminded of how many times in New York I would close down a bar with my co-workers, sipping at the watered-down tequila dregs in our margaritas before we swayed out into the night and onto the subway home. Although I'm just as tipsy now as I had been a dozen other times with them, tonight feels nothing like my old city happy hours. For one, hanging out with Jules and Morgan is . . . *fun*. We aren't drinking to forget our boss's terrible pettiness, or to numb the stress of an overlong day. We certainly aren't bitching for hours on end, either, which is all I ever did with my co-workers, our complaints about our jobs, bad dates, rent prices, and roommates tasting more sour than our mojitos.

Morgan and Jules's company feels easy and comfortable. With each new sip from my Jar of Bees, I allow myself to sink into the warmth of it, half listening to their debate about dwarves versus elves while rocking my head along with the music.

Morgan notices the dreamy, sleepy smile stretched across my face at the same time that the brewery's lights come up, signaling that they're now closed. "I think that's our cue, girls."

Jules yawns her affirmation.

As Morgan stands and threads her arms through mine and Jules's, Noah comes to flank my other side. "Can I walk you all out?"

Of course I offer him my arm.

Stumbling slightly over our four pairs of feet, we snake out toward Morgan's car in a line, our kind sober friends patiently steering me and Jules despite our giggles.

"You've got a really great place here, Noah," Morgan finally says. "I'm sure you'll see us again very soon." Our linked arms fall as she reaches for her car keys, but I keep my arm entwined with Noah's. There's no rush to let go. He's keeping me steady.

"Oh, I do hope so!" Jules gushes. "I want to see every step of Sadie's mural."

For once, I welcome the blush that warms my cheeks.

Morgan's gaze pans across the three of us but pinballs briefly between me and Noah. I watch an idea form in real time: for an instant, her eyes narrow, and then her lips press into a sly smile. She nods to herself, and she reminds me so much of Liam in this instant. He wears the same exact poker face every time he throws a complete plot twist at us in D&D. "Well," she says with a sigh. "I suppose we should get on the road. We've got a long way to go, with Jules on one side of town and Liam on the other . . ."

I'm too slow and tipsy, and I don't see it immediately. Morgan's trap is well laid, and Noah's ever-present kindness—or genuine interest, if Morgan and Jules are to be believed—ensures that he takes the bait.

"I live close by Liam's. I can take Sadie home," he offers. Then, to me: "If you want."

"Oh, are you sure?" Morgan rocks from one foot to the other. "It's up to you, Sadie."

Jules is so drunk she can't hide her shit-eating grin. She hiccups a laugh as she climbs into Morgan's car.

"Okay," I say, turning back to Noah. "If you don't mind."

CHAPTER
Thirteen

It feels a little like flying.

My curls whip around my face as the world slides past us in a blur. I've tucked my glasses into my bag for safety, and all I can see are the halos of car headlights, the back of Noah's neck, and the brief golden twinkles of fireflies in the grass. I've wrapped my arms around Noah's middle like a vise, with my cheek and nose pressed hard against his shoulder—*there it is again, sandalwood and pine*—and the strap of his helmet digging uncomfortably into my chin. He'd had only the one, and he'd given it to me. Even though Noah's pedaling slowly, the hardest part is keeping my wobbly legs straight as I brace them atop the back pegs of his bike.

"You doing okay back there?" Noah asks, and god, I can feel the rumble of his voice against my chest.

"I'm fine," I call. No, I'm more than fine. I'm great. I'm doing wonderfully. I'm *flying*. I'm tempted to straighten and throw my arms out *Titanic*-style as Noah sails down the road.

But I can't bear to let go even for a second. I'm dizzy on more than one level, the sweetness of the moment directly at odds with the way the alcohol in my stomach flips and spins every time we take a sharp curve.

The wind almost carries his voice away completely. "It looked like you had a lot of fun tonight."

"I love them." It's out of my mouth before I have a chance to think it through. "They're so great, Noah. Everyone in our group is just the best." At the last word, I give him a squeeze.

There's a small, persistent voice in the back of my head, a sober voice that certainly hasn't had four beers, but I don't pause long enough to listen to what she has to say.

His laugh vibrates through my whole body. His smile is so *loud*. "I think so, too."

Too soon, he's slowing down, though I don't realize we're back at Liam's house until we've stopped next to the mailbox. The deck's outdoor lights are still on, casting a soft bubble of warmth over the porch and front yard.

Noah helps me off the bike with a steadying hand between my shoulder blades then props it up next to the curb. As we walk to the door, he keeps his hand where it is, and the weight of it is all I can focus on until we're standing on the doormat. I can't get the damned helmet off. There's a button-type latch, but it's stuck, and I can't figure out which part of the plastic to press—

"Oh, Sadie," Noah says, in the most endearing and gently pitying tone I've ever heard. "Let me help you. It's a little tricky." I'm sure it's not—he's just being sweet. He bends forward until his eyes are aligned with mine. His knuckles drag along my jawline as he tucks his fingers underneath the helmet's straps and then— *click!*—it's off.

Everything goes still. The leaves in the trees hush their rustling, and the fireflies are suspended in midair. Our mingling breaths freeze in the narrow space between us. Words unspoken catch in the back of my throat, and I don't know what to say next.

Thanks for the ride.

I'll see you tomorrow.

Is what Jules said about you true?

Do you want to come in?

Or, I could say nothing at all. I could simply lean forward and close the distance. I wouldn't even have to go up on tiptoes to reach him, not with his face so close. His hair is a messy red cloud around his face, tousled by the wind. His eyes are wide and awake, and his dark brows are slanted upward. His head is canted slightly to the side, and his lips are curled in a questioning, tentative half smile. He rocks slowly forward, or maybe I do, and his lips—

The front door creaks open, and the spell is broken. The world starts to spin again. My *head* starts to spin again, and Noah straightens suddenly and steadies me with a hand on my arm.

"Liam," Noah says in greeting as my best friend—and worst enemy, in this moment—suspiciously peeks his head through the door.

"Noah was just giving me a ride back," I say.

Liam gives me a good once-over, taking in my flushed cheeks and slight wobble. He exhales a short laugh through his nose. "Good thing he did, huh?"

"A very good thing," I agree.

"Happy to chariot you home anytime," Noah says. My attention darts back to him as his hand slides down my arm; he squeezes my fingertips twice before letting go and then fastens the helmet to his own head. "I'll see you two bright and early tomorrow?"

"Of course."

I float my way inside and up the stairs, out of my clothes, and into bed. The next morning, I'm only slightly hungover. In truth, I still feel a little drunk—drunk on the magic of last night, on all the possibilities that hung in that moment on the front porch.

I wonder if I can re-create it or if the moment's already passed.

I head downstairs and into the day's session with only one goal in mind: *roll for initiative.*

After three more days of traveling—*three dull days kindly summarized and skipped over by a benevolent DM*—Morgana spots something in the distance and points. Half a day's journey away, rolling green-and-yellow hills give way to the only man-made building for miles: Shira's tower. It's built with white brick and covered in curling vines, capped with a purple roof sporting a black flag flapping merrily at the top. Jaylie did not expect it to look so *friendly*. She's of half a mind to walk right up to the front door and ask nicely for the safe return of Alora when a loud, guttural croak shocks her into stillness.

Morgana puts her hand on her dagger defensively just as Kain bares his fangs in an intimidating snarl. Everyone tenses, ready for another attack.

But when Jaylie catches sight of the figure approaching on the trail ahead, she has to press her fingers to her lips to cover her smile. The stranger grumbles under his breath, head hung low as he angrily kicks at pebbles in his path. His glittering attire clearly marks him as a wizard—but he's got to be the cutest little wizard Jaylie has ever seen.

He's also a frog.

About the size and height of an average halfling and dressed in brilliant purple robes, the little wizard waddles up on webbed feet. Between his bulging eyes sits a conical hat embroidered with silver and white moons and stars. The entire party dissolves into *ooh*s and *aah*s of admiration until he opens his wide mouth.

"You lot ought to fuck right off in the other direction."

Loren lets out a surprised guffaw.

The frog's eyes narrow to slits. "Let me guess—you're on your way to pay Shira Soros a visit, aren't you?" He throws his arms up in exasperation. "Not like there's anywhere else to visit in this blasted forest."

"We're here for the witch," Kain confirms, his low voice gravelly and irritated. "Not for you."

"Aye, and I'll be the first to tell you that you don't stand a *chance* against her," the frog sneers.

Morgana huffs. "What are you, her *guard frog*? Don't you dare tell me what I can and can't handle—"

Jaylie steps forward, hands held out helplessly before her. "We really don't have much of a choice, sir. We don't need to kill her or anything gruesome like that. We just need her to release her captive."

"Is that right? And are any one of you talented in the arcane arts? In wizardry?"

Loren splays his palm out in front of him and shakes it in a *so–so* motion while Jaylie self-consciously fingers her holy symbol.

"I'm going to take that as a *no*," the wizard snaps harshly.

"Why the bad attitude?" Loren asks. "Are you here to defend her against us?"

The frog folds his hands atop the curve of his large belly. "Hells, no. I'm here to warn you that if I, *Alastair Darkthorn*, can't handle her, then you haven't got any hope at all." He pauses, but when no one reacts to his name, he deflates slightly. He wrings his webbed fingers in agitation, and Jaylie can't help but notice just how slimy they are. "This morning, I arrived at Lady Shira's tower to challenge her to a duel."

"Did she wrong you in some way, too?" Morgana asks.

Alastair narrows his glassy black eyes, anger causing his throat to bulge with a sudden and surprising *ribbit*. After an embarrassed moment of silence, he says, ". . . No. See now, when one wizard challenges another to a duel, the winner receives their defeated opponent's spellbook—"

"What's the spellbook do?" Loren interrupts.

Alastair exhales a long-suffering sigh. "Why, a spellbook is what every wizard needs to cast spells. Without their spellbook, they're useless—they can't do much more than light a candle. The book guides every spell they cast, every day."

Jaylie shares a smug look with Loren; their magic has no such limitations. All Jaylie has to do to be granted a wealth of spells to cast is send up a little prayer to Marlana, and Loren seemingly just bursts into song and his spells follow after. It occurs to Jaylie then: "Well, why would any wizard willingly enter into a duel, then? A spellbook seems too precious to risk."

"But the reward is just as great," Alastair insists. "As powerful as she is, her spellbook would give me access to a whole host of new spells. I wanted her spellbook, and I thought I was talented enough to get it. But she won, obviously, and turned me into *this* as punishment." He gestures to his body, disgusted. "Typically I'd be able to turn myself back with a snap of my fingers, but without my spellbook . . ." Alastair shakes his head. "I've got to find one of my apprentices, convince them I'm *me,* and have them return me to my original form. At the very least, I must undo this curse."

"But you're so *cute* in this form." Jaylie slaps her hand over her mouth as soon as the words are out. Alastair looks like he might explode with indignation. *The nerve!*

"You know, I heard a tale about this once," Loren says, rescuing her from the stormy silence. He leans forward slightly, batting his eyelashes and tossing his hair from his eyes. "Might a kiss get rid of this curse? I could try, if you like."

Alastair cuts him a withering glare. "Imbecile."

Jaylie stares thoughtfully up into the sky. It's a beautiful day, with puffy clouds floating carelessly across the blue expanse. "If you know her well enough to challenge her to a duel, then you must know something of her tower or her weaknesses, Alastair. If we don't return to our employer with Shira's captive, Alora Clare, he won't be kind to us." She lowers her gaze back to the small wizard. "We'll go to Shira's tower with or without your blessing, so why not help us out? Give us some guidance?"

He shoves his webbed hands—feet? Paws?—sullenly into his pockets. "And why should I?"

"Well, you seemed happy enough to warn us *away* from certain folly, and you didn't have to do that. You could have let us wander on to our doom," Morgana says. "Why not help us, if for no other reason than to spite her?"

"We could try to get your spellbook back," Loren adds. Immediately the party all begin to nod. It's a good offer. "Should we have even a sliver of success, we might be able to return it to you. Otherwise, it will take you, what . . . years to collect all the spells that you had before?"

Alastair's gaze locks onto something just over Jaylie's shoulder, and his eyes suddenly widen in horror. "No, no, not again, *please*—"

A ribbon of pink shoots past Jaylie's cheek with alarming speed. She yelps in surprise and stumbles backward, tripping over a rock. Mid-fall, she realizes with disgust that the pink rope was Alastair's *tongue.* Loren dexterously steps to the side and winds an arm around her waist just in time to catch her. He flashes her a quick wink before setting her back safely on her feet.

Alastair is gagging, having just swallowed the poor bug that his froggish instincts compelled him to catch. "Fuck," he groans. "Fuck, every *time*! Fine. Fine! I'll help you. But I really don't know how much of a difference it will make." Alastair fists his webbed hands on top of his head as if he were tugging at his hair. "Come. Sit. We'll strategize."

Alastair leads Jaylie and her companions off the path and through waist-high ferns until they come to a mossy fallen tree trunk, which makes an excellent seat for the party to perch on. Morgana sits to Jaylie's side and begins sharpening her daggers while Kain stands behind the group, muscled arms crossed threateningly across his chest.

"Clearly your greatest weakness is that you're defenseless against her magic." Alastair eyes the party. "Her tower is riddled with arcane traps. She's carved glyphs into the trees surrounding her land—they'll explode if you come within thirty paces of them.

There are alarm spells woven into the wildflowers, alerting her to any uninvited guests who pass her border. She can summon barriers over her front door, her windows, and the damn basement on a whim. Lady Shira herself is a force to behold, and her home is as armed to the teeth as she is.

"You need something that will get your foot in the door—literally. Something that will allow you at least to have a conversation with her. My spellwork allowed me to dispel her defenses, but . . ." He pretends to wince sympathetically. His frog mouth forms one big squiggly line. "You haven't even got that," he condescends.

"But I've heard a rumor of a great artifact hidden in the corrupted caves to the west, an artifact that—if used correctly—can nullify the effects of even the strongest of magics. I'll tell you exactly where to find this legendary orb, and if you can brave the craggy tunnels where it's hidden to retrieve it, Shira won't stand a chance against you."

CHAPTER
Fourteen

"Good morning, sunshine," Noah says warmly, dodging raindrops as he jogs to meet me at my car. It's a sweet greeting for a gloomy Monday, but I don't mind the weather. It's impossible to dampen my enthusiasm now that I'm finally getting started on this mural.

"Hey!" I'm usually a ghost without my first cup of coffee, but my excitement has me practically dancing on my toes with energy. I can't imagine what caffeine will do to me next. With my latte in one hand, I offer Noah an identical paper cup. I don't know how he likes his coffee, but Busy Bean's cinnamon spice latte is my favorite, so I got two. "Had your wake-up potion yet?"

His expression brightens. "I have, but I'll never turn down another."

Noah helps me gather my supplies from the back of the car, hefting Liam's borrowed projector under his arm with ease. As we walk into Alchemist, I hold a yardstick out before me like a sword while shouldering a small bag of masking tape, chalk, and pencils. It's not much, but it's all I need for the first day of work.

Armed with a piece of chalk and my half-finished latte, I balance the projector on top of the bar and turn it on. My finalized outline for the mural flashes to life on the opposite wall above the fireplace.

Making use of the deep green that already coats the brick, I drew out a scene centered in a forest. Dark emerald and violet trees creep up the edges of the wall, looming over a small clearing. A horse is left to graze to the side, tied to a tree branch. Far off in the distance and deep into the trees are two glittering yellow eyes set in the face of a white, golden-antlered stag, hidden among the foliage. Near the middle of the image sits a traveler with a steel tankard in one fist, his features shrouded by his cloak's hood.

But it's the campfire at the center that's truly the star of the show. I drew it so that tongues of orange, gold, and white flame appear to emerge from Alchemist's electric fireplace, illuminating the traveler and warming his outstretched hands. A campfire is a place to take a break, to sit and rest for the night. It's home, even if just for a little while. That's the sense of comfort I want people to feel every time they visit the brewery.

"I get so excited every time I look at it," Noah breathes, his eyes wide as he takes in the projection. "But seeing it like this—fuck, it's going to be incredible, Sadie. It's spooky for a second, if you only look at the trees and the shadows, and then . . . it's warm. It's welcoming."

"That's what I'm going for." I roll my coffee cup between my hands, letting what heat is left seep into my palms. Seeing a glimpse of what the art might look like in a few weeks . . . I can't tell if it's the coffee or the project making me giddy. Probably both.

Probably Noah, too.

All morning we've done a graceful dance around each other, but with each moment of contact—my shoulder bumping against his side as he holds the door open for me, or his fingers brushing mine when he passes over the projector—I'm transported back to Saturday night. I can still remember the way his laugh felt while my arms were wrapped around his waist, and how he was close enough on the porch that I could feel his breath against my cheek. I wonder if the memory of it hangs over him, too, but before I can determine whether I'm brave enough to ask, the bell over the entry door tinkles merrily.

Noah takes a sudden half step in front of me; he'd locked the door behind us. But it's just Dan, smiling sheepishly as he takes off his damp beanie and walks over. "I know I told y'all I won't be comin' in on Mondays, but—I just couldn't help myself. Wanted to get a peek of your first day at work."

"It's incredible, isn't it?" Noah says, gesturing to the projection.

Dan lets out a low whistle, rocking back on his booted heels until his back connects with the bar. "You really found us somethin' special, Noah."

My cheeks warm as Noah tosses a wink in my direction. "We got very lucky," he agrees.

Dan pulls out his laptop while Noah and I set to work on our separate jobs for the day. Noah wanders off to the back of the brewery to do *beer things*—I remind myself to ask him sometime what happens in those great big vats where he brews the stuff—as I start outlining the projected sketch with white chalk. Dan sets the speakers to fill the building with a funky, jazzy indie band I've never heard of while I allow myself to relax into the blissfully mindless task of tracing.

Hours later, I stand atop Alchemist's small ladder, finishing the stag's curling antlers in the upper right corner of the wall when someone clears their throat below me. I nearly jump out of my skin, and Dan lurches forward to hold the ladder steady.

"Sorry—didn't mean to scare you. Just wanted to give you a heads-up that we'll need to start wrappin' things up soon."

I check the time—nearly evening. *Already?* "You got it. I'm almost done here."

He nods but insists on staying, with one hand braced on the ladder. He seems content to let me continue working in comfortable silence, but my curiosity gets the better of me. "Noah says you've been friends for a long time."

That brings out a grin hidden only somewhat by his overgrown mustache. "Oh hell, it's gotta be a decade at this point."

"What was he like? In college?"

Dan pauses. "Different," he says eventually. "You'd think most folk—me included—would've had their wildest days back in college. But I think he's livin' them right now, what with all of his adventuring and such. Back in school, he spent a good deal of his time keepin' *me* out of trouble."

I laugh at the thought as I descend the ladder. Dan trades places with me so that he can install the temporary curtains that will hide my work in progress from view. He'd insisted on keeping the mural a surprise until it's complete.

I pass up the dark curtains as he needs them. "It must feel great to work on a project like Alchemist together after planning it for so long," I say.

Something in Dan's gaze softens. "It's a dream come true, Sadie," he admits. "Now I've just gotta try and keep him around long enough to really get it off the ground."

"He seems to love it here, though. You really think he'd take off so soon?"

When Dan shrugs, he does it with his whole body. He tosses his hands upward. "Couldn't say," he says with a laugh. "I've never known anyone who could slow him down. And who am I to ask him to, anyway?"

Dan's words burrow uncomfortably into the back of my mind. But Noah interrupts my thoughts as he comes to stand behind me, squeezing my shoulders and taking one last look at the chalk outline before Dan tugs the curtains into place.

"Looking good, Sadie," Noah says. "Supply run tomorrow?"

"Tomorrow," I agree.

The second day of working on the mural leaves me squeezed with Noah in the back of his van, out of breath and soaking wet.

We're halfway through checkout at the home improvement store when a peal of thunder cracks above us, causing the teenage employee wielding the scanner to cast a worried glance toward the door. With our cart piled high and heavy with an assortment of paint cans, brushes, primers, and more, we head toward the exit and are brought to an abrupt halt by the mess outside. From where we cower under the awning, Noah's van is nothing more than a distant smudge of blue through the near-horizontal sheets of rain that pour from the sky.

"We could wait it out," I suggest.

Five minutes pass, and—somehow—it only gets worse. The cart shivers in a gust of wind.

"Fuck it," Noah huffs, tightening his grip on the cart. He looks to me, raises his eyebrows. "Fuck it?"

Feeling reckless, I laugh. "Fuck it."

We sprint across the concrete. Noah plows through puddles and potholes, bracing the cart as a battering ram before him while I run ahead to throw open the back doors of the van. It has tons more space than my little Civic, which had been the whole reason we'd brought it at all. But I don't have the keys—of *course* I don't have the keys—so I just stand there, laughing my ass off in the rain until Noah arrives to jam the key into the lock, his slick fingers fumbling the whole way through. "Shit, Sadie!" I can't tell if he's breathless from running or from laughing. "Terrible idea. Worst idea!"

Finally he swings the doors open, and we shove the bags and cans in as quickly as we can. Although Noah's mattress frame takes up the width of the van's interior, he'd cleared out tons of storage space underneath. When the cart is empty, I quickly look to Noah—and then to the lightning that illuminates the clouds above us from within. A clap of thunder follows soon after, and Noah snorts. "Like hell I'm driving in this. Just get in, Sadie."

"What?"

"Get in!"

There's really nowhere else for me to go but right on top of the blankets, so I scramble inside, and Noah slams the doors behind me and runs to return the cart.

On the way here when we'd ridden in the front, the interior was shielded from view by a curtain. Now I sit with my knees pulled to my chest, my drenched clothes soaking a folded quilt, a shocked loop of *Oh god, I'm in his bed* running on repeat in my head until Noah swings the doors back open and clambers in next to me. He doesn't bother to try to minimize the damage of his wet clothes. He just flops back onto his pillow, panting, and laces his hands behind his head.

We share one long, silent stare before dissolving into rib-cracking laughter.

As another rumble of thunder joins in, we stop to catch our breath, and I take off my glasses and wipe the lenses dry with the corner of his blanket. He reaches for something under the bed. There's a click, and dozens of tiny bulbs light up above us.

As I take my first real look around, I can't help but inhale a surprised gasp.

I didn't expect it to be so *cozy*, especially when the van's faded blue exterior looked so worn. It looks like a tree house—or, better yet, a hobbit hole. Handmade shelves full of books and tools and supplies dot the walls, with mismatched multicolored fabric drapes weaving in between each, covering the two windows and separating the cabin from the interior. A cleared desk with cabinets above is tucked close to the wall on my left, while the bed takes up the remaining middle and right side of the space.

"Lay back," Noah says gently. "Look."

I lie down, but even with my hands folded over my stomach, the bed is small enough that it's impossible not to immediately be shoulder to shoulder with him.

Wooden slats lie across the ceiling, some sporting tiny hooks to hang the string lights on. In the center, the slats are cut to make room for the van's vent, now shut tight against the rain. Handwritten postcards and pictures are stuck all over the ceiling, pictures of Noah in a dozen different places with a dozen different people. Noah in ski gear, his cheeks flushed and alarmingly clean-shaven. Noah with a group in hiking boots posing with Delicate Arch in the background. Noah with a beer in hand, his face smooshed up against a corgi's. I recognize Dan in more than a few of the photos, and I'm crestfallen to realize that he's sported the caterpillar mustache for as long as he's been able to grow it.

In more ways than one, the space feels . . . intimate. Like I'm seeing some part of Noah I haven't before. "It's beautiful," I say honestly. And then, more quietly, "This is home for you, isn't it?"

His answering smile is so sweetly fond. "This is home."

I reach up and trace my finger along the arc of a waterfall in one of the bent photos.

"Where to next?" I ask. Dan's joke about his inability to keep Noah rooted in one place echoes in the back of my mind again, despite my efforts to shove it down.

"No idea," he says with a laugh. "Any suggestions?"

I pat the wall of the van with teasing affection. "Think she could make it in the streets of New York?"

His eyes shine with amusement, and he turns onto his side until he's fully facing me. "To visit you, Sadie—I'd brave it."

I let my gaze skate past Noah's face to the window behind him. Rain no longer drums against the glass but instead dribbles down in slow streams. The storm's passed. It takes me a moment to realize that Noah has stopped speaking. He lies with his head propped on his fist, considering me thoughtfully.

His words are soft, daydreamy. "What are you thinking about?"

I turn to mirror Noah's position, and our knees knock together in the small space. I don't know if it's the rush of adrenaline from running through a downpour with him or just the fact that we're trapped together in our own bubble, waiting for the world outside to slow down—but the words rise to the base of my throat, begging me to let them out.

The uncertainty comes in a wave again, twisting my stomach and making me feel foolish for even considering asking.

But then I think about what I'd said to myself when I was feeling braver and drunker. *Roll for initiative.*

I'm lucky we're lying so close, because I can't get my voice to come out louder than a whisper. "Tell me I didn't imagine it. What almost happened Saturday night."

When Noah brought me back to Liam's, I'd thought there was something in that moment on the front porch. A spell half-cast, a magic ritual left incomplete. But when viewed through the lens of four drinks and the beauty of a twilit evening, anything could feel magical. I remember his hesitation, when I had leaned forward and he'd stayed still—

But then, very slowly, Noah's hand edges forward to cover mine. "You didn't imagine it."

I open and close my mouth several times, and when I'm able to speak again, all I manage is a quiet "Oh."

Noah presses on. "You were drunk. I didn't want to . . ." He pauses, tilts his chin down until his eyes are absolutely level with mine, so that he's sure I'm meeting his gaze. "I wanted to be sure. I wanted *you* to be sure."

"I'm sure." I say it too quickly. I don't even think.

"But how sure, Sadie?" His tone is so tender. He reaches up to smooth down the wet curls stuck to my forehead, tucking them neatly back behind my right ear. His fingertips linger on the side of my neck and trace slow, soothing circles. The interior of the van suddenly feels very, very warm. "After this summer, you're leaving.

I might be, too. We could ride it out, see how things go. But if we try this . . . are you really okay with that kind of uncertainty?"

His words cool me down. Am I? I want to insist *yes, of course!*, to jump in with the same abandon as when I raced out into the rain with him. I want to slip back into that moment from Saturday night and pull him toward me without pause. There's something about Noah that makes my brain turn off, that has me wanting to act on instinct and trust my gut feelings before I have a chance to talk myself out of them.

But he's asking me to slow down and think it through. He's hesitating, too.

Maybe he thinks this is a bad idea.

And maybe he's got a point.

Every aspect of my life feels uncertain right now: my job prospects, my bank account, and now this wild, wanderlust-filled boy. I've been managing to take things day by day, but I'm not sure I can handle any more unpredictability. So I tell him the only truth I can: "I don't know."

It's impossible to tell whether he's disappointed or relieved. "Think about it. We can talk when you're ready." His small smile is gently apologetic. "My shift starts soon anyway."

". . . Okay."

I glance at my phone to check the time—which turns out to be the worst thing I could do.

I can't look away, once I've seen it. The email notification is a bright bubble on my lock screen.

To: Josephine Brooks
From: Addison Marshall
Subject: Interview Invitation with Paragon Media

Noah must feel me go rigid under his hand, because he sits up suddenly, brow creased in concern. "What is it?"

My lips part, but it's like someone else is speaking for me. "I got an interview."

His eyes trace my features, searching. His mouth bends in a worried frown. "Is that a good thing?"

But my mind's gone blank. Once again, I tell him the only truth I can.

"I don't know."

CHAPTER
Fifteen

I should feel relieved—excited, even. But I haven't gotten past the shock. Most of my half-assed applications have been for jobs at companies I know nothing about, but Paragon is a gem, a stellar and competitive agency with a growing reputation. My application to them had been a shot in the dark, and I hadn't expected to get an interview at all—especially not this soon. Not to mention, one phone call to my old manager and Paragon could learn the truth of how I'd left Incite. Why would they bother to take a chance on me?

I didn't open the email until I got back to Liam's. On the drive back to Alchemist to unload Noah's van and pick up my car, he'd been so kind. Rather than try to untangle the complicated conversations we'd broached lying next to each other, he'd instead distracted me by playing a new band he thought I'd appreciate, sometimes peppering in easy questions about what the next steps were for the mural.

Back at Liam's, I'd stood in front of the pantry for ten minutes trying to figure out what I wanted for dinner before caving in and ordering delivery to save myself the effort of making a decision.

Tomorrow, I'd thought, curling up in bed after picking at my burrito bowl and staring at my phone, the events of the day replaying in my mind. *I'll have an early night and figure it all out tomorrow.*

But now it's nearly midnight and I'm reading through the email for the hundredth time. *I'll do the first step of the interview, of course, there's no harm in that,* I think robotically. *That's it. That's all I've got to decide right now.*

Well. It's not all I've got to decide.

My thoughts circle back to him, as they so often do lately. I open up my messages.

> I can't sleep

Noah responds in seconds.

> how can I help? more anime? the chess app? you've owed me a rematch for weeks now

> what's the point of a rematch when you won?

> it's hardly a win when your opponent gives up

> I fell asleep!

> . . . I see your point

> don't think that'll work this time tho. something else, maybe?

> like what?

I exhale noisily, frustrated.

> I wish we were playing tonight.

I've fallen in love with Liam's game for more reasons than one, but at this moment, I just miss the way it gets me out of my head and into Jaylie's. I drum my fingertips on the back of my phone as I watch Noah's text bubbles appear and disappear, over and over again.

do you like to write?

it's . . . okay?

hmmmm

when Liam first started the game, did you fill out the backstory document he sent around? the one with all the questions about Jaylie's history, motivations, weaknesses, etc?

of course

I'd spent days on that questionnaire, thoroughly laying out Jaylie's story with deliberation and care. This might be my first D&D game, but it's not my first time building a character. Sometimes I would go back into my cringey middle school sketchbooks to look at all my original characters and the backstories I'd built for them. RIP Desdemona Rose Evelyn Cullen, shy and misunderstood vampire queen.

so

i write fanfiction sometimes. i also used to roleplay on legends of lore. it was a little similar to dnd, but different

how do you mean?

it might be easier just to show you, but

instead of speaking for our characters like we do in dnd, you just write it out. so it'd be like, i type

"Loren blows Jaylie a kiss"

and you'd type

"Jaylie rolls her eyes"

and then you write a scene together
and it just goes on from there

My brows knit in a knot on my forehead. I'm confused but curious.

so you sexted in legends of lore?

Noah's miles away, but for a moment I can almost hear his smile-groan and picture the way he's pressing the heels of his palms to his eyes.

very funny, Sadie

just let me show you

if you hate it, we'll stop. or i'll just
bore you to sleep. win-win either way

sure, okay. let's try it

Noah sends a winking emoji along with a link to an online server. I shove my pillows into a nest behind my back and settle my lap-top on my thighs.

i'll start. you'll see what i mean!

Loren sits on a moss-covered log, facing away from
the campfire that had long since been put out. He

doesn't need the light, of course—as an elf, he's always been able to peer far into the dark, though in a forest as dense as this one it's difficult to see farther than ten paces ahead. He drew the short straw this evening, so it's his job to take the first watch as his companions rest. It's dull work and he's not very good at it, prone to distraction. Even now he flips through one of his songbooks and hums quietly under his breath.

Jaylie can't fall asleep. Ever since they left Belandar, she can't get used to the feeling of roots and rocks pressing into her back as she tries to rest. She longs for her feather bed. She's not cut out for adventuring, not like this. So she stares at what little she can see of the sky through the canopy of leaves above her and eventually gives up on sleep. She stands with a sigh.

Loren's long ears perk up at the sound of approaching footsteps, though as soon as he sees that it's just Jaylie, he relaxes. No threats there. "Still can't sleep, can you?"

"It's not getting any easier," Jaylie complains. "It's embarrassing."

Loren smiles sympathetically. "I remember my first trip on the road. It was hell. I can help you rest more easily, if you want. I know a few tricks."

Jaylie narrows her eyes suspiciously.

Loren rolls his eyes. "Trust me." He gestures for her to come closer. "Come here, sit down. We don't want to wake the others." Loren leads Jaylie to a dry patch of clover in front of the log. He tucks away his songbook and draws out a carved wooden comb, holding it out for her to see. "May I?"

Jaylie's brows rise in surprise before she smiles. "I suppose you can, if you really want to. It's a rat's nest in there, though."

"I'll make quick work of it." Loren sits behind her, gently placing his hands on her shoulders and guiding her until she faces forward. He gathers her hair, fingers brushing along her collarbones and the sides of her neck as he lays her curls to fall in waves down her back. He takes a small section in his palm and begins at the ends, working slowly through the tangles.

Jaylie laces her fingers in her lap and allows herself to relax under his capable hands. "How are you finding all this traveling? No offense, bard, but you seem as much of a city girl as me," she says dryly. "I thought you'd wilt like a flower the second a bed and a drink weren't within an arm's reach."

Loren winds one lock of hair around his finger and tugs it playfully, chastising her. "I'm a *traveling* bard, Jay. Where do you think I get all of my songs? All of my stories?"

"I assumed you made them up."

"No, love. All of the best ones are true." With most of the tangles taken care of, he brings the comb down from the crown of her head through the ends in slow, even strokes. "Are you from Belandar originally?"

"I grew up on the outskirts of the city, but—yes. It's home." She sighs softly. "This is the first time I've ever left."

"Were you always with the church of Marlana?"

"Not always, but for most of my adult life. I don't
like to think about the times before," she says
stiffly. She tries to relax a little, resting the
small of her back against Loren's shins. She allows
the sensation of the comb's teeth threading over her
scalp to calm her. "Where do you call home?"

Despite his curiosity, Loren doesn't pry. "Funnily
enough, I'm from Belandar, too. But I was born many
years ago, and likely left the city before you were
even a thought in your parents' heads."

Jaylie twists to squint at him over her shoulder.
With the darkness so thick around them, it's
difficult to make out much more than the deep maroon
sheen of his hair and the brights of his eyes. It
makes it even more difficult than usual to read him.
"What are you, then? Over a hundred?"

Loren simpers, placing his palm flat to his chest.
Among the elves, one hundred years would be barely
into adulthood. "So young? You flatter me." Loren
sets the comb aside and begins to braid her hair with
well-practiced motions. This way, it won't tangle as
she sleeps. "But to your question—Belandar isn't
home. *This* is." He gestures to the sky, his sleeping
roll, his lute, and finally the campfire sitting cold
in its ring of stones.

Jaylie wrinkles her nose. Her mind wanders back to
Marlana's temple. Wistfully she recalls the meals
shared with her fellow clerics, the familiar pink-
and-gold marble arches surrounding the stained glass
mosaics, and the little black kitten, Charm, she
rescued last month. He's probably missing her by now,
and her chest aches with the thought. "But what of

the adoring fans you told me about? Don't you worry that they'll miss you?"

Loren chuckles under his breath. "That's the point, actually."

"How do you mean?"

Loren clutches Jaylie's shoulders and squeezes. "Don't you see, Jay? I *want* them to miss me. I want my songs to get stuck in their heads, and I want them to look forward to seeing me play again. To wonder when I'll come back." He loosens his grip and gently circles his thumbs in the curves between her shoulders and neck. "If I stay somewhere for too long, I'll get stuck. I'll get boring. The world will pass me by, and all of the great legends and adventures will happen without me." As he massages her shoulders, the pressure increases with his resolve. "I want to be the one to tell those stories. I don't want them to forget me."

Jaylie is quiet for a moment. His hands are hot on her skin, and though her muscles unwind under his touch, the pads of his thumbs press too deep to feel soothing. There are aspects of his words that resonate with her faith in Marlana—luck has everything to do with opening yourself up to opportunity and new experiences—but she's not wholly convinced. "That's not true," she murmurs. And then, teasingly, "You're impossible to forget, Loren."

"Is that right? Do you think of me often, Jaylie?"

"I can't help it when you never shut up. Constantly talking our ears off or waking us up in the morning with a burst of song," she says with grudging fondness.

"Stop it, you'll give me a big head." His touch becomes light, gentle. His fingers sink into her hairline at the base of her skull and gently weave in circling motions.

"I couldn't possibly make your head any bigger than it already is." Despite the way her mind races, her eyelids begin to droop. Hair petting has always been her weakness; she melts completely into his touch. "You'll have to tell me of your other stories, Loren, but . . . you're off to a pretty good start with this one."

"You think so?"

"A daring tale of a stolen bride, blood magic, and a team of adventurers vanquishing an evil witch while saving a beautiful woman? Utterly compelling. You'll have damsels throwing themselves into distress just for the chance to be your next muse."

Loren exhales a gentle laugh. "You must be very sleepy indeed, priestess, to be complimenting me so much. Is your guard down so completely?"

Jaylie's expression goes stormy, but she can't keep up the act for long; a smile peeks through as her eyes drift closed. "You said you'd send me to sleep, but here you are again, chattering away."

"Allow me one last try, then. Lie down."

"Don't try your luck, bard," she warns, though her threat is half-hearted. She lies down on the faded blue canvas of her sleeping roll. Already she can feel the roots press into her back, tempting knots back into the muscles of her shoulders that Loren just smoothed out.

"I wouldn't dream of it." He comes to sit beside her in the dirt and gently lifts one of her hands to hold it in his lap. He leans close to her face, so that his hair falls in a sheet of red between them, and cups his palm around the shell of her ear. He casts a spell—and begins to sing. It's a lullaby of a sort, a magic charm to ease someone quickly and gently into slumber. He sings it slowly and draws her softly down into a dream.

It's a language that Jaylie does not recognize. As the spell sinks into her bones and embraces her like a warm bath, she concentrates on the sound of Loren's voice. When everything else fades, it's the last thing she holds on to.

When he is sure that she is asleep, Loren presses his lips to Jaylie's forehead. "Good night, Jaybird."

CHAPTER
Sixteen

On Friday morning, the interview goes so well that I think I might throw up.

It had taken HR only a day to schedule the call with Addison Marshall, my potential manager, though I'd entertained the hope that maybe they wouldn't reach back out at all. If they hadn't, it would be so easy to pretend that the end of summer was still some far-off thing. If they hadn't, I wouldn't have to face reality for a few more weeks. But HR had responded, and the interview went great, and Addison was lovely.

"I'm already charmed by you, Josephine, and I know the team will be thrilled to meet you, too," she had said. "I'll be in touch soon to schedule the next round. It was *so* nice to meet you today." Her honey-brown hair, expensively dyed and styled in a topknot on her head, bounced from side to side with her little shimmy of enthusiasm.

I'd exchanged some pleasantry I can't remember now and kept the smile frozen on my face until I was sure that the virtual meeting had ended and my camera was off. Then I'd leapt into my unmade bed with Howard curled up next to a pillow, buried my face into his belly, and silently screamed. Liam had found me like that after work and tempted me downstairs with the promise of milk-shakes he'd picked up on his way home.

Now I slouch into the couch cushions and squeeze the bridge of my nose until the pain forces me to let go. Liam sits across from me with Howard on his lap, the two of them patiently waiting for the rundown.

"It went well," I say. "It went really, really well. It's everything I could ever want, Liam."

With this job, I'd have more agency in which projects I worked on, my own direct report, a seat of leadership among the team . . . everything I never got when I was at Incite. Everything I'd spent so many years working toward.

God, and so much money.

I push my glasses into my hair and cover my eyes with my hand. "I could afford my own apartment," I say wistfully before looking at him. "I could ditch my bitchy roommates and get a little studio. My commute would be shorter, I could find a grocery store that's not seven blocks away, I could adopt the cat I always said I wanted, but . . ."

His head dips gently to the side. "But what?"

"I just didn't think it would happen this fast."

The thought of sliding back into a marketing role so soon . . . There would be familiarity in the routine, yes. I know the industry inside and out, and I'm aware of its expectations, intricacies, and weaknesses. Just like slipping into Jaylie's skin, I know exactly how to shift back into Josephine. I've got a costume and everything: my killer black pencil skirt that makes my ass look amazing, the magenta blazer that I always wear when I need an extra burst of confidence, and tall clicking heels that make me feel powerful. I know the steps to the song and dance, I know how to pitch, and I know how to convince and when to push.

Addison's description of the job sounded simple. Theoretically, I could do it in my sleep.

But I'd thought the same about Incite. And then, when they really increased the pressure, I couldn't take it. I broke.

"After everything that happened, I don't—Liam, I don't know if I can handle it."

Liam's expression goes gentle in a way that immediately has my hackles up. "Just because Incite didn't end well doesn't mean it'll be the same this time. Sometimes layoffs—"

"It wasn't layoffs," I snap. I can't believe I'm finally saying it.

"What?"

"I wasn't laid off from Incite," I say carefully. It's the first time I've ever given the words voice, and each one tastes more bitter than the last.

"I was fired."

He exhales a soft laugh, as if to ease the sudden tension. "Isn't that the same thing?"

"It's not," I insist. "I wasn't let go because of budget cuts or whatever, like I'd said. I—I lied, Liam, I'm sorry. But it was my fault. I deserved it."

I squint, as if that might be enough to keep the tears currently flooding my eyes from escaping. The stress of the interview, of these choices, of holding the truth of this in—

"It wasn't bad luck at all. It was *me*."

Liam's brows draw together in concern. "Tell me what happened."

And I do.

My vision narrows and I'm suddenly back there again. I'm on the subway at 9 P.M., heading home after a long day of bombing a pitch meeting, being chewed out by my manager, and forgetting lunch. It's not the worst day I've ever had at Incite, but it's top five at least. There's a coffee stain on my magenta blazer from where I spilled my fourth cup of the day. My laptop is tucked into the tote bag at my side. Even after I stayed so late, there is still so much of my presentation I have to fix, and my team needs the new draft in their inbox by tomorrow morning.

I go home, burrow myself under the comforter of my twin bed (it's the only size that fits in my tiny room), and pull open my laptop. I keep the other lights off, so the square screen alone illuminates my face. My mind blank and empty, I stare at the screen for a good hour before I drift off to sleep.

The next day, I don't send the presentation. I don't go to work, and I don't get out of bed except to pee.

The following day is the same. I don't even open my laptop, but it glares at me from where I've pushed it to the corner of the bed.

A week passes like this. My manager sends me dozens of texts and calls me twice as many times. I email to tell her I'm sick. I never pick up the phone. I haven't showered yet. Last week's paycheck funds food delivery after food delivery.

During the second week, HR gets involved. They are extremely puzzled. How is it that one of their top performers has fucked up so badly? *We have resources,* they soothe, *for whatever it is that you're going through.* But I already burned through my two allotted mental health days back in early February and used more than double my sick time. I think about calling a friend to come over, but I don't know who I would call, and I know even less about what I would say. *I can't do it anymore!* I imagine announcing. *Every time I try to turn on my laptop I feel so panicked that my muscles lock up and I forget how to breathe.* Liam's all the way in Texas, and calling my parents is out of the question. All of my other friends are co-workers, and "friends" is probably too generous of a term for them anyway. Lunches and happy hours spent bitching about work doesn't leave a lot of room for real friendship to grow.

"At the end of the third week," I finish eventually, "I was allowed to resign. 'We don't see you growing with our team,' they said. I could tell they felt bad about it all, enough that they didn't fire me outright in a way that would have gone on my record. But in the end I was still encouraged to leave."

Liam is quiet for a moment. "Did something happen to make you disconnect from it all so suddenly?" he asks.

"Not at all." That was the worst part. There was no event that I could map my feelings back to, no tragedy to justify the way I broke down. "One day, it just . . . got to me. One day, it was just too much."

I press my knuckles to my eyes, attempting to stem the flow of tears. "I didn't know how to tell you. I haven't told anyone, and I've barely admitted it to myself. I—I feel like I've taken advantage of you this whole time, Liam, when it's always been my fault that I'm even in this position. It's not fair that I—"

"Sadie, shut up."

It's like a slap in the face. My jaw falls open and I gape at him, stunned. "What?"

"Shut up." Liam's grinning. He shrugs dramatically. "So you messed up."

"Badly."

He waves one hand flippantly. "Maybe. Maybe not. Maybe you regret how you left, and maybe it wasn't the most graceful exit, but—do you regret leaving?"

I hate how easy a question it is to answer. "No."

"Do you think I'm a bad person because I didn't move to New York with you? Because I chickened out? Does it make me a failure?"

"God, of course not, Liam."

He looks at me meaningfully. "Sadie, listen. Whatever the world throws at you or whatever choices or mistakes you make on your own, I'll always be here for you." He leans to brace his elbows on his knees. "You could have told me the truth from the beginning, and it wouldn't have changed a thing. You would still be welcome for as long as you like."

And just like that, the knot in my chest loosens, and I pull Liam into a rough hug. My voice is muffled against his shoulder. "I love you so much."

Liam wraps his arms around me, and we pull each other close in a Howard sandwich. "Love you, too. Stay forever. I mean it."

I laugh and wipe at my eyes. "That's what makes this so complicated," I say thickly. Maybe part of me even wants to take him up on his offer. "I don't know what to do."

"At the end of the day, there's no pressure either way," Liam says slowly. "So why not just see how things go?"

Even as I nod, I can't help but smile. "You sound like Noah."

He blinks in surprise. "You told him about this?"

"No, it was—" I have to pause to clear my suddenly dry throat. "We were talking about something else."

Liam's not letting me get away with that. He leans backward, regarding me down the bridge of his nose as his mouth curls into a teasing smile. "You've been spending a lot of time together." Not a question.

"We wrote a story this week. About the D&D game." It's carefully laid distraction bait, personalized specially for Liam.

He bites, eyes narrowing. "A story?"

"He called it roleplaying."

Liam's eyebrows climb to hover over the lenses of his rimless glasses. "Oho, okay. Whoa. What sort of roleplay? The handsome scoundrel and the celibate priestess?"

I snort. "Jaylie's not *that* sort of priestess—"

Liam's brows rise even higher. "Not celibate? So then it was definitely a spicy role—"

"No!" I snap, laughing. "It wasn't *that* sort of roleplay."

"Not yet, anyway," he says under his breath, snickering. "Better you write that part privately with him than subject my game table to witnessing it."

"Oh god, Liam, I wouldn't dare." Feeling sheepish, I reach forward to run my fingers over Howard's fur, which immediately starts up the purr engine. "Do you think—am I playing wrong?"

"Wrong? How do you mean?"

"Like—is it normal for two players to roleplay privately?"

Liam pauses to pick up his milkshake, which had sat forgotten on the coffee table as I'd had my afternoon breakdown on his couch. What little is left is all but melted at this point, but he sips noisily from the straw in a valiant attempt anyway. "Honestly, one-on-one roleplay is pretty advanced for a couple of first timers," he says thoughtfully. "Not a lot of my other players do it, unless they're wanting to explore their character dynamics more seriously. But it's just another way to engage with the game. I'm honored that you're so invested."

I nod to myself. "What about . . . romance?" My pitch drops dramatically on the last word.

He grins. "Go on."

"Is that something that happens in other games? Flirting between characters?"

"Of course it is. Hell, I've seen characters get married, have kids, try to seduce the villain . . . all sorts of things. Some DMs won't allow romance at their tables, but I've always thought that's ridiculous. As long as everyone's having a good time—and no one's being, like, fucking weird about it—I welcome it."

I don't respond, but I don't have to. Liam elbows my ribs. "If you do decide to pursue romance, you have my blessing." He pats my hand. "Roll with advantage, Sadie."

CHAPTER
Seventeen

"If anyone dares to step foot in this room before I say it's ready, I'll give you disadvantage on all rolls for the entirety of today's game." Liam's using his teacher voice again. Even through the shut door of the game room, we can hear him with perfect clarity.

I hover near the dining room table with the rest of the players, picking at Jules's snickerdoodle cookies and waiting for Liam's go-ahead to enter. Morgan appears at my side and bumps her hip against mine. "Sounds pretty serious, huh?"

"What, disadvantage?" It would be a massive punishment, meaning we'd have to roll our dice twice but be forced to use the lower of the two numbers.

"Yes, but no," Morgan says. "I'm talking about whatever it is he's setting up in there."

"Did you see today's map, Sadie?" Noah asks as he comes to stand by me. There are snickerdoodle crumbs caught in his beard. I consider brushing them out but keep my hand at my side. "Got any insider info?"

Catching on, Jules and Morgan lean toward me, too.

But I'm going into this session just as blind as everyone else. Whenever we have an exploration session like this one, where our characters voyage into new territory, Liam brings out a lovingly crafted map so that we can better visualize how the adventure plays out in real time. He even gifted us with miniature figurines of our characters. I'd spent years in high school and college helping him paint miniatures for his games, but for this campaign, he'd done it himself as a surprise.

"I have no idea," I say honestly. "He's locked himself in there all day; Howard and I aren't allowed in."

Jules presses her ear to the game room door as Noah shuffles excitedly from foot to foot. Liam must hear his antsy dancing, because he finally emerges.

Our DM stands silhouetted in the doorframe, backlit by purple, green, and blue lamps scattered atop the table. Eerie music seeps from speakers planted in each corner of the room. The map is covered with a thin sheet of black fabric, though I can see the peaks and valleys of figurines and landscape pieces set up underneath.

"Come in, adventurers," Liam intones. "Your quest awaits."

At the base of the mountain lies a cave, and within ten paces of it, no plants grow. Jaylie has become used to the lush waist-high grasses of the rolling fields, but here they've withered to brittle yellow stalks, and the tree roots have calcified hard as stone. Shadows pour from the cave's entrance, reaching out purple tendrils of darkness that seem to suck at the light. The worst part is how quiet it is. Jaylie can't pick up any skittering sounds of insects underfoot, and even the breeze hangs still, ominously frozen around their shoulders.

"Well, this feels evil as shit," Loren says cheerfully. "Are we sure *this* is the cave Alastair told us the crystal orb is in? Are we positive he's not just trying to get us killed?"

"It does reek of dark magic," Jaylie says slowly. "But I don't think Alastair was lying. He's too proud—and too desperate."

"We'll be fine." Kain's voice rumbles above Jaylie as he slides past her to lead the group into the cave, axe balanced over his shoulder. Morgana swallows audibly as everyone follows him inside.

It's worse when the sun goes away. The light disappears entirely, and the silence feels like a blanket smothering all of their senses. Although Jaylie's companions have the ability to see in the darkness, her own human eyes see nothing at all. Loren offers to hold her hand, but despite the temptation, she needs more guidance than that; she summons a ball of pale pink light between her palms.

"I could sing, if we want?" Loren's voice sounds very far away, though he stands right at Jaylie's shoulder. "Just to chase away the bad vibes, if nothing else."

"And alert every creature in this cave to our presence? I don't think so," Morgana hisses.

Too late for that.

From out of the gloom there's a sudden screech, made infinitely more terrifying by the way it echoes against the slick, curved walls of the cave. Like nails on steel, the skittering of dozens of legs follows the inhuman howling, clattering closer with each heartbeat that thunders through Jaylie's chest.

"Fuck fuck *fuck*, get ready!" she warns.

The light between her palms spreads in a gentle circle around them. She sees the beady eyes first, then the oily shine of fangs, and lastly the furred, spiny bodies with far too many legs attached.

Of course it had to be spiders.

Of course it had to be *giant* fucking spiders.

Which makes it all the more astonishing when Jaylie and her companions cut through their ranks like knives through butter.

Surprisingly Loren steps forward first, lute held before him. With a strum of his strings, tongues of fire leap from the bowl of the instrument and set each creature aflame. Morgana sinks her knives into several pairs of eyes, popping them like wet black bubbles. Kain follows soon after, and one swing of his axe is enough to take off at least six waving legs. With Kain crouched in a defensive stance, Jaylie focuses a preemptive healing spell on him, forming a shield of pink light.

But he never needs it.

In less than a minute the spiders are sprawled dead in a semicircle around them, limbs and eyes and legs scattered in puddles of black and orange goo. Quickly Jaylie scans her companions for any sign of injury, but no one has been touched.

"Damn, maybe we're actually good at this." Even spoken in a breathless whisper, Morgana's words are easy to hear in the stunned silence that follows the slaughter. Jaylie lets out a relieved laugh.

"*Hell yeah*, we are," Loren boasts.

And as they delve deeper into the cave, it only gets easier.

Kain carves through hordes of spiders while Loren plays a purposefully misleading tune that causes a group of reptilian kobolds to distractedly turn down a side tunnel, avoiding confrontation with them entirely. All the while Jaylie consults the map she hastily drew using Alastair's descriptions of the cave system, directing the party closer and closer to their goal.

With only a few tunnels left between them and the crystal, the caves grow quieter. Pressure builds in Jaylie's ears, and her breaths become quick and shallow regardless of how hard she tries to keep them even and slow.

"We've already traveled a great deal," she says eventually, sighing and slowing to a halt.

Loren and the others continue ahead before they realize that the sphere of light from her spell has stopped along with her, no longer illuminating the way forward.

"Perhaps we should stop for a while," Jaylie suggests. "Take a rest."

Kain frowns. "You want to quit already? Are you losing your nerve?"

Loren frowns at his tone and turns to Jaylie. "Are your spell reserves low?"

Jaylie tugs lightly at her holy symbol, twisting it between her fingers. She can perform only so many feats of magic per day, and although the path has been easy on them so far, she's not sure how much more she can manage. "Not completely, but if things go badly, we'll be in trouble."

"But this has been a walk in the park. If we stop now, we risk giving whatever shit crawls these tunnels a chance to regroup and attack again," Kain says, crossing his arms over his broad chest.

That seems to put Morgana on edge; she casts a wary glance over her shoulder. Loren regards Jaylie with his brows drawn low over serious green eyes. "I think it's up to our lovely priestess. She's the one keeping us all alive." He raises his voice and turns to the rest of the group with his hands on his hips. When Jaylie doesn't move, Morgana winces, and Kain audibly groans as he rolls his black gaze to the ceiling, which is thick with dripping stalactites.

Frustrated, Jaylie shakes her head, causing the gold coin charms woven into her braids to tinkle gently. "It's fine. We can continue." She tightens her grip on the holy symbol. "Just don't get too hurt, all right?"

Please, my Lady, watch over us. We're nearly there.

Loren studies her for a moment, but his mouth twists toward a frown as his gaze slides past her to take in their ugly surroundings. He's eager to leave this place, too. "We'll make quick work of it, then. I've also got a few healing spells up my sleeve, just in case."

The light from Jaylie's spell catches on one of Kain's fangs as he grins. "Let's fuck 'em up."

They continue forward, and although Jaylie's steps are slower than before, she follows. Eventually they arrive at a narrow passageway in the wall at the end of the cave, just barely tall enough to accommodate Kain's height—horns and all. Its walls are covered in a blood-red moss, and the water running in rivulets down its surface makes it look like an open wound. Jaylie wrinkles her nose delicately.

"This is where the crystal should be," she says.

"One at a time, then," Kain grunts.

He leads, with Morgana offering to take up the rear. Situated just behind the hulking tiefling, Jaylie winces at the sound of his horns scraping against the sharp stone of the tunnel. Kain gives a hiss of discomfort as he shuffles through, turning his body to the side and leading with his shoulder. After what feels like forever, the barbarian finally exits the tight tunnel, though what he sees makes him freeze just past its opening.

"Oh *gods*."

It's the first time Jaylie has heard him speak with reverence.

Pushing her way past him, she steps out into a large and surprisingly well-lit space. The air feels fresh against her skin, and for the first time since entering the caves, she takes a full breath in. The scene spread out before her is so beautiful, so undisturbed and *intimate*, that for a moment she's certain it must be a shrine to some god. From the darkness above pours an unending stream of water that flows into a glowing green pool. Though sparkling grains of black sand surround the pond, the water occupies the majority of the space, lapping gently along the shore. The moss disappears from the walls as soon as the tunnel ends, replaced with huge chunks of sharp white and mint-green crystals. Though they give off a dim glow of their own, they're no match for the beam of light shining from the orb buried under the water's surface. It's gorgeous, and the thought of stealing it from its resting place feels like a violation. Even witnessing this holy space feels sacrilegious.

Loren is the first to echo Jaylie's thoughts. "Well, that's got to be it, right?" He jerks his chin toward the orb.

Everyone murmurs in agreement—but no one steps forward.

Even Kain looks skeptical, his eyes slitted as he peers into the depths.

Jaylie's painted lips curl into a wry smile. "Shall we flip a coin?"

Loren laughs, and it's only half-forced. "You'd like that, wouldn't you? But you have too much luck on your side, and it would surely be one of us who'd have to fetch it."

"A volunteer, then?" Jaylie asks.

Again, the room is quiet.

Eventually Kain rolls his eyes, lowers his axe to the ground, and steps toward the water. "Cowards," he grumbles. Morgana unsheathes a couple of throwing knives strapped to her thighs and holds them at the ready. At Loren's questioning brow, she shrugs and whispers, "Just in case. It can't be this easy, can it?"

The others nod and ready their weapons as Kain wades farther into the water. His loose pants billow in the clear pool as the surface rises past his belt and up his bare, muscled chest. It's up to his shoulders by the time he reaches the crystal orb, the waterfall gushing in a steady stream directly atop it. Kain gives the party a grin and a quick thumbs-up as he inhales deeply and prepares to dive under.

But it's at that moment that the orb begins to rise.

There's a pulsing rumble from below the pool's surface, sending dozens of bubbles streaming upward. As soon as the orb peeks above the waterline, the thunderous sound can be heard clearly for what it is—deep, rolling bouts of gleeful laughter. The sound fills the chamber, echoing painfully off the walls as the giggling grows shrill with barely contained madness.

"Oh, it has been so *long* since I have had visitors."

What appeared to be a glowing green orb from under the waterfall resolves itself into the form of one huge, unblinking green eye. Below the bulge of the eye grins a grotesque mouth full of dozens of thin, needlelike yellow teeth that drip with water and thick saliva. The monster floats above the pool without the aid of limbs, its spherical body suspended magically in the air as it drifts out from underneath the cascade of the waterfall. From its slimy folds of green-blue skin sprout thick tentacles that reach toward the ceiling, each capped with a single smaller version of its central eye. The awful creature makes direct eye contact with each one of Jaylie's companions, its individual stalks reaching out to peer at them, though it keeps Kain held in the gaze of its continuously glowing central orb.

It takes all of Jaylie's strength to keep her knees from giving out as her breath freezes painfully in her chest. She's heard stories about creatures like this, but they're not meant to live this close to the surface. They're supposed to be buried deep in the darkness of the underground far below. How far down had Jaylie and her party traveled? These are the creatures of stories that keep children awake at night, that keep adventurers constantly visiting Jaylie's church to pray for protection.

Here is a creature of nightmare.

A beholder.

"And while it's so kind of you to visit, I'm not much in the mood to host guests." The thing's lips move horribly around the knives of its teeth as it speaks, its voice shrill and booming all at once. Again it bursts into terrible laughter that rises in volume until it reaches one continuous screech.

A single dagger finds its way into the beholder's jaws, sticking in its gums like a discarded toothpick. Every one of the beholder's eleven eyes narrows to a slit simultaneously and locks on to Morgana.

"You'll regret that, dwarf."

In the brief moment Jaylie has to consider whether she might prefer to flee back toward where they came from, her party leaps into action.

"Motherfucking *shitballs,* gods have mercy . . . What in the *Hells*—" Loren fumbles at the strings of his lute as he rushes to get an offensive spell in motion. Just as flames begin to gather in the instrument's bowl again, the beholder turns its gaze on the bard. "Not so fast," it chides him. Caught in the cone of sickly green light emanating from the creature's central eye, the magic Loren weaves at his fingertips fizzles away to nothing. Loren stares stunned at his lute as his spell disappears.

Jaylie's heart twists with the sickening realization that they can't run—if they want to stop Shira's magic, they need the orb. They need the *eye*.

And yet despite her newfound resolve, she's shaken by Loren's scream as the beholder lunges forward to sink its teeth into his shoulder, tearing through his beautifully tailored coat to the skin and muscle beneath. At the same time, one of the monster's eyestalks shoots a sizzling ray of magic toward Kain, who, dripping with water, has just raised his axe to cut into it from behind. The spell hits him in the chest, and the tiefling seizes as dark magic rolls in agonizing waves down his body. Inhaling a ragged gasp, Kain shakes off the pain and cuts the blade of his axe deep into the beholder's skull, severing one of the stalks.

Morgana takes advantage of the momentary respite, peppering the creature with knives as it howls in pain. Jaylie's gaze flicks between the bard and the barbarian, both men bloodied and hurt. For once Loren hasn't succumbed to dramatics and stands with his spine as straight as Kain's. Everyone walks the edge between panic and determination as the reality of the danger of their situation sinks into their stomachs like stones. At the last moment, while the beholder is still distracted, Jaylie throws her first spell of healing at Kain despite her fondness for Loren. She's willing to bet that Kain is their best bet for killing the monster as quickly as possible.

As she wills another spell of healing to her fingertips, the beholder stops screaming and gasps in labored breaths that shake the walls. With dread, Jaylie watches the beam of green light pan across the wall's sparkling crystals before pinning her to the ground in its glare. She swallows audibly as the warmth of her healing magic flees from her palms, leaving her fingers feeling cold.

"Ah-ah-ah," the monster scolds her, its thickly scaled brow lowering over its eye threateningly. "I won't allow you to *cheat* with your healing magic, cleric."

Jaylie raises her hands before her as a beam of shadow from one writhing eyestalk lances through her chest. Her heart thuds painfully just as her throat tightens. She gasps in a breath of air at the pain, and her lungs freeze. With each heartbeat, numbness radiates from her chest and seeps into her bones. First, she finds herself unable to exhale. Then, her spine turns to stone, locking her back in a painful arch as she struggles to twist away from the monster. She tries to take a step, but her feet sink heavily into the sand and refuse to move. Her eyes roll in a panic until they, too, freeze in place, her gaze forced to behold the creature as it looms over her. When paralysis fully takes hold of her body and numbness replaces the pain, she watches in horror as her skin is transformed into stone.

She is a statue. *Marble.* In place of human flesh and the blue lines of veins is smooth white stone threaded with pink and gray. Although she can't feel her heart racing in her chest, or the adrenaline and fear coursing through her, her mind rattles against its cage in terror. She is forced to watch as her companions continue to fight—and bleed—without her help. Unable even to blink or shed the tears that build like pressure in the back of her head, she witnesses the battle in what feels like horrible slow motion.

"Jay, no!" Jaylie thinks it's Loren's voice, but she can't be sure— he's out of her line of sight. But the twang of a string snapped in fear confirms it.

The beholder grins at its latest victory, but it doesn't have much time to celebrate. Even though Kain's and Morgana's eyes grow wide with fear and anger to see Jaylie petrified, they redouble their efforts to destroy the creature. As Kain's axe slices off two more tentacles and carves a bloody tear into the beholder's massive eyelid, Morgana sinks her knives into the monster's back, using them as leverage to climb up its head.

Again Jaylie hears the plucking of strings to her left. The frantic and stressed tempo of the music is at odds with the cheery melody. Little darts of sparkling yellow light shoot toward Kain and set to knitting up some of the worst wounds left in the wake of the beholder's spell. Jaylie would raise her brows in surprise if she could move them.

"I don't know if you can hear me, Jay, but—stay awake, okay? We'll get you out of this. I've heard songs about how to treat this petrification curse. It'll be all right. We'll figure it out." The warm assurance in Loren's voice has Jaylie's eyes swelling with the memory of tears again.

But the howl of the beholder distracts her from his soothing tone. She focuses her gaze on Morgana's prone form as Kain takes a defensive stance over her. With a last thrust, Kain sinks his axe deep into the right side of the beholder's mouth, and with one wet tug, he tears the lower half of the monster's jaw clean off. The tiefling steps back, inhales, and releases a bloodcurdling yell as he twists his axe in a gorgeous arc behind his head and swings it around to sink the blade deep into the beholder's skull.

The beam from the monster's great central eye flickers as its body tumbles through the air, shifting dizzily from side to side. But before death claims it entirely, before its light goes out, it twists in slow motion and narrows its eye, weeping blood, directly at Jaylie. She imagines she can feel the hate rolling off of it in waves. With one last cry, the monster throws itself forward, and its body grows horrifically large in her vision as it barrels toward her.

Halfway there, it collapses entirely, the teeth on its unhinged lower jaw raking through the ink-dark sand below. It comes to a stop right at her shins, spraying blood and green gore along the white marble of her skirts. Her vision wobbles as the force of the blow sends her body swaying.

She sees rather than feels the brush of Loren's fingers against the stone palm of her hand as her vision pans dizzyingly upward. *I'm falling,* she realizes. As Loren yells out her name, his hazel-green eyes are the last thing she sees before the back of her head collides with the wall behind her.

It doesn't hurt at all when her body shatters.

"What do you mean *when her body shatters?*" My hands are clutched around my dice so hard that I can feel the points of the d4 digging into my skin.

Liam sits very still, his hands steepled before him. For a few moments, he just silently taps his pointer fingers against his lower lip where it peeks out from his beard. Suddenly, he stands and leans over the game board laid out on the table before us.

Honestly, I've never seen our chaotic group so quiet and still.

The map turned out beautifully. Liam decorated it with chunks of LED-glowing crystal lamps, scattered rocks, dozens of spiders with bendable legs, a terrifyingly realistic beholder model, and each of our characters' miniatures.

But I can't appreciate any of that right now. All I can do is watch in horror as Liam reaches forward to where Jaylie stands resplendent in a pink dress with tiny gold coin details—and knocks her prone. He raises his head and meets my gaze evenly. "Her body was destroyed." He takes in a deep breath, and when he exhales, he says exactly what I dread hearing most.

"She's dead."

I almost expect him to whip out a hammer and smash the little figurine to pieces just to drive the point home.

"Just like that?" An unexpected wave of grief has my voice sticking in my throat.

Finally, the other players stir, shaking themselves out of a fugue state of shock.

Morgan suggests, "I've got healing potions, though—is it too late for that?"

"And I have a healing spell or two left, or a restoration spell, though I've never used it before . . ." Noah says. He stands, his body shot with energy. He braces one palm on the table and the other on my forearm.

Jules sits back in her chair and winds one brown curl around her finger thoughtfully. She looks calm. Strategic. "Could we take her back to one of Marlana's churches, maybe? Could the other clerics revive her?"

Fuck Liam and his excellent poker face. His eyes don't so much as twitch as everyone chimes in with new ideas on how to save my girl. I glance down to where I'd doodled a drawing of her mid-battle with her hands outstretched, sunbeams burning in her open palms.

I have to ask. "Do I need to make a new character?"

Liam slides his gaze around the room, meeting all of our eyes in turn. "There may be several paths forward, and we can consider them all." He looks at me last. "But for now, Sadie . . ." He gestures toward the door. "I'm going to have to ask you to leave the table."

Liam's features are unreadable, but his eyes are bright. *This is for dramatics*, I tell myself. It's all part of the theater of the game—right? I know Liam loves a bit of theater. He wouldn't do this, surely. Especially not after the week I've had. Would he?

Stress has me gnawing a hole in the inside of my cheek.

Noah makes a noise of protest. "That's a little harsh, isn't it?"

"It's what I always do in these situations—" Liam starts.

"*These situations?*" Morgan looks stricken. "You've had characters die before in your games?"

For a heartbeat, Liam's face goes dark—and a little smug—as the lives of all the characters he's killed flash before his eyes. Then his expression softens, and his voice is soothingly gentle. "A few times," he says easily, "and every time, I ask the deceased character's player to leave the table. Since Jaylie is not present, Sadie should not be, either. It will give the remaining characters a chance to choose what the next course of action may be. Afterwards, we'll of course invite Sadie back in and continue from there."

No one looks convinced, but I hold out a placating hand. The old folding chair creaks as I stand. "It's okay. That makes sense to me."

Noah catches my fingers as I turn to go. "We'll get her back, Sadie." His blue eyes are so wide and earnest that I let myself believe him.

I give Noah's hand a quick squeeze before letting go and gathering up my things.

"See you all soon," I say. "I hope."

CHAPTER
Eighteen

Loren

Loren watches as she falls apart.

Horrifyingly, her neck is the first thing to break. It snaps off with a clean *click* as the back of her head connects with a green crystal jutting out from the wall behind her. Her head cranes forward, as if bending toward him, before rolling away into the sand. Her arms go next, each one shattering as her stone elbows crack against the wall. He sees one thick fracture run through her torso from her right shoulder to her left foot. It widens suddenly, and that's when what's left of her crumbles.

For the span of three heartbeats, everyone is silent.

Then Loren is kneeling, careful not to further crush any of her broken pieces. *I've done puzzles like this before,* he thinks numbly. *It's like when I was a kid. If I can just figure out what goes where, I can put her back together.* He reaches for her sandaled foot and the biggest piece of her polished marble calf that he can find and places them together. The break is smooth, so the pieces fit seamlessly. *Next, her knee. Where's her other foot? She's missing toes . . .*

"Loren."

He doesn't register the voice. He's too busy crawling toward where Jaylie's head rolled away. At least it hasn't broken entirely. Her features are beautifully intact, her curls captured in masterful little spirals and her lips parted in a small "O" of surprise.

"Loren." The tone is so gentle. It's unexpected, spoken through the fanged mouth of Kain. "She's gone."

"She's right here." *Obviously.* "This would go much quicker if you lot would help me."

Silently Morgana kneels beside him and begins to gather what pieces of the cleric she can recover. Her touch is reverent as she works alongside Loren to fit all the shards of marble back together. In time, they have Jaylie's body laid out, all the shards approximately in the places that they should be. The hands are the hardest part—all that's left of her fingers is dust.

"Loren, this isn't Jaylie anymore," Kain says. Loren shudders to feel the giant tiefling lay his broad palm on his shoulder. It's still slick with the beholder's blood.

"There's nothing we can do?" Morgana's voice is small, but in the silence following Kain's statement, her words seem to echo in the chamber. For a moment, the only sound is the trickle of water where it continues to flow from the ceiling.

"She's just a pile of stones now," Kain says thickly. "I don't know what we *could* do."

Loren gently sets Jaylie's head back in the sand before his hands erupt into flame. He calls the magic to him in a burst of emotion, in a rush of *rage*. He feels the heat of the magic flow through his veins like lava, and his teeth grind near to breaking in the effort to hold back a scream. Instead, he fuels it all into the flames, flames that crawl up his arms and wreathe his shoulders in a mantle of fire.

And it's the flames that give him the idea.

"I want to speak with your father," he demands.

Kain blinks a few times as the words take time to register. The black orbs of his eyes narrow to slits. "Like Hell you do," he snarls.

"Summon him. Let me talk to him."

"You don't know what you're dealing with, bard. You may think you've got a silver tongue, that you can bargain with the likes of him, but you don't know the price. You don't know the *cost*."

"So then *you* ask, *you* make a deal with him." Loren bites off each word. "It would be better than admitting defeat, that this—that this is *it*. When we first met, I didn't think you had a cowardly bone in your body." Loren knows the words will hurt. It's why he says them. "Now I'm not so sure."

The tiefling still isn't moving, and Loren's hands clench into fists at his sides. He points to a cluster of crystals buried in the sand. At his beckoning, flames rush down his arm and follow his extended finger toward the rocks. Surprisingly, the fire catches, burning as hot and bright as if it were kindling. The quartz crackles with tongues of blue and green.

Loren turns back to Kain, who is breathing heavily through flared nostrils. "Well?" the bard asks sharply.

Kain bares his teeth. "I'll do it. But you must know—he takes advantage of people in this state. Your emotions are high. You feel like you have nothing to lose and everything to gain. If you let him, he'll take everything from you."

Loren's lips press into a grim smirk. "You wound me, Kain." He dramatically lays his palm on his vest even as his grin stretches dangerously wide. "I've always had a way with words."

Kain shakes his head, kneels next to the fire, and begins to speak the infernal tongue.

CHAPTER
Nineteen

I'm twenty minutes into my game room exile when I really start to get worried. I told myself that I'd spend the time drawing or brainstorming new character ideas, but within five minutes of pacing circles around the living room I'd already scrolled through several D&D forums and determined that Jaylie is truly in deep shit.

From what I can understand from the discussions I find online, within D&D lore and rules, there are a few different ways a character might be resurrected. High-level clerics and some other spellcasters are capable of the feat, but Jaylie isn't a high enough level to access spells that powerful, never mind that she can't cast them anyway when she's *dead*. In other cases, clerics in cities can be paid to resurrect a character for the price of a hefty donation to their church. But our characters are days away from Belandar, and we don't have enough gold to pay for such a service—not until we get paid for completing Donati's job.

Even if we could manage to find a cleric willing to resurrect Jaylie for a lower fee, there is the issue of her body. If a character spends too much time dead, it becomes more difficult to resurrect them, as theoretically their spirit journeys further and further into the afterlife. Their body becomes less, well, *hospitable* the more it decays. Jaylie doesn't have a body anymore, though . . . she's a pile of rubble. She's been Humpty Dumpty-ed. Even if her spirit wanted to return to the mortal plane, there isn't anywhere for her spirit to *go*.

The most powerful spell in D&D is the Wish spell, which seems to be exactly what it sounds like: one can simply wish for something to be true, and the universe will rework itself and bend the rules in order to make it so. But because it's the most powerful spell in the game, it's also one of the most inaccessible, reserved for only the most accomplished wizards, demigods, or others so deserving and learned. High-level shit.

In other words: impossible for our little band of misfits.

Liam is the type of Dungeon Master who would happily fudge rules in favor of telling a good story—but those are rare exceptions, and he needs to be absolutely convinced that it's necessary. He calls it *the rule of cool*. Liam believes that the most important part of playing D&D is telling a good story and having fun with your friends, and if one silly rule is wasting everyone's time and making it so they aren't having fun, it can be ignored. But Liam also understands that the rules give everyone a level playing field and a sense of challenge. Rules give structure to the stakes. I can see this being a situation where he might stick to his guns. All things considered, we're still a pretty new party—maybe he wants to use a player character's death to emphasize the risks involved in our quest?

But, fuck, why did it have to be *my* character?

I put more of myself into Jaylie than I realized, and the fact that I've lost her hurts more than I expected it to. She's not me, exactly, but she's made up of many qualities that I idolize. Qualities I wish I possessed—or maybe even qualities that I'm building toward. She is confident and sensual, witty and flirty, and entirely uncaring of others' opinions of her. She takes risks, laughs loudly, makes the first move, and indulges in her passions. Her devotion to her goddess isn't a burden; it's a privilege. She embraces the magic of possibility, of opportunity, of *luck*.

She is bold and brave, and she doesn't look back.

As my throat gets unexpectedly tight and my vision blurs, footsteps pad down the hall toward me. They aren't the familiar quick, quiet steps of Liam in his house shoes but the heavy footfalls of boots. Noah appears from around the corner in his Docs.

He gives me a tentative smile. "Liam told me to come get you. To ask you to come back."

"Is Jaylie going to be okay?"

There's a beat of silence. "You'll have to come see."

I inhale shakily. Noah watches me expectantly, and I take a moment to study his features, to capture them in my mind. His stance is tense, almost energetic—just on the edge of something. His blue eyes are crinkled at the corners, and I just barely catch the way his mouth curves up on one side in a small, hopeful smile.

Something in my chest unfurls, like a flower stretching toward the sun.

Whatever time Jaylie has left—whatever time *I* have left with this campaign, this town, these people . . . I want to make the most of it.

"Noah." My voice is soft. "I'm sure."

He blinks a little, and then the furrows bracketing his eyes suddenly deepen as he smiles. He stretches out his hand toward me.

I lace our fingers together and don't let go.

Jaylie stands next to a well. It's familiar, built with gray stones worn smooth by long years of use. Though she cannot remember how she got here, she can't help but smile to see it again.

It's the well where she first made her escape.

A decade ago she stole her handmaid's drab uniform and snuck out of her locked tower room to run for the rolling green hills past her father's estate. She didn't know where she was going or how she would get there—all she knew was that she had no choice but to leave. Better to make a run for it than to marry the old, cruel man her father had promised her to—a union meant to solidify their trade partnership. Jaylie remembers hearing the guards behind her raise the alarm to signal that the heiress was missing, and she collapsed next to the well and threw in a handful of coins.

"Please, get me out of here," she had gasped between sobs. "I'll go anywhere. I'll do anything—I swear it."

Marlana had saved her then. One of the goddess's clerics had given her shelter and then a new name and a new life in the temple of Belandar. Jaylie had never looked back.

Now, ten years later, Jaylie peers into the well again. She must be in a dream, of course. She has not set foot on her father's land since the day she left. All around her, servants and guards busily pace the length of the yard, dressed in the mustard-yellow livery Jaylie always hated. Women chatter with buckets of water in hand while stable boys give the horses their breakfast. No one takes notice of Jaylie. In fact, they don't seem to see her at all. Dressed in her ceremonial garb, with wide pink sleeves that brush the dirt and a deep hood embroidered with dozens of dangling coins, Jaylie should be the glowing center of attention. Instead, she is undisturbed as she watches her reflection ripple in the well's depths.

"You're a lucky girl, my dear. You're getting a second chance."

Jaylie startles. The voice is resonant and rich—and it's coming from the bottom of the well. Jaylie peers suspiciously again into the water, but her reflection is the only thing to look back.

When Jaylie straightens again, she nearly jumps out of her skin. The yard is suddenly empty of all souls save for herself and a stranger standing next to her.

She's beautiful.

It's the first thought in her stunned mind. Standing a good two heads taller than Jaylie, the woman is resplendent in rippling robes of cream, peach, and gold. Dark gold medallions clasp the fabric at each of her shoulders and hang in a shining belt at her waist. Her skin, too, is dark gold, and the blaze of her red hair falls in perfect ringlets past her waist. Jaylie has never seen her before—but she has seen her likeness reproduced in a dozen different ways. Woven into massive tapestries. Painted on tiny keepsake canvases. Patiently pieced together in great windows with stained glass of red and gold. Stamped onto the face of every coin in Jaylie's possession.

The priestess falls to her knees and presses her forehead to the dirt. "My Lady," she gasps.

"My cleric," Marlana says warmly. "Please, stand. We must speak." She gathers Jaylie's hands in her own and helps her to her feet. Marlana's skin is inhumanly warm. Jaylie feels as if she's standing before a hearth in the middle of an inn. It makes her feel safe.

Marlana leads Jaylie to the other side of the well and leans gently against its foundations, facing away from Jaylie's father's squat little castle. The two women peer into the distance to where the setting sun has painted the tree line with rays of orange and pink. Staring out across the fields of wildflowers and into the forest, Jaylie can almost imagine that she's somewhere else entirely.

"What am I doing here?" she asks. "What happened?"

"You died, my love." Marlana's lips move, but Jaylie hears the goddess's voice envelop her from all directions. It's the only sound in the world.

"Oh." She can't think of anything else to say; she can barely remember how it occurred. She recalls magic coursing through her veins, freezing her solid, and then nothing at all. She tries to look directly into the sun. So close to the horizon, she can almost stare at it without squinting. "What happens next?"

"You have a decision to make." Marlana reaches for Jaylie's fingers and holds them between her palms. Jaylie's hand is dwarfed in Marlana's, but it's a soothing gesture. "You can choose to leave this realm, and I will guide your spirit on to the next. Your soul would rest for a time. Then one day, if you are lucky, it could be reborn." Marlana gestures toward the forest at the edges of Jaylie's father's land. A narrow dirt path that Jaylie does not remember from her childhood leads directly into the sunset. She imagines she can see a ripple of water in the distance, beckoning her. Tempting her.

"Or you can go back," Marlana says. The water is suddenly hidden, obscured behind the sway of the trees as the wind stirs the leaves. "Your friends have opened a doorway for you. Should you wish it, you can go back. You can continue living."

"How did they do that?"

"It is not my place to say."

That puzzles Jaylie, but she does not question it. As comforting as it is to be in the presence of her goddess, there is something about this place that Jaylie does not like. It's *too* comfortable. The softness of the grass under her feet invites her to lie down and rest. The gentle breeze threading through her hair is the perfect temperature, cooling sweat before it even has the chance to bead on her brow. The longer she remains here, the easier it would be to allow her eyelids to droop, her body to relax, her bones to sleep forever.

Jaylie violently shakes the fog from her head. "I want to go back. I want to *live*. I'm not ready to go." Despite her vehemence, her eyes flood with tears. "But I don't want to leave you, my Lady. There are so many things I want to ask, so much I want to learn. Will I see you again?"

Marlana takes Jaylie's face between her hands and presses a kiss to the crown of her head. "You see me every day, child. You see me in the sun that chases away the storm clouds, and in the smiles of young lovers who have found each other at last. You see me when you find the shortest path through the darkest forest, and in a babe's first cry when it is welcomed to life." Teasingly, the goddess taps the tip of Jaylie's nose. "I am always with you."

Marlana guides Jaylie to step carefully onto the edge of the well. Before she can stop herself, Jaylie wraps her goddess in a fierce hug. "Thank you," she whispers into the fall of her hair. "Thank you, my Lady, for everything."

Marlana holds Jaylie gently, full of warmth and light and love. "Good luck, my darling."

Jaylie turns, takes a deep breath in, and jumps.

She's so cold, and it's so dark.

The pressure *hurts*. Every part of her body aches to move, but every muscle under her skin is tight and cramping, frozen just on the edge of breaking. Pain sears along each of her bones, swelling in her ears and between her temples, and just when she thinks that every joint is about to *pop*—

Warmth blooms on her lips.

It's like the first breath of sunshine in spring, come to thaw the winter. It's the first taste of soup after a long, grueling day. Better—it's the taste of hot spiced cider at her favorite tavern, surrounded by friends, raucous laughter, and the promise of a lantern-lit night full of dancing. The warmth seeps into her limbs with the enveloping embrace of easing into a steaming bath. It chases the ice from her veins and urges life back into her skin.

As the sensation fades, she begins to feel where chunks of raw crystal and stone press uncomfortably into her spine, where her arms and legs sting from the memory of recent wounds. There's a specific pain in the back of her neck that feels particularly out of place, throbbing horribly. The warmth recedes as she settles back into reality.

But the heat is still on her lips, tasting of fire.

Jaylie's eyelids flutter open to find Loren close to her face—*touching* her face. Touching her lips. This close, she can see where his brow is creased in concentration, his eyes screwed shut. The air around him hums with powerful magic—and where his skin touches hers, he burns like the sun.

It takes her three thudding, glorious heartbeats to realize that he's kissing her.

It takes him three thudding, glorious heartbeats to realize that she's alive.

He draws back from her in a rush, and his green eyes flash open in surprise. Tentatively he reaches forward, tracing a line from her temple to her jaw with his calloused musician's fingers.

"Jay." He says her name so tenderly, and she's shocked to feel tears gather in the corners of her eyes.

For a moment, it's the only sound she hears. Then all at once, as if time catches up to her, noise fills the small cavern. The rush of the waterfall into the pool, the crunch of gravel underneath boots as her party rushes forward, Kain's shout—or maybe Morgana's—as they realize that she's okay.

Loren's sweet, unguarded smile is soon replaced with an uncharacteristically sober expression as he holds his palms up defensively. "I know what you're going to say, but listen, I swear that was part of the spell. The exchange of breath is a crucial element in the process of resurrection, and—"

She silences him. Reaching upward, she curls a fist in his waves of red hair and pulls him down until his lips meet hers again. There's a surprised noise in the back of his throat that swiftly dissolves into a deeply satisfied chuckle. Jaylie kisses him hungrily, chasing the rush of every sensation that floods her body—every reminder there is blood racing through her veins, breath caught in her mouth, a heart fluttering against her ribs. It's a kiss to remind her that she's alive. *I'm here,* she gasps to herself. *I'm here!*

It's the laughter that finally makes her pull away. She can't contain the way it bubbles up out of her in a stunned, wondrous cloud. "Goddess," she exclaims, unable to tear her eyes away from Loren. "Thank you. Thank you, thank you, *thank you.*" She punctuates each statement with a kiss.

Then, "What the fuck happened?"

"You died," Morgana chirps helpfully as she pretends to wipe dust out of her watering eyes. "Spectacularly. The beholder turned you to stone, rammed forward in one big rush, and—" She splays her fingers wide and throws her hands above her head in a bursting motion.

"But you brought me back." Jaylie's gaze searches the face of each party member, landing last on Loren. His expression softens at the same moment that hers hardens quizzically, and she tilts her head. "You don't have access to that kind of magic," she says slowly. And then, uncertainly: "Do you?"

"What can I say? Sometimes the music just . . . comes to me." He smiles winningly. "What, do you wish I hadn't brought you back?" His words are teasing, but Jaylie notices a twinge of tension in his tone, like a lute string tuned too sharp.

"Of course not." She lets out another laugh, marveling at how it feels to have the air move through her lungs. She will never take the sensation for granted again. "I just don't know why you lot bother to have me around if you've got that kind of magic in your repertoire. You'll have me replaced in no time."

Kain, who up until this point had been sitting in the shadows, leans forward from his perch on a boulder. A muscle feathers down the length of his jaw. "You heal with much more reliability than the bard does." His tone is flat. Factual. His gaze cuts toward Loren, made all the more unnerving by his pupilless black eyes.

Loren rolls one shoulder in a shrug with forced nonchalance. "I always keep a few tricks up my sleeve. For emergencies."

Kain nods his head heavily, seemingly weighed down by his great horns.

Morgana crouches near the embers of a dying fire, covering it with sand. Jaylie's gaze swings toward them, bewildered. "Were you thinking of making camp? *Here?*"

"We considered it," Loren answers quickly as he stands, bracing his hands on his knees before straightening. He offers Jaylie a hand up. "But on second thought, I think we would like nothing better than to get out of this place."

Jaylie takes his hand and rises. Though she wants nothing more than to sprint headlong out of the cave and back into the sunlight, she pauses and looks around. "The orb," she says. "Did we get it?"

"You bet we did." Morgana hefts up the beholder's eye. Her arms barely reach around its total circumference. Strangely enough, it's hardened and crystallized, reminiscent of the chunks of quartz in the cavern's walls. Somehow they're dimmer now, but the orb glows with the same sickly green light.

Jaylie nods. "Good. Let's get the fuck out of here."

CHAPTER
Twenty

"Hey, you."

The words are a low rumble in Noah's broad chest, a playful greeting as he eases the glass door open with his shoulder and welcomes me back into Alchemist on Monday morning.

Even as a part of me melts to see his crooked smile, I'm careful not to let our fingertips brush as I hand over his latte. "Morning, Noah." I'm worried the contact would ignite the sparks of anxiety crawling under my skin.

It's the first time we've spoken since yesterday's game.

There's a sense of expectation that buzzes inside my skull, a tension that has my head spinning and my heart punching inside my chest. Truthfully, I'd wanted to see Noah—alone—immediately after our game, but the girls had stuck around to gush about the session's events, and Noah ran off to work after an unnervingly quick goodbye. He'd stressed to us that Dan was keeping him busy with all sorts of ideas for events to host at Alchemist, hoping to entice new customers, and his eyes had grown big and apologetic when he'd caught my gaze on the way out the door.

It had almost been enough to convince me that my semi-confession hadn't scared him away.

Almost.

But now he comes to stand at my side, hands on his hips and face tilted up toward the wall. "Today's the day, isn't it?"

"Today's the day."

As I stare up at the looming expanse of brick, dusty with lines of chalk, a sense of calm focus soothes some of my nerves. It's just me and a blank canvas.

Today, I start painting.

I already know exactly where I'll begin, which layers I need to map out first, which can of paint to crack open—but before I get lost in the exercise, Noah draws my attention back to him, brushing his knuckles against the skin between my shoulder blades.

"I need to run a few errands for Dan," he says. "Anything I can get you before you start? More containers? Some music to work to? The ladder?" He pauses, and his jaw flexes briefly. "Actually, please don't use the ladder until I get back."

His concern almost distracts me from the dim disappointment of him leaving again.

"No, I'm good," I say, my eyes still on the wall. But then the corner of my mouth ticks upward. "Actually, can you play some fantasy shit before you go?"

Noah barks out a laugh. "Can you define 'some fantasy shit' for me?"

"Yeah, you know, like—the stuff Liam plays during games."

"You've given me too much to work with, Sadie. There are so many subgenres to 'fantasy shit.' Do you want to feel like you're riding into battle, or like you've been invited to Her Majesty's midwinter masquerade ball? Or maybe you're in a tavern, being serenaded by a handsome elf bard?" He sips at his coffee, and his sky-blue eyes do that blissful squint again. Overcast. "Mm. Or maybe something to make you feel like you're wandering through the forest, exploring. On an adventure." It isn't a question. He knows.

"Yeah. *That* exact brand of fantasy shit."

Before ducking out the back door, he turns on a video game soundtrack I don't recognize. For now it's enough to distract me. I let the ethereal chords from a harp lull me into a dreamy daze, setting the perfect tone for the scene I'm about to bring to life.

At the end of the day, this is what I'm really here for.

I turn and set my brush, dripping with inky indigo paint, to the wall for the first time.

"But how scared were you?"

"I spent that half hour of exile pacing around Liam's coffee table and trying not to shit myself," I admit.

I'm surprised Noah had actually been able to hold back from talking about it for the past few hours of work. He'd returned around lunchtime with sandwiches for us, but with one look at my focused, determined brushstrokes, he'd left me to my task and gone back to work in the office, an amused smile curling at his lips.

I'd been so engrossed in painting the base layers of the mural that I hadn't made space for any other thoughts. I was shocked that I'd managed to curb my own lingering questions and nerves, but everything went blessedly quiet while I painted. The curiosity behind Jaylie's resurrection, the need to check my email for news about my next Paragon interview, the pull of Noah's orbit and my fears about why he was keeping me outside of it . . . Gone. *Quiet.* All I'd been able to focus on was the whisper of the brush against the wall. It had always been that way.

Now I sit atop one of the kegs with my half-eaten sub, admiring my progress. I'd managed to lay out the entire mural in thick blocks of free-form color. The trees that border the scene are a pale olive green cut down the middle with broad strokes of violet-black trunks. The campfire circles the unlit fireplace in approximate tongues of pale yellow flame, which I'll darken and give depth. The subjects of the mural—the lone wanderer, his horse, and the stag in the background—have only been outlined in a soft gray. I could have taken them further, but I want them to be the last things to come to life. I glance down at the tablet in my lap, referencing the mural's original design in my files.

"Did you think there was a chance she wouldn't come back?" Noah presses, his voice drawing my attention back to him. He stands in front of me, his gaze intent on my face.

"Sure did. I tried to plan for it, too—tried to brainstorm ideas for a new character. But it started making me too sad, so I stopped."

"So you're glad we brought her back?" I love how earnest his voice sounds.

From my vantage point atop the keg, I have a good couple of inches on him for once. I narrow my eyes, skeptical. "I've been meaning to ask how you did it."

Noah's face freezes. His lips are still parted from when he'd initially asked the question, and he closes his mouth with a snap of his jaw and lets out an amused exhale through his nose. He still has that open, honest look in his blue eyes.

"Did what?"

Coy.

"How did you bring Jaylie back from the dead?"

"I told you, Loren's got tricks."

"Unless you've paid off Liam for some secret magic that we don't know about, then there's no way any of his *tricks* would have worked. Jaylie was too far gone."

"Clearly she wasn't."

Though the words themselves are irritating, his tone is gentle and goading. He's poking fun at me—and avoiding the question.

"Uh-huh." I lean forward, bracing my elbows on my knees. I press at his shirt with one stiff, accusing finger. "I'll make it worth your while if you tell me." My hand relaxes, palm unfurling until it lies flat against his chest.

Noah's eyebrows shoot up as whatever implication he's imagining plays out in his mind. "And how might you do that?"

I ball my fist in his shirt and tug him toward me. "If you tell me," I promise, "I'll use the secret to make sure that when *Loren* dies, he's not left in the dirt." I push forward suddenly, and Noah stumbles back with a laugh.

"Blackmail, Sadie? I thought you were above that."

"The curiosity is killing me."

"Can't you just be grateful that she's not dead?"

"No, I need details."

He paces forward, arms crossed over his chest. As much as I like all his flannels, I like it more when he doesn't wear them. I like to see how his biceps stretch the seams of his shirts.

Forget it, Sadie.

I'm reluctantly tearing my gaze back up toward his face when he releases a whistling sigh and says, "I suppose I could show you how Loren did it."

"Really?" I frown, suspicious.

He tilts his chin up, playfulness etched in every line of his face. "Sure, if you really want to know."

He's up to something, but I'll play along. "Show me," I urge. I hold my tablet out toward him. I've already queued up the D&D reference guide, full of spells, magic items, and other secrets, ready for him to unlock the mystery.

But he sidesteps the tablet and gently nudges my arm out of the way. He moves forward until his boots knock against the wood of the keg I sit on, until his eyes are a few inches from mine. With his free hand he curves his fingers behind the nape of my neck, tilting my head gently to the side. "It went something like this." As his breath curls against my cheek, I catch the musky scent of some sort of dark caramel beer before his lips press—just *barely*—to mine.

There's a moment where I think he might have reversed the spell as the shock of the gesture freezes me to a stonelike stillness. And just as the urge blooms in my chest to reach for him, just as my lips part to deepen the kiss—he pulls away.

A beat of silence hangs between us. His fingers toy with the small hairs at the base of my head while my hands flex rapidly where they sit in my lap. He wears a small smile nearly hidden by his beard, while his eyes are bright with a curious, nervous sort of energy. I realize after a moment that he's gauging my reaction.

I swallow. My voice comes out just above a whisper. "Now show me how Noah would kiss me."

It's a challenge—and a question. I have to know.

He doesn't hesitate.

The first difference I notice is the pressure. Where his imitation of Loren's kiss had been gentle and light, full of reverence and respect, Noah's touch is hungry. Confident. His palm skims along the side of my jaw, calloused fingers gripping my chin to pull my face down toward his. This time when he kisses me, I can feel the tickle of his beard against my cheek as his mouth moves against mine, and I can't help the hum that escapes the back of my throat as his tongue traces a line of heat over my lower lip. I deepen the kiss immediately, suddenly desperate to taste the caramel I'd gotten a hint of before.

His free hand runs down my spine, curls around the curve of my waist, and *tugs*. I gasp in surprise as he pulls my body forward on the keg, my legs parting to either side of his torso as he presses his chest to mine. I can feel Noah smile against my lips before he draws back enough to meet my eyes.

A surge of amused frustration courses through me. Fucking *tease*—always pulling away just when I'm getting started.

But I won't let him get away with it.

"You did that on purpose," I accuse. I try to sound harsh, but my breathlessness makes it difficult.

"Yeah, I've been wanting to do that on purpose for a while now."

"No, I mean—" My cheeks heat, and I fix him with a wry smile. "You did it to distract me. You're avoiding telling me how you brought Jay back."

"Is it working?"

Damn him.

I don't bother to respond with words—it's enough of an answer to lean forward and press my lips to his again. I can feel more than hear his laugh in the vibrations of his broad chest, and I twine my arms around his neck as I wrap my legs around his middle, hooking my ankles together behind his back. Taking my hint, Noah brings his hands from my waist to curve under my thighs. Without even a grunt of effort he lifts me from the keg, and before I know any better, I breathe a moan of delight into his mouth. I tighten my arms around him, but he holds me as if I weigh nothing at all, his fingers digging into my paint-stained jeans and sliding down to cup my ass.

My eyes had fluttered closed ages ago, so when my back meets the cold brick of the wall—*the wall I've been hired to paint,* I think distantly—I inhale sharply in surprise. "You're okay," Noah murmurs into the shell of my ear. "I've got you." He draws a line of kisses down the side of my neck to my shoulder and then hums against my skin on the way back up. I bite back a whimper as he exhales against my throat, goosebumps rising on every spot of bare skin that his beard brushes.

An eternity later—or perhaps just a few heartbeats, I can't tell— Noah slowly eases me back to the floor. My knees are weak, and it takes a moment for me to feel grounded. Even as Noah takes a small step back, the air between us feels charged, like one more stray spark will send us colliding again.

I draw in a shaky breath and glance sidelong at the part of the mural I've completed. "So," I say, a note of laughter threading through my words, "same time, same place tomorrow morning?" It's a joke, in part—and a gentle test of the waters. How much does he want from . . . this? From me?

And how much am I willing to give?

Noah huffs out a quick laugh then shakes his head. "Let me take you out, Sadie." He reaches forward and gathers my hands in his. "This weekend."

"Oh." My chest is so full of heat and warmth and *light,* it feels like I've swallowed the sun. "Okay."

He bends his head so that his gaze meets mine evenly. I worry the heat from my cheeks might fog my glasses, as much of an impossibility as that is. "Like a *date,*" he says meaningfully. He squeezes my hands on the last word for emphasis.

"Like a date," I echo. I let the words hover in the air between us before I nod my head. "So you're sure."

He laughs. "I'm sure."

"Then—I'd like that."

"Good." He uses his hold on my hands to tug me forward a little until he can press another kiss into my cheek. I love the way his beard feels against my skin. "Me, too."

CHAPTER
Twenty-One

"Well, it's about goddamn time."

I groan at Liam's comment. He snickers from where he stands at the kitchen counter, struggling to uncork our second bottle of Trader Joe's discount wine. Neither of us really knows shit about wine, but we generally agree that anything that's either white or rosé with a pretty label is good enough.

"You're not upset? You don't think that my seeing him will, y'know—mess up the party vibes, or make anyone feel uncomfortable?" I ask. I'm sprawled against the arm of the couch, swirling the remnants of my wine.

Liam's stare is so aggressively deadpan that I can't help but hunch over in a fit of giggles. "Sadie," he says flatly, barely managing to contain a smile. It's the same tone he uses to chastise Howard when he's being a little shit. "You two have been flirting for the whole campaign—in character *and* out of character. I think we've all been waiting for this from the start, and it hasn't disrupted our dynamic yet. If anything, you two have made it all that much more enjoyable to witness. For all of us."

"Uh-huh," I scoff, smiling despite myself. I finish the rest of my glass, savoring the overly sweet prosecco as it bubbles its way down.

My head is swimming pleasantly, and everything seems a little bit brighter.

"But what if things go badly?" I continue. "What if it's a disaster and he reveals that he's secretly been a terror this whole time?"

"Then I kick him out of the game, and we're down a bard. Mechanically, it wouldn't be a huge loss," Liam says. His tone is carefully indifferent, and I smile. D&D would be much less fun without Loren's witty quips and hilarious whining, and we both know it. But Liam's always on my side, and if things go poorly with Noah, Liam will be the first to jump to my defense.

He finally comes to sit on the couch cushion next to me, uncorked bottle tucked carefully under his arm while he balances two bowls brimming with warm ramen in his hands.

"But he's not a terror, Sadie," Liam continues, placing each bowl on the coffee table. His cooking skills have come a long way since our microwave ramen days in college: the bowls are brimming with pork belly, chili oil, carrots, mushrooms, and—my personal favorite—soft-boiled eggs. "I think you'll have a good time. He's good people."

I think again of Noah—hell, I'd spent all fucking *week* thinking about Noah, stealing kisses in the back room of Alchemist after every morning painting session—and a familiar warmth blooms in my chest. I push off from my lounging spot on the couch.

"It complicates things, though," I say as I lift noodles from the broth, letting them cool before slurping them down.

Liam pauses with his noodles halfway to his mouth. "How so?"

"Summer's halfway over. I don't know how much longer I'll be around."

The bubbles in my stomach churn uncomfortably at the thought.

"You know you can stay as long as you like, Sadie." Before I can protest, Liam holds a hand up to stop me. "But I know that's not your plan, especially with how well the Paragon stuff is going. As long as Noah knows where you stand, too, then there's no harm done."

I refill our glasses with rosé and sip mine for a good twenty seconds before speaking again. "Why did you stay, Liam? In Heller. What changed your mind?"

I still remember the day he told me that he wasn't coming back to Connecticut—that he wasn't coming back to the East Coast at all. It was the summer after we'd graduated college, and he'd gone down to Texas to be with his grandpa before he died, and to settle all of his affairs after he passed, too. After the tears, he'd joked with me over video call that he was going to sell the giant house he'd inherited for a buttload of money—the house where he'd spent so many summers and Christmases—and get us a swanky apartment in the middle of Manhattan. Then one week away from home turned into three, and then two months, and then the whole summer.

Liam kept claiming that there was more to his grandpa's affairs than he'd realized, and that he needed more time to organize them and decide what to do. And then he'd called, his wavering voice lacking the confidence and absolute assurance it always had, and admitted to me that he wanted to stay. I could tell he felt awful. We'd made so many plans: to find the perfect apartment, to finally go to the Mermaid Parade at Coney Island, to visit every wine bar in every borough until we found the best one. But of course I'd been supportive. I was disappointed, but I understood. Or I could at least try to understand.

He snorts, and the sound surprises me out of my memories. "I stayed in Heller because I knew there wasn't any other way I'd get a house within the next ten years on a teacher's salary," he says dryly.

"Sincerely, though."

He sits quietly for a moment, rolling his newly refilled wineglass between his palms. "I liked it here," he says eventually, and he makes it sound so simple. Maybe it *is* that simple. "When I was a kid and my dad moved back to Texas after the divorce—honestly, I thought he was literally moving to the Wild West. I believed all the stereotypes." Not the funny ones, I knew, about cowboys and boots and riding horses to school—the ones about intolerance and prejudice. Shit that made Liam's dad keep his distance, while Liam's grandpa welcomed him in. "And while some of them are true, I fell in love with Heller. It has a small-town charm that reminds me of home, and all of Grandpa's friends were so kind, inviting me to barbecues and block parties and offering to send my résumé to their kids' schools. They were asking me to stay."

He pauses to take another drink.

"And New York scared the shit out of me," he says finally. "When we made all those plans, Sadie, I just—I relied so much on you. I knew it wouldn't be all bad, not if you were there. I knew I'd find my place eventually if we could just get through those first couple of years. But I don't think I even had that much in me. I couldn't get used to the idea of being surrounded by so many people and having to pinch every penny, or having to fight for space on the sidewalk and in the subway. I felt like the city would swallow me whole. I felt like I would disappear."

I used to love how crowded the city was. It reminded me that I was surrounded by people who were also striving to carve out a place for themselves in a city of dreams. There was community in that beautiful, passionate struggle. And though his words twist my heart, I know there were times when I'd felt the same—like if I wasn't careful, I'd be swept away.

"But why not just stay in Connecticut, then?" I ask. "If you wanted something small-town, you could have found it there, too."

Liam shrugs, picking up a chunk of the soft-boiled egg from his bowl. "I don't know." His mouth twists into a wry half smile. "I got sick of New England winters. I like the parks here. I like the calm energy of the town." He pauses. "And I suppose I wanted to stick around awhile to see if I could understand my dad more, and his dad—to figure out why he might have chosen this place." I don't point out what Liam doesn't say: *to figure out why he might have wanted to live so far away from me.*

"It's warm here," I agree after a moment of quiet. "And not just in terms of the weather—though it is hot as balls—but the people are warm. You've really built a good community for yourself, Liam."

He sips at his broth happily. "I'm glad you think so, Sade. I'm glad you're a part of it." I open my mouth again, but he beats me to the punch, smiling mildly as he corrects, "For now, at least."

He juts his chin in my direction. "But what about you? Do you miss it?"

"Miss what?"

"The city."

I take two thoughtful sips before I speak.

"I do," I admit. "Parts of it."

"Like what?"

I circle my finger around the rim of my wineglass. "Is it really crazy to say that I miss riding the subway?"

"Honestly? Yes."

I grin. "There were plenty of times when it was gross, sure, but— I liked to just sit there and imagine where everyone was heading, y'know? What was their story? And in the summers, I would always get off a stop or two early, just to enjoy the walk. It felt like everyone in the world was outside, sitting at coffee shops or running across the street or reading on the grass in Bryant Park. There's no better place on earth to people-watch than New York."

I set my glass on the coffee table and hold my hands in front of my face, fingers curled as if I'm cradling a ball. "Really, Liam, I just felt like I had the world at my fingertips. Growing up, I always thought that New York was where things *happened.* That it was where people went to *make* things happen, right? I believed you could find whatever you were looking for in the city."

It would have helped, perhaps, if I had known what I'd been looking for in New York. Even now I still don't know what exactly I want—from the city or otherwise—and it leaves me feeling directionless. Unmoored.

"There was something so energizing about living moment to moment. For so long, I loved the rush of it, until . . ." My lips twist sourly. "Until I couldn't keep up."

Liam lets the words hang between us for a moment. I'd surprised myself with the admiration in my voice, the way I'd gushed about a city that had left me feeling so bone-tired.

He smiles gently. "Texas is good for that," he says. "Slowing down."

I let my head fall back against the couch's cushions, let my eyes shutter closed. "It's been so nice," I admit. "You've been so nice. Everyone's been so *nice*."

"I get it, Noah's very nice."

I swat at his hand. "I adore Morgan and Jules, too, and we text all the time. We keep meaning to hang again soon, but I've been . . . distracted."

"Uh-huh."

I press my lips together to try to hide a smile before consuming my next mouthful of ramen. With so few noodles left in the bowl and my fine motor skills deteriorating with each glass of wine, my chopsticks are becoming unwieldy. Disadvantage on dexterity.

"I think you've needed this break for a long time, Sadie—and I'm glad you're spending it with us. I couldn't have asked for a better group of newbie players. I've never had a group take to the game as easily as you all have." He exhales a whooshing sigh. "I'll miss you guys, once it's over."

"Are we that near to the end?"

Liam lifts his shoulders in a sloppy shrug. "Depends. I suppose you're not too far off from confronting Shira . . ." His mouth twists in a lopsided grin. "We'll just have to see."

"No hints? Not even for another hefty pour?"

He reaches for his glass and drains it completely. "I'll never break."

I know it to be true, so I don't press.

CHAPTER
Twenty-Two

> can you at least tell me what I should wear?

Noah:

> watch out, you're giving me too much power

> wear whatever you want, but definitely comfortable shoes

> like strolling-through-downtown comfortable shoes or two-mile-hike comfortable shoes?

> shoes you'd wear in the dirt

> we're going to get dirty?

> I hope so 😉

For half an hour I debate whether to wear my expensive running shoes or a pair of old athletic sandals, and eventually the sandals win out. I tug the last strap over the back of my heel and take a good look at myself in the mirror. Teal-green Spandex running shorts, tight black sports bra, and an unbuttoned sunflower-patterned shirt. Finally, I pull a black baseball cap over the loose curls of my bob. It really completes the hot-vacation-mom look.

I've just pulled my phone out to ask Noah where we're meeting—he *still* hasn't told me—when the doorbell rings downstairs.

And god damn him, Liam beats me to it.

I'm halfway down the stairs when I see him silhouetted in the doorway, wearing his house robe. He and Noah are already shooting the shit when I sidle up next to them. Liam's got his glasses pushed down his nose, and he's peering at Noah from over the rims. "And you'll have her back before curfew, yes?"

"Yes, sir. Wouldn't dream of missing it." Noah's hands are clasped seriously in front of him. From the line of tension in the side of his jaw, I can tell he's trying hard not to laugh.

"All right, then," Liam huffs dramatically. "You kids have fun." He pats me on the back, pushes me into Noah's chest, and closes the door behind us.

"Hey, you." Noah skims his palms over my shoulders and down the sides of my arms. Despite the immediate shock of the Texas heat, goosebumps follow the path of his hands.

"Hey." I curl my fingers over the fabric of his shirt. He's wearing a sleeveless green tank top, gray shorts, and a stuffed backpack. His hair's tied up into a knot, shining copper in the sunlight. I like how short his shorts are. They show off his thighs. "Is this the part where you finally tell me where we're going?"

"Nope. Where's your sense of adventure?"

I stretch up on my toes to peer over his shoulder. His bike's propped up in the middle of the driveway. Noah reads my mind before I have a chance to ask. "Saddle up, Sadie. I'll be driving again today." Leading me out into the sun, he swings one leg over the bike and holds it steady as I step up onto the pegs. I wrap my hands around the straps of his backpack and shake them once.

"All right, then. Giddy up, cowboy."

Noah sets off. It's late morning, so the heat's not so bad yet, but

I can feel it emanating in waves off of the dark pavement. Noah tries to keep us under the shaded parts of the road, and as he picks up speed, the wind rushing past almost feels cool. We wind through one of Heller's oldest neighborhoods, and as we pass by the well-loved houses, I imagine who lives in each. The sage-green house with the wraparound deck belongs to a retired elementary school teacher with dozens of grandkids. The brooding maroon house with the awkward spire jutting from the second floor is the home of an introverted professor who surrounds himself with books; he's secretly a vampire who checks his mailbox only at night. The purple-painted house covered in vines with an overgrown lawn full of flowers obviously belongs to a witch. As I yell my theories into Noah's ear, I wave at kids with dripping popsicles gripped in their fists and at old folks watering their carefully cultivated flower patches. Noah's right; biking really is the best way to get to know a place.

Eventually the houses become more spaced out and then disappear entirely, and we're left under the glare of the open sun. I look up. The sky is so *blue;* it's never this blue in New York, where you can barely see the sky for how the buildings crowd around you. Noah takes a sharp turn at what I thought was a dead end and swerves onto a dirt path, and I have to clamp my mouth shut to keep my teeth from chattering against one another. Soon we arrive at a small unpaved parking lot under a canopy of trees, empty save for two cars and a bike rack. There's a board with a yellowing map of the surrounding trails posted behind scratched plastic.

"We *are* going on a hike," I realize, delighted.

"A short one, but yes. I want to show you my favorite spot."

After Noah locks his bike into the rack, we set off onto one of the trails—though, truth be told, it barely deserves the name. The worn dirt path is narrow and overgrown in spots, and the red trail markers painted onto the tree bark every twenty feet or so are faded and difficult to spot. Vegetation presses in so tightly around us that it's like I'm crawling through a tunnel. But Noah doesn't even look for the markers; he already knows the way.

I try not to jump too much at the sound of rustling in the overgrown grass and focus my attention on Noah's topknot bouncing ahead of me.

"You know, the first time I offered you a ride," I muse, "I considered whether you were an axe murderer. This is the perfect opportunity."

He turns just enough for me to see the flash of his teeth as he smiles. "Damn. I was hoping you wouldn't catch on this quickly."

"You've been playing the long game, haven't you?"

"You got me."

He chooses this moment to veer off of the trail. The trees are farther apart here, so theoretically there's more room to step in between them, but still I blanch. Noah's five steps ahead of me when he realizes I haven't moved. He turns and reaches toward me. "It's okay, Sadie. I know where I'm going."

I take his hand. He squeezes once and then holds on, drawing me deeper into the leaves and shadows. I focus on the warmth of his palm instead of the childhood memories of Animal Planet that flash unwanted in my mind. Don't rattlesnakes live in Texas? Spiders do—I'm sure of that. Is it true that everything's bigger in Texas? Does that apply to venomous bloodsucking insects, too? I gasp at a sliding, rustling sound in the bush to my left.

See, I've always been an admirer of nature—from a distance. I regularly run on carefully paved trails in perfectly groomed parks, and I enjoy vacationing in a cabin in the woods from time to time. But I'm usually the one sitting on the deck sipping a glass of spiked cocoa instead of bushwhacking my way through uncharted wilderness.

So maybe a small park a few miles from Liam's house isn't *uncharted wilderness,* but close enough.

"I'm not making a very good first-date impression, am I?" Noah's tone is amused. He takes each step with slow assurance, as if to prove to me the safety of our exploration. I'm careful to step only in places where I can see the imprints left behind by his sandals.

"I just think you might be confusing me with Jaylie." She might prefer the comforts of the city as I do, but she's braver than I am. I try to tap into that, picturing our trek as the start of a quest.

Surely Marlana would smile down on my adventurousness.

"We're almost there."

At the sound of flowing water, I start to relax, and curiosity wins out over fear. The trees part to reveal what can only be described as a hidden gem. Gently the earth slopes downward, growing rockier until it dissolves into sand leading into a clear stream. The water trickles by unhurriedly, and though it's deep in spots, I can almost see to the bottom. It's the perfect swimming hole. I look around, expecting a family to come bursting out of the bushes to picnic, or high schoolers to swing wildly from the branches and jump in, but it's quiet. Empty. As far as I look, I can't see anything but trees and water and glimpses of blue sky through the leaves.

As Noah watches my eyes go soft, his face breaks into a smile. "You like it." It's not a question.

"It's lovely."

"One more thing." He tugs at my hand again—*he hasn't let go,* I think distantly—and leads me away from the stream. We're climbing again, and he's pulling me up steep rocks along a winding path until we're on a ledge overlooking the water. One tree leans dangerously over the ridge, as if peeking into the stream below. I can see half of its root system, old and gnarled, shooting out from the earth to either curl back into the rocky foundation or dangle like wind chimes in the air above the water.

We stop at the base of the tree, and Noah gives it a friendly, welcoming pat. Briefly I worry that it's just enough of a push to send the old thing tumbling into the water, but it stays strong. Noah shrugs off his backpack and begins pulling all sorts of shit out of it—a blanket, one water jug, a glass bottle full of a mystery amber-colored liquid, containers of fruit, a towel (suspicious), pencils, a sketchbook—as if it's a goddamn Bag of Holding. He must be a packing pro.

I shrug out of my sunflower shirt and toe off my sandals, moving to sit in the center of the newly spread-out blanket. "You're good at this, aren't you?"

"Good at what? First dates?"

I grin. "Hiking, backpacking. You look like you know what you're doing."

"Oh, this isn't anything like backpacking," he says with a laugh, "but yes. This . . ." He spreads his arms wide, encompassing every tree and leaf and rock that surrounds us. "This is my favorite thing in the world. I'm always outside."

"Really?" I say, surprised. With sweat already running down my back and pooling under my boobs, I can't help but ask why. "You're so outgoing. So *social*. Doesn't it get lonely out here, with just the birds and the bugs?" I imagine him alone in his camper van, driving off into the horizon.

But his smile is sweet, and he looks all too eager to let me in on his secret. "I think I'd go crazy without a hobby like this to help me recharge. Every day, I wake up full of all this pent-up energy." He clenches his fists as if wrestling an invisible pickle jar. "But when I'm on my bike, or on a walk, it's just . . ." His fingers release the jar and flutter off into the air. For the first time since I've known him, he's at a loss for words—opening and closing his mouth, tilting his head to the side thoughtfully . . . and then shaking his head. "I don't know how to describe how it feels to me. Here. It would be easier to show you. Stand up. Close your eyes, Sadie."

I let Noah pull me to my feet, and my eyelids flutter closed. Standing behind me with his palms on my shoulders, he guides me forward until the soft blanket under my bare feet gives way to warm dirt and hard roots. With a squeeze of my shoulders, Noah holds me back before I can walk off the ledge.

"Listen." His voice is warm against my neck. His beard tickles my skin.

It takes a while for my thoughts to fade into the background, for my breathing to even out. The first sound I hear is of course the water, tinkling its way around rocks as it winds its way out to Lake Travis. The birds are next. Every few heartbeats one will call out a few ringing, harmonic notes—and just when it's quiet again, another will answer. But it's the wind that really grounds me. It's like the air is breathing. On an inhale, the breeze cools the sweat on my forehead and threads its way through my hair. On an exhale, every leaf stirs, whispering against one another in one great *shhh*.

Noah begins to run his palms down my arms with an aching, gentle slowness. I keep my eyes closed, which sets my other senses on high alert. Grounded by his touch, the music through the trees, and the clear smell of everything green, I feel as if we are the only two people who exist.

Noah steps away to stand by my side. His big hand circles my wrist easily. I exhale one more time then open my eyes to look at him.

He's discarded his shirt next to his backpack, but before I can fully process this wonderful new development, his gaze captures mine forcefully. There's a wildness in his eyes, and they spark like wildfire. "Can you swim?"

My usual internal alarms feel numbed. In this space, I'm untouchable. Bold. I can do anything I want to.

"Yes."

"Do you trust me?"

". . . Yes."

Noah jumps from the ledge. I hurtle after him.

It's *cold.*

As I submerge, I nearly inhale a lungful of water in shock. In this heat, I'd expected the water to feel like jumping into a cup of tea left out too long. I can't feel my hands or my feet, but I kick up to where I can see the sun's warped shimmer on the surface. As soon as hot air touches my cheeks, I suck in a breath. As I begin to sink back under, I belatedly realize how deep the water actually is. I tread the surface with only a little difficulty and scan for Noah.

I shriek a cloud of bubbles into the water as something brushes against the back of my thigh and comes to wind around my ribs. Finally he emerges, broad hands scooping under my arms and kicking us toward shallower water. Once he has both feet planted on the bed of the stream, I grab on to him like he's a tree in a flood.

"You did it," he laughs. His chest is pressed tight against mine, and it shakes with the rumble of his laugh.

"You make it sound like you thought I wouldn't!"

He shrugs; circled in his arms, I am gently lifted and lowered with the motion. "I wasn't sure." He leans to rub the bridge of his nose against my cheek. "But I'm glad you did." His hair has fallen out of his topknot, and it fans out on the water's surface like a red lily pad.

Flush with adrenaline and breathing heavy now that I have the taste of air in my lungs again, I take a moment to just look at him. Thankfully I didn't lose my glasses in our leap, and the water droplets clinging to the lenses look like tiny orbs bobbing in the open air. I push my glasses up into my hair, and suddenly he's the only thing in focus. The world fades into soft greens and browns, while Noah is in front of me with his sun-kissed skin, dripping beard, and lake-blue eyes.

"Me, too," I say finally. And then I lean in to kiss him.

Within moments, it's as though I'm drowning again. I can't get enough air; I can't get enough of *him*. As the water streams past us, I hold on to him as if he might slip away with the current, like the only things tying him to me are my toes pressing into the tops of his feet, my arms wound around his neck, my fingers tangled in his hair.

Just like with every greeting and enthusiastic "Sadie! It's you!," Noah kisses me like it's the first time. Like I've been gone for ages, and all he's thought about in the time I've been away is me. *It's so good to see you,* his hands say, gently cradling my face, his fingers sliding into my hair. *It's been only days since I've tasted you, but I missed you.* His tongue swirls against mine, and there's this contented, possessive hum that vibrates out of his chest and makes my nipples pinch. *Will you stay longer this time?* One hand slides around to the back of my neck and grips hard, holding my head above the water. The other pans down my lower back, squeezing gently as he passes over my ass and then holding tight as his fingers curl under my thigh. *I'm so happy you're here.* His kisses grow gentler as he sighs under his breath, gently tracing my jawline with parted lips.

As he climbs his way up to my ear, he murmurs, "Take a deep breath in for me, Sadie."

I'm already panting, so it's easy to do.

But the moment my lungs are full of air, he drags me under.

On instinct, I close my eyes. Some old high school biology lesson leaps to mind—something about infections and contaminants in freshwater bodies of water. *What the fuck?* It's the silliest thing in the world for me to think about when I'm tangled in the arms of a beautiful man, but I can't help it. And then, as soon as Noah's lips meet mine again, all thoughts save for him evaporate like bubbles to the surface. Swaddled in voluntary darkness, my body suspended in the water, my chest already growing tight, I'm a hundred times more aware of his touch—and a thousand times more aware of *mine.*

My hands paint him in the dark. My palms press against the muscles of his chest, fingers brushing through the cluster of soft curling hair underneath his collarbones. Next I trail my hands across the expanse of his shoulders—*god, he's got to be as wide as at least two of me, right?*—and think about how easily he could snap me in half if he wanted to. But instead, he just cradles me in the water, allowing me to explore. Finally, as I press my cheek to his chest, feeling the way his heart thunders at the same frantic pace as mine, my arms wrap around him to allow my fingers to dance along the muscles of his back. So many curves, divots, and bumps—so much definition. *Why a bard?* I think again, wildly. *Why play a bard, when he's built like a barbarian?* Experimentally, I dig my nails into the meat of his shoulders, and it's enough to send all the air rushing from his lungs.

Just before we crest the surface, I allow myself one tiny peek. Noah floats above me, ringed in light, sunbeams stretching warped lines through the surface of the water. His hair flows around his face like a halo, and his face is all laughter as bubbles of air flow out of the corners of his mouth. He reaches for me where I still hover at the bottom of the stream. I reach back, and he pulls me up with him, back toward the sun.

We both break the surface with gasping laughs.

"I could do this all day," he pants.

"You can. If you can catch me."

I manage to swim exactly two strokes away before he grabs my ankle and tugs me back to him with a delicious jerk. Within moments I'm caged in the circle of his arms again as he envelops me from behind. Even as I squirm, his grip is like iron. He drags us back and away from the middle of the stream until we're swallowed in shadows. I look up to see the gigantic root system of the tree that leans over the stream; Noah's tucked us underneath its ledge. Even as the water grows shallower, Noah draws me with him until he's sitting with his back pressed to the rock and I'm firmly caught in his lap. "Good try. But you're no match for me, Sadie." His voice is a low rumble in his chest, and his lips draw back in a smirk before he captures my mouth with his again.

I let my head crane back as his lips move against mine, reaching above my head to twine my arms behind his neck. I press my back against his chest, and as soon as he's sure I'm not going to run again, he relaxes his hold. His hands glide over my sports bra, circle teasingly around my belly button, and trace over the curves of my hips. Finally, his fingers play along the waistband of my shorts, curling against my skin. He's waiting for me. He's asking for permission.

Again I surface for air, drawing back from his kiss just enough to beg, "*Please.*"

As my head falls back into the crook of his shoulder, he presses languid, burning kisses against my neck and jaw. Slowly, he slides his fingers underneath the fabric of my shorts while his free hand skims along my ribs and moves up to cup my breast. I arch into his hold, urging his hand farther *down*, and something heavy presses against my ass. I swallow thickly.

"Is this okay?" His teeth are grazing along my neck. His fingers hover just above my burning skin, stretching the fabric of my underwear.

"Keep going, Noah." My voice is thin—snappy.

He chuckles into my shoulder. "Bossy." I make an ungodly sound in the back of my throat as he teases me, tracing the sensitive line between my legs while his thumb moves in slow circles around the space above. Gently he presses his lips to the skin right behind my ear. His tongue traces a slow, aching circle against my neck—just as his middle finger begins to do the same to my clit. At any moment I expect all of the water in the stream to start boiling. Already I can feel tension winding through my body as it chases after the blessed ache that suffuses my limbs.

He's sliding his finger into me when a twig snaps.

We both freeze.

Slowly, Noah's hand withdraws from under my bra and comes up to wrap around my mouth. I inhale through my nose, and he draws us both beneath the surface.

Under the water, neither of us can help the way our laughter escapes upward in a rush of bubbles. Noah takes my face between his hands and presses a rough kiss to my cheek. He kicks backward and resurfaces a polite three feet away from me.

I peek my head above the surface, and as the breaking of twigs and the rustling of several pairs of feet come closer, a group of four college-age kids emerges from behind the trees. The girl at the front, blue hair piled in a bun on top of her head, lifts her brows in surprise. "Oh, I'm so sorry. Usually this spot's empty, we don't mean to inter—"

The water surges upward in a massive splash as one of the boys hurls himself into the stream. The other boy follows soon after him, whooping. The last girl, sporting a pink bikini, hefts a cooler and shakes her head in resignation, as if used to their antics.

"The more the merrier." Noah grins. Always friendly, forever outgoing.

I wade up next to him and swallow hard. "We should probably—"

"Y-yeah." Thank fuck he sounds as out of breath as I feel. "Could you, ah—could you grab me the towel?"

For once the heat is soothing as I emerge from the stream, and the shivering and the goosebumps that aren't completely the fault of the icy water soon begin to fade. I can't help but feel a little smug as I toss Noah the towel, which he wraps around his waist immediately after climbing out of the water.

We head back to our spot and splay out on the blanket, Noah leaning against the base of a tree and me on my back, head resting on his thigh. It gives me the perfect vantage point to watch rivulets of water run from the ends of his hair down the planes of his chest.

"Just our luck, Sadie," he sighs dramatically. His chest swells with the motion. "I've been out here half a dozen times now, and this is the first time I've ever had to share the space."

I shrug helplessly. "Jay hasn't taught me her secrets yet." His forearm stretches across my chest, and I trace along the tendons on the back of his hand. His skin is starkly warm against my paleness. Later I'll pay for forgetting sunscreen. "What would we have done if I hadn't jumped?" I almost hadn't.

"Oh, I had lots of options." He gestures toward the items spread out around his backpack. Strawberries, books, a card game, art supplies. My heart squeezes a little.

"A choose-your-own-adventure date?" I tease.

"Fitting, isn't it?"

"What's in the bottle?"

"I'm so glad you asked."

I sit up on my elbows as he plucks the bottle from beside his backpack. He holds it out for me to sip from, but I narrow my eyes a little.

"It's something I brewed up," Noah explains.

"From Alchemist?"

He shakes his head. I wait for him to continue, but he just smiles. I crane my neck to take a testing sip of the amber liquid. Immediately I know it's not beer. It's definitely alcohol, but it's far too sweet to be beer. It's got the same fruity undertones as cider, too, but it's not so bubbly. I take a deeper drink, let it pass over my tongue. There's a heavy smoothness to it—thick, almost. I've never tried anything like it. It's too unfamiliar to be enjoyable yet, but I'm compelled to keep drinking it.

"Is it cider?" I guess.

"It's mead."

My eyebrows form a confused knot on my forehead. "Like, old-timey medieval mead? Like D&D tavern-type shit?"

"Sure," he says, laughing. "That kind of mead."

"Is that what you've been working on in the back of the brewery?" I remember the times we've been at Alchemist this week; when I'm actually working on the mural and he's not busy pressing me up against the wall in the back room, he's hard at work monitoring the huge metal tanks full of brew. A true alchemist.

"No, actually. Mead's the first thing I ever brewed, way before I even worked at Alchemist. It's the easiest of all alcohol." Noah always sounds enthusiastic when discussing his interests, but this is one of the first times I've seen his eyes really passionately light up. His tone is almost as reverent as when he's talking about backpacking. "All you really need is honey, yeast, water, whatever fruits or flavors you might like, and a few weeks' patience. I used oranges and raisins for this one. It's so low-maintenance, I can even keep a gallon brewing when I'm on the road." His voice softens a little, and he leans closer. "Do you like it?"

"I think so. It's growing on me." I take another small sip—got to be careful with the pacing on this one—and set the bottle upright next to me.

"Don't feel like you have to finish it now," he teases. "Take it home with you. Enjoy it."

My cheeks warm. "Thanks, Noah."

Despite the shrieks and laughter from the group playing in the stream below, we relax into an easy, comfortable silence. Noah stares with half-lidded bliss into the canopy above, one hand plucking strawberries from the container while the other plays gently with my damp hair. I've nestled back into my spot resting on his leg, Noah's sketchbook propped in my lap. The pages are empty and pristine, and the sticker from the store is still on the back. I'm flattered by his thoughtfulness.

Maybe an eternity later—I can't tell how much time has passed in our bubble, but my hair has completely dried by now into its usual waves—I'm sketching a scene of water nymphs tempting a traveler into their pond when Noah speaks up again.

"I want that on my ceiling." His thumb taps the side of the sketchbook. "What's your next project after the mural's finished? Should only be a week or two left, right?" The expression on his face is soft and daydreamy. "Morgan should hire you to paint bluebonnets at her store. Or maybe I'll hire you to paint my van." He twirls one of my curls around his pointer finger. "What do you want to try next?"

I'm surprised by how quickly unease cramps my stomach, how my heart sinks further with each new suggestion. "I think the mural is a onetime thing for now."

"Oh? I thought you were really enjoying it."

"I am. Of course I am." I think back to how I crooned off-tune into my paintbrush as we blasted music from the speakers yesterday morning. I swallow. "I just—I don't know how much time I'll have for another project. It depends on how everything with Paragon goes."

"Oh," he says again. "How was the first interview?"

"It went really well."

"Are you excited?"

I poke my tongue into the side of my cheek. "It's a good opportunity."

"That's not what I asked."

I don't answer. He acknowledges it by mussing my hair again, but he doesn't press.

"Well, I think Dan would hire you again, if he could," he says.

"For what?" I laugh. "There aren't any walls left."

"He's considering opening up another location."

"Here?"

My eyes are on my sketchbook, but I recognize the smile in his voice. "In Colorado," Noah says. "Our old college buddies in Boulder are getting jealous. They think he could do the same thing back there. At least, they want to be a part of it if he decides to go that route."

I hum thoughtfully as I take a sip of mead again. "Is Dan thinking about moving?"

"He's not sure. Maura would love it if he did. Either that, or he asked if I would be interested in leading the charge."

The mead is suddenly too sweet, and the flavor clings to the back of my throat. I put too much pressure on my pencil, and the next line I draw is bold and dark. "Are you?" I hope my tone sounds calmer than I feel.

Noah tilts his head from side to side. "I don't know. So far as a rule I haven't lived in the same place twice, and I spent years in Colorado—but I've got a lot of friends out there. We'll see. He's given me a few weeks to think it over."

He says it so simply, like it's the smallest thing in the world. *Just a few weeks? Does he make all of his decisions that quickly?* I wonder if he can tell that my brain is bluescreening, so I distract myself with sliding the pencil into the spiral binding of the sketchbook and folding my hands on my lap. I glance toward the sun through the leaves; already it's far past its peak, arcing back down toward the earth.

"I felt like all of the days dragged, when I first got here," I say quietly. "I hardly knew what to do with myself. But now—" I'm impressed by how level I keep my voice despite the tightness in my throat. "Time is passing really fast, isn't it?"

Already his hands are moving. He's lifting me up, wrapping me in his arms from behind. It's like I'm filled with bees—the anxious, awful energy buzzes underneath my skin. But he's still. Quiet. I love how enveloped I feel in his arms, pressed against his broad chest.

"It is," he murmurs, his chin nuzzling against my hair. "But it's nothing to worry about now, Sadie. We take it one day at a time."

Part of me takes comfort in his calm approach—and part of me resents how he seems to take everything in stride. I question whether seeing him get all worked up over what I see as a massive decision would help justify how torn I am. How seriously is he considering driving off to his next adventure? And would the answer make me feel better or worse? Maybe I want him to ask me to stay—and maybe I want to ask him to stay, too.

But instead he just holds me and whispers into my hair, "It'll all work out."

It makes me want to jump out of my skin.

In time, I match my breathing to his. I close my eyes for ten heartbeats. I still have weeks left of D&D to play, and weeks left of the mural to paint. And despite Addison's enthusiasm and pep, she hasn't yet reached out to schedule my next interview.

I remind myself that I'm cradled in the arms of a gorgeous, shirtless man who wants nothing more in this moment than to feed me strawberries and pet my hair and take me on pretty walks. I can save the worrying for later.

"Okay," I say, touching his cheek and drawing him down for a kiss. "Okay."

CHAPTER
Twenty-Three

They had tried everything, but it was useless. The orb wouldn't work.

"Went through all of that trouble," Morgana huffs, her tone sharp with frustration, "and we haven't got a godsdamned clue how to use it."

The women stand together and watch their companions lunge in an awkward dance before them. Loren strums a little jig, swaying from side to side as colorful motes of light flash and bounce around his head. Kain stalks in a circle around him with the orb clutched between his clawed hands. Every few steps, he thrusts the orb forward toward the bard at a different angle. But no matter what, Loren's magic merrily persists.

Jaylie pinches the bridge of her nose. "There must be something we're missing."

Morgana squints up at the sun, blazing bright in a cloudless sky. It's a beautiful day again, now that the party has camped as far from the cave as possible while still keeping Shira's tower in their sights. "Maybe there's some sort of ritual to it? Or a magic word?" The dwarf clutches her beard. "Hells, you don't think we'd be so unlucky as to have it just quit working once the creature's dead, do you?"

But Jaylie's caught on her earlier suggestion. *A magic word.* "Most spells do have a verbal component of a sort," she muses aloud. She gestures at Loren, who's currently sticking his tongue out at an increasingly frustrated Kain. "He accesses his magic through music. I pray to my Lady." She frowns. "But I haven't a clue what beholders do."

She beckons the boys over. Loren comes to stand close to her side, and Jaylie presses her lips together to keep from smiling. Since the events of the cave, he'd barely let her out of his sight. When they had made camp the night before, she'd caught the reflection of the fire dancing in his eyes as he watched her unblinkingly, as if concerned she'd crumble to dust again.

"Kain, would you hold that *just* there, please?" Jaylie guides his wrists until the orb is held extended before him. "Thank you. I'm going to try something."

It's not a spell she's done before, but she's seen clerics at her temple conduct small rituals to reveal the magical properties of holy artifacts. This dark sphere is the furthest thing from holy, but she hopes the trick might work nonetheless. Plucking a gold coin from her purple leather pouch, she flips it into the air, where it catches the sunlight and gleams a dozen different colors as it spins. It lands in Jaylie's palm, and she slaps it against the top of her free hand, revealing Marlana's winking face. Jaylie beams.

Please, my Lady, she prays. *Show me the way.*

Rainbow light arcs between her palms. As Jaylie spreads her hands outward, the magic stretches from her fingers like the delicate skin of a bubble. Jaylie holds her hands above the orb, peering through the colorful oily sheen of the spell like a looking glass.

She gasps as information floods her mind, flashes of memories playing out between her hands. *Glorvalk.* The word rings in her head like a bell, and she sees an adventuring party pinned in the sick green glow of the beholder's central eye. *Glorvalk.* An obsidian tower, stark against a stormy purple sky and held aloft in the air by magic, crumbles to the ground under the monster's green gaze. *Glorvalk*. While laughter shrills in the background, a wizard's skin disintegrates to ash, leaving only his bones as the magic keeping him young fades away.

"Glorvalk," Jaylie says. She tastes sulfur in the back of her throat as she speaks the word aloud. "*Glorvalk* is the word that will activate it." Kain straightens immediately, his great horns whistling through the air as he swings toward the priestess.

On cue, the orb begins to glow, casting Jaylie's features in poison green. She tries to summon up a quick light spell, but the magic fizzles out. Loren claps his hands together excitedly just as Kain bursts into rumbling, thunderous laughter.

Loren looks up at him, bemused. "What's so funny?"

Kain pretends to wipe a tear from his eye. "You're kidding. Glorvalk? That's embarrassing."

"Oh?" Jaylie posts her hands on her hips.

Kain's mouth twists into a smirk, showing just the barest hint of one long fang. "In the devil's tongue," he says dryly, "*glorvalk* means *behold*."

Faced once more with the friendly exterior of Shira's vine-covered white tower, Jaylie wonders again whether to abandon their plan of attack and simply knock. It's even more welcoming up close. There are wrought iron gates fashioned in friendly curlicues, an array of rosebushes surrounding the tower's base, and a gold door knocker held in the cheerful grin of a chubby gargoyle. All things considered, it's adorable. Jaylie thinks that maybe, on the inside, there's a little sign that reads LIVE, LAUGH, LICH, a cheeky nod to the greatest form a dark wizard can take.

But none of that stops Kain from thundering up to the gates, the orb-capped wooden staff held in his fist. With some makeshift crafting on Morgana's part, the orb had been attached to a fallen branch as tall as Jaylie. Experimentally, Kain presses one clawed hand to the gates. They don't budge.

"*Glorvalk,*" he intones.

It sounds much better when he says it.

Glitter rains down from the iron as a warding spell that neither Jaylie nor Loren noticed dissolves to nothing. Kain bares his sharp teeth in a grin. "Follow me, little ones." The muscles of his back strain as he holds the glowing staff out in one hand and unstraps his axe with the other.

As the party advances, Jaylie half expects to see the charming display of flowers and vines wilt under the beam of green to reveal the dark truth beneath the pretty illusion. But while the orb does successfully disarm the glyphs and alarm spells hidden in the vegetation, the beautiful greenery remains the same. Jaylie can't help but admire Shira's natural green thumb as they pass a peach tree, perfectly pruned and ripe with dozens of pink and orange fruits.

On the wind, Jaylie catches the tinkling sounds of chimes and laughter as they approach the tower's entryway—though the sounds are coming from the garden toward the back. As Kain raises his axe to slam through the purple-painted wood of the front door, Morgana hastily shakes her head and points: off to the side, under an archway of trellises heavy with roses, a dirt path leads in the direction of the voices. Loren places one hand on Kain's forearm and steps through, leading the way with Jaylie trailing after him.

They take their time now. Even as magic continues to shrivel in the wake of the orb, Jaylie and her party step quietly and stealthily. She imagines that Kain and Morgana are eager to catch Shira off guard—the rogue has always been a master of surprise attacks— but Jaylie finds herself more curious than anything. As she pauses behind one trellis wall, thick enough with greenery to hide their advance, Jaylie can hear the voices well enough to finally distinguish words. Intrigued, she bends to peek through the leaves.

"You're unhappy here, aren't you, my dear?" Jaylie immediately recognizes Shira's deep voice. The witch is dressed casually, with a billowy violet shirt tucked into high-waisted black trousers. The heels on her knee-high boots, however, are vicious. She reclines in her chair, sipping delicately from a pink porcelain teacup.

"I wouldn't call it *unhappy*." Jaylie never got a good look at Alora underneath all of her lace at the wedding, but upon recalling Donati's description of her, this woman certainly fits the bill: pale, pretty, and redheaded, with her curls cropped short right under her ears. She wears a dress of light blue that leaves her shoulders bare and sparkling. *Sparkling?* Jaylie leans forward for a closer look. Where the sun shimmers on Alora's skin, especially on her cheekbones and shoulders, Jaylie swears she can spot a light pattern of scales.

"It's only that it's lonely, Shira. It's quiet," Alora says with a sigh. "I miss my family. I miss our parties. Hell, sometimes I even miss my stuffy office in the Academy."

Shira nods, and her black hair falls over her shoulder, hiding her expression from Jaylie. She plucks the teapot from the table and refills Alora's cup.

"I miss when you'd come to me in disguise at my father's balls and sweep me off my feet . . ." Alora delicately walks her fingers across the table and strokes the inside of Shira's wrist.

"You liked that, did you?"

"You always used the most charming accent. I loved the stories you came up with, pretending it was our first time meeting."

"I was the best dancer there," Shira preens, lips ticking up in a smile.

"Oh, I think you just loved to watch the others seethe with jealousy at the way you commanded my attention."

"Oh my god." Loren's voice is barely a whisper in Jaylie's ear. He presses himself close to her side, just as enthralled as she is.

"Oh my *god*," Jaylie agrees.

"Oh my god!" Loren sighs wistfully.

Shira bends forward, just enough so that she can lace her fingers in Alora's. "I could take you back, you know. You could stay with your family until we figure out what to do next."

"No. You know there is nowhere else I'd rather be than by your side." Alora squeezes Shira's hand gently and leans forward to press their foreheads together.

Shira angles her jaw for a kiss just as Kain hefts his axe over his head, sweeps it forward at a savage angle, and carves the trellis to kindling. "Murderer!" he bellows, charging toward them. "Enchantress! Free her from your spell before we free your head from your neck!"

Three inharmonious shrieks erupt simultaneously from Jaylie, Alora, and, hilariously, Loren. Morgana holds out her knife uncertainly while Shira immediately jumps into action. Her teacup shatters against a wall as she desperately flings it away to begin casting a spell.

But Kain is faster. He slams the base of his staff into the ground. "Glorvalk!" he thunders.

The two women shiver under the sudden beam of green, and Shira hisses in anger as her spell flees her fingertips. Kain advances forward to take advantage of her weakness, but Alora steps between them, hands planted firmly on her hips.

"What is the meaning of this?" She sounds nearly as imperious as Donati.

"We're here to rescue you, miss," Kain growls. "You are free now. You are no longer enraptured by her dark hold over you."

Shira's face is a storm cloud. "You think I would enchant her against her will? Like some fucking love spell? You've got me confused with some other—"

Gently, Alora presses her hand to Shira's side. The witch stills then quiets.

"*Enraptured?*" Alora laughs. "No, it's nothing like that."

"It's not?"

"No, of course not," Alora says, exasperated. "Shira and I—we're in love."

CHAPTER
Twenty-Four

"*What?*" Kain's hold on the orb staff wobbles slightly, then straightens resolutely. He continues to pin Shira and Alora in its beam. "Prove it. Prove you're not under her spell."

"First of all, your *thing* would have dispelled it immediately." Alora waggles her fingers toward the staff and rolls her eyes—but Jaylie can see how they gleam with playfulness. "And if I were a poor damsel, and Shira was a nasty, mean witch . . . do you suppose I would do this?" Suddenly she trips Shira—who's a good deal taller than her—with a swift kick, sweeping the woman's feet out from under her. Shira gasps in surprise, but before her ass smacks against the ground, Alora catches her with one arm around her waist and the other behind her head. "My darling," Alora says sweetly before diving down and kissing her passionately.

Loren claps delightedly.

Kain blushes a deep, dark shade of purple.

Shira stands and composes herself, brushing her hands along her pants. After a moment, her flushed smile fades. She narrows her eyes. "Lord Aurelio Donati sent you, didn't he?" Her tone drips with contempt.

"Of course he did," Morgana says. "But you have to admit how bad this looks for you. You stole his bride right from the altar.

Made quite a scene, too." Somehow, she looks grudgingly impressed, even as she keeps her daggers out and ready for stabbing, just in case.

Alora and Shira share a smug smile. "We did, didn't we?" Shira sounds wistful. "But I did not steal anyone. I *rescued* her. It was Aurelio who stole my love from the start."

Behind Shira and Alora, Loren circles back toward the table where they were having breakfast and begins to pour himself a steaming hot cup of tea. He catches Jaylie's eye and raises a single eyebrow as if to ask whether she'd like any. *Drama!* he mouths.

Jaylie rolls her eyes, sends a prayer up to Marlana, and sharply extends her palms outward. "*Enough*," she says. Five pairs of eyes fix on her face. "We need to start from the beginning. Clearly we've all arrived here with different versions of what happened, but we need to learn the truth."

Shira surprises Jaylie by nodding vehemently. "Of course." She gestures toward the holy symbol hanging from Jaylie's neck. "I've seen priestesses like you cast spells that have a way of drawing the truth out of people. Can you do that?"

Jaylie opens her mouth then snaps it closed. It's the same spell she offered to cast for Donati after the chaos of his ruined wedding. But he'd waved her off. She hadn't thought it suspicious at the time, but . . . her brows knit together, and she clears her throat carefully. "Of course. We'll start there."

As Jaylie traces a wide circle on the ground with glittering gold dust, Alora turns to Kain. "For us to participate in your priestess's spell, you'll have to let us out of this beam. I can tell it nullifies magic." She taps her pointed chin thoughtfully. "And if this all goes well, perhaps you'll let me pick your brain about how it works. It's a fascinating contraption . . ."

Kain's tail snaps back and forth irritably. "How do I know you won't attack us the moment you're free?" He's not speaking to Alora. His slitted eyes are fixed on the witch.

Shira's dark gaze is steady on his face. "You'll just have to trust us that far."

"Or you can simply trust *me*, big boy," Morgana quips. She pokes the tip of one of her knives just under Shira's ribs. "One wrong move and I'll bury this in your heart, aye? Faster than you can cast any spell."

Shira scowls but nods.

Jaylie finishes constructing her ritual circle, and as she sprinkles the last bit of gold dust to connect the lines, the ring glows with a rippling pink light. "All right, everybody in." At the looks of hesitance from her party, Jaylie points emphatically to the circle. "If Shira's willing to be honest with us, the least we can do is meet her halfway."

Jaylie takes the first step in. Marlana's magic is always warm, gentle, and comforting, like being wrapped in a soft blanket while sitting before the hearth. But this time is different. The heat immediately cuts through to her core, like a sunbeam magnified by a glass many times over. It's almost painful, but as she opens herself to it, the intensity lessens. Just to test it, she says, "My name is Loren Ros—" Pain spikes violently at her temple, so agonizing that she can't bring herself to finish her sentence. After a few panting breaths, she tries again. "My name is Jaylie."

It wasn't always her name, but it is now. The sunlight-warmth embraces her truth.

Loren steps into the circle next. "Have I ever told you how beautiful you look when you cast your magic?" he muses. "You've got this . . . glow. You sparkle."

"Flatterer."

"I mean it." Jaylie can see the smile lines in the corners of Loren's eyes as the spell testifies to the honesty of his words.

One by one, everyone steps into the circle, with Shira and Alora escorted by Morgana. Finally, Kain gingerly places the staff on the ground outside of the ring before he shuffles in last. "Fine," he says, crossing his arms over his bare chest. "Speak. Before my patience runs out."

"Right now? You're stopping the game *right now*?" Morgan slams her fist on the table, causing all of the dice to shiver. "C'mon, Liam, you can't do that to us."

Meanwhile, Jules leans back in her chair, clutching her chest as she giggles. "I can't believe I thought she was charmed. I was about to cut Shira's head off!"

I meet Liam's eyes from across the table. He has his hands folded neatly on top of his spiral DM notebook, and it warms my heart to see how fucking pleased he looks. He told me years ago that every Dungeon Master's greatest wish is simple: all he wants is player engagement—player *investment*. This must be bliss for him. He gives me a little eyebrow bounce and a quick flash of a grin, and in return I fire at him with my finger guns.

"What can I say?" he teases. "We've already played over our allotted time, and I like to leave you guys on a cliff-hanger. That way you're hungry for more."

"Oh fuck off." Noah lets out one of his booming laughs and waves a hand at Liam. "You've had us hooked from the start, DM; no need for such petty carrot-dangling strategies."

As the three of them hound Liam for more game time, I glance down to my notebook. With an ink pen and a sick neon-green highlighter, I'd sketched out a portrait of Kain. The orb illuminating him from below highlights his more devilish features.

Suddenly, Liam thuds down his half-empty can of beer to get everyone's attention. "I want to prepare you guys," he warns. "We only have a few sessions left."

I sag into my chair. "Already?" When Liam first put the campaign together, he mentioned to me that he'd purposefully planned

it to be brief for several reasons. For one, it's easier for newer players to commit to a shorter storyline. And second, it was only ever
intended to last for the summer. It's another anxious reminder that
my days here are numbered.

"Yes, just a few more weeks," Liam confirms. Just as everyone
starts to deflate, he jumps in. "But I want to do something to celebrate. Let's plan an end-of-campaign outing the weekend we finish. That way, after I've slaughtered you all in the final boss fight,
you'll at least have some sort of consolation prize."

I snort and toss my head. He wouldn't.

Would he?

He looks to each of us. "Any ideas?"

Morgan passes her palm over her curls, looking thoughtful. "A
new axe-throwing bar opened up a few towns over." Her red-painted
lips spread into a grin. "I hear they've got daggers, too."

Noah presses forward on his elbows. "We could have a *real*
adventure. We could go camping. S'mores, beer, trails, campfire
songs—we'll be just like our characters, out on one last journey
together." Noah beams expectantly.

Everyone is horrified.

"Camping? In *this* heat?"

"Noah, it's the middle of July. What the fuck, *no*—"

"Do you mean, like, actual tents? We'd be sleeping on the
ground?"

"My sweet summer child, is this your first year in Texas?"

Everyone speaks up at once, and pressing the back of my hand
to my mouth isn't enough to cover my laughter. Always good-
natured, Noah grins and holds up his hands in surrender. "Fine,
fine—not our cup of tea. That's okay." Under the table, I squeeze
his thigh consolingly.

Jules smiles kindly at Noah, a little patronizing but still sweet.
"I do like the idea of connecting with our characters one last time,
though," she offers. "What about the Renaissance Faire?"

Liam strokes his beard. "I've always meant to go."

Morgan hums. "I could be down for that. Bet they'll have axe-throwing there, too."

Noah nods with interest.

I'm the only one who has to ask. "What's a Renaissance Faire?"

Jules brightens, her cheeks rosy. "It's a medieval fantasy festival, of a sort. Originally it was meant to celebrate Renaissance culture, but most people just like to dress up as knights, wenches, fairies, elves, and other fantasy-inspired creatures. They've got jousting, turkey legs, music . . ." She trails off, a little sheepish. "Me and my husband go every year with the kids. It's our favorite."

"Do we have to dress up?" I ask.

Jules smiles. "It's more fun when you do."

"We could dress as our characters," Noah suggests.

Morgan pets at her imaginary beard as Jules reaches up to adjust her headband, probably already imagining how she might fashion horns from it.

"I like it," Liam announces. "Though I'll have to figure out which character to be."

"You would make a very convincing Donati," Jules says.

"Or Shira," Morgan teases.

Noah's eyes go wide. "It's got to be Alastair. Alastair or bust."

I'm losing my mind over the thought of painting Liam green when Jules smacks her palm against her forehead. "I'm so sorry, y'all, I forgot—the season doesn't start until the fall. It won't be open for a few more months." She casts a doe-eyed, apologetic look specifically toward me.

Disappointment settles around the table, and I add the Faire to the list of things I'll miss.

Noah jumps in with a forced optimism. "We'll keep brainstorming. We'll figure something out, yeah?"

Liam nods. "Just another cliff-hanger to resolve next time, folks."

CHAPTER
Twenty-Five

"I'll go camping with you."

"Hm?" Noah's face is buried in the scoop neck of my paint-spattered tank top, his thigh pressing me against the door to the supply closet while his knee eases my legs apart. I don't know how he can breathe with his nose so deep in my cleavage, but the way his tongue swirls around my nipple sets my nerves on fire in an ungodly way, so I don't complain.

"I said—" I inhale sharply at the feel of his teeth tugging. Gently, then harder. "I said I'll go camping with you."

That gets his attention. He straightens so suddenly that his forehead knocks against my chin. I wince, but it's not his fault. The closet is cramped.

"Really?" His tone is a weird mix of doubtful and hopeful. It makes his pitch go high.

"Yeah," I say. Why not? "I think it could be fun. I've never been, but I want to go with you. Are you working this weekend?"

"No." He looks thoughtful as he drags a knuckle down my chest, from the base of my throat down between my breasts, ending at my belly button. "We could go this weekend."

I won't lie. I have ulterior motives. Ever since we were interrupted by the college kids, my mind's been swimming with thoughts about what might have happened if we'd been left completely alone and gone on just a bit longer. Would Noah have continued whispering in my ear, his fingers moving inside of me until his touch had me dissolving like thousands of bubbles chased to the surface? Or would he have slipped his shorts down lower, lower until—

It's probably for the best that we were interrupted, all things considered. Indecent exposure and all that. That being said, it does have me aching to be alone with him—more chances to make up for lost time. But this week is turning out to be a scheduling mess, full of "When can I see you again?" and "When are you free?" on both of our parts.

I told Liam I'd go to the game store with him after he's done working tonight. He wants another set of dice, even though he's got hundreds.

Tomorrow Dan has me staying late, experimenting with the new food menu he's launching soon. Don't hold your breath—so far, it's all shit. Wednesday?

Fuck. I'm supposed to catch up with my mom that night on Face-Time. Thursday?

I didn't say that Wednesday is also the day of my next interview with Paragon—this time with the whole team. I know there's a good chance I'll be a mess of emotions afterward, and I don't want to see him then.

When I'd suggested Thursday, Noah had shaken his head. He'd broken my gaze, and his lips had curled into a little smile. "I can't Thursday," he'd murmured into my ear, "I'm working on a secret recipe. I'll show you soon."

Eventually we agreed on meeting over the weekend, but this is the first time I've proposed solid plans. After a week of breathless make-out sessions cut short by Noah's work schedule, I need assurance that our next date is set. I need something to look forward to. Noah is the type to spontaneously come up with a plan the morning of, but I'm always desperate for early details to key in to my Google calendar.

"Do you have an idea of where we could go? To camp?" I still haven't even left Heller yet.

"I'll figure it out."

"Do I need to bring anything? Like—a tent? Bear spray? Fire?"

"*Sadie.*" He says my name so playfully—half laugh, half groan—as if I've said the funniest thing in the world. He hides his grin by burying his face in my hair. "No, you don't need to bring anything. You don't need to bring *fire*. I have plenty to share."

I pinch the side of his thigh. "Don't mock me. This is my first time, I want to be prepared."

He runs his hand over the crown of my head. "I'll make sure we're prepared. I'll teach you everything."

There's another reason why I want to go camping, too. On our hike, I felt like I got a glimpse of a side of Noah I'd never seen before. During D&D, or at Alchemist, or whenever we're together in public, there's this boisterous and infectious enthusiasm to him that lights up every room. He has a talent for effortlessly pulling anyone into conversation, making them feel warm and welcome and listened to. He's a great big ball of sunshine.

But when he was leading me through the trees, his hand laced in mine, he was quiet for the first time. Peaceful. He didn't have to put on a show for anyone, regardless of how much he embraced playing the part. He didn't have to put on a show for me.

He just *existed*.

Watching him during our hike reminded me of where I go when I paint. It's a separate pocket realm where my thoughts are gentle, where my anxious spirals loosen up and become nothing more than soft ripples atop the still pool of my mind. Sometimes, if I really hit the flow, I don't think of anything at all. I am only an extension of my brush; I am color and movement, gliding along.

It had been so long since I'd found that peace. Drawing exclusively smut and anime fanart over the past few years hadn't exactly gotten me there.

But the mural does. Painting it gets me out of my skin, especially as I've focused on adding the details this week. It helps me breathe.

I want to see what that looks like for Noah, too. I want to peel back his layers of paint and see what lies beneath.

"What are you thinking about?" Noah hums, nuzzling the crook of my shoulder.

"I'm thinking I might like to see you naked." In a figurative fashion. But, as his teeth nip against my skin almost chidingly, I admit that I'm eager for a literal interpretation as well.

Noah laughs low in his throat. "That can be arranged."

The team interview with Paragon feels like another D&D game.

I'm Josephine again, with my black thick-rimmed glasses, magenta blazer, and hair curled so tight and bouncy that it barely reaches past my ears. Before the call, I hadn't really recognized myself in the mirror, but that's okay. I'm just playing a character for now.

A youngish man situated in a little video box at the top of my screen asks the first question. "Can you tell us more about the projects you worked on while you were with Incite, Josephine?" His hair is so gel-slicked to his skull that he looks like a Lego figure.

Intelligence check. Roll with advantage. I give a brief overview of the projects I'm proud of, including a rebranding campaign for a clothing line that switched gears to prioritize sustainability, a surprisingly successful launch campaign for a company that made formalwear for dogs, and a local marketing passion project for a new ice-cream shop in my neighborhood in Queens. As I run through each campaign, I make sure to highlight the data, metrics, and revenue and my own lightning-fast project turnaround time.

"And how do you like to connect with new clients? What is your outreach strategy like?" A woman with warm brown skin and hair twisted into a cute side bun smiles at me, her chin propped on her fist.

Charisma check. I talk through my networking strategy, which includes a mix of sending personalized emails to new clients I admire, scouting out conferences and events, and wooing new local connections at my favorite charming coffee shops and wine bars. I throw in a formulaic but endearing joke for good measure.

They continue to pepper me with questions, and I juggle them all as best I can.

"Tell me about a time you experienced a challenge or a disagreement with a client. How did you handle it?"

Wisdom check.

"How do you balance many competing priorities in your day-to-day schedule?"

Dexterity check.

"How well do you work in a team environment?"

Charisma check, again.

There's a man in the bottom right corner of the screen who hasn't spoken up yet. He sits with his arms crossed over his dark suit jacket, shifting from side to side in his swivel chair. He's older than the rest. Finally he clears his throat and speaks directly into the camera, and it's like he's locking eyes with me. "Can you give us a little more insight into why you left your previous role?"

Constitution saving throw. Roll with disadvantage. My throat is suddenly dry, and I use it as an excuse to stall and take a sip of water as I rush to gather my thoughts. My stomach roils uneasily. "I loved my time at Incite, but I'm eager for a change of environment," I say. "I'm hungry for new challenges, a new atmosphere, and a new team to learn from."

Deception check. Of course I don't tell them the truth. Incite felt suffocating. I wasn't sleeping. I met my deadlines only by regularly staying up into the early hours of the morning. I was exhausted, and I couldn't handle the pressure.

Dark Suit looks like he wants to dig deeper, but Addison cuts him off, a cheery smile on her face. "I think that's all the questions we have for you today, Josephine. I'm happy to discuss next steps with you now, but everyone else—feel free to drop the call." As the other team members wave goodbye and wink out of existence, Addison's face fills the screen, expertly painted with what I can tell are expensive cosmetics. "As I said at the beginning, the last step of this process will be an in-office visit. If anything, it will be *your* chance to interview *us*—and for us to show you everything we have to offer." She beams. "The whole team will be there. We'll also meet with my director, Cary, but it's more of a formality than anything . . ."

I nod and laugh along obediently. *Performance check.*

"I need to compare everyone's schedules—and of course see when the best time is for you," Addison says. Her gaze pans off to the side, away from the camera. She must have another screen up somewhere. "I'll get in touch with you as soon as I know more, and we'll have our assistant book your flight out."

"That sounds good to me, Addison. Thank you so much. It's been a pleasure."

"Wait."

Addison leans toward her camera like we're just two girls gossiping over coffee. "Just so I know, dear . . . between you and me. Have you given any thought to when you'd be available to start?"

My mind blanks. It's not a question I prepared for. My thoughts spinning, I try to do quick math around when the campaign will end and when I'll finish up the mural, then calculate a week out from that. From a technical standpoint, it would work fine. My apartment is still there, waiting for me. My roommates text me sometimes, asking whether I'm going to renew the lease in the fall. But it feels wrong. *That's still too soon,* I panic. *Don't say it, I'm not ready to leave.*

I swallow and say it anyway. "August fifteenth?" Three weeks and change from today.

Addison clasps her manicured hands together. "That would be perfect," she gushes. "Mid-August would be ideal!"

"Of course," I say smoothly, trying not to stumble over my words. "Thanks for everything, Addison."

She gives me a little nose-scrunch smile and logs off of the call.

I barely give myself enough time to shrug off the blazer and slip into my running shoes before I'm hurtling down the stairs, hopping over a snoozing Howard, and running out the door.

The first time I ran, I did it because it hurt like hell.

A meeting had gone south at Incite. I'd pitched a new idea for a campaign, and my boss harshly shot it down in front of my colleagues. It wasn't new behavior from her, but it was the first time her dissatisfaction had been made public. Before that point, I'd felt like a star—the new girl with new ideas and new perspectives, beloved by my co-workers and clients. Always willing to go the extra mile and work the long nights needed to prove myself and succeed. Later on, I justified that her behavior meant that she was starting to take me more seriously—like she trusted me enough to know I could handle criticism.

But really, she'd just been shitty.

I'd returned home, changed into my cheap pair of all-purpose sneakers, and gone on a long walk toward the park.

It was a good forty-minute hike from my apartment, yet it had always been a trek I was willing to make. Sometimes the smells of the city and invisible smog made my throat tighten in the same way it did whenever I was anxious or nervous. But in the park, the surrounding greenery made it easier to breathe for a while. If you squinted a little and put in headphones to block out the ever-present noise of the cars and the subway crossing the bridge overhead—well, then you might find a sliver of peace. I'd often walk there, pick up an iced coffee along the way, then sit and people-watch and sketch until the coffee forced me to find a nearby bathroom.

But that day, I skipped the coffee, crossed under the bridge, and took off the second my feet touched grass.

I hated it. At first, I really fucking hated it. I'd never been an athlete, never played any sports. I was out of breath within the first two minutes and my feet screamed at me to stop. It was the middle of the summer, and I'd worn shorts, but I knew immediately from the way my thighs chafed together that I'd chosen the wrong out-fit.

But as I homed in on how much the movements hurt, how un-used to the exercise I was, how each step felt like a new and worse challenge—I forgot about my workday. My boss's words were noth-ing in comparison to the fire in my lungs. I'd had to cancel a first date in order to stay late and finish my project, only to have that work discarded during the meeting—but the disappointment faded as I pumped my arms at my side, hoping the momentum would distract from the pain in my legs. I had to focus so hard on putting one foot in front of the other that my brain had no room left for anxiety, worry, or feeling bad about myself.

Ever since then, running has become a habit. It's a switch I can flick whenever I need to turn off the buzzing of my thoughts, to smother the anxious bees that needle me with overplanning and overthinking and overstressing. It's still difficult, sure, but it's not absolute hell. And after the fog of those first few weeks at Liam's house, I've unearthed my old running routine day by day. Some-times I go in the morning, before the summer heat has had a chance to sink into the asphalt, or I wait until the cusp of twilight when everything is shaded a soft blue.

But the second I step out of the door today, I know this run's going to be misery. Texas's midafternoon heat is especially brutal, and already I can see the hot air sizzling over the concrete farther down the road. Immediately I start to sweat.

I begin with a light jog to warm up. I'm sorry, I text my mom. I don't feel well today. Can we talk later? I think about texting Liam to ask if he'll pick up a bottle of wine on his way home. I think about texting Noah to tell him that my evening has freed up. Maybe if he can kiss me hard enough, he can chase all of these thoughts into the void where they belong, where I can pretend I've slotted them away and ignore them forever. I think about texting Addison and wonder if there's a professional way to tell her to go fuck herself, despite how accommodating she's been this whole time. I think—

I have to stop *thinking*.

Fuck it, warm-ups be damned. I have to move. If I don't start running now, I'll actually have to grapple with all of the feelings that interview brought rushing to the surface.

I run like I'm racing my shadow. I run like there's someone chasing me. I'd fled from Liam's house so fast that I hadn't even bothered to grab my headphones, and I can hear every frantic slap of my shoes pounding against the sidewalk. Thankfully, I don't see anyone. No one is insane enough to be outside in Texas when the temperature is at its peak. So it's just me, the cloudless sky, and the orb of the sun glaring down on me.

It takes a while for the pain to come. Even with the brutal pace I'm setting, my body has become used to this. At first I'm like a bird freed from its cage, marveling at the release. If I can just run fast enough, maybe I can escape into the sky and never have to return to figure all this shit out. Energy hums through every limb, pushing me forward farther and faster.

And then the sides of my thighs start to burn.

My lungs can't move fast enough, can't pull in oxygen quickly enough to supply my screaming muscles. Sweat pours down my face, and with each step I take, the heat sucks away at my energy and resolve.

Within five minutes of my sprint, I'm forced to stop in my tracks.

I suck in great gulps of air. I gave too much in the beginning, and now I have nothing left.

Just like at Incite, I think ruefully.

As I stop and hunch over, my hands braced on my knees, the emotions come flooding back.

What the fuck am I even *doing*?

Why the hell do I continue to pursue a job when I've dreaded every single interview I've had? Every time I slink back into the role of Josephine, it's like I'm tugging on a jacket that I've long since grown out of. The seams are frayed and stressed. The buttons strain all the way up to my chin and I can barely breathe. Every time I log off of an interview, I want to hide. Why do I continue to pretend that I might enjoy a job I'm literally running from?

I could stop running. I could rest. It's been two months in the Lone Star State, what's two more? What's five more?

What's a year?

Maybe I can rent Liam's second floor from him. We could live together again, just like we did in college, and I wouldn't feel so much like I'm taking advantage. I can bounce around between jobs, figure it out as I go, try something new. Maybe Morgan can show me around Austin, and we can all go out dancing. Maybe Noah will discover he loves it here just as much as I do, and he'll stay, too.

Panting, I stare at the crack in the pavement where a shoot of green grass has burst through.

Give me a fucking break, Sadie, I snap internally. *You're overreact-*

ing. You're stronger than this. It's my voice, but with my old manager's tone. *What are you going to do, just give up on your career? After everything you've worked for?*

The seed of doubt takes root, tangling my thoughts and squeezing my heart miserably.

I flip to the other side of the coin. The darker side.

What the fuck am I even doing in *Texas*?

I'm fooling myself if I think that I could live here long-term. Sure, I'm making good money from the mural—but it's not exactly full-time work. It pays the grocery bills, but it wouldn't pay rent. And would I even want to do it full time? I'd have to do several murals a *month* just to get to the level I'd been at Incite. And I'd bet having to financially rely on my passion in that manner would suck the joy right out of it.

Maybe Paragon doesn't spark the same level of enthusiasm that art currently does for me, but I'd be lying if I told myself that it's not a good fit on paper. I try to rationalize my terror, try to tell myself that all of my panic surrounding this new job is rooted in the fear of how my old one ended. Just because things were shit at Incite doesn't mean that Paragon's bound to be the same. Right?

Right?

I'm fully spiraling now, but I can't stop myself from riding the wave.

If I could just figure out how to overcome my fear that I'll fail if I try again, my dread that maybe I'm just not cut out for this industry or for New York—I'd be fine. If I could just drag my perspective back into shape, build a healthier relationship with my work, forge a new relationship with—

A new relationship.

Noah.

I clench my jaw. My thoughts sour.

At the very least, I shouldn't be making any plans where Noah is concerned.

He's the antithesis of a plan. He's everything that's chaotic and good, hopping from state to state with careless abandon, always seeking adventure and never staying long enough to grow roots. He's the dictionary definition of *winging it*. He could be plotting out Alchemist's new location with Dan right now. Maybe he's sitting at home, mapping out our camping trip just as he starts to wonder which trail he'll disappear down next.

He makes everything feel so easy—so effortlessly simple. But days like today prove that things are much more complicated than that.

As I sit with my head between my knees, the heat burns away all the delusional daydreams I've had during my time here until I'm left with hard, bitter facts.

Stop.

I swallow thickly.

Take a deep breath in for me.

I follow the memory of his voice, scrunching my eyes closed and sucking in a deep breath.

Take it one day at a time, okay?

I press the heels of my hands into my eyes and shake my head. And then, finally—something breaks.

One day at a time.

Okay. I exhale in a rush.

I'm soaked like I've run for miles, but I'm not very far from the house at all. My formerly bouncy curls stick limply to my face as I start to walk back to Liam's. Every time my thoughts creep back toward the decision I'll have to make in the next few weeks, I focus instead on my breathing. In. Four steps forward. Out. Four steps more. In . . .

One day at a time.

"Do you know any campfire songs, bard?" I ask.

The campsite Noah chose is perfect for a first timer like me. It's only an hour outside of Heller, and it's private enough that we don't hear yelling from the truck full of frat boys I saw pulling in after us, but modern enough that Noah's got an electric hookup for his van and I've got showers and restrooms in case I'm not ready to shit in the woods. Not to mention, it's gorgeous. Situated up in the hills surrounding the river, we've got an incredible view of the water below. It's late afternoon, but I can still spot a few boats lingering on the lake, soaking up the last hours of sunshine.

"Do *I* know any campfire songs?" Noah's tone is teasingly mocking. "What do you take me for, Sadie, an amateur?"

He starts to sing as he unpacks the back of the van. His voice is charmingly off-tune, but he makes up for it with a good helping of enthusiasm and a fantastic memory for every line of an old Decemberists song. I make myself unhelpful, sitting in the bed of the van with an open bottle of mead cradled between my thighs, my legs dangling above the ground and my heels keeping the beat against the bumper.

"I'm surprised you were able to get the weekend off," I say, watching as he kneels to coax a fire to life on the kindling. Half the reason we tend to play D&D on Sunday mornings is because of Noah's busy weekend evening work schedule. "I'm sure Dan's missing you."

"Oh, he'll be fine. I've put in more than enough hours this week anyway." Noah exhales gently onto the budding fire. Sparks fly up and around his face. He reminds me of Loren, casting magic.

"What's the sudden rush?"

"We're a bit of a hot spot around town lately, Sadie," Noah says, not a small amount of pride in his tone. "Dan's got tons of ideas for events to bring people in, and they seem to be working. He's got me in charge of at least half of them."

"Like what?"

"Game nights, live music, art markets, private events. The game nights are a hit so far. He's looking for someone to DM a D&D campaign, actually. Do you think Liam might be up for it?"

"It would be hard for him during the school year, but we could ask." I tilt my head back against the wall of the van. "Honestly, Noah, I think you should DM."

Noah lets out a low laugh. When I don't echo it, he looks up and considers me with surprise. "You really think so?"

"You're a natural storyteller."

"Liam does so much prep, though. So much research and planning, I . . ."

"Make it all up. Improvise. Your style doesn't have to match his."

He seems to consider this as he watches the kindling finally start to spark. "I'll think about it," he muses. His knees pop when he stands, and he wanders over to pluck the bottle of mead from my lap. "But yeah, Alchemist is doing great."

Of course I can't help but wonder whether Alchemist's buzzing success is doing more to attach Noah to Heller or to convince him of how successful another location in Colorado would be.

As if he can sense the direction of my wandering thoughts, Noah ducks into the van and distracts me with a quick kiss to my

cheek—just as he gathers my hands and tugs me from my lounging space. "Come on, show's over. I need your help."

I want to press him with questions, but as soon as he pulls out
the folded-up tent, I'm distracted. "We're not sleeping in the van?"
I'd really been looking forward to testing that mattress out.

"Hell no. You asked for an adventurer-style camping trip. You're
getting one."

He begins to flap a tarp out over a little square of space where I
realize a tent is meant to go. It looks awfully small. Awfully *cozy*, if
I'm being optimistic.

Noah scoffs playfully at me. "Do you think Jaylie would sleep in
the van?"

"Given the choice? Of course."

"Well, this is how Loren would do it. And there are no vans in
D&D."

I won't admit it, but I'm grateful to have a task as involved as
setting up the tent to occupy my mind. I follow each of his directions as best I can, but there are still half a dozen times where I
nearly poke his eye out with a tent pole, the fabric almost rips, or
the whole thing deflates entirely.

After we manage to set it up, we start prepping for dinner as the
sun begins to dive down toward the lake. I drop a blanket and a
couple of pillows in front of the fire while Noah breaks out a surprisingly fancy-looking Dutch oven. He proceeds to fill it with
tortilla chips, beans, salsa, avocado, and an absurd amount of
cheese. "Nothing beats campfire nachos," he assures me. "Nothing."

I purse my lips. "There are no nachos in D&D," I point out.

But Noah audibly guffaws. "You're telling me D&D has fire-
balls, beholders, and magic beyond our comprehension—but no
wizard ever thought to make nachos? What else is arcane knowledge *for*?"

I consider that but then shake my head. "I thought we were

supposed to be imitating our characters and what it's like to adventure through the forest. I doubt either of our characters are a high enough level for nacho-sorcery."

Noah ponders this. "I could probably catch a fish," he says eventually, eyeing the lake down below. "But it would take me a few more hours than nachos would."

It's a concession I'm willing to make. "Nachos it is."

Although the nachos may not be canon food in Liam's fantasy world, the rest of the evening feels positively magical. After we take turns disentangling chips and stuffing our faces, I lean against Noah's side as he strums ineffectually at his ukulele. From our perch on the ledge, we watch the dying light to the west paint the water a dozen shades of orange and purple. As we pass the bottle of mead back and forth—"This one is a special wildflower recipe," he boasts—everything begins to blend together. The shadows cast by the trees stretch longer, the darkness deepens, the temperature finally lets up, and I'm hyperaware of all skin contact: Noah's shoulder against mine, his hand tucked between my thighs where I have them curled against his hip.

Annoyingly, my mind wanders to the furthest thing from peace. "I made it to the final round of interviews," I say eventually, as if set on ruining the mood. Earlier this week, Addison sent through my tickets for the last interview on Tuesday.

"Are you excited?"

This time I don't deflect. "No."

"Then why are you going?"

It's a question I've asked myself a hundred times this week alone. "I think . . . there are parts of the job I would like. Aspects I could grow to love, even. My manager is very sweet, and I'd have more control over my own schedule. I'd be able to set better boundaries." I prop my chin in my hand. "I just feel like I've got to see it again. Like I've got to stand in the middle of Manhattan and look up at all the skyscrapers and ask myself if I'm really ready to leave all of it behind."

Noah's expression is understanding as he looks at me. Firelight ripples across his chin and flickers in his eyes. "Then I think you should go."

I frown. "That's not the advice I thought you would give."

"Why not?"

Maybe it's the mead. Maybe it's the fact that he never dodges any of my questions that makes me brave. "Maybe I want you to tell me that you don't want me to go. That I should stay."

Gently, he cups my hand in his and leans forward to kiss the inside of my wrist. "If you decide to stay, Sadie," he says quietly, "it should be because you explored every option and found the one that's best for you. I would never hold you back from that. If you decide to stay in Heller, wouldn't it mean so much more if you made that choice after seeing everything this job has to offer? It'll make the decision harder, sure, but at least you'll make it knowing you left no stone unturned."

"But what if it's the wrong decision?" My throat feels thick. "What if I love the job, but I lose you guys?" *What if I lose you?* "Or what if I stay, and the art doesn't work out? Or, worse, I start to resent it? What if I stay, and you . . . don't?"

Noah squeezes my hand. "Then we just make the next right decision," he murmurs, like it's the simplest thing in the world.

For a few heartbeats, all I can hear are the crickets and the crackling of the fire and, very far off, the hush of water lapping at the stones below. It's the type of advice that rings with obvious truth, despite how difficult it is to actually follow. I stand up suddenly, dig through our supplies, and bring back the s'mores ingredients. This time, it's my choice to change the subject.

"Have you been to New York before?"

"There are some places in the Adirondacks I want to visit . . . but no, I haven't been to the city itself yet," he says with a laugh. "Believe it or not, though, I used to live in downtown Chicago. For a few years, actually. That's New York–ish, isn't it?"

"Really?" I turn to him, curious. "I figured you were incapable of living anywhere more than half a mile from a trail."

"You'd think, right?" He pokes a stick into the fire. "I mean, obviously I bounced off pretty hard from it. It was after that when I bought the van and really started traveling."

"What were you doing in Chicago?"

"I'm from Illinois, actually. But I moved into the city when . . ." He pauses and looks at me seriously. "Don't laugh."

"I won't laugh."

"I was an accountant."

It's too much. At the thought of him with his shirt buttoned to his chin, a tie wrung around his neck, beard neatly trimmed and hair slicked back into a professional bun—well, I don't laugh, but my grin is impossible to hide. "It's hard to imagine you as a fancy businessman, Noah."

"I'll save you the trouble, then." He pulls out his phone and starts scrolling through old pictures. I catch flashes of selfies at Alchemist, shots of Noah and a group of strangers posing at the summit of some mountain, pictures of beer and random dogs on trails. Finally he taps one of the photos to enlarge it on the screen and passes his phone over.

It's a professional headshot of a serious man in a white button-up shirt.

"Is this your dad?"

"You're so funny, Sadie. Have I ever told you?" His tone drips with endearing sarcasm.

I barely recognize the Noah in this photo. For one, he's clean-shaven; I bet I could cut myself on the lines of his long, angular jaw. His red hair is trimmed short on the sides, and though it's longer on top, it's too short to show off any of his natural curls. He's thinner than he is now, too. Without any of the masculine raggedness of his long hair and beard, he almost looks pretty. Elegant. His features remind me of Loren, smooth and elven, but his unsmiling expression is nothing like Noah. The Noah I know is always smiling.

"I liked my imagination better," I admit.

He presses his lips to my temple. "And what were you imagining, hm?"

"I was trying to remember whether I remembered how to undo the knot of a tie."

"Mm." He slides his hand up the side of my ribs, his thumb skimming the underside of my breast through my shirt. "It's easy. I could show you."

But I'm not ready to be distracted yet. "Why did you leave?"

"Truthfully, I liked the work fine. Accounting's like a puzzle if you look at it the right way. Even now I still do some work for Dan. But the culture I was part of in Chicago wasn't much fun. And I got tired of how cold it was."

I don't know if he's talking about the people or the city—maybe both. His gaze pans away for a moment as he looks into the fire. He's so beautiful in this light. The golden glow from the flames makes his hair shine that much redder, the light catching on each individual unbound curl. I'm so glad he grew it out.

When Noah looks at me again, there's a soft vulnerability in his expression that wasn't there before. I fix my attention on the way his lips part hesitantly.

"I moved away after a tough breakup," he says eventually. "When I left, I didn't know where I wanted to go. All I knew was that I wanted to get out."

I don't have time to ask whether he wants to talk about it. He just does.

"We were high school sweethearts, both grew up in a tiny suburb outside of Chicago. I begged her to come with me to Colorado for school, and I was really excited to try something different from what we were used to. She liked it fine, but the plan was always for us to move back home to be close to her family. That was always The Plan."

He smiles at me like it's an inside joke, but I'm on the outside of it.

"We went back after we graduated, and I followed all the steps as she laid them out. We'd live together in the city for a few years, her as a nurse at the hospital and me at a firm. We'd adopt a dog, save up as much money as possible, buy a house, I'd get a ring . . ." He ticks off each step on his fingers as he speaks.

"I loved her enough, I thought, that I was happy to go along with it. I don't know how she got so sick of everything, when it was all her idea." He reaches over to pat my thigh consolingly, as if I'm the one experiencing the breakup.

"She cheated on me with a guy from the hospital," he says finally. "Took the dog and said she couldn't keep living such a 'railroaded life.'"

"Not the dog." My voice is small. What else am I supposed to say?

"That part was for the best, at least," he says with a laugh. It's an empty echo of humor. "God, he was the most pitiful little thing, Sadie. The tiniest, laziest dachshund. I couldn't take him on a walk longer than a mile. He was devoted to her anyway." Noah scratches his beard and clears his throat. "So I decided that if she wasn't going to live a railroaded life, neither was I. When I first decided to leave, I just wanted a big change, you know? Something that would give me the same open-air adventure feeling that college had." He exhales sharply, and I can't tell if it's another laugh or a frustrated sigh. "I got over her, but I haven't gotten over the rush of traveling. I haven't slowed down since. I don't know if I know how.

"So." He exhales the word in one great big rush. He reaches

toward me and threads his fingers through my hair. "That's why I left."

I lean into his palm. "Thanks for telling me. I'm sorry—I'm so sorry it happened like that."

"It was shitty. But I don't regret anything I've done since." He caps a stick with a marshmallow as he continues. "She gets the lion's share of the blame for how things ended, sure, but if I'm honest, I was going through the motions as much as she was. Of course she shouldn't have cheated on me, but I wasn't a good partner, either. By that point, we'd both stopped trying. For years."

"Did she ultimately shake things up, like you did? After it ended?"

Noah snorts. It's loud enough that I jump. "No, she settled down with the PA. Last I heard from my sister, they're still in Chicago with their second kid on the way."

Fucking hell. As soon as Noah sees my sympathetic wince, he musses my hair. "It's fine, Sadie, really." He hands me the prepped marshmallow stick before getting to work on his.

"Have you ever been tempted to stay anywhere since then?" I ask.

We both stick our marshmallows into the fire. I let mine roast gently atop the tallest flames and watch it darken to a pretty golden brown.

Noah sticks his marshmallow right where the fire's hottest. It immediately catches aflame, and he lets it burn. "Not really. Everywhere I've been, I've always hit a point where it's made sense to get moving again. When I was a park ranger, I waited until the season was over. In Montana, I left when my landlord started losing her marbles. When I was a camp counselor, I left after the summer ended. Or sometimes my friend groups would start to drift apart, or other people would start leaving, so. Maybe I'm worried about getting stuck—rolling stone and moss and such. I'm afraid to stay in one place long enough for it to get boring."

"Are you bored of Texas? Of our friends?" *Are you bored of me?* I don't say it, but it hangs unspoken between us.

"No, Sadie, of course not. I'm waiting for people to get bored of *me*."

He's squinting at the stars like the light pains him. My chest clenches. Suddenly, my perspective on his extroverted demeanor and aggressive friendliness shifts. What part does he feel like he has to play to keep people's interest? I wonder if that's how his ex made him feel, when their relationship ended. Like betraying his trust was somehow justified because she'd lost interest in the life they'd built—because she'd lost interest in *him*.

Just as I'm about to reach for him and draw his face back down to me, Noah jerks suddenly and blows out the flame boiling his marshmallow. It's completely charred, and it bubbles and drips like white lava. He barely manages to nestle it in between the graham cracker and chocolate piece that I hold out for him before it melts clean off the stick. I eye the obliterated marshmallow with suspicion and a sudden surge of affection.

"No one could ever get bored of you, Noah," I say gently. *You're impossible to forget, Loren.* "Not when you make s'mores like a psychopath."

He finally turns back to me, and his expression is like sunshine again. "It's the best way. Try it."

Hesitantly, I trade the golden-brown perfection of my s'more for his monstrosity. I carefully bite into it. There's a definite smokiness to it, and I'm alarmed to hear the crunch of the char flaking off. But once I reach the gooey part in the middle—

"*Fuck.*" Except my mouth's full when I say it, so it just comes out as a grunt of satisfaction. Melted chocolate dribbles down my chin.

"I told you. I tried to tell you."

I hold up the s'more. "This one's mine now."

"Consider it a gift."

Within moments it's gone, and I gaze into the night with eyes half-lidded in bliss.

"Sadie." Noah laughs, turning fully to face me. "Sadie, you're a mess."

Even as I start to smile, I can feel the sticky remnants of the marshmallow on my lips.

"Let me help you."

He grabs for my hand, his fingers easily circling my wrist as he presses a teasing kiss to the pad of my thumb. He sucks at it lightly, and his tongue draws a swirling wake of warmth along my skin, catching the last rivulets of dripping chocolate. I shiver on instinct, and he tugs me forward.

"You've got some here," he murmurs, pressing another kiss to the corner of my lips. "And here." He traces a line of heat down my jawline. "Here, too." His teeth skim down my throat.

My laugh is low and breathy. "There's no way."

"You just taste so sweet, maybe I can't tell the difference." He burrows his nose in the space behind my ear and inhales. His hands move to snake behind my back, and once he's wound his arms around me, he tugs again. I'm pulled flush against his chest as he hums into my shoulder, "Much better."

Not quite. The line of my hips is tilted at an awkward angle against his, and a hidden rock under the blanket digs uncomfortably into the meat of my thigh. I twist further into his hold, swinging my outside leg over his waist until I'm straddling him, my knees nestled on either side of his thighs. Leisurely I twine my fingers behind his neck, my forearms resting lightly on the tops of his shoulders.

"Listen," I say, leaning forward until we're cheek to cheek. My voice is barely more than a sigh exhaled into his hair. "I feel like we were rudely interrupted last weekend."

His words are muffled by the way his lips press to my neck. "Go on."

I roll my hips deliberately forward against him. "I was thinking we could pick up where we left off."

Something hard presses into the back of my thigh again, but this time I'm certain it's not a rock.

He doesn't answer immediately. Instead, he skims his palms down my back, and his touch is light, soft—just the barest brush of his fingertips. I swear I can feel his grip tighten as his hands round my ass, but then it's gentle again as his fingers trace the sides of my thighs, the backs of my knees, the arches of my calves. His touch is slow and studious, like he's trying to memorize the shape of my body. He lightly pinches my heel, and I wonder if he's hesitating.

I wonder if I read the situation wrong.

It wouldn't be the first time.

But then he's inhaling again, and his beard brushes against my bare skin as he noses the neckline of my crop top to the side. He bites into the dip of my collarbone just as his grip tightens suddenly, his arms winding tight around my waist and anchoring me to him. On instinct I rock my hips against him again, and he barely muffles the groan that rumbles against my chest. Through the thin fabric of my tight athletic shorts and the navy-blue nylon of his . . . fuck, it's like we're not wearing anything at all. Heat gathers between my thighs, and I can't help but clench them tighter against his legs—except his are so much *larger* than mine, and an ache builds in my hips where they stretch to make room for him. Where the hardness of him strains against his shorts, I slide myself forward in a slow arc, desperate for the friction.

It's not nearly enough. I need more.

"The tent," he says roughly, his voice strangled. "Get into the tent."

CHAPTER

Twenty-Seven

Blood and mead rush to my head as I bolt upright and we scramble for the tent. I sway in place for a moment while Noah hurriedly tugs at the zipper to the entrance. When it catches against the plastic, he curses, nearly tearing it off in his haste to get inside. I wonder briefly why we're bothering with the tent at all. I peer out into the night, but with no moon in sight and the sun gone hours ago, I can't see anything farther than the bubble of light cast by our own dying campfire. Before I have a chance to fully think it through, Noah finally unlatches the flap and tugs me inside.

Thank fuck we'd already prepped everything when we assembled the tent. Noah had lined the floor with cushioned sleeping pads, two separate sleeping bags (just in case—what a gentleman), the quilt from his van, several pillows, and a small solar-powered lantern. "It would have been too heavy to carry all this on a real backpacking trip," Noah had teased earlier. "But for your first time, Sadie, I've ensured maximum comfort."

As I move to step in after him, Noah stops me with an outstretched hand. "No shoes."

I kick off my sandals. "Anything else you'd like me to take off?"

His eyes darken. "All in good time."

As Noah zips up the tent behind me, I realize how intimate the space is. It's smaller than the bed in Noah's van, and even crouched as I am, my head brushes the top where the poles intersect in the middle. Already Noah's sprawled out in the nest of blankets and sleeping bags, peering up at me through half-lidded eyes. Curling his hand around mine, he gently leads me down until I'm lying at his side, propped up on my elbow. The space between us feels charged with electricity, but I'm not sure how to make the connection again.

I'm not sure where to start.

Noah closes the distance between us. He reaches out to run two fingertips down the curve of my cheek. "Tell me what you want, Sadie."

I short-circuit at the question. What do *I* want? I'm used to following someone else's lead. I hadn't seen anyone seriously in the years since college—I was far too focused on my career for romance, I'd told myself—but I'd had a handful of half-enthusiastic hookups. They'd all known what they wanted from me, whether it was a rough make-out session pressed against the wall in the corner of a sticky dance floor, or ten minutes of quick, unsatisfying missionary on a mattress (sans bed frame) in a Williamsburg apartment. No one had ever asked me what I wanted.

But then, I'd never bothered to ask for it, either.

I'm not sure how to answer him, so I try for the obvious. "I want you." It's the simple truth. To stave off any more questions, I lean forward to kiss him—but he stops me with a finger between our lips. I can smell sugar and chocolate on his breath.

"Tell me what you like." His voice is pitched low, and there's this rough undertone to it that makes my chest ache. "Where do you like to be touched?"

Everywhere, my mind screams. But I chew on the inside of my cheek, quiet.

"What makes you feel good?"

I feel a rush of annoyance that isn't directed at him. I don't—I don't *like* being put on the spot. I like it when someone else is in the driver's seat, making the decisions. While I might not like the destination, it saves me the anxiety of having to decide for myself. What if Noah doesn't like the same things I do?

As I retreat further into myself, Noah runs his palm over my shoulder. "You don't have to say it," he murmurs, butting his nose up against mine. "But can you show me?"

The knot building in my chest stills—then loosens slightly. I lift my hands and splay my fingers experimentally over his chest. The uncertainty drains away, replaced by curiosity. Boldness.

Hunger.

"Can you take this off, please?" I ask, with a finger to his dark gray tee. It comes out more politely than I intend.

Noah chuckles quietly as he shoulders out of his shirt. At the same time, I slip out of my cropped tank. We return to the same positions, both lying on our sides, facing the other, and I reach out again, tracing upward from the softness of his stomach to the wide, muscular plane of his chest.

Again I'm caught off guard by how much lighter and redder the coils of hair clustered here are than the dark curls falling around his face. I reach up to run my hand over his hair as it falls around his neck and shoulders. He looks wilder with it down, more untamed. I like it. As my fingers skate back to his chest, they still over his heart. Although his breathing is carefully even, I can feel his pulse race under his skin.

My hand strays lower. I tuck a finger under the waistband of his shorts and tug—the same motion Jaylie had used to tease Loren. "These, too."

We both peel out of our shorts, and as soon as he's tossed his from his ankle, I roll on top so that I'm straddling him again. His briefs are tight and black and leave nothing to the imagination. I still don't know how to answer his question, but I know from earlier that I like this. It's as good of a place to start as any.

I press my chest to his as I roll my hips against him again. Noah squeezes his eyes shut, jaw clenching as he releases a shaky breath. There are so few layers left between us, I wonder if he can feel the heat rolling off me in waves. With him pressing incessantly between my legs, I wonder if he can feel how wet I am. Gently, I tug at his lower lip with my teeth before kissing him. He groans into my mouth as his hips buck upward to meet mine where I arch against him, and the friction is almost magical. It feels like hours pass this way as our bodies move against each other in the heat of the tent, sweat slicking our skin until we're gliding together. Noah is the first to deepen the kiss, and he tastes like sweets and mead and honey and *him*. As his tongue tangles with mine, warm and slow, I can't help but fantasize about the way it might feel on my—

With a little gasp, I pull back. And then I lean upward.

We come to the same conclusion at the same time.

"Can I . . . ?"

"Yes, Sadie. *Please*," he gasps, like a drowning man who's just been offered water. My mouth goes dry at the naked need in his voice. I lick at my lower lip, swallowing carefully.

"Okay."

I lean backward, enough so that Noah can hook his fingers under my panties and slide them down my legs. I sit up a little, balancing on my knees as Noah shifts his body down. I pause, hesitant, but then his warm palms are on the backs of my thighs and he's easing me forward, guiding me until my knees are by his ears and I'm hovering above him. His breath curls against my inner thighs. Looking down, I see only the top half of his face.

Even in the dark, his eyes sparkle.

"Please," he says again. Every calloused finger brushes against my skin as he drags his hands up my inner thighs. He draws one thumb up between my legs, between my lips, barely touching— but it's enough to make me bite back a whimper. "Please?"

My spine relaxes, and I sink down lower over his face.

The first thing I feel is his beard. It tickles against my skin—so *sensitive*—as he exhales against me. It almost makes me straighten again with surprise.

But it's the first swirl of his tongue that makes my mind go blank.

I forget how to breathe. His tongue moves with the same slow curiosity that it had when he'd licked my fingers clean, when he'd chased the line of melted chocolate down my neck. He tastes me in the same way—sampling, savoring, *sucking*.

I can't help myself. I drop my hips even lower, grinding myself along the line of his tongue, into his jaw. Noah makes a low, pleased sound in the back of his throat. Distantly, I hope he can breathe, even as I struggle to suck oxygen down myself. I sink my fingers into those messy curls, worrying that if I don't have something to hold on to, the ecstasy of it will have me floating off into the night sky like a ghost. As an extra anchor, he slides his hands over the tops of my thighs, pulling me even more solidly down against him.

There's no way he can breathe.

He moves against me in slow, aching circles, and each pass of his tongue sends me closer and closer to the edge. The pressure building in my core feels so heavy with coiling tension that I can barely imagine what will happen when I finally fall in. But Noah, who never rushes anywhere, takes his time. Noah could do this all day, probably. Noah has all the time in the world.

I wonder if he knows that I've got only seconds left.

"Stop," I gasp. The word comes out dry and quiet, like I haven't spoken in days. "Stop."

He draws back immediately. "Is everything okay?" Warmth rushes over me at the concern in his tone.

"God, yes, of course. I just—" I have to swallow twice before moisture floods my mouth again. Even then, I struggle to string together more than five words. "I want more. I want to feel you, before I—I want to feel you first."

I can hear more than see his smile when he speaks. "Okay." He lifts his hands from my thighs but otherwise doesn't move.

Huffing, I swing my leg over his body; my knees are so weak, it's a lot more difficult this time. As I lie on the nest of blankets and stick myself to his side, I press a series of kisses to his ear. "It's your turn, Noah. Show me what you want."

Unlike me, he doesn't need to be told twice.

Gently he snakes his arm under my neck, cradling my face on his shoulder, close to his. God, it's where I'd always dreamed of being—pillowed by his biceps. With his free arm, he reaches for whatever corner of the tent he discarded his shorts in while sliding out of his underwear at the same time. After a moment, there's the familiar crinkle of a little square of foil.

"You really thought of everything," I tease.

"I never venture into nature unprepared."

Suddenly, Noah digs his fingers into my hip and pulls me against him, until my back is flush with his chest and we're spooning. I feel the heaviness of him against the small of my back and my mouth goes dry all over again.

I shift toward him, angling myself a few inches upward and then back again, back until he slides in between my thighs with a groan. I rock forward slightly, and the tip of his cock strokes against my clit. Noah hisses through clenched teeth as I inhale sharply. This close, it's almost enough to unravel me.

But then, Noah draws back slightly, and I know that with just one roll of his hips he'll be inside of me. His free hand slides between my breasts, and his fingers curl gently around the base of my throat. The muscles of his arm flex against my chest. His grip is strong but not choking, just holding me close—holding me so that no matter how I arch against him desperately, he's the one in control.

I understand. We're moving at his pace now, not mine. Impatience and need flare hot in my chest, but the way he makes me wait only makes me want him more.

I swallow, and I know he can feel it. My pulse throbs at my neck, and I know he can feel it.

I turn my head until our foreheads are touching, the bridge of my nose crossing with his. "Please." It's my turn to beg, to ask nicely.

He brushes his lips against mine, back and forth. "Take a deep breath in for me, Sadie," he murmurs.

I inhale.

"Very good."

He sinks into me.

He's slow about it, but he doesn't stop. I don't have a chance to gasp for air or bite down onto something or brace myself. Inch by fucking inch, he doesn't stop until he's buried inside of me, hips flush against my ass. And then he's pulling back again, in and out, steady and measured, and each stroke has me seeing stars.

Despite his even pace, Noah's panting, and we're both sucking air out of the same small space. The air tastes thin; I'm lightheaded. He bends his head to bite my shoulder, muffling a groan that climbs out of his throat. "*God,*" he sighs against my skin. "I can't even begin to tell you how good you feel."

I reach back to tangle my fingers in his hair as the hand on my throat snakes down my sweat-slicked torso. His fingers round my hip, gripping briefly, and then come to hover at my waist. Flexing his other arm, he twists my face back to his. "Stay with me," he says against the corner of my lips, his gaze locking on mine. "Right here." He captures my mouth, swallowing my moan just as his middle finger begins to circle my clit again.

It's like my brain breaks. I'm feeling too much at once. The insistent, rolling thrust of him spreading me apart, the slow dialing of his finger as he winds me tighter and tighter, the slide of his tongue against mine until I don't know where I end and he begins.

It's too much. It's just enough. As he sinks into me again, I fall apart.

I imagine this is what it feels like to be at the bottom of a waterfall as the weight of an entire river cascades over you and breaks you apart until you're nothing but sparkling bones. I gasp his name against his mouth as each violent, shuddering wave of pleasure spears through my limbs. Somehow he presses even deeper into me as I clench around him. Somehow he's still circling his damned finger, coaxing from me every last whimper and pulse and shiver, and fuck me if I never knew it could feel this *good.*

And still he doesn't stop.

His hand skates back up my body and curls at the curve between my neck and shoulder, his arm a heavy brace across my chest. His pace becomes stuttering, ragged. A little off-tempo, a little rushed—and more than a little desperate. Every thrust has my eyes going out of focus, each one an aching echo of the pleasure he wrung out of me. And then suddenly he's biting down hard into my shoulder, every muscle in his body constricting around me like he might just absorb me entirely as he falls from the same cliff I did.

We both collapse boneless onto our backs, panting into the darkness. We stare up through the tent like if we could just squint hard enough, we might see the stars again.

We have no choice but to wake up with the sun. There are no curtains to hide behind, no windows to shut it out. Early in the morning, sunlight shears through the thin fabric of the tent and floods it with light.

Just like Jaylie out in the wilderness, I barely slept, but it wasn't because of any sort of discomfort. Throughout the night, every time I felt my eyes drift closed, I worried he'd disappear. I worried that he was just a dream, some wild fey forest prince who would return to his realm under the cover of darkness. So I'd reach for his hand, or nuzzle into his shoulder, or knock my ankle against his shin just to assure myself that he was still real. It wasn't until he'd gathered me into his arms and folded his body securely around mine that I'd allowed myself to finally drift off.

Noah's eyes are already open when I finally blink awake.

Warmth rushes over me at the sight of him.

It's you.

You're here.

"I am," he murmurs, pressing a kiss to my forehead. I blink rapidly. I didn't realize I said it out loud.

"You're still naked."

He looks down. "I am."

Good, I think, raising my head to press my lips to his. We might not be sleeping in, but I'm not getting out of bed anytime soon.

Hours later, we're finally having a breakfast of granola bars and excellent cold brew coffee from Noah's giant water bottle. I'm wrung out in the best way, and I lounge in one of the camp chairs with my feet propped up on the cooler. We've already cleaned everything up and tucked it all away, and all that's left is to enjoy the morning as it stretches out before us.

"It's true, y'know. What they say," I observe.

From where he's seated on his own chair, Noah tilts his head down to look at me over the rims of his sunglasses. His hair's a mess. We're facing the ledge over the lake, and the sun is already dancing across the water. "What do they say, Sadie?"

"About having sex while camping."

"Please, no," he begs.

I drill my gaze into his. "It's intense." I gesture to where the tent sits, already disassembled and packed up in its bag behind us. *In tents*, I mouth, meaningfully.

His fingertips cluster around his temple as he groans. "Psychic damage. Critical hit." He looks as if he's aged ten years.

I twine my fingers with his, partly because I'm desperate to touch him again, partly because I'm worried he'll run. Maybe that joke was the last straw. "I'll heal you."

He smiles, and his mustache tickles my knuckles where he presses a kiss to the back of my hand.

For a while, we're quiet, and there's peace. We're far enough away from the roads that I hear engines only whenever other campers drive by our site on their way out. Otherwise it's just the birds, the whistle of the wind through the leaves, and the distant lapping of the water below.

There's an ache in my chest fingering its way between my ribs that feels a lot like dread. I'm not ready for this weekend to be over. At the thought of the flight I have to take in a few days, the memory of New York's annual summer reek fills my nose, smothering the fresh scent of the dewy grass surrounding us. I start to mourn that I have only a few sections of the mural left to paint, a few sessions of the campaign left to play, and my mind starts replaying the last conversation I had with Addison. *Have you given any thought to when you'd be available to start?* The memory of her voice is reedier, more demanding.

With the same steady patience as always, Noah pulls me back to earth. He tugs gently on my hand. "Look." He points.

A butterfly flutters around the patches of grass surrounding our site, looking for flowers. It's a common enough sight, but for now it's enough to distract me. To ground me.

Noah squeezes my hand again. "Listen, Sadie." His tone is quiet; it almost blends in with the sounds of nature surrounding us. "Whatever happens over these next few weeks, wherever we end up . . ."

His gaze drifts down to the water again, where a kayak skims the surface of the lake behind a group of ducks.

"Right *now*," he says, "I can't imagine anywhere else I'd rather be."

My muscles unwind, and the knot of tension between my brows unravels. I sigh.

"Me, too."

CHAPTER
Twenty-Eight

Within the circle of Jaylie's spell, the truth is brought to light.

Loren is the first to speak. "Here is the story as we know it thus far . . ."

What follows is a tale that Jaylie can't help but be enraptured by—even though she was present for nearly every second. Shira smirks as Loren describes her rescue of Alora as dashing and dangerous, though she scowls to hear Donati's retelling of their time together at the Academy. She starts to interrupt, but Loren holds up a finger and assures her, "Your turn is next." He continues, weaving a tapestry of the quest that Donati and then Alastair sent them on, and of the party's epic battles against roadside bandits, spiders, and, finally, the beholder. There's real emotion in his voice as he recounts Jaylie's death. *Is he simply a good actor,* she muses, *or did he really miss me that much?* She notes how purposefully vague he is about the details of her resurrection, rushing to summarize the rest of the tale until he arrives at the current moment.

"And that, my friends," he says with a sweeping bow, "is where we find ourselves today."

Shira nods thoughtfully as Alora gazes at Jaylie with wide eyes. "Gods, I didn't know you *died*," she says with a gasp.

"Just for a moment, I'm told," Jaylie says. She thinks back to

Marlana's face, the warmth in her smile. She hadn't told anyone of her meeting with her Lady. The memory feels so holy, maybe she never will.

Shira looks off into the distance, smiling wryly to herself. "Alastair was an apprentice of mine, once. He left when he decided he'd prefer to hoard his secrets and conduct his studies independently," she says. "Obviously that hasn't worked out well for him, since he's clearly coveted my spellbook this whole time. It doesn't surprise me he's helped you all along, hoping to get back at me for his minor punishment."

Jaylie thinks that being turned into a frog is a great deal more than a minor punishment, but then again, she's not a wizard. "We did promise him his spellbook back if we, ah—defeated you."

Shira waves a hand, unconcerned. "I hardly care. Maybe I'll give it back to him, if he asks nicely."

Loren extends his arms in a wide arc, encompassing the circle of the spell. "Whenever you're ready, my lady," he says to Shira, "the floor is yours."

Shira's confidence seems to dim as everyone's attention turns to her. Gently, Alora draws Shira's arm over her shoulders and supports her with a hand on her back. Alora's a good head and a half shorter than Shira, but it's a sweet gesture nonetheless. "I've got a good feeling about them, love," Alora says. "It's all right."

Shira reaches up to brush some of her long hair out of her face; the sunlight catches on a few strands of gray. Her undercut is growing out in uneven patches and needs a fresh shave, and her eyes are ringed in dark circles.

Eventually, Shira sighs, dark violet eyes trained on the ground. "You should know that Donati was telling the truth—in some cases. In school, I did practice dark magic. I still do." She lifts her gaze and casts it around the circle. "But it was Aurelio who introduced me to it.

"He was the one who would knock on my door with an armful

of tomes he'd 'borrowed' from the forbidden sections of the library, or bartered for in the dark alleys of Belandar. From the very beginning, it fascinated me. I was as hungry for the secret knowledge as he was, and so long as we weren't harming others, I was more than willing to immerse myself in our studies. We were both very good at it, but he especially took to it like a duck to water. Our divination spells kept me up late with nightmares. When we cast a ritual spell to speak with one of the cadavers from our biology seminar, I heard the dead's voice for days and days after. One time, using a bit of Aurelio's blood, we summoned a little imp from Hell itself. It lashed out with its claws, and it took weeks for my gash to heal. But Aurelio's wound was no more than a scratch by morning.

"Over time, Aurelio became very interested in blood magic. In retrospect, that's where I should have cut off our studies. Talking to the dead and summoning portals is one thing, but using the life force of other creatures to fuel your magic?" Shira shakes her head vehemently. "It was a line I wouldn't cross. But there was a scholar we had heard of, studying up in the Great North . . ." Shira pauses and smiles a little. She slips her hand into Alora's. "I regret the part I played in furthering Aurelio's experiments, but I don't regret the decisions that led me to her."

"I don't think he knew at the time that we were seeing each other," Alora adds, her voice bright and amused. "He's so dense when it comes to these things. I'm not even certain he knows it now."

"We kept it a secret for a long time," Shira agrees. "In the North, Alora's family is . . ."

"Old-fashioned?" Alora tries.

"Famous."

"Powerful!"

". . . Traditional."

The women go back and forth, then Alora snickers. "I was never destined for a love match," she explains. "They always tried to stress to me how important it was to carry on the bloodline and whatnot. I always planned to run away one day, before that happened."

Jaylie smiles to herself as a rush of admiration and kinship for the woman fills her chest, but her attention snags on the sorceress's sudden scowl.

"Aurelio beat me to it," Alora huffs.

"You're skipping ahead in the story, darling," Shira says, running her hand over Alora's cap of red hair. "Anyway. Around the time we started seeing each other, I'd ferry books back and forth between Alora's personal library and the study Aurelio and I shared in Belandar's Academy. My professor, Lazlo, had taught me the trick of teleportation by that time. And I had taught Aurelio." Although Shira's expression is hard enough to be carved from stone, Jaylie is close enough to watch her dark eyes grow wet. "I wasn't there when it happened—I was with Alora. When I returned, Aurelio cornered me in our study, his eyes dilated and his face flushed with excitement. He said he'd finally done it. His summoning spell had worked. He showed me where he'd trapped the thing—this ugly devil with black spines—behind the shining bars of a magical cage.

"Immediately I started throwing open the closets, searching every room. I'd read the books. I'd seen the spells. To perform feats of magic this powerful . . . I knew the cost."

Jaylie understands now why Alora pressed herself so close to Shira's side. For a moment, it looks like Shira might collapse, but Alora holds her up while the wizard presses her palm to her eyes. "I found him in Aurelio's office, in the summoning circle. There wasn't a drop of blood left in his body.

"Aurelio came up behind me and put a hand on my shoulder. 'He would have reported us immediately,' he said. 'We would have been expelled. I had no other choice.' And he pointed to Professor Lazlo's body and set him on fire. He let him burn until there was nothing left but ash."

Shira straightens and wipes her eyes. "He beat me to the dean, weaving his story of Lazlo's false disappearance, how his experiment might have gone wrong. Desperate, I tried to tell them my story—the *real* story—but as soon as Aurelio realized we weren't a team anymore, he turned against me. And he was always one step ahead—it was like he'd planned for what he called 'my betrayal' all along. He showed them my spellbooks, my studies, my notes. My research into dark magic wasn't at all on the level of what he was capable of, but it was enough to get me expelled. It was enough that they didn't trust my word when I tried to convince them that he was the real danger.

"For years I've been trying to prove that he is at fault. Lazlo's is not the only life he's taken. I've collected so many reports of missing people in Belandar. The gardener at his estate, one of the students from his class, two maids from the Academy. Dozens more. But when Lora was taken, I—" She swallows thickly. "I know how it looked when I stole her from their wedding. I know what it does to my reputation. But I couldn't let her stay with him, not when I know what he's capable of."

There's a ringing silence following Shira's words. Kain has his arms crossed, a pensive look sketched into his hard features, while Loren writes down a few notes. *Likely composing the next chapter to our story,* Jaylie thinks.

But there are gaps in the tale.

"I still don't understand your part in this, Alora," Jaylie says gently. "Why did you agree to the wedding at all?"

"Oh! I didn't. Of course I didn't." She points to Kain, his axe still held threateningly at his side. "Hilariously, he was right about the whole enchantment thing. But it was Aurelio who enchanted me, not Shira. When he first made his proposal, my parents were delighted to accept. He had it all: power, prestige, political standing. And he arrived with *so* many gifts." She grimaces at the memory, full lips pressed in a pout. "I hated him, of course. Shira had told me everything by that point. But for appearances' sake, before the proposal was finalized, I accepted his gifts. And when my maid clasped the necklace around my neck—" She snaps her fingers. "My mind was gone, locked under his charm. Honestly, I can't recall anything that happened between that point and when Shira disenchanted it."

"It was a hell of a thing," Shira mutters. "It would have been a lot easier if I'd had something like *that*." She juts her sharp chin in the direction of the orb.

Again, the circle is quiet. Jaylie can't think of any other questions to ask, and the others look properly satisfied. Kain is the first to speak. He strikes the butt of his axe loudly on the cobblestones. "Well," he rumbles. "I suppose we'll just have to kill him, then, won't we?"

Loren frowns to himself. "He does deserve it, I think."

Jaylie blanches. "We'll want to clear Shira's name first," she stresses. "Or they'll paint us all as the villains of the story."

Kain bares his teeth in a fanged grin. "I've been the villain many times before. It's made no difference to me, so long as I can sleep at night."

"Wise words, Kain," Morgana barks with a laugh. "I'm in."

Loren rubs his palms together. "Well, then. We'll need a plan, won't we?"

Shira ducks her head in one sharp nod. "Of course. Yes. Come with me."

As the others rush away to begin their preparations, Jaylie stops Alora and draws her to the side. They stand underneath an awning covered in vines raining purple leaves as Jaylie wrings her hands nervously.

"I just want to tell you how sorry I am," she starts. Her throat is tight and there's pressure behind her eyes, making it difficult to continue. "If I had known what Donati had done to you, if I'd known that you were under that spell . . . I would have never gone through with the wedding. It's such a sacred ceremony, and I hate that you were forced into it. However unknowingly, I hate that I played a part in it."

Alora reaches forward and clasps Jaylie's hands in her own. "There is nothing to apologize for, priestess. As you said, you had no idea." She squeezes Jaylie's hands comfortingly. "The ceremony was never completed, anyway. We are not married. I am not bound to him."

Jaylie releases a breath she hadn't known she was holding, feeling an invisible weight lift from her shoulders. She bows her head over Alora's hands and presses a brief kiss to her knuckles. "Thank you."

When she lifts her head again, a small smile curves at the corners of her lips. "I was thinking, if you ever do desire to be married . . . Well. I would be honored to bless your marriage. I imagine your allegiances may be with other gods, or you may not wish for it to be *me* if it would remind you of all that's happened, but—the offer stands. Should you ever wish it."

Alora is quiet for some time. She peers upward at the purple vines swaying around them, and when she looks back to Jaylie, her gaze is intent. "How soon could you conduct the ceremony?"

Jaylie blinks. "As soon as you like."

"Come with me."

As per Alora's instructions, Jaylie waits to enter the garden until the moon is at its highest peak in the sky. On her way down the spiraling stairs of Shira's tower, she gently knocks against Loren's door. The tower is much bigger on the inside than it appears—impossibly so, really—and Shira had gladly provided rooms for each adventurer. As Jaylie waits for him to answer, she gently cradles a ball of pink light in her cupped hands.

The light illuminates the bard flatteringly when he opens the door wide, seemingly careless of the fact that he wears nothing more than his undergarments. He poses in the doorway, arm propped against the frame, hip jutted out to the side.

"I've prayed this day would come," he says confidently, his voice pitched low. "Are you here to finally answer my prayers, priestess?"

"Marlana's mercy, Loren," Jaylie hisses. "No!" She pauses. Considers. *Maybe later* . . . "Not now. I need your help with something."

Loren deflates, but as Jaylie steps close to whisper her plan in his pointed ear, his expression brightens with intrigue. ". . . It's what she wants, but it also means her parents never get to make the choice for her," she finishes. "How quickly can you get ready?" Her dark eyes take in Loren's state of undress, though this time, she lets her gaze linger.

"You'd be surprised by how many times I've had to dress quickly to make a grand escape."

"I don't think I'd be surprised at all, actually."

Loren huffs. "Give me a few moments." And then, teasingly, "Would you like to watch?"

Jaylie rolls her eyes. "Loren, *hurry.*"

In an impressively short amount of time, Jaylie and Loren rush down the staircase hand in hand. Loren has his lute strapped over his shoulder and sports a beautifully embroidered emerald jacket and black dress pants. Jaylie herself is dressed in her ceremonial robes of peach, pink, and cream. She steps carefully to keep her garlands of gold coins from clinking noisily as they descend.

When they exit the tower, Jaylie leads Loren through the gardens, following the directions that Alora gave her earlier. *Right at the pond with the water lilies, left at the daffodils, and then right again at the white roses—but the second bunch, not the first, all right? The ones next to the wind chimes.*

Finally, they arrive at the curtain of pale purple wisteria that Alora described as the final turn. Gently, Jaylie pushes the flowers aside and steps into a small, enclosed space. Between the walls of greenery and the lattice of flowers hanging from above, there's barely enough room for three people to stand shoulder to shoulder. Tucked into the center of the square space is a small smooth shrine: a stone bowl of water, an offering of honey and flowers, a mirror, and several lit candles. The shrine is dedicated to no god in particular, but the ritual materials are there, available for anyone who needs a moment to pray.

Alora and Shira stand before the shrine, and they both turn as Jaylie and Loren approach. Silver moonlight catches in the dark strands of Shira's hair, newly cut and woven into a complex braid sprinkled with pale white flowers. She wears a black dress with embroidery of such a dark purple that it's difficult to pick out the patterns. Alora wears none of the lace or frills that Jaylie had seen at her wedding with Donati. Instead, she's fashioned tulle and silk into the shapes of flowers that flow down the back of her white skirt. Both women look at Jaylie with wide eyes, as if they're two teenagers caught kissing in the garden hours after dark.

Jaylie smiles softly. "Are you ready?"

"I think so," Shira says. Her tone is nervous and light, void of its usual deep, commanding growl.

"Yes." Alora's voice is so full of warmth that Jaylie's heart aches just to hear it.

Shira asks, "What do we need to do?"

At Jaylie's nod, Loren positions himself behind her and begins to pluck lightly at his lute. It's a gentle song, and at first, Jaylie can barely pick out the melody. But as the song flows from his fingers—light and tender, soft and sweet—she breathes out a peaceful, happy sigh. Even Shira's shoulders ease, falling from where they were hunched nervously at her ears. Alora's eyes sparkle with unshed tears.

"Now," Jaylie says quietly, "I will cast the ritual spell, and Loren will pay witness. But this promise you are about to make—it is between you two and no one else. We will not hear the vows you speak, but you will be bound to them nonetheless." Hours before, when Jaylie had planned everything out with Alora and Shira, they had both stressed their desire for as private a ceremony as possible. None of the pomp, frills, or spectacle of Donati's wedding—just the two of them and the love they shared, as it had been between them since the beginning. "Join hands, please," Jaylie murmurs.

As Loren's music swells, Jaylie removes a ribbon of coins from around her waist and begins to bind Shira's and Alora's hands together, palm to palm. With each loop of the ribbon, gold and pink magic swells from where their hands touch. A sphere of light blooms between the women, expanding until just the two of them are bound in a bubble of gold. The light catches on Shira's jewelry and on the subtle pattern of dragon scales underneath Alora's skin. Jaylie smiles, ties the knot across Alora's knuckles, and nods.

Haltingly, Shira begins to speak, her eyes darting sidelong toward Jaylie and Loren. Jaylie watches her lips move, but she can hear nothing other than Loren's playing, the tinkling of a far-off fountain, and the chirping of crickets in the distance. Shira's eyes widen with realization, and when she turns back to Alora, her expression is earnest.

Jaylie cannot tell for how long they speak. Time passes strangely within the influence of the spell, and the small space feels charged with emotion and divinity. Slowly, Jaylie takes a few steps back until she stands at Loren's side. She allows her head to fall onto his shoulder as he plays, though she never takes her gaze from the couple as they make their vows. Though Jaylie does not know what promises they make to each other, at the end, there is one phrase she recognizes as it flows from Alora's lips.

I love you, she says. *I love you* and *I love you* and *I love you.*

CHAPTER
Twenty-Nine

"You had me in tears, Sadie! It was so sweet!" Jules gushes.

I turn to look at her in the back seat, where she's fanning at her eyes dramatically. Morgan is smiling, too, but she keeps her gaze on the road. Each member of the D&D group had offered to give me a ride to the airport Monday afternoon for my interview. I was unexpectedly touched, but I'd missed Morgan and Jules. Not to mention, a gossip-filled drive with them seemed the best way to distract myself from my complicated feelings about returning to the city.

"Remember, I *told* y'all Shira and Donati were never a thing." Morgan slaps the steering wheel for emphasis. "I *knew*."

"And for Shira to whisk Alora away like that?" Jules swoons, her eyes full of stars.

"I loved the secret wedding, too, Sadie," Morgan says with a sigh, her tone wistful. "When I first signed on to play this game, I never expected that it could be like this. I thought it'd be a lot of fighting and shenanigans, not . . ."

"Emotional character deaths, magic frogs, and heart-stopping romance?" I say helpfully.

"Exactly," Morgan says, laughing. "I never realized D&D was going to be this *involved*."

"That's the best part!" Jules says, dancing in her seat. After a beat of silence, she taps her fingers together mischievously. "Speaking of involved . . ."

"Oho." Morgan catches on immediately. Her eyes flash sidelong to me. "How was that camping trip, Sadie? Was it as hot as we warned you it'd be?"

"Steamy, even?" Jules pokes.

"What was it like, pitching a tent for the first time?"

"Did you have enough wood for a fire?"

I groan loudly and cover my face with my hands, but my friends have my ribs aching with laughter in no time. Although I tease them with hints, arriving in the drop-off lane saves me from sharing too much detail. Jules and Morgan are sweet enough to not say goodbye as I stand on the curb. Jules rolls down her window and waves enthusiastically, setting her charm bracelets jingling. "Good luck, Sadie! We'll see you soon!"

Morgan blows me a kiss. "Saturday morning, right?"

"Right at noon," I say.

It had been a last-minute decision to stay in the city for a few more days after tomorrow's interview. *No stone unturned*, I'd thought, remembering Noah's advice. I haven't yet figured out what I'm going to do with all the time, but for once, I don't mind not having a plan. This is all about feeling things out anyway. Besides, the mural is nearly finished, and I'm confident I'll complete it next week without any rush. I have time.

Morgan wiggles her fingers at me as she rolls the car's window up. "We'll be here."

The flight is long, but I sketch the time away as afternoon bleeds into evening. On my tablet, Noah's van and tent are tucked into the trees, glowing in sunset colors of orange, yellow, and pink. When the city comes into view through the tiny plane window, thousands of lights sparkling like beacons against the night, I look up on instinct. That familiar tug of awe blooms between my lungs.

Whatever my feelings for New York may be, the glittering view of the city from above will never get old.

To avoid my Craigslist roommates, who dislike me almost as much as they dislike each other, I drop off my things in my dusty bedroom and immediately leave. Even before I went to Heller, I didn't spend much time here, opting instead to busy myself with after-work happy hours, runs in the park, and late nights in the office . . . Okay, so mostly late nights in the office.

But if I'm going to give this job every last opportunity to woo me, as Noah suggested, then my first step is a romantic night of taking myself out to dinner.

I start the evening five blocks down from my apartment at my favorite rooftop sushi bar. It's by far the most impressive date night spot that I know of, with happy hour cocktails to die for and little candles lit on every table, and yet I'd never invited any dating app boys here. I saved this spot for every time Liam visited me in the city. We'd pay extravagant prices for half a dozen drinks and nearly every app on the menu, then play a game of guessing which other diners were tourists and which were locals. It was usually easy to tell based on who was staring out toward the water, trying to spot peeks of Manhattan.

After a half hour's wait, I'm seated at a small table against the railing; it's the best view you could ask for. There's a thin sliver of open air visible through the last cluster of buildings in Queens, and I'm able to see far enough through the clear night to pick out the twinkling yellow lights at the top of the Empire State Building.

I remember the first time Liam and I visited New York on a high school field trip. After the afternoon showing of *Wicked*, we'd both stared up at the massive skyscraper. I pointed at the top. "We're gonna live up there one day, you and me."

Liam rolled his eyes. "There aren't apartments in the Empire State Building, Sadie. Nobody lives there. Anyway, it would be the worst place to live in the whole city."

"Why? Everyone would be jealous."

"What if the elevator goes out?"

I pressed my lips together. "That's a fair point."

I smile at the memory; it makes me miss Liam. I can't help but feel like I'm looking at New York through his eyes now. The city is always worth admiring, but there's something about it that also feels inaccessible and intimidating. At least I can admit that, laid out before me as it is tonight, the skyline paints a pretty picture.

It's almost as pretty as the view of Central Park from my new office.

Well, what *could* be my new office.

The next morning, after I've drifted through coffee at my favorite café, a sticky subway commute into the city, a crowded but scenic walk up Madison Avenue, and a truly perfunctory last interview with Addison's boss and the marketing director, Cary, Addison shows me to my office.

It's gorgeous. It's immediately clear to me that it's the cherry on top of their offer.

"It used to be Cary's office, actually," Addison chirps, her heels clicking as she circles the desk, an expensive cloud of perfume trailing in her wake. The fact that she makes it a good six paces before the wall stops her is a testament to how massive the space is. At Incite I'd been given only an open-office cubicle. "But when they moved our team down to this hallway . . . I asked them to save it for you." She beams at me.

"It's beautiful," I say truthfully. "I love it." And I do.

"I'm going to run downstairs to grab some coffee. Can I get you anything?" Addison asks.

"No, thank you. Is it okay if I just . . . ?"

"Of course," she purrs. "Take a look around."

As her heel clicks fade away, I look outside. The window takes up the top half of the wall to my right, and for the first time, the buildings don't crowd outside my window. Instead, I can see almost the entirety of the southern half of Central Park, all open air until my gaze hits Central Park West. It's strange to see it from this angle, like I'm peering down at New York's little slice of manicured nature through a telescope, admiring it from the sky rather than immersing myself in the greenery. It's a little green snow globe. Grass globe.

I sit down at the L-shaped desk and run my palms along its dark wood as I cast my gaze around the room. It's almost easy to imagine myself working here; the wide desktop monitor is dark now, but I pretend it's bright with my bold presentation drafts, open reports, and full inbox. The office is currently bare, but just as I had with Alchemist's wall, I picture what it might look like if it were *mine*. The first thing I'd do is put lots of plants in the window, let them soak up all of that uninterrupted sun. Next I'd hang the photos and posters I'd painstakingly framed over the years, though none of them are my artwork. I didn't want to risk clients asking questions about them; it felt too intimate for them to even witness my art at all. I'd fill up the desk space with all of my best pens and stationery, and maybe add a few books to the shelves. I'd have space for a few pics of me and Liam, of my parents and their foster fail, Meatball, on vacation.

Maybe I'd take a picture with the D&D crew at the Renaissance Faire, all dressed up and grinning. Something to remember our summer by.

Just like Noah, I think ruefully. *Surrounded by so many pictures and memories, but thousands of miles away from the people we made them with.*

Then I remember that if I take this job, I won't be in Texas long enough to go.

I'm considering snapping a picture of the office to save when Addison returns with her coffee and two of my potential co-workers, Imani and Derek, in tow. I recognize them from the team interview—Cute Side Bun and Lego Man—and they both beam at me from the doorway.

Imani's the first to speak. She has on adorable wide-leg red pants and a sweater vest. She juts her thumb back down the hall-way. "Hey, neighbor. I'm right next door." She flashes a conspirato-rial grin. "Pretty, isn't it? This office is half the reason I even agreed to work here, honestly."

"Oh hush," Derek snorts. "We all know you've been here since the start, back when we were just a couple of folding chairs in Cary's basement."

"Well, obviously it was worth it."

Obviously.

I laugh along with their banter, and when Addison finally walks me back through the glass doors, down the long elevator ride, and into the building's entryway, I give her warm handshake an extra squeeze. "Thank you so much for having me, Addison. You and the team have been so welcoming."

"I hope you've enjoyed your time here, Josephine." She paces backward effortlessly despite the height of her heels. "Keep an eye on your phone, okay? I'll be in touch soon."

I nod. Even after she disappears back into the elevators, I stand still in the lobby, watching as people dressed in smart suits and dark skirts flow in a current around me.

As soon as she's off the train she comes running at me, and then I'm enveloped in a near-painful hug that's all elbows, wild gray-blond curls, laughter, and a cloud of cucumber melon body spray.

"Oh, Sadiebug," she sings right into my ear. "It's been too long!"

"Just a few months, Mom," I say sheepishly. But when I hang on to our hug for a touch longer than I need to, she doesn't pull away.

"I am just *so* happy to see you, honey." She threads her arm through mine and tugs me along.

Despite the dozens of times I've seen it, I spare a glance for Grand Central's iconic turquoise-and-gold celestial mural as we walk toward the street. I try to picture what Noah would think of it, imagine him elbowing me and grinning as he says, *I bet you could manage something like that, huh?*

As my mom squeezes my arm, I drift back down to earth. "We have so much to catch up on," she says, beaming.

Mom and I cut across Manhattan all the way to Times Square, where she pauses to take a few pics to share with her book club before we begin a long, meandering walk down Broadway. Inspired, I snap a shot of the *Hadestown* marquee for Jules and text Is this where Kain's dad lives??? She responds with a string of laughing and heart-eye emojis.

My mom had insisted on coming to spend my last day in the city—for now, at least—with me, and as we traipse down the crowded streets, I update her on the events of my week. After the interview, I'd spent the next day and a half revisiting all of my old haunts. Experimentally, I'd mapped out my commute to Paragon twice, to see which subway line made for the quickest trip. Yesterday, I'd optimistically taken a run through a couple of Manhattan's neighborhoods, daydreaming about leaving Queens and finding a new spot in the city. I vastly prefer to run in a park rather than down long avenues—I hate the way I have to bounce on my toes as I wait for cars or pedestrians to pass—but it helped me note which streets have the shadiest trees, the closest grocery stores, the cutest corner wine bars and breweries.

I'd wondered, for a moment, how Noah was filling his time at Alchemist without me there to keep him company as I finished the mural. But then the crosswalk turned green, and I'd turned my mind back to my jog.

"When will you accept?" Mom asks as we peruse the bookshelves in the basement of the Strand. I can't help but feel that it doesn't have the same warmth and cozy quiet as Bluebonnet, but my mom loves the store nearly as much as Liam does. Their love of reading is something they share more closely than we do; to this day, they still regularly exchange recommendations.

"I don't know," I answer, running my finger along the cracked spine of an old fantasy book. Paragon's formal offer had come in this morning.

"Best not to keep them waiting, though, right?"

"Addison told me to take the weekend to think about it."

Mom laughs. "What is there to think about, honey? You made it sound so wonderful."

I had, hadn't I? I suck on the inside of my cheek bitterly. If anything, I suppose I do know how to make a good pitch. Noting my silence, Mom pokes her head around the bookshelf. Her brows draw into a puzzled cluster above her wire glasses. "Are you still on the fence?"

All of the air in my lungs comes out in a rush. "Is it crazy that I am?"

She doesn't answer immediately and pauses with her mouth open. Her lips press together after a moment, resolute. "No," she says slowly. "But I do think I'm missing some part of the story here, dear." Her dark eyes, made wider by the thick lenses of her glasses, touch on the other shoppers weaving through the shelves. "Why don't we get some coffee and chat?"

After we pay for our purchases—Mom's four romance novels and a memoir, and my tote bag of souvenir gifts for Morgan and Liam—we duck into the nearest coffee shop and fight for a small table in the corner.

The first sip of my iced latte has me wincing.

"No good?" Mom pouts as she sips blissfully at her tea.

"A little too sweet." I swirl the ice with a straw as I'm unexpectedly hit with a pang of longing for my regular order from Busy Bean. I've gotten to the point where the baristas recognize me on sight, prepping my coffee before I even make it to the register. I smile to myself, and Mom tilts her head to the side, curious.

"There's this coffee shop I like, back at Liam's. I think they've perfected my order," I explain, laughing. "I go every morning and get coffee for me and—and a, ah . . . friend."

That earns me a stare charged with curious intensity.

". . . I get us coffee before I work on the mural," I finish.

"You keep on promising to show me more pictures."

"I keep on getting distracted."

"Mm."

I ignore her pointedly raised eyebrow and turn my phone screen toward her, where I've pulled up a photo of my latest progress. I'm rewarded with a quiet, awed inhale of surprise. "So lovely, Sadie. I'm so glad you've gotten back into it. You've always loved painting."

"It's been incredible, Mom. The man who hired me seems to love it, and I've learned so much about the process. I really think I've outdone—" I pause, then swallow. I laugh a little and turn my phone face down on the table. ". . . Sorry. We were going to talk about Paragon?"

There's a tiny shift in my mother's features that I would have missed if I'd blinked—a slight lean forward, a loosening of the lines on her forehead. She smiles gently, and her warm fingers wrap around my wrist.

"No, go on," she says. "I want to hear more about Texas."

CHAPTER
Thirty

Noah arrives early for the game on Sunday to wrap me in a crush-
ing hug that sweeps me off my feet. He presses a loud kiss into my
cheek. "Missed you," he says warmly. "How was your trip?"

"It was really good." It feels nice to hear how relaxed I sound
when the words ring with truth. "I visited some of my favorite
spots, got to see my mom, and—oh, I brought you something."

I fetch him the four-pack of local beers I'd brought back from
the brewery near my apartment in Queens. "They're not as good as
Alchemist's," I say quickly. "But in case you want to try something
new."

"Trying new brews and food is the best part of traveling."
He snaps one beer off and opens the can with a hiss. "You know
me well." He squeezes my hand then drops his voice. "And Paragon?"

I just nod. "They've given me the weekend to think about it." I'd
told him about the offer, of course—but not much more than that.
I'd kept our texts during the trip lighthearted, and he'd kindly followed my lead.

I don't think I imagine the way his lips linger as he plants another kiss on my temple.

Shortly after Morgan walks in, Jules arrives wearing the pair of chunky yellow taxi earrings I'd given her that I'd found at an art market in Chelsea. We all descend upon her latest batch of treats: dice-shaped sugar cookies. Half of them are decorated immaculately and frosted with tiny numbers, while the others are smeared with messy colors.

"My kids helped." Jules glows with pride.

As I search for a gold-painted d20, Liam shoulders his way into our frenzied feeding circle. "Y'all better have left some for me," he grouches. I gape at him and mouth, *y'all?*

He grins and shrugs. "What can I say? It's grown on me."

He plucks two natural twenties from the top of the pile—which doesn't bode well for us—and turns back toward the game room. "Let's get started, shall we?"

Noah fires off a crisp salute. "Ready when you are, DM."

Hearing a knock, Jaylie opens the front door of the tower to find Alastair on his knees, webbed hands held awkwardly clasped together above his pointed hat. His bulging eyes are fixed on the dirt.

"Lady Shira Soros," he intones, voice thick with feigned obeisance. "I have tried everything I know, and I cannot rid myself of this curse. Please consider me thoroughly humbled. You may keep my spellbook, as is your right, but if you can find mercy within the depths of your black heart to free me from this slimy cage—"

He finally looks up when Jaylie can no longer suppress her giggling.

He drops his arms to his sides and stands immediately. "Oh. It's you," he says flatly. And then, very meanly: "*Fuck* you, you said you were going to help me!"

Jaylie cuts off her laughter with an indignant gasp. "Well, fuck you, too! You got me killed!"

"You seem fine now!"

"Only because they brought me back! It was a godsdamned *beholder*, you nasty little amphib—"

"What's going on here?" Shira snaps. Over Alastair's roaring ribbiting, Jaylie hadn't heard her approach. The others peek their heads around the corner with curiosity.

"Alastair has come to beg for mercy," Jaylie summarizes. She glares down at the frog. "Pathetically, I might add."

The green wizard takes in a deep, bracing breath before he turns his flat black eyes to Shira. "Please just turn me back," he pleads, exasperated. "I am at my wit's end."

"Do you promise never to return?"

"I'll promise to be your personal court jester, if that's what it takes."

Shira wrinkles her nose. "No, thank you." She beckons him inside. "Very well. Come along."

Jaylie considers the whole jester affair to be a missed opportunity on Shira's part, but she follows as Shira leads them into the library. Like a moth to a flame, Loren's taste for theatrics has him falling into step behind the priestess, and the other members of the party are not far behind.

Shira's library is unsurprisingly gorgeous. Glossy black shelves piled with books and artifacts stretch impossibly high toward a ceiling shrouded in light. Alora is curled into the corner of a plush purple couch, her slippered feet tucked under her.

"Another guest?" Alora calls. "My love, you've grown so popular."

Shira's lips twitch. "Not by choice," she says dryly.

Alastair pauses in the center of one of the library's many elegant rugs, tracing his gaze over the shelves. It's difficult to read a frog's features, but Jaylie can't imagine that he's looking upon Shira's collection with anything other than naked hunger. Something catches his eye, and he freezes.

"Hells." A note of reverence creeps into his tone. "Is that it?"

Shira plucks the orb-capped staff from its resting place against the shelf. "It most certainly is."

Over breakfast the day before, they had all agreed that with the orb in hand, confronting Donati would be a walk in the park. All they needed to do was pin him in its beam, tie him up, and then flip a coin to see whether they would turn him in to the City Watch or chop his head off themselves.

What Jaylie's companions had meant to be Shira's downfall would work just as well on their employer.

Shira's fingers curl over the spine of her spellbook, bound in a leather harness at her side, but she pauses. Her fingers wrap around the wood of the staff. "Would you like to see it at work?"

Alastair swallows. "Please."

Jaylie and Loren exchange a glance. They shrug. *Wizards.*

Shira extends the orb toward Alastair, fixing him in its sights. "Glorvalk."

Green and yellow tendrils of light swirl momentarily around Alastair's froggy form, forming a twisting cyclone that swirls briefly upward. As it dissipates, Jaylie's jaw drops to the ground.

He's magnificent, she thinks, more than a little guiltily. But by the way Loren's green eyes bug out, too, she guesses she's not alone in her thoughts. She'd fully expected Alastair's exterior to be a match for his terrible rudeness and poor attitude.

But with dark golden skin, piercing indigo eyes, a jaw cut from marble, and long jet-black hair that curls behind his slightly pointed half-elven ears, he paints a gorgeous picture. Somehow he manages to make the purple star-studded robes and hat appear more mysterious and artistic than adorable and cute. As he takes a spin, marveling at his unwebbed fingers, silver embroidery shimmers in his wake. Jaylie catches a whiff of dark, smoky cologne.

"I am in your debt, Shira." Even as his full lips bend toward a scowl, his voice is a deep purr in his throat—nothing like his former croak.

Loren bends close to Jaylie's ear. "He would have made a killer bard."

Jaylie huffs. "Might have had better luck with it, too."

Alastair casts his burning violet gaze to the ground. "I suppose that's all, then," he says, despairing and broody. "Thank you for your mercy. I will be on my way, to begin . . ." A long-suffering sigh. "Rebuilding."

From where he leans next to Morgana on the far side of the room, Kain rolls his eyes heartily at the wizard's dramatics. But with Alastair's back to her, Alora slowly turns a wide set of doe eyes on Shira.

Shira purses her lips and shakes her head vehemently.

Somehow, Alora's eyes only grow larger and dewier.

"Darkthorn." Shira says his name through clenched teeth, re-signed. "My wife has decided to take pity on you."

He turns. "Oh?"

Shira plucks a seemingly random book from the shelf and strides forward. Stiffly, she thrusts it toward him. "After this, I never wish to see your face again. Understood?"

Alastair's eyes flick quickly between Shira and Alora as he curls his fingers around his spellbook.

"Oh, I can promise you won't," he murmurs. There's an under-tone of deep, frantic amusement that threads through his voice. Jaylie can't pinpoint the reason—until she catches his gaze snap-ping to the orb.

In a blink, Jaylie rushes toward him—but Alastair is much faster. His spellbook begins to glow just as he shoots his free hand forward and tears the staff from Shira's grasp.

The last Jaylie sees of him is a flash of too-white teeth as he teleports away in a cloud of smoke.

In the silence that lingers in the library, Kain finally gives voice to all of their thoughts.

"Well, shit."

Shira paces violently from wall to wall. At the rate she's going, Jaylie reckons she'll carve a valley down the center of her kitchen by sundown. For hours they had all sat in the dining room, strategizing what the Hell they were meant to do without their most powerful weapon.

"If it were a duel between me and Aurelio alone, I could likely best him," Shira mutters. "It would be difficult, but possible."

"I won't risk you like that," Alora insists. Despite Shira's tired assurances, Alora still wrings her hands in her lap, feeling responsible. Guilt hangs around her in a cloud.

Shira shakes her head. "I doubt I could get that close to him anyway. The situation is much worse. We know from the wedding that his estate is crawling with guards. And I'm sure given my last entrance, they'll attack me on sight."

Loren clears his throat nervously. "You don't think Alastair would give the orb to Donati, do you?"

Shira bares her teeth at the mention of the traitorous wizard, but she shakes her head quickly. "He cares little for Donati. I imagine he's holing away in some dark cave, happy to conduct his experiments alone."

"Can we go to the City Watch?" Jaylie asks. "You said you had reports, and piles of research. Would it be enough to convince them to act?"

Shira sighs. "We can try. But with your party gone this long, I expect Aurelio has realized that something's gone wrong. He's probably spinning tales and preparing for the worst as we speak."

Morgana steps forward, muscular arms crossed over her chest. "Why don't we play his game, then?"

Shira narrows her eyes. "How do you mean?"

"He's got allies, wealth, power." Morgana ticks off on her fingers. "Do we have friends we can call on? What about all of the citizens he's wronged—don't they want to fight back, too? Fuck the Watch. We'll go straight to the people. We'll spread the word, see who shows up, then knock his fucking front door down."

Her words are met with a heavy, thoughtful quiet—and then the energy in the room shifts. Loren's lips slowly stretch into a grin. "I do know a thing or two about circulating a good story."

"And as soon as I tell my father what Donati has done to me, we can certainly expect my family's allies to show en force," Alora adds.

Suddenly everyone's full of ideas.

"We could tell Dorna, too," Jaylie muses. "She'll be eager to shake off the reputation of ever having worked with him. And she'll have plenty of fresh young faces looking to make a name for themselves." She knows because she was one.

"I have friends, too," Kain says. He offers nothing more.

Shira sighs. "I suppose it's a start. Let's give it a week, then. We'll do all we can, and then we'll return to Belandar with whatever we've got."

For the first two days, no one answers the call.

But on the morning of the third day, a stern-looking elf clad in shining plate armor raps a demanding beat into Shira's front door. As soon as Alora sees him, she jumps into his arms, elated.

Three dozen soldiers from the Clares' personal guard are the first to arrive. Alora was right; once she told her family of Donati's crimes, their offended pride and need to protect their own was nearly enough for Alora's father to declare war.

Next are the students from the Academy, led by a tall elven woman with a sparkling enchanted sword at her hip. She's flanked on either side by a raven-haired enchantress with fire in her eyes and a smirking sorceress with bright red hair bound into twin buns at the back of her head. The trio makes quick work of setting up camp for the crowd of students that follows in their wake. Some had heard whispers of Donati's crimes, while others had always remained secret allies of Shira. They hail from magical circles within the realm's major cities, and they appear on her lawn through portals, by flying carpet, after transforming into winged animals, and more.

But it's Dorna's connections who really answer the call. When Jaylie had first approached her, agreeing to meet at a small tavern not far from the tower, Dorna had nearly killed her with the daggers in her eyes alone. "You've got a lot of fuckin' nerve showing up here when you are at the very top of my shit list." But after the priestess had quickly explained the whole story, Dorna's features had calmed, her brows drawing low over her eyes. "Fuckin' Hell," she said with a sigh. "It's short notice. But I'll see what I can do."

After that, they come from all over the realm.

Adventurers, always hungry for a chance at fame, glory, and gold, show up in droves. As Jaylie walks through the makeshift camps set up outside of Shira's tower, she watches them spar. A half-orc with her hair pulled back into dozens of braids dances circles with her rapier around a laughing blond boy wielding a sword. Across from them, Kain trains with a woman with a gem embedded in her greatsword. When he scores his first hit—a shallow cut to her upper arm—a boy in a green hood rushes out with a small crystal gripped in his fist to heal her wound. Morgana hovers off to the side, trading daggers and tips with a blue-haired halfling, an emerald-eyed elf, and a human woman with a scar across her freckled nose. Morgana waves at Jaylie as she passes, and the freckled woman meets her eyes and offers a friendly smile.

Where a makeshift firing range has been set up, adventurers test a variety of weapons against the targets. One curly-haired halfling ducks behind a box of supplies, firing her crossbow from cover. A redheaded half-elf with a green bandanna knotted around his forehead competes with a noble human man to his left, both of them taking turns aiming at the bullseye; the half-elf slings axes while the human fires glowing magic-tipped arrows. In between turns, an excited wolf pup and a dog with shadow-dark fur bound out to fetch all of the expended arrows, bolts, and axes.

At the sound of music, Jaylie turns—and immediately laughs. Loren looks to be conducting what can only be described as a rehearsal, and by the sounds of it, it's not going well. He's surrounded by a semicircle of bards: a purple-haired tiefling with a harp, a human woman with pigtails and a trumpet, and two cheerful halflings. As soon as the music starts, the bards compete to play louder than their companions, none of them used to sharing the spotlight. It doesn't matter, of course. As long as they continue to share the scathing song Loren wrote about Donati and the quest they're on to defeat him, well—they'll have done their part.

Hilariously, many of the other spellcasters play together just about as well as the bards do. They don't group as one in the makeshift camp like the others, preferring instead to ready for battle alone. Jaylie spots two sorcerers sulking in the shadow of the tower, one with a scowl carved deep into his haggard features and the other with a pleasant, forgettable face, both of them weaving dark magic away from the sun. An elf with olive-brown skin adjusts his glasses as he flips idly through his spellbook, while a tiefling with arcane symbols tattooed in spirals up her arms feeds roaring flames into her personal campfire. Near the edges of camp, a woman with blue skin and seashells woven into her dress trades sparring spells with an elven sorceress whose dark curls are threaded with brilliant gold chains.

Jaylie returns to the tower to find Shira leaning heavily into the doorframe, her expression thoughtful. She casts her gaze across the dozens of adventuring parties surrounding her home and sighs wistfully. As she turns to Jaylie, her eyes sharpen, and her lips curl up into a small, determined smile.

"I think we may stand a fighting chance."

CHAPTER
Thirty-One

It's supposed to be finished.

I sit shoulder to shoulder with Noah on the bench, and together we stare at the mural. For the last couple of days, I'd single-mindedly thrown myself into painting the final touches. I'd avoided speaking to anyone about my pending offer from Paragon—Addison included, though I knew she was waiting on me—and instead allowed myself to be absorbed in my mission. It looks exactly as I imagined it would, with purple-and-green trees encroaching from all sides. The ethereal gold-and-white stag, perfectly posed atop a hill in the background, the night sky rich and dark behind him save for the pinpricks of stars and fireflies. The traveler, weary from his journey but enjoying his evening drink at his campsite. And finally, the fire, warm and welcoming and bright with every shade of red, orange, and yellow.

But something's missing.

I turn to gauge Noah's reaction.

The energy between us is different today. His *hello, good morning!* kiss lasted a touch longer than usual. My fingers lingered on his as I passed him his favorite latte. When I had to reach the top of the mural and needed the ladder again, his hand curled possessively around the back of my ankle.

Now he stares open-mouthed at the mural, fingers laced under his chin. His features have gone soft and sweet, and his eyes are full of stars. But then he pauses to tap his thumbnail against his lower lip and looks sidelong to me. "Is it finished?"

The fact that he has to ask at all tells me that my instinct is right. "No." I adjust my glasses and rock forward.

And that's when I see it. What it still needs.

Biting my bottom lip, I glance at my watch. Already noon. I usually don't work past noon.

"Think I could steal a couple more hours today?" I ask.

"Sure, so long as you're done by the time we open at four."

Filled with renewed purpose, I pluck the paintbrush from behind my ear. "Okay."

"I'll be in the office with Dan if you need me."

With my final vision for the piece consuming me so that it's the only thing I see when I close my eyes, it takes me only a few more hours to complete it. I barely register the hushed, tense voices muffled by the thin walls of the office, or the sound of Dan's car as he pulls out of the parking lot. I hardly feel the way the muscles in my neck and upper back start to lock up as I stretch to make final adjustments and additions. I am in another world entirely.

Usually when I finish a piece, I toy with it for a while. I'll put it under different lighting, add in some extra lines. Or I'll be hit with inspiration days after I thought it was done and rush back to include new details. But for this mural, I know exactly which paint stroke is my last. It's an arc of brilliant gold—the same shade as Jaylie's holy symbol—that contrasts beautifully with the field of purple behind it.

Footsteps echo quietly behind me.

"Sadie, it's perfect. It's beautiful." Noah wraps his arms around my middle, chin propped on the top of my head.

"I love it." I'm surprised to hear the words come out of my own mouth. I'm often the type to constantly fish for feedback and reassurance, but in this moment, I don't need it.

"I can't believe you added so much."

"I knew what it needed. It felt unfinished without it."

"Are you going to sign it?"

I hesitate. But as pride surges through my chest, I kneel at the corner of the wall and sign my name along the curve of a dark green leaf.

Sadie Brooks.

Noah helps me adjust the curtains to cover the completed mural, and a little twinge of sorrow ripples through me as we tuck the art away for the final time.

"Well," I say, my throat suddenly tight. "I'm sure I'll—I'll be back soon." I still need to get my last payment anyway. But even without that as an excuse, I've developed a taste for beer over the past few months.

And a taste for the brewer, too.

I don't want to act like this is goodbye. So, instead, I simply twine my fingers around Noah's neck and pull him down for a kiss. "I'll see you soon?"

"Whenever you like, Sadie." His forearms squeeze against my lower back.

It almost sounds like a promise.

The bell hanging over the doorway rings as I walk out. The heat, as always, wraps me in its usual warm, humid hug. As I stand outside with my back pressed against the Civic, I scroll through my emails until I find Paragon's offer again.

I inhale a deep, bracing breath.

It took me a while to realize that Addison isn't insidious, not at all like the fire-breathing dragon that was my last manager. No, truthfully, Paragon *is* a wonderful company. Their office is beautiful, their turnover rate is low, the projects are engaging and inspiring, and every single employee I met was an absolute delight. And if things got out of control again and I became overwhelmed and stressed, I could pick up strategies to help. I could set better boundaries. I could grow.

I could move back to New York and try again. This time, I'd be more prepared. I could prove that Incite hadn't broken me.

It's taken me much longer to realize, though, that I don't have anything to prove at all.

I press the green call button and lift the phone to my ear.

After the call, I sit in the car for a long time as dusk softens the sky to a sleepy blue. I watch Noah through the brewery's windows as he welcomes in patrons with his usual enthusiasm and consider stepping back inside to tell him the news.

But for now the small seed of joy settling in my chest feels too fragile—too new. I need a moment to myself to give it time to take root and grow.

I pull out of the parking lot and drive home.

I know the way by heart by now, but a sudden rush of sentimentality convinces me to take the long way back. I roll down the darkening road, past fields that Jules told me grow thick with bluebonnets in the springtime, past the beacon of the Mama's sign farther down the way. I slow as I drive under the twinkling lights of downtown and smile at the bookstore where I know Liam and Morgan are working the closing shift. The scenery grows more mundane as I near my neighborhood, but even the sight of the bank, the library, and my preferred grocery store inspires a surge of sharp fondness.

After reheating a quick dinner, I take my time brewing tea, selecting a playlist, lighting Brooding Love Interest, and arranging all of my pillows into a cozy nest on my bed. I even hunt down

Howard and purposefully carry him upstairs with me. After grabbing my tablet, I climb into bed.

Blissful contentment immediately settles around my shoulders like a warm blanket.

I sit and draw for hours, my fingers still crusted in paint from the day's work at Alchemist. It's a wonder that I still have energy left for more art after rushing to finish the mural, but for once, I don't work on a paid commission. This is a personal project. Something just for me and my friends.

Something I'm choosing to do for myself.

With our last session penned for this Sunday, I want to celebrate the adventure we've all been on together.

My phone buzzes in the pocket of my sweatpants. Howard lifts his head from where he's pressed to my leg, annoyed at being woken up.

Noah:

will you write with me one more time, before the campaign ends?

I'm going to miss these characters:(

My gaze flicks to the time and I inhale in surprise. Already after ten.

Tonight?

if you're up for it!

I am 😊

I add a few more swaths of color to the illustration on my tablet before trading it out for my laptop. I navigate to the private server between me and Noah and sink back into our world.

It's the night before the final confrontation.
Tomorrow, they will set the plan in motion and attack
Donati in his home. All week Jaylie has prepared for
this moment, ensuring that every possible outcome has
been planned for. She should be able to rest easy,
knowing that she's done everything she can. Not to
mention, the bed Jaylie lies in is a thousand times
more comfortable than the bedroll she's grown used
to. Yet still she cannot find sleep, her eyes pinned
on the canopy of silk that cascades over the four-
poster bed frame.

Loren cannot rest. He sits on his bed, plucking
through the chords of the song he wrote about
Donati's crimes—not that it matters anymore. There's
no time left to spread the word any farther than he
already has. Sighing irritably, he sets his lute to
the side, shrugs on a loose nightshirt, and walks
into the hallway. After peering both ways down the
dimly lit corridor, he makes his way to the
priestess's door. Inhaling deeply, he knocks gently
three times.

The knock echoes in the darkness of Jaylie's room.
She summons an orb of gentle gold light, and it
follows in her wake as she pads to the door. As she
peeks out, she smiles. "It's you." She widens the
door. "Can't sleep?"

Loren shakes his head. His features are drawn, and
there's a tightness around his green eyes, but seeing
her makes him smile all the same. "Can I come in?"

Jaylie lingers in the doorframe for a moment before
she steps aside. "Of course."

Loren steps in and closes the door quietly behind
him. He casts his gaze around her room—it's twice

the size of his. "Shira must like you more than she likes me," he murmurs. And then, before he has time to think about it, the words he's been pondering for weeks now come out in a rush. "Why did you kiss me, Jay?"

Jaylie blinks. Her lips part in surprise, and a few moments pass before she responds. "What do you mean?"

"After I brought you back. In the cave. Why did you kiss me?"

Jaylie thinks back to when her eyes cracked open after she took that painful first breath. Loren was the first thing she saw, and the emotion she had felt in that moment was so strong she'd thought she would burst into thousands of pieces all over again. "I don't know," she says softly.

His face falls.

"No—I mean, I didn't even think it through, Loren. You were the first thing I wanted to see when I opened my eyes. Kissing you felt like the most obvious thing in the world. I couldn't help myself." She laughs a little and smooths her palms down her nightgown, fiddling with a loose thread on the lace. "I was just so happy to see you."

Gently, Loren reaches forward and takes her hands between both of his. His thumb runs across the backs of her fingers, catching on each of her golden rings. "And what about now?"

Jaylie lets her head fall forward until her forehead meets his. "I'm always happy to see you, Loren."

Loren lifts her hand and presses his lips to her skin. "Are you nervous about tomorrow?"

"That depends. Is your secret resurrection spell one that you can repeat?"

He snorts once, and his gaze skates away from hers. "Unlikely."

"Then, yes. Of course I'm afraid."

He tucks a stray golden curl behind her ear. "You'll be fine, Jay. You've learned so much since then. We all have. You'll keep us all together."

She tries to smile, but her expression is shaky. It's difficult to see through the tears that gather on her eyelashes. She clears her throat and tries for levity, to distract her from the battle on the horizon. "I'll bet it's going to be difficult for you to top this one."

"This what?"

"This *story*." Jaylie glances toward her window. Even now she can see the glow of dozens of campfires burning in the shadow of the tower. "After we've defeated Donati and saved the day, you'll finish your song." She gestures outward. "And then you'll be off on your next big adventure." Her tone was meant to sound wistful, but there's a note of regret that she can't mask.

Loren follows her gaze, staring off into the night. The campfires mirror the brilliance of the stars scattered across the sky. "No, I don't think I will," he murmurs.

Slowly, Jaylie turns until she's facing him again. "No?" A ghost of a smile passes over her features. "That's what you told me last time—that you wanted

to write the next great adventure. You wanted people
to miss you."

Loren shakes his head hard enough that strands of his
hair escape from his braid. "I don't want *you* to miss
me." He grips her hand hard enough to hurt.
"Jaylie . . . I want to be the first thing you see
when you open your eyes. Every time. I want to be the
one to rescue you when you fall—just like you do for
me, after every battle. I want to be the last sound
you hear before you fall asleep at night. I don't
just want my songs to get stuck in your head, Jay. I
want you to be the reason I write them." His throat
is so tight he has to clear it a few times before he
continues. He tilts his head down until his gaze
bores into her warm brown eyes. "I don't want to miss
those moments. I don't want to miss *you*," he insists.
"I won't go anywhere without you by my side."

Jaylie's lip trembles. "I want that, too. I could not
bear to see you go." She presses a kiss . . .

No. No, that's not quite right. I delete my drafted post. My foot
bounces restlessly as I try to think of another.

Jaylie gasps. "Take me, then. Take me with you. I
want to see the world you're always talking about. I
want you to show it to me." She throws herself
into . . .

But that's not it, either. I scowl at my laptop as I delete my
words and read through Loren's declaration again. I imagine that
I'm staring at Loren through the screen, my hands clutched in his
as he stares earnestly into my eyes. The pointed ears fade until Noah

sits in his place, thick fingers drumming against his keyboard as he whips up a string of flowery words that he surely knows will cut straight to my heart.

I won't go anywhere without you by my side.

The filter of our in-game romance had been a welcome amusement from the beginning, an opportunity to flirt and explore our interest in each other without having to wade in too deep. But now it's like I'm back at the stream Noah showed me, thinking it was shallow before I jumped—only to find that the water stretches far deeper than I could have known.

It's too much. It's too much, to have only Loren say the words I long to hear from Noah's lips.

My phone vibrates at my side, and I glance at it.

Noah:

everything ok?

It's been a while now since Noah's last post; I left him hanging, and he's probably wondering where I've disappeared to.

Biting my bottom lip, I text back immediately.

I need to see you.

I twist the ring on my middle finger in tight, nervous circles until Noah opens the front door of his duplex.

Still damp from a shower, his hair hangs longer and darker around his face. He wears nothing but a pair of sweatpants, but I force myself to keep my eyes on his face—right where his brow is creased in concern.

After sending that text, I hadn't looked at my phone again. I'd just hopped in the car and pressed on the gas.

"There's something I have to tell you," I say.

"By all means, come in."

I follow Noah down a long hallway, and my heart leaps suddenly into my throat.

Deeper in the house, the living room is crowded with boxes. Dusty outlines where picture frames used to hang stamp each wall, and the only furniture that occupies the space is one lonely gray couch. Noah passes through without stopping, and I follow in his wake, trying to ignore the pressure building in my chest.

Although there are no boxes, Noah's room is somehow worse. It looks like a hotel room, ascetically clean and completely bare of personality, with a dull blue bedspread and empty walls. The only real signs that he lives here are the small closet full of clothes and his massive brick of a gaming laptop plugged into the outlet behind the desk. Within twenty minutes he could pack up every part of himself and no one would know he'd ever been here at all. Even my room at Liam's, which I was meant to stay in for only a few months, has more personal touches.

Gingerly I sit on the edge of his bed. Noah's desk chair creaks as he sinks into it and swivels to face me. He pulls one of my hands into both of his, tethering me.

I consider asking about the boxes, the empty room, the gutted house—and I will, before the night's over. But it wasn't my first intention, and it's not what I'll start with.

I didn't come here to ask him questions or demand answers. I just came to tell him.

"I'm staying."

It's the first time I say it out loud, and I feel the rightness of it all the way down to my bones. It feels like staying up for days on end and finally allowing myself to sleep. It feels like crossing the finish line after a half-marathon.

"In Heller?"

I nod. "In Heller."

Noah opens his mouth to speak again, but I touch my fingertips to the corner of his lips, settle my palm against his bearded cheek. "Just let me get this out"—*while I'm still brave enough to say it*—"and then I want to know. Okay?"

He leans into my hand and nods.

"After I finished the mural today, I called Paragon and declined their offer. I think they were . . . mystified, honestly, but they were kind about it. They asked whether I had a competing offer, or if my plans had changed, and—and that's the thing. I have no plan. I don't have *any* plans, Noah." I let out a bewildered, wondering laugh. "I have no idea what I'll do. All I knew was to make the next right decision, and that's what I did." I drop my hands back into my lap and set to fiddling with my ring again.

"I don't want it anymore," I say quietly. If I'm honest with myself, that had been the hardest truth to come by. My career in New York felt like something I was supposed to hold on to, because all I'd done for the past decade was dream of that damn city, and changing my mind felt more like a betrayal of myself than I was ready to accept. For so long I'd convinced myself that I was avoiding New York because I just wasn't ready to return yet, or I hadn't healed enough, or I wasn't good enough for it—when really, I just couldn't come to terms with the fact that I wanted to let it go.

"What I do want," I say slowly, "is what I have right now. What I don't want is—" I steal the line directly from Loren. "I don't want to miss you."

Noah's eyes widen in recognition, and he slides one hand along the outside of my thigh. "Sadie . . ."

"I wanted to hear it from you, Noah. All of the things you were saying as Loren were so beautiful and lovely, but they weren't from *you*. I couldn't tell if you were trying to tell me something, or just staying in character, or . . ." I exhale sharply. "Even now, I still don't know. But for everything to still be up in the air between us while Jaylie and Loren get their happy ending, I just—I think we deserve . . ." It doesn't feel right to say *a happy ending*, because what I really want with Noah is a happy beginning, isn't it? An adventure we agree to embark on together, without knowing where we'll end up.

I stop playing with my ring and take his hands in each of mine. "You deserve to know where I stand," I finish. "So, I'm staying, with or without you. But I hope it's with you."

Noah lets my words float in the air around us, lingering in the space between us. Once he's sure I've said all I need to, his thumbs come to rest on my temples as he threads his fingers into my hair.

"Oh, Sadie."

His kiss is gentle—just the barest brush of his lips against mine—before he draws back again. But whatever he's about to say, I'm not ready to hear it yet.

Even now, I still want more.

I curl my fingers around his wrists and capture his mouth with mine again. I want to sink my teeth into his lower lip, to taste him, to tie him to this moment and this place—

But just like always, Noah meets my frantic, restless energy with steady, slow assurance. Without pulling away, he rises from his chair. The palm of one hand presses against the side of my neck as his fingers stretch to circle my jaw, and he tilts my face up toward his as the other hand folds around my shoulder and guides me back until I'm lying on his bed. With one knee pressed to the inside of my thigh, he parts my legs and climbs on top of me. Although he braces his elbows to either side of my head, the deliciously heavy weight of his hips pins me underneath him.

His kisses are deep and slow, but there's an insistence in them that steals my breath. Every time the tide seems to pull back, when I think we might take a moment to breathe, he surges forward again, his tongue tangling with mine as his arms wind around my ribs and pull me close. In the back of my head, I get the sense again that he's trying to communicate something to me, his lips moving against mine in a language he's teaching me how to speak. But I can't yet tell whether the iron circle of his arms around me means *I'm here, I've got you*—or if it's the last embrace before he finally lets me go.

I feel his smile before I see it. It's tucked neatly into the corner of his mouth, right where my lips skim along his dimple.

I draw back and blink up at him. "What?"

He rests his head against my brow, his beard tickling my cheek. "I already told Dan last week," he murmurs against my ear.

"Told him what?"

"That I'm not going back to Colorado. I want to stay, too."

Lightness fills my chest. If it weren't for Noah pressing me into the mattress, I might float right up to the ceiling. I draw back from him, just enough so that I can see his eyes—so that I can watch his expression soften. My voice comes out breathless. "Why didn't you tell me?"

"You were in New York," he says gently. "You had a decision of your own to make, and I didn't want to add any pressure to that."

I swallow. "The boxes?"

"Are Dan's. He's leaving for Boulder in a few weeks." He laughs as my eyes immediately narrow. "Well, most of them are Dan's. Some are mine. I'll spend a few weeks in the van, until I find a new place to stay."

"What about Alchemist?"

I've never seen Noah's eyes this bright. "It's mine now." His voice is a hushed, excited whisper. "While he's in Colorado, I'm the manager. He's left it all to me."

I can't help the way my mouth hangs open. "All of your late nights, the extra prep he's had you doing—"

"*Yes.*"

So many words crowd my throat that I hardly know what to say. But I grow still as Noah's palms rise to cup my face again, anchoring me as only he can. The lake blue of his eyes goes liquid as he trains his unblinking gaze on mine. "Listen. Hear it from me, Sadie. This is not a fantasy, or a one-off adventure, or just a bard's declaration. This is real." He presses his forehead to mine. "I won't go anywhere without you by my side. I'm tired of running, and this is the only place I want to be. Right now, this . . ." He sweeps his thumb in an arc across my cheek. "This feels like home."

I press my fingers to the bare skin of his chest, feeling how his heart beats against my palms. The smile sneaks up on me, stretching wide until my cheeks ache with it. But I can't make it go away.

"It grows on you, doesn't it?" I murmur.

"What does?"

"This place. This town."

"Not just the town, Sadie."

Noah's fingertips glide under the hem of my shirt as he presses his lips to my forehead. "I can't promise that I won't want to leave again one day to explore, or to try something new. If that time comes, I hope you'll come, too. But for tonight—" His arm snakes under my neck, cradling my head in the crook of his elbow. His damp hair shrouds half of his face, his eyes half-lidded in the dark. "Will you stay with me?"

"I will," I promise. "I'll stay."

CHAPTER
Thirty-Three

I stare at the sign hanging from Alchemist's glass doors, the letters written in a heavy hand with orange chalk.

> CLOSED FOR A PRIVATE EVENT

I stop in my tracks.

"What did you do?"

Noah can't tell a lie to save his life. So he just bites his lips to hide his grin and lifts his shoulders in an overdramatic, comedic shrug.

We'd spent last night together—and several of the ones before it, too—and Noah had asked me to stop by Alchemist on our way back to Liam's to play the last game of our campaign. Said he'd forgotten something.

When I push through the glass doors, I'm met with the pounding drums and heroic trumpeting of tense battle music spilling from the speakers. I find Liam with his fingers steepled, sitting at the head of a table decorated with the most extensive battle map I've seen yet.

Donati's gardens are reproduced in exquisite detail, with fake greenery, hedges, and flowers spread out over the surface area of

two long tables pressed together. Half a dozen white mini figurines float atop tiny bowls of water scattered across the grounds,
representing the wizard's ridiculous fountains. Dotted throughout
the shrubbery are decorative plates piled with some of Jules's very
best pastries, including a brand-new and most welcome addition:
cinnamon rolls. Morgan circles the table and sets down freshly
poured pint glasses brimming with golden beer. Confused, I glance
to the bar. Dan catches my eye and waves before returning to his
laptop.

"Took you two long enough," Liam says wryly.

Morgan and Jules sit on either side of him, looking far too
pleased at my shock. "We were going to throw you a going-away
party," Jules admits. "But I'm really glad we didn't have to."

"Figured this was much better," Morgan agrees.

I laugh, delighted. "You booked the whole day?"

Noah slings his arm across my shoulders and pulls me to his
side. "You forget, Sadie," he says. "I'm the boss man now. I can do
whatever I like."

"Not for another two weeks, Mr. Walker," Dan warns teasingly
from the bar.

Liam catches my gaze and shakes his head slightly. "He's had
this on the books for a while," he corrects.

Noah's arm at my back keeps me from melting to the floor as I
will my eyes to stay dry. Looking quite pleased with himself, he
squeezes my shoulder and takes a seat at the table, drawing his
notebook from his backpack. I gasp, dismayed. "But I don't even
have my—"

Liam wordlessly hands over my tote bag. My lips twist into an
amused grin. "Really thought of everything, didn't you?"

Noah catches my wrist before I sit, speaking low. "Do you want
to show them? Before we start?" His shining gaze slides past me,
and I turn to see Dan standing by the curtains.

Dan nods, one thumb hooked into the belt loop of his jeans. "It only makes sense, y'know. For y'all to be the first to see it."

Jules's eyes have gone wide, and I don't bother to hold back my smile. I nod.

Dan draws the curtain back with a flourish.

As my friends turn to take in the mural for the first time, I'm gratified to hear their gasps of surprise. My eyes linger on the elements I'd added at the last moment—the parts that made the project finally feel complete. I can't help but think that the scene I've painted doesn't look all that different from the one before me.

The traveler isn't alone anymore. A woman in robes perches on the fallen log across from him, smirking into her own mug, while a man in armor stands just outside the campfire's ring of light, slightly shrouded in shadow as he peers into the night. Another woman leans dramatically over the campfire, arms outstretched and lips parted as she recounts a story to the group. I'd even given the traveler a dog to curl at his feet, his dark eyes hopeful that he might be given the night's scraps.

The traveler no longer sits by himself at his campfire, staring moodily into his drink.

Instead, he's surrounded by friends.

"Before we put our lives on the line today, I'd like to tell you all a secret," Jaylie begins.

She stands before the ranks of gathered adventurers at sunrise, dressed in her ceremonial robes. Her hands are clasped neatly before her, cradling her holy symbol. It was Loren's idea for her to make a speech before the battle began. *Give them a little faith,* he'd said as he'd kissed her good morning.

"There is no such thing as luck," she announces.

Off to a great start.

"At least," she amends, "not in the way that you believe it to exist."

She eyes her friends, gathered at the very front of those assembled. Kain wears his billowing pants and leather harness across his always-bare chest. Morgana is decked head to toe in shadow-black armor. In one glance alone, Jaylie counts six knives on her person. Someone let Loren borrow a breastplate of his own, and somehow he's managed to make the dark boiled leather look stylish when paired with a forest-green shirt and knee-high boots. Morgana looks doubtful of Jaylie's pep talk, but Loren offers her a wink and a thumbs-up.

"Many people believe that luck is random. They believe luck is as simple as something wonderful happening to you when you least expect it. Some people even come to rely on it, gambling away their hard work and hoping—always hoping—that one day they'll finally have their lucky break.

"But luck does not find those who sit around waiting for it. Luck is for the seekers, the adventurers, the lovers, and the dreamers. Luck is for those who chase after it, those who open themselves up to new experiences and new challenges every day of their lives. As one of the great clerics of my order once said, luck is where preparation meets opportunity."

Years ago, trapped in her tower, Jaylie had wished every night on the brightest star that she would be freed from her father's plans. Nothing happened.

It wasn't until she made her escape to the well, when she had taken the first steps toward freedom, that luck had truly found her.

"Luck is for all of you, my friends, if you are brave enough to seize it," Jaylie finishes, spreading her arms wide. "May Marlana bless us all today."

She's met with a roar of approval and dozens of coins tossed into the air. Shortly after, the portals begin to open. To Jaylie's right and left, teams of wizards led by Shira step forward to activate the runes carefully chalked into the earth during the early hours of the morning. One by one, the runes light with an electric-blue glow, and arches erupt out of the dirt and tear holes in reality. Through the portals, Jaylie can see the familiar sight of Donati's wrought iron gates and his garden beyond.

Shira is the first to step through, but Jaylie, her party, Alora, and all the others are not far behind.

Just as Shira suspected, Donati waits for them behind the gates, his arms crossed over a beautifully designed blue-and-white doublet with lilies embroidered along the sleeves.

His eyes, bloodshot and violent, are trained on Shira.

"You were not invited," he says through clenched teeth. "But I've been expecting you."

It's obvious he's bolstered the ranks of his guard, but Jaylie notes the absence of anyone from the City Watch. *That's a good sign,* she thinks. *Perhaps they took our story seriously, then.*

Perhaps we will not be arrested after we are done with him.

"I think I've had quite enough of you for one lifetime, Shira Soros. We've had our fun, but I tire of our games. This will be the last." Donati lifts his hands upward. It's a clear day, cloudless and beautiful, but lightning spears down from the sky all the same. Beyond the gates, every bolt lands at the same exact moment with a resounding *crack,* each one striking a different statue.

Jaylie watches in horror as every statue in the garden comes to life. Razor-sharp teeth sprout from grinning mouths, and stone fingers grow into long black claws. They leap from their foundations—a Donati wielding a wand, a Donati with a pair of bat wings, a Donati three times the size of the wizard himself, and at least a dozen others—and surge forward.

"You can try to kill me," the true Donati says, seething, his eyes alight with a new red glow. "But you'll have to find me first."

And with a snap of his fingers, he turns invisible.

Surprising Jaylie not in the least, Kain leads the charge. Spit flies from his mouth as he opens his jaws in a bloodcurdling roar. Over and over again he clashes his great axe against the estate gates, joined soon after by the front lines. Eventually the metal bends to the barrage and the gates crumple and fall. Shira's small army rushes through.

"Remember your orders!" Shira bellows as adventurers, guardsmen, students, and more race past her. "Stay together, stay smart, and everything in his fucking castle is *ours*."

Jaylie, having never been in an actual godsdamned *battle* before, is grateful for Shira's level of organization. Keeping to the discussed strategy, she hangs back as the fighters spill into the gardens, weapons at the ready. She trusts that Kain will command them wisely while Morgana leads a small strike team through the estate, keeping to the shadows as they track down the true Donati.

Meanwhile, Jaylie stays close to what Shira lovingly referred to as "the support group": the healers, most of the bards, the youngest volunteers, and a very grumpy Alora. "Shira didn't want me to come at all," Alora told Jaylie earlier that morning. "But I'm not about to let you fight on my behalf without lending a hand." She's frustrated that Shira forbade her from joining the front lines, but she loves her well enough that she agreed to stay near the back.

She understands, too, just how much of a target she is.

The gardens are chaos as Jaylie and her team are the last to enter. She spots a trio of Alora's guardsmen hacking ineffectually against a gray Donati statue wielding a lance. Farther down, a blond dwarf with two swords strapped to her back wrestles with a grinning stone Donati in the shallow waters of a fountain while a bald halfling fires arrows from the hedges. Jaylie's head snaps to the side when she hears Kain's familiar roar again, and she grins to herself as a statue shatters under his axe. In the far distance, she hears and then feels the rumble of massive magical explosions. Shira's doing, she expects.

Perhaps they do stand a chance.

Jaylie and her group back up into a small clearing where all of the hedges have been carefully trimmed to resemble an array of magical creatures: a gryphon, a unicorn, and a particularly thorny and large dragon. As Loren and a few of the students launch spears of ice and fire at any guardsmen who try to approach, Alora weaves a complicated spell that immediately summons three seething fire elementals. Her scales glow as she casts, and she laughs when Jaylie asks where she learned such a spell.

"Spellbooks are for fucking nerds," she brags. "I was *born* with my magic."

Eventually, word spreads of the support group's location, and bloodied warriors limp toward them in search of healing and sanctuary. Jaylie aids as many as she can, though she's careful to keep a few emergency spells on hand. As she tends to a wound on a tiefling's shoulder, she sees a ripple of shadow out of the corner of her eye.

"There!" she shrieks, pointing ahead.

Donati—not stone, but flesh and blood—materializes out of the shadows to slit the throat of a poor Clare soldier thirty paces away. The woman collapses backward, and Donati shoots a vicious grin in Jaylie's direction. Immediately, he disappears again.

Within heartbeats, he blinks back into existence, this time closer. Shoving his extended palm into the chest of a half-orc wielding a dagger, he sends pulses of dark energy into the man's body until he collapses, dead, into the dirt.

And again, shadows take him.

"On guard, everyone!" Jaylie shouts, a note of panic in her voice. "He's close."

Alora's jaw clenches, and Loren summons motes of fire to his palms.

An awful quiet settles around Jaylie as each of her companions holds their breath. But it's Alora's pained gasp that breaks the silence.

"Hello, my dear," Donati purrs, materializing behind her.

Jaylie turns in a rush, but she's too late. Donati has the tip of a serrated dagger pressed to Alora's throat, his hand wrapped tightly around her forearm where he's already sliced through her skin from wrist to elbow. Blood pools around his fist where he digs his thumb into the cut. It's not enough to kill her, Jaylie realizes with relief.

But he doesn't need her dead.

He just needs her blood.

A laugh starts low in the back of the dark wizard's throat. It's a terrible, grating sound, and it grows louder with each moment that passes. The blood coating Donati's palms glows a deep red as he claps his hands together and begins to chant in a language Jaylie does not recognize.

Suddenly, the rosebuds serving as eyes for the dragon-hedge catch fire. Every leaf rustles at once and then, as if in a great wind, lies flat against the hedge's form.

Just like scales.

Roots creak and branches screech as the dragon begins to move. The thorns elongate into talons just as tiny branches weave together to form the webbing between its wings. As the blood spilling from Donati's palms flows into the earth, the dragon becomes more real, shedding the fragile leaves in favor of hard green scales. As it lifts its head to the sky, it lets out a roar that pierces through the garden.

"*No.*"

Jaylie does not recognize the voice—but she sees Loren's lips move.

Loren's green eyes disappear as flames pour out from the sockets. Fire wreaths his wrists and hands as he raises his arms to the clouds, his lute forgotten where it hangs from his shoulder. As he tilts his head backward, a column of fire erupts from his mouth, and he screams into the sky.

Horrified, Jaylie watches as he summons an inferno between his blackened palms. What starts as the size of a marble soon grows, swelling until it's a meteoric sphere twice the size of the dragon crouching ahead. Just as Donati and the monster leap forward, Loren hurls the fireball in a great, burning arc.

Jaylie's world turns red. The last thing she hears is Donati's cry before she blacks out.

"We did it. Gods, we actually did it."

Marlana?

No. Morgana squeezes Jaylie's hand as the priestess blinks back to life.

She lies on the edge of a crater. Steam rises from the gaping hole in the earth, spiraling upward. The hole is so deep that even as Jaylie arches her neck, she can't see the bottom of it.

"Donati's dead?" Jaylie asks. Her voice cracks, dry in the heat.

"No, even better. Loren wounded him—gravely—but Shira captured him in the end. She's taking him to the Assembly now. They'll deal with him there." Morgana barks out a low laugh. "Painfully, I hope."

"Where's Loren?"

"I'm right here, Jay." *Good. His voice is normal again.* The bard leans forward, and Jaylie can see his sparkling green eyes upside down from where he kneels above her, her head in his lap.

"Your eyes were on fire," she croaks.

"Were they?" he says mildly, his smile crooked. "I don't remember."

Jaylie casts a gaze at her surroundings. Within her direct vicinity, trees and roses and shrubs still burn. But farther than that, the garden looks intact—as do most of her allies, which she is grateful for. She doesn't have the energy to heal even if she wanted to.

"Can you help me up?" she asks.

Together, Loren and Morgana hook their arms underneath each of Jaylie's and ease her into a seated position. From here, she can see the fire still burning at the crater's center. It seems to be growing larger, but Jaylie can't tell what might be fueling it.

To her left, she hears Kain's sigh. He is painted in blood. He crouches with his forearms on his knees, tail flicking back and forth in agitation. "It's time," he rumbles, turning to Loren.

Pain flashes across Loren's elegant features. "No." His voice is so small. "Can't I have a few more hours?"

Kain shakes his head, his horns cutting through the air. His expression is severe.

Frantically, Jaylie looks between them. "Time for what?"

Neither man answers her. But from the core of the crater, a voice she hoped to never hear again calls out.

"*Your bard must like you very much, little priestess.*"

Suddenly, the crater glows with fire. Morgana whips out her daggers, but Kain remains unmoved. When the face forms, it's much worse than the last time Jaylie saw it, full of cruelty, intrigue, and *victory*. This time, it stretches across the whole of the pit, a massive grin cutting through the crater's center.

"Maglorbizel," Jaylie breathes. Kain's father. One of the most powerful devils in Hell.

"*He made a deal with me. Now that your little quest is complete, it is time for him to pay his price.*"

Jaylie's gaze swings to Loren. "A deal to kill Donati?" She remembers the way the flames crawled along his arms. The way they consumed him.

"*No, my dear. He made a deal for* **you.**"

Jaylie's voice wavers. "What are you talking about?"

"*If it were not for me, you would still be dead. He bargained for your life.*" Clouds of smoke rise from the crater as Maglorbizel bellows out a dark laugh.

"Loren, you didn't. Tell me you didn't."

Even as his lips tremble, Loren's jaw is set with determination. "I would do it again, given the choice."

Gently, Jaylie reaches up to wipe away a smear of ash on the center of Loren's forehead. That's when she sees it.

Underneath the grime, an infernal rune glows bright.

Her voice breaks. "What did you trade?"

"Nothing so bad, love," Loren says gently. He reaches to run his knuckles across the line of her jaw. "A year and a day of service. In the span of my lifetime, it's less than the blink of an eye."

An awful chuckle boils from the crater. "*And yet you do not even know what demands I might yet make,*" he says with a cackle.

Feeling dumb and romantic and resolved all at once, Jaylie shakes her head viciously. "I'll go with you."

Loren blanches. "Jay, I would never ask—"

"You didn't ask," she cuts him off. "This is my decision. I would go to Hell for you, Loren." She clears her throat delicately, then laughs. It comes out a little breathless. "Literally."

The color drains from Loren's face. "Jay, no. This was my bargain to make, and I'll gladly pay the price, but you—"

"I'll go, too," Kain says darkly.

"*Finally coming home to visit your father, then?*" the crater hisses.

Morgana's dark eyes are wide as her gaze jumps among her party members. She looks of half a mind to run, but her features soften as she looks at them. "Well, fuck me, then," she says, throwing her hands in the air with a laugh. "I guess we're all damned."

Jaylie takes Loren's hand and squeezes it. "On to the next adventure, then? Just like we said?" Her smile is small but determined, and her eyes are lit with fierce passion. She pitches her voice lower as she leans in. "We'll find a way to get you out, all right?"

Loren's eyes shine. "You do not have to do this for me."

Jaylie plants a kiss on his cheek. "After everything we've been through, Loren—there's nothing we can't face. We're coming with you."

As cackling fills Jaylie's ears, flames rise from the crater in a column of orange-and-red fire. Suddenly, a tongue lashes out, circling Jaylie and her friends in a fiery portal.

In the next moment, the gardens are gone, and all Jaylie sees is darkness.

Heat licks up the side of her neck, and Maglorbizel's voice rasps in her ear.

"Welcome to Hell."

CHAPTER
Thirty-Four

THREE MONTHS LATER

It's been only a few weeks since he moved in, but already Noah's new studio has more character than his old room at Dan's ever did.

A funky thrifted green-striped couch slouches comfortably in the corner across from where his bed nestles against the wall. Above his desk stretches a large corkboard, already crowded with dozens of pictures, postcards, and ticket stubs. Bottles of fermenting mead cluster together on the shelves above his fridge next to four-packs from the brewery, and a candle burns merrily on his tiny dining room table. As I wait for Noah to finish getting ready in the bathroom, I glance to where the portrait of Loren I'd painted for him hangs in a leafy golden frame above the couch.

I smile to myself. It had been his first decoration.

I'd gifted everyone portraits of their characters at the end of the campaign, but Loren's especially had been a labor of love. He sits with his lute cradled in his arms, posed in front of a campfire. I'd also added a few tiny details of my own: the reflection of fire in his eyes, one of Marlana's coins hanging on a cord from his neck, and a small collection of individually unique feathers woven into his traveling cloak.

When Noah emerges from the bathroom, my brain stutters.

"Well? What do we think?" he asks.

I take a sip of water, unsure of when my mouth suddenly became dry.

Noah's booted heels click against the hardwood floor as he spins in a slow circle, his dark green cloak fluttering in his wake. Tucked into his boots, light linen pants hug his calves and billow out around his thighs. His olive-green shirt is downright swashbuckling, with its loose sleeves and wonderfully deep, open V. Noah's left most of the laces undone so that the costume-jewelry amulets he'd found are on the best display.

"I'll never get over this," I say, cupping his face in my hands. To my light horror, he'd shaved his face completely yesterday to better do his costume justice. But already he's stubbly again, which I admit looks particularly dashing.

The latex elf ears stuck over his own are the cherry on top.

I press my palm to my chest. "Consider me *thoroughly* charmed, bard."

He catches my fingers, bowing slightly as he lifts my knuckles to his lips. I wonder if he knows that the way he's looking at me through his long lashes is making my knees go weak.

"I'm almost ready," I say. Jules helped me order a petal-pink corset online, and I pick it up from where I'd tossed it to the couch. "Can you help me put this on?"

"Only if I can help you take it off later."

Oh, I have every intention of it.

While Noah navigates the maze of ribbon laces at my back, I scroll through our D&D crew's group text.

Jules:
Y'all ready for your very first RENAISSANCE FAIRE?

Morgan:
Hell yes

Morgan:

> This beard already itches like hell but it looks too good not to wear

Jules:

> How did the green turn out, Liam?

> Liam???

Liam doesn't answer; he just texts a mirror pic of himself decked out in a sparkling purple robe with gently mussed hair and a home-made green orb-capped staff at his side. I'd spent hours helping him paint it last week.

What he didn't paint, though, is his face.

Liam:

> I can't commit. It would all melt off, anyway!

Jules:

> Awwwww

Morgan:

> COWARD

I let out a quiet yelp as Noah pulls the corset tighter. "Almost there," he promises. I drum out a response to the others.

> Howl's moving castle vibes. You killed it.

Morgan:

> He's just doing hot-Alastair because I'm bringing my brother

Jules:

Oooooo

☺☺☺☺☺☺☺☺

I've met Morgan's twin and my new co-worker Marcus only a handful of times since he returned from his summer abroad, but I can already tell that he shares his sister's earnest friendliness and blunt, infectious humor. He'd trained alongside me at Bluebonnet as Morgan showed us how to manage the café, where I've been picking up a few shifts when I'm not working on my next project: a storybook mural for the kids' section. I couldn't have asked for a better opportunity than to work with them while I explore day-dreams about what comes next for me.

But it's Liam who's been the most keen to spend time with Marcus. After a few instances when I caught sight of his car pull-ing into Liam's driveway—*our* driveway—just as I pulled out, I'd gently encouraged Liam to invite him to join our game. It hadn't taken much persuading for Liam to agree to extend our current campaign—especially after the hellish cliff-hanger he'd left us on—and I knew from Morgan's delightfully meddling hints that Marcus would love to play, too. So, starting in a few weeks, he'll embark on the next chapter with us, and already I can't wait to see what he thinks of our rowdy crew as we battle to escape from Hell.

Jules:

Sadie? Noah? How are things coming for y'all?

Liam:

I'll be there in ten, so you better be ready

we're ready!!

With one more great tug, Noah ties off the corset and settles his hands tiredly on his hips, looking for all the world like he's just finished a workout.

I hold my phone out at arm's length. "Pic for the group?"

Noah ducks in for a selfie by pressing his cheek to mine, and I take a moment to marvel at how incredible we look together. Although my hair isn't as long as Jaylie's, I've started to let it grow out, and my curls bounce underneath the circlet I'd fashioned with gold coins. My face is fuller, and the dark circles I'd arrived in Texas with are long gone. I painted my lips to match the pink layered skirts of my dress, and my corset—

I glance down in alarm to where it looks like my boobs are about to spill out my front.

For someone who can regularly get away with going braless, it's not a problem I've had before. I never thought it was even possible to get them to look like this.

Noah, too, seems momentarily caught in their orbit. "Huh," he says thoughtfully. "We should go to Renaissance Faires more often."

Three sudden raps at the door startle us out of our fit of giggles.

"Hah! Almost forgot." Noah ducks back into the kitchen to fetch a bottle of mead. Jules had insisted on the importance of a little pregaming in the parking lot before heading inside the Faire. Something about tradition.

Noah's eyes light up with sweet mischief as he points the neck of the bottle at me. "Want to try a little? Before we head out?" I've noticed him brewing batches more and more often, both at home and in kegs at Alchemist. He has plans to put some on tap soon, to test it out with the patrons. After that, well—maybe then I'll show him the pitch I put together for fun, proposing Alchemist as a vendor at the Faire next year.

I circle my arms loosely around his waist, my fingers linking behind his back. "What's it this time?"

"Vanilla." His tone is thick with amusement.

"Forever a classic," I tease.

He fishes two glasses out of his cabinet. "You know," he muses, "they've got Faires like these all over the country. If we really like it, maybe next summer I'll take you on a whole tour."

He pops off the cork and pours a splash of sparkling gold into each of our cups.

"Off on another adventure, then?" I say.

"Every day is an adventure with you, love."

We raise our glasses to the ceiling and clink them together.

"To adventure, then."

ACKNOWLEDGMENTS

I could never have made this journey alone, and I am eternally grateful for my wonderful adventuring party.

To my incredible agent, Rose Ferrao—thank you for being *Roll for Romance*'s biggest fan and fiercest champion, and for all of your guidance, assurance, and wisdom every step of the way. Your boundless enthusiasm for this book, advocacy on my behalf, and kind thoughtfulness make me feel so supported, grounded, and grateful. I am so lucky to get to work with you, and I can't wait for all our adventures yet to come!

All my thanks to my brilliant editor, Wendy Wong! Wendy, you are such a joy to work with, and I am immensely grateful for your editorial wizardry, warmth, and keen insight throughout every stage of this process. From the beginning you saw immediately to the heart of the story I was trying to tell and helped me dig it out until the book became the best version of itself—I could not have done it without you. Thank you for everything!

A huge thank-you as well to every member of the Dell, Ballantine, and Random House teams who played a part in creating this book and connecting it to readers. To the broader editorial team, including Kara Welsh, Jennifer Hershey, Kim Hovey, Kara Cesare, and Shauna Summers, thank you for your support! To the art team, including designer Sarah Horgan and illustrator Chloe Quinn, thank you so much for the cover of my dreams! To my marketing and publicity team, including Megan Whelan, Taylor Noel, Brianna Kusilek, and Jennifer Garza, thank you for being the ultimate romance matchmakers by helping introduce this book to its readers. To my production team, including Christa Guild, Saige Francis, Erin Korenko, Alexis Flynn, Nicole Ramirez, Taylor McGowan, and Laura Dragonette, thank you sincerely for your careful work (and for correcting my nerdy references!). Thank you as well to the wider Random House team, and everyone who's had a hand in helping this book become a reality: design, sales—especially my bookselling bud, Uriel Perez!—and all others. I'm grateful for all that you do!

To booksellers and librarians, I am so thankful for all of your dedication and hard work. The community spaces that you create and the magic that you do by getting books into the hands of readers is so special and important.

All my love and gratitude to *Roll for Romance*'s first readers Stephanie Hess (thank you for being the first to love this book!), Marty Cahill, Tomoko and Will Bason, Mason Sparkman, Megan Harley, Sara Leonard, Paola Crespo, and Mom. In the beginning, I was terrified of sharing this book with anyone—but your kind feedback and love for this story made every second spent writing it worth it. To Anne Perry especially, thank you for your encouragement, guidance, and vision in the early days of this project—I am so grateful.

Writing became an infinitely less lonely endeavor once I discovered so many welcoming online writing communities. My first thanks to the SmoochPit Mentorship Program and my ever-enthusiastic and incredibly kind mentor, Audrey Goldberg Ruoff. Audrey, you've held my hand through every scary step of this wild journey to publication, and I'm so thankful for you! Thank you as well to every member of TTWD, SF2.0, the Rose Buds, and 2025

Debuts for fostering such supportive and hilariously fun communities. Emily Daluga, I'm so thankful for all the time we've spent together in our Discord Writing Hut—but I'm even more grateful for your friendship!

Although I never thought I'd write a book one day (even now, drafting these acknowledgments, I have a hard time believing this is *real*!), there are a few people in my life who always believed I would. Mrs. Popelka and Mrs. Adams, thank you so much for inspiring my lifelong love for reading and writing; I don't think you would be surprised to learn that I ended up here. Zalisa and Jenna, thank you for teaching me how to find my voice and learn how to listen to it. Mom and Dad, thank you for encouraging me to chase even my wildest dreams; because of you and your unwavering support and love, I never believed that anything was impossible. Jake, it meant so much to me to share the news with you first—thank you for always believing in me, bro, though I am sincerely sorry for all the times I kicked you off the computer as a kid so I could "practice writing." Zoë Butler, my beloved friend, my loudest cheerleader, my fellow Chili's slut: thank you for being there for me at every turn, and for always pushing me to pursue my passions and joys. Let's celebrate with margs soon.

And to Angelo. You know, I first fell in love with writing in the tavern where we met. We've come a long way since then, and though we both still love storytelling, through you I've learned that the best stories are the ones we're living today. Thank you for your support, belief, and love. It is such a gift to adventure by your side.

Lastly, I want to extend a big, warmhearted thank-you to everyone I've ever rolled dice with—you have all brought so much magic into my life! Without your friendship and love, this book would not exist. Special thanks to Will Bason, for making me cry in nearly every campaign and letting me romance the NPCs; Tomoko Bason, for your brilliant, heartfelt characters and art to capture our adventures; Nathan Andrada, for always being game to push the Big Red Button and keeping us on our toes; Marty Cahill, for your fantastical world-building, incredible homebrew, and fierce friendship; Mason Sparkman, for your mechanical prowess, timely memes, and keeping us all alive despite our best efforts otherwise; Dan, for constantly pawing dice off the table, and for keeping me company for every pandemic online game and in all the years before (I miss you, buddy); and Angelo, Megan, Zoë, Hideo, Rocio, Danielle, Steph, and every other adventurer I've ever had the pleasure of playing D&D with. This book is for all of you, because there is no greater joy than telling stories with your friends.

ROLL FOR
Romance

LENORA WOODS

A BOOK CLUB GUIDE

Dear Reader,

Whether we know it or not, we're all playing characters. You may be playing the part of a bard adventuring from tavern to tavern, a dutiful eldest daughter, the brightest and busiest employee at your office, or something else entirely, but we all take on roles as we move through the world.

Games like D&D give us the opportunity to embody any sort of character we want, and for over a decade, it's been one of my favorite escapes. In creating *Roll for Romance,* I wanted to write about a woman who uses the game and the character she plays as a way to feel brave, lucky, adventurous, and capable during a time in her life when she feels otherwise helpless to stop everything from falling apart. And while I wanted to explore how empowering it can be to embody a strong persona through a roleplaying game, I also wanted to think about all the roles we play in our day-to-day lives—and what happens when we can't play the part anymore.

I wrote *Roll for Romance* after experiencing the worst period of burnout in my life. I'd wrapped up so much of my identity and worth in my work that I felt incapable of ever taking a step back—and when I finally had to leave my job behind, I hardly knew who I was outside of it. This book came to life when I finally gave myself permission to do something just for fun—just for me.

And now, for you.

At its heart, this book is about discovering who we are underneath all the roles we play. It's about how important it is to surround ourselves with people who see us as we truly are—and love us for it.

Thank you so much for reading *Roll for Romance*. I hope it inspires you to chase all your joys and seek out adventure at every opportunity.

With love,
Lenora

QUESTIONS AND TOPICS FOR DISCUSSION

1. In many ways, *Roll for Romance* is a story about recovering from burnout and reconnecting with the world around you. Have you ever experienced burnout? How did you navigate it?

2. Sadie explores many different identities in the book (as Sadie, Josephine, and Jaylie). What different roles do you play in your own life? When do you feel the most yourself?

3. *Roll for Romance* combines a real-life romance with fantasy world interludes. Do you feel these worlds worked well together? Did you have a favorite storyline?

4. Sadie's and Liam's dreams for their lives changed and diverged throughout the course of their friendship. Did any parts of their journey resonate with your experiences?

5. Even before the events of the book, Noah finds joy in fanfiction and online roleplay. Have you been a part of any online communities, or what hobbies have you found your own community in?

6. Noah defines "home" as more of a feeling than a place. How do you define what home is to you?

7. Each member of Sadie's D&D party creates characters that explore different personality types. What type of character would you play in a D&D game? What personalities would you be interested in exploring?

8. For a large portion of the book, Sadie struggles with determining where she belongs and how her job informs her identity. If you were her friend, what advice would you have given her?

9. Noah has spent the last few years exploring North America. If you had a van like his, where would you go?

10. When Sadie is given the opportunity to return to the path she felt like she was always meant for, she realizes her perspective and desires have changed. Do you think Sadie made the right choice in the end?

11. If you could design your dream set of dice, what would it look like?

ALCHEMIST'S NEW SPECIALS

SNACKS

CAMPFIRE NACHOS
*Skillet-cooked fresh corn tortilla chips covered in cheese,
black beans, pico de gallo, jalapeños, salsa, and avocado*

SECOND-BREAKFAST CHARCUTERIE
*Seasonal fresh fruit, mini cranberry muffins, French toast sticks,
maple syrup, sourdough bread, assortment of jams,
gouda and cheddar cheese, and bacon*

FIREBALL QUESO
*Beer cheese queso topped with hatch chilis,
served with fresh corn tortilla chips*

ON DRAFT

WIZARD'S WELLSPRING
IPA | 5.5%
Citrusy, hazy, and downright magical

FROLIC TONIC
Wildflower Mead | 6%
Floral, crisp, and bright

LONG REST
S'mores Imperial Stout | 7%
*Warm & rich, brewed with chocolate, marshmallows, and
graham crackers. Best enjoyed by a campfire*

COCKTAILS

BARCANE KNOWLEDGE
Wizard's Wellspring IPA, spiced rum, pineapple juice, and grenadine

THE BEE STING
*A Renaissance Faire classic; mead, hard cider, and
a cinnamon sugar honey rim*

DIRTY TWENTY
Gin, dry vermouth, olive brine

LIAM'S QUESTIONS FOR CREATING A CHARACTER'S BACKSTORY

1. What does a normal day in the life of your character look like?

2. What is one hobby or interest that your character has? Where did they pick it up?

3. Does your character have any important relationships in their life (friends/family/lovers/enemies)? Describe them.

4. What are your character's immediate and long-term goals? What motivates them?

5. What is your character's proudest achievement? Their biggest regret?

6. Is faith important to your character? What do they believe in (a god, a force of nature, a patron, themselves, etc.)?

7. What qualities does your character value in the world and in other people?

8. How did your character acquire their skills/spells/magic?

9. What are your character's greatest strengths and weaknesses?

10. What events in your character's life led them to the start of this adventure?

© JADE PIERCE

LENORA WOODS is a writer hailing from Austin, Texas. When she's not writing, she spends her free time hiking, rolling dice, and pretending to be an elf at her local Renaissance Faire.

lenorawoods.com
Instagram: @lenorawoodswrites

ABOUT THE TYPE

This book was set in Caslon, a typeface first designed in 1722 by William Caslon (1692–1766). Its widespread use by most English printers in the early eighteenth century soon supplanted the Dutch typefaces that had formerly prevailed. The roman is considered a "workhorse" typeface due to its pleasant, open appearance, while the italic is exceedingly decorative.